UNINTENDED CULTIVATOR

VOLUME 7

ERIC DONTIGNEY

CHAPTER ONE
HELP

"There you are," squealed Misty Peak in, what Sen assumed, was feigned joy.

She dashed across the room, wrapped herself around him in a manner that Sen thought was probably inappropriate for any situation outside of a bedroom, and kissed him. Sen felt the hateful looks from at least three other men in the common room of the inn where he'd left the fox woman and her grandfather. It had been one day. One day! How could she have possibly ensnared three men that fast? *She's a fox*, Sen reminded himself. *It's what they do.* He wasn't sure how much longer the kiss might have lasted, but an icy wave of danger washed over him and Misty Peak. The fox froze. Her eyes snapped open, and her head swiveled over to where Falling Leaf was smiling at them. A smile that was *all* teeth and no friendliness.

"Ghost panther," whispered Misty Peak in a hushed tone of fear and no little awe.

Sen shook his head and took a half step back. His eyes scanned the room and fell on Laughing River. The elder fox was looking on with unrepentant glee in his eyes at the scene unfolding before him. The old fox had been the source of a lot of trouble in Sen's life just recently. Trouble that had culminated in Sen taking possession of an extremely potent spatial treasure and fighting a true devil. He gritted his teeth a little at that thought. The results of that fight were mostly a mystery, and Sen didn't like the idea of a devil out there biding its time and plotting vengeance. Not that he could do much about it right now. He gave Laughing River an annoyed glare. The elder fox had clearly decided not to tell his granddaughter they'd meet a ghost panther, probably so he could enjoy this very spectacle.

Falling Leaf took a step closer to Misty Peak, her smile growing even bigger if that was possible.

"Prey," said Falling Leaf.

The fox woman took a hasty step back, clearly unprepared to pick a fight with something she saw as a superior predator. Then, Misty Peak turned an accusing look on Sen.

"What?" he asked in an annoyed tone. "I didn't tell you to make a spectacle of yourself in front of strangers."

"You could have warned me," she pouted.

Sen shrugged. "Probably."

Before anyone could do anything that everyone in the vicinity would regret, he started walking over toward Laughing River. Falling Leaf kept glancing at him with looks he couldn't interpret. That struck him as odd. He thought he'd learned most of her expressions. Misty Peak trailed behind them, looking very put out by the recent turn of events. He didn't know what to make of that either. What had she been expecting? It wasn't like he'd been enthusiastic about her presence. Once they got close enough, Laughing River opened his arms wide. His appearance at that moment had a strange quality to it like he was a sly but benevolent grandfather. This time, it was Falling Leaf who looked uncertain in the face of a superior predator. She gave Sen a questioning look.

"He'll behave," muttered Sen. "He's paying off a favor to me."

The ghost panther instantly relaxed. She eyed the elder fox with open curiosity. He supposed that spirit beasts at her level didn't often cross paths with spirit beasts of Laughing River's level, at least not and live to tell the tale. The old fox seemed almost as curious about her as she did about him. He eyed the ghost panther in a way that Sen did not like *at all*. That displeasure must have been written clearly on Sen's face because Laughing River held up his hands in a gesture of surrender.

"Easy, nephew. I'm here to help, not indulge myself. I'll keep it professional," said Laughing River.

"Do that," said Sen in a tone hard enough to shatter steel.

Sen was amused to note that the three men who had been glaring hatefully at him earlier abruptly decided that they had pressing business elsewhere. They fled the inn, two of them leaving half-eaten meals behind. Sen sat down without an invitation. A moment later, Falling Leaf and Misty Peak joined them. Both the ghost panther and the fox woman wore expressions that told him they wouldn't have dared speak to the elder fox that way. Already weary of the foxes and their silliness, Sen got right down to business.

"Falling Leaf, this is Laughing River and Misty Peak," said Sen, gesturing at the foxes.

Falling Leaf inclined her head to Laughing River in a gesture of muted respect. She eyed Misty Peak askance for a moment before issuing a little sigh and nodding to the other woman.

"Hello," said the ghost panther.

"Laughing River, Misty Peak, this is Falling Leaf. My friend," said Sen, before he added something he thought was necessary. "I will note that should I discover she's been drawn into any kind of fox plot, scheme, or foolishness, I will become *profoundly unhappy*."

The foxes looked a little sheepish at that last statement. Maybe they'd both been thinking of some way to rope the all-but-mythical ghost panther into something. More to the point, they'd both gotten a good look at what it meant when Sen decided he wasn't happy about something. Misty Peak already knew that she couldn't take him in a fight if he got serious about it. Sen sincerely doubted he could win in a fight with Laughing River, but that didn't make the elder fox eager to soak up whatever damage Sen could dish out. He reasoned that simply suggesting there would be consequences ought to be enough to keep the foxes in line for now. At least, he hoped it would. The last thing he wanted to be doing was chastising the foxes when he had other things to do.

Sen had been a little worried that Falling Leaf might take issue with him issuing threats on her behalf. She was plenty dangerous in her own right, but he'd been worried that the whole spirit animal hierarchy might inhibit what she said to Laughing River. He worried a lot less about how Falling Leaf would deal with Misty Peak. He expected any friction there would be solved with swift and bloody action. He snuck a glance at the ghost panther to try to gauge her reaction. She seemed perfectly content with how things were playing out. If anything, she might have even looked a touch smug. Laughing River spoke up again.

"Like I said, just here to help."

Sen wasn't sure he actually believed those words, but his next thoughts disappeared as someone burst through the inn door. A look over his shoulder revealed someone vaguely familiar. A young man that Sen thought was a local. The young man was battered and even a little bloody. The man looked around the room with wild eyes.

"I need help!" the man shouted. "A tree came down bad. My father's trapped under it."

Damn it, thought Sen. He'd crashed through enough trees to have a sense of how heavy they were. It'd probably take a dozen of the local men to move it, and then only with the assistance of ropes. That was assuming that they could even set them up properly. On top of that, the man would likely be injured. Depending on where the tree landed, the man might be too injured to move safely. *This isn't my problem*, thought Sen. *I can't help everyone.* The excuse sounded weak even to him. No, he couldn't help everyone, but this problem was right in front of him. More to the point, he was probably better equipped than anyone else to actually render aid. He gave Falling Leaf an apologetic look, but she just shrugged. He gave the foxes a flat look.

"Behave," he ordered, before standing up and walking over to the frantic young man. "Let's go."

"Thank you," gushed the young man. "As soon as we gather up—"

"You'll only need me," said Sen, and then added, "I'm a cultivator."

The young man looked, in order, surprised, elated, confused, and then worried. He abruptly bowed, as though remembering something very important. "Honored cultivator, we have no treasures to offer."

Sen waved it off. "I don't need anything from you. Just take me there while there's still time to help."

The young man looked very uncertain but nodded. Sen followed as the young man led him outside and then out of the town. The pace seemed excruciatingly slow to Sen, despite the fact that the young man was all but running. Sen kept his spiritual sense extended and soon felt the flickering life of someone ahead. They didn't have time to move at the young man's pace. Sen grabbed the guy, threw him over his shoulder, and activated his qinggong technique. The guy shouted in surprise and fear as they sped through the trees. In no time at all, they were there. Sen put the young man down and focused on the scene before him. There was a mortal man in his middle years pinned beneath a tree. A quick look around showed that the man and his son had been doing some logging. There were a few other felled trees nearby along with discarded axes.

Sen suppressed the urge to simply lift the log away with brute strength. That could make things worse just as easily as make them better. It could shift broken ribs, which might then pierce the lungs or heart. Instead, Sen knelt down next to the man and did a quick scan with his qi and spiritual sense. He still lacked anything even remotely like Auntie Caihong's skill at discerning injuries, but he got the general picture. The young man was almost vibrating in concern and his desire to *do something*. Sen decided to explain himself before the guy acted out of sheer impatience.

"I need to make sure moving the tree won't hurt him more than help him," said Sen. "Just give me a moment."

Having looked at the man's injuries, Sen was pretty confident that moving the tree was the worst thing they could do at the moment. Instead, he started searching the elixirs in his storage rings. *Too strong, too strong, too strong*, he thought as his mental fingers brushed the vials he had stored. It had been a long while since he last made something intended for a mortal. Anything useful to heal him would rip a mortal apart. He finally found some older elixirs tucked away and summoned one. He pulled the cork and slowly tipped the liquid into the pinned man's mouth.

"What are you doing?" demanded the young man, trying and failing to sound respectful.

"It's a minor healing elixir," said Sen. "It should help some of his injuries. Make it safe to move the tree."

The young man looked dubious. He obviously believed moving the tree *right the hells now* was the right answer to this problem. Sen paused at that. He supposed that for anyone who didn't have a ready store of high-quality healing elixirs, that probably *was* the right answer. It was probably the only answer, now that Sen considered it. Fortunately for the man under the tree, Sen did have a ready store of elixirs. The young man grew increasingly impatient and even angry as they waited. Sen's attention was taken up with monitoring the pinned man's condition. The elixir was doing its work and stabilizing the man. Right around the time that the young man looked like he might tear out his hair, attack Sen, or try to move the tree by himself, Sen rose.

"Alright, it should be safe to move the tree now," he announced.

"What should I do?" asked the young man.

"Just stand back," said Sen.

Sen repositioned himself, grabbed the tree, and lifted it off the man. He tossed it over by the other felled trees. Once the tree was gone, the young man was kneeling next to his father, interspersing whispered prayers and pleas for his father to wake up.

"Let's get him back to the town," said Sen, waving a hand and lifting the injured man on a platform of solid qi. "No reason he shouldn't heal somewhere more comfortable."

CHAPTER TWO
THE PROBLEMS OF OTHERS

Sen was a little relieved that the tree cutters lived near the edge of the town in a truly modest but well-tended home. He wasn't looking forward to making a show of carrying the injured man through the town on a qi platform. He would have, but it would have been inconvenient. Cultivators made mortals rightly nervous, and overt displays of cultivator power made them very nervous. Fortunately, the young man was much more concerned with his father's well-being than with anything that Sen was doing. When they arrived at the house, the young man simply called out for his mother. She was distraught to discover her husband was injured, but it seemed she was cut from a similar cloth as Grandmother Lu. She focused on the practicalities, rushing around to set up a pallet near the stove they used for cooking and heating the little home. Sen settled the injured man on the pallet. Before he could make good an escape, though, the young man dropped to his knees and started kowtowing.

"That really isn't necessary," said Sen.

"This Wang Bo can never repay the kindness of the honored cultivator."

Wang Bo's mother, who had been crouched and fretting by her

husband, whirled to stare at Sen in mixed shock and horror. She scrambled over to mimic her son.

"This Du Fen begs a thousand times for the honored cultivator to forgive her disrespect."

"Please stop," Sen almost begged the pair.

He wanted to think that they'd heard one too many stories about arrogant and petty cultivators, but he didn't really believe it. He'd met plenty of cultivators who would have, if they noticed this mother and son at all, treated them like trash. He imagined that those cultivators expected this kind of behavior. He had no stomach for it. It always took him right back to the streets of Orchard's Reach. Always hiding in dark corners to avoid the notice of the noble brats. Pleading with the shopkeepers who caught him lurking around their businesses to spare him a beating. He had no need or desire to harm the mortals he encountered, unless they were violent bandits, and this family clearly wasn't in that category. He didn't know if it was the pleading tone in his voice or a total lack of hostility on his part, but Wang Bo and Du Fen looked up at him hesitantly. It was almost like they were testing to see if he was trying to trick them. He quickly gestured for them to rise. Du Fen's eyes went immediately back to her injured husband.

"Tend to him," said Sen in the gentlest tone he could manage.

She didn't need any more encouragement. The woman swiftly returned to her husband's side. Sen looked at Wang Bo, who was looking uncertainly at him. Sen felt at a loss about what to say now that the immediate crisis was over. Instead of standing there in awkward silence, Sen fixed his attention on the injured man and checked the wounds again. They seemed to be healing up fine, but it was clear that the pace of healing was slowing. Sen pursed his lips. It could be that the elixir was wearing off, but he suspected it was more likely that the man simply didn't have the physical reserves in place. While it didn't look like this family was starving, it was clear that they didn't enjoy any kind of wealth. They probably weren't eating all that well. *No doubt eating whatever they could afford and nothing else*, thought Sen.

This family's problems weren't his problems. Sen knew that. But he had intervened. The first elixir he'd given the man would almost certainly ensure his survival. Of course, he also knew that survival came in a lot of forms, not all of them good or advantageous. It wouldn't really cost him anything he cared about to help a little more. *I've already come this far*, he thought. *I may as well finish the job.* He searched through his storage ring and found another weak elixir. He summoned it and held it out to Wang Bo. The young man stared at the vial like he didn't dare touch it. Sen waited a little longer before he rolled his eyes.

"Take it," he instructed.

Apprehension on his narrow face, the young man gingerly took the vial. He held it in his hands like it was a fragile infant. Sen realized that the young man probably had no idea what it was, let alone what to do with it.

"Give that to your father tomorrow at midday," said Sen. "No sooner."

His eyes going wide, the young man nodded furiously.

"It will be done as you say, honored cultivator," said Wang Bo, almost shouting the words.

Sen looked over the young man's mother.

"Madame Du," he said, causing the woman to shoot to her feet and look at him. "Your husband will need hearty meals for the next several days."

The woman exchanged worried looks with her son.

"I... I will do what I can, honored cultivator," she said.

Sen nodded as though he expected nothing less because this attitude was what the mother and son seemed to expect from him. He adopted a very mellow version of what he thought of as his young master mask.

"I have taken some small interest in this matter as your husband has received the benefits of my alchemy. I cannot have the elixirs' effects diminished by inadequate meals," he said, tapping his chin thoughtfully. "No, I will have to ensure he is properly fed in order to test the quality of the elixirs on a mortal."

Sen waved a hand and summoned a truly absurd amount of food from one of his rings. Bags of rice and piles of vegetables appeared. Wang Bo and Du Fen gaped at the food, stunned by the good fortune that had seemingly dropped on their heads out of a clear sky. Sen continued to put on his young master act. He frowned at the pile.

"No," Sen muttered to himself. "That won't do. He needs meat to heal properly."

Sen peered around the room as if looking for something. He didn't see anywhere to store meat, even if only temporarily. He searched his rings and found a small table. He usually used it for tea, but he decided he could sacrifice it. After all, he could just make a table from stone if he really needed one. He summoned the table and piled several kinds of meat on it. He gave Du Fen a vaguely stern look.

"Hearty meals," he ordered solemnly. "I will return in three days to see the results of my elixirs."

The woman nodded slowly like it was taking her body a while to translate the commands her mind was giving it. "I will do as you say, honored cultivator."

"Good. Good. I have other business to attend to now," announced Sen.

Wang Bo and Du Fen offered hasty bows. While they weren't looking at him, Sen seized the opportunity to activate his qinggong technique and run away through the still-open door. He expected that they would just assume he did some mysterious cultivator magic to disappear. Which, he realized on reflection, was what he *had* done. It was a relief to escape from their general awe and palpable fear of him, though. Reassuring people who were certain you might kill them at any moment was a mentally exhausting exercise for Sen. It was so much easier to deal with people who either didn't know he was a cultivator or had some experience dealing with cultivators. It gave him more and more respect for inn owners who managed to maintain some equanimity when they realized he was a cultivator.

That thought reminded him that he'd certainly left Falling Leaf alone with the two foxes for longer than was wise. He walked back to the inn. Before he even reached the door, he knew something was wrong. Sen would have liked to say that he picked up on subtle indications like changes in the ambient qi or telltale noises, but it was nothing like that. The door to the inn had been knocked completely out of its frame and had what looked like an injured mortal sprawled across it. There were also the general sounds of fighting and yelling coming from inside the inn. Sen pinched the bridge of his nose, just certain that Laughing River and Misty Peak were somehow responsible for whatever disaster he was going to find inside.

"This is what I get for thinking that I could leave them alone for any length of time. You brought this on yourself, Sen," he muttered.

He spotted a stray dog that looked at him curiously from a nearby alley.

"You don't know how lucky you are," he said to the dog. "I bet there isn't a single nine-tail fox making any trouble for you."

The stray didn't comment, just kept giving Sen a vaguely happy and curious look. Sen considered just walking away from the mess and letting the foxes sort it out for themselves. If it were just the foxes inside, he probably would have done exactly that. Unfortunately, there was a good chance Falling Leaf was in the middle of whatever mess they had made. She had direct and absolute ways of solving problems that he thought were probably overkill for whatever situation had developed in his absence. *Best to get her out of there as fast as possible*, he thought. Mentally imploring the heavens for a problem he could solve quickly, Sen squared his shoulders and stepped through the empty doorway.

CHAPTER THREE
SURPRISES

Sen didn't quite know what to make of the scene that greeted his eyes. The foxes, who he had just assumed were going to be the problem, were still sitting at the table where he'd left them. Of course, that didn't mean they hadn't caused the problem. In fact, he found it odd that they hadn't gone somewhere else. Sen didn't imagine that Laughing River really wanted to discuss the secrets of transformation in front of mortals. However, after he thought about it for a second, Sen realized that Falling Leaf had probably proven unwilling to go somewhere private with the immensely powerful nine-tail fox. Sen didn't think the fox would have tried anything. Especially not with Sen holding the spatial treasure hostage. He couldn't fault Falling Leaf's caution if that had been the reason, though. Only a fool offers their hand willingly to a predator's teeth.

By all appearances, however, it seemed that the ghost panther was the source of the trouble. There were bodies scattered everywhere amid the wreckage of shattered tables and splintered chairs. A quick scan with his spiritual sense revealed that those people were still alive, even if some of them were probably thinking they'd rather be dead. The thing that truly captured Sen's attention was

Falling Leaf. She had a foot planted firmly between the shoulders of a man, keeping him pinned face down on the floor as he thrashed. Meanwhile, she had seized the robes of a man nearly three times her size in one fist, while savagely beating him with the other fist. Sen couldn't even tell if the man was still conscious or if the ghost panther was holding his unconscious body up to continue the punishment.

Frowning a little, Sen picked his way over to the small bar and peeked over the top. The inn owner was crouched behind it looking like he believed that the end of the world had come. The man looked up, saw Sen looking down, and flinched like he'd been struck. Before Sen could get a word in edgewise, the inn owner started babbling.

"I'm sorry. I'm sorry. I didn't know she was a cultivator. I didn't know!"

When it became clear that he wasn't going to get anything useful out of the inn owner until after the fighting was over, Sen made his way over to the foxes. He had to step over some groaning, battered people to do it. He sat down at the table and gave the foxes an expectant look. Laughing River started to chuckle.

"I expect you think we did this somehow, but we didn't. This is all on the mortals."

"Oh, is it?"

Misty Peak quickly nodded. "We were minding our own business. Then, that pack of idiots came in here. One of them decided that Falling Leaf was too pretty to sit with us and should sit with them."

Sen suppressed the groan he felt coming on. He could guess what happened, but he gestured for Misty Peak to continue. The fox woman glanced over to where Falling Leaf was still administering object lessons.

"Shouldn't you stop her?" asked the fox.

"Not until I know the whole story," said Sen.

"Alright," said Misty Peak a little uncertainly. "Well, she said no. She was quite firm about it. The man didn't like that, and he grabbed her. I think you can put together the rest."

She gave the destroyed common room a halfhearted gesture. Sen nodded before he glanced over at where the inn owner was cowering.

"Why is he so afraid?" asked Sen, hiking a thumb at the bar.

Laughing River shrugged. "He didn't do anything to stop it. He probably figures that once she's done with them, she'll turn her attention to him. Or maybe he thinks that you'll burn the place to the ground because he let it happen."

"Oh. I guess that's not an unreasonable assumption," said Sen.

Misty Peak got an interested gleam in her eyes. "*Are* you going to burn it down?"

Sen thought it over. "No. I don't have anywhere else convenient for you to stay. I've taxed the patience of my teacher already. I'm certainly not adding to that by bringing you two there. Besides, it's going to cost a lot to replace all this broken furniture. I don't know if that's punishment enough, but it is some kind of punishment. If Falling Leaf decides to do something to him, though, I'm not planning to step in."

Laughing River lifted an eyebrow. "I thought you were all soft-hearted about the mortals. Didn't you run off to save one an hour or so ago?"

"Soft-hearted? Not so much. I went to help that young man's father because it was probably a life-and-death situation and because I could. A tree fell on the man. *Maybe* it was karma coming around on him, but I doubt he was doing anything objectionable at the time. The idiot who runs this place lets some of his customers grab other customers. Whatever he gets, he deserves," said Sen before glancing over to where he could hear someone blubbering.

Falling Leaf had seemingly grown tired of beating the big man and had turned her "gentle" attention to the one she'd pinned to the floor. He was on his knees, crying, and pleading with the implacable ghost panther. The man's words were so garbled by his sobbing that Sen couldn't even understand most of it. Then again, he didn't need to hear the words to understand it. It all boiled down to one key idea. *Please don't kill me.* One look at Falling Leaf told Sen that those pleas were largely falling on deaf ears. Her eyes were still blazing with cold fury. She probably wouldn't kill him given that she hadn't killed any of the others, but Sen didn't imagine that man was going to feel healthy anytime in the near future. When she started in on the man, Sen turned back to the foxes. They were both giving him mildly surprised expressions.

"You're really not going to do anything?" asked Misty Peak.

"I didn't tell those men to be stupid," said Sen. "They aren't innocents. If they grabbed Falling Leaf here, they've almost certainly done the same thing in other places to people who couldn't fight back. Besides, I don't know them. They aren't allies. Why should I get in the middle of it? More importantly, why do you care what happens to them?"

"She doesn't," observed Laughing River. "Neither do I. Understanding you, on the other hand, is of interest."

Sen gave the elder fox a dubious look. "Why is that?"

"The better we understand you, the easier it will be to avoid truly angering you," said Laughing River.

"Is that really a matter of deep concern for you two?" asked Sen with a small snort.

"Of course, it is," said Misty Peak. "You can summon vengeful, terrifyingly powerful nascent soul cultivators. Do you think that they'd say no if you asked them to kill someone for you? Equally important, all the evidence suggests that *you* will be a vengeful, terrifyingly powerful nascent soul cultivator. Probably sooner rather than later. Teasing you is one thing, but I don't have a death wish."

Sen opened his mouth to speak but found he didn't have a ready response to that. She wasn't wrong about him being able to summon nascent soul cultivators. Master Feng and Uncle Kho probably would kill someone for him if he asked them to, not that he would. But he supposed that there was no way that the foxes could know that. He wasn't as sure about Auntie Caihong. She would likely hunt down anyone who did him true harm, but that wasn't the same thing as killing someone just because he asked. He was less than comfortable with the idea that he might be perceived as a vengeful figure of terror and doom. He sighed. It was probably too late to avoid that since so many of the stories painted him that way.

"I suppose I can understand your concerns," admitted Sen.

There was a particularly sharp sound of fist on flesh that drew Sen's attention. He saw Falling Leaf casually toss aside the limp form of the crying man. His spiritual sense revealed that she had spared even him. The ghost panther stalked over to the bar where she glared down at the inn owner.

"Bring me food," she commanded.

"Whatever the honored cultivator wishes," cried the inn owner before he fled toward the kitchen.

Falling Leaf nodded to herself and returned to the table. She sat down and picked up a cup of what had to be cold tea. She took a sip before she turned her gaze on Sen.

"Did you save the tree man?" she asked, all signs of violence gone save for the blood on her hands and speckled across her face.

"I think so," said Sen.

He retrieved a piece of fabric and a water gourd from his storage ring. He wet the fabric and handed it to the ghost panther.

"That's good," said Falling Leaf.

She took the cloth and wiped at her face and hands.

"I'll check on him in a few days to make sure," said Sen. "Sometimes, these things are trickier than they look at first. I wish Auntie Caihong were here. She's better at reading injuries than I am."

Falling Leaf nodded. "The Caihong has great talent in healing."

17

Sen took no small measure of amusement from the increasingly baffled look on Misty Peak's face. Laughing River did a better job of controlling his expression, but Sen could tell that the elder fox also wasn't sure what to make of the conversation he was listening to.

"So, I heard someone tried to grab you," observed Sen.

Falling Leaf glared at the unconscious men she'd left in her wake. "They thought to force me to sit with them. Force *me*. A ghost panther. The fools," said Falling Leaf before she sat up straight and gave Sen a concerned look. "You must teach the kit to protect herself from such as these. She has no claws. She must be shown, as you were shown."

"Kit?" asked Misty Peak and Laughing River in unison.

Falling Leaf eyed the startled foxes warily before she glanced at Sen. He lifted a shoulder in a half-shrug.

"Sen has taken in a lost human kit," announced Falling Leaf.

"He did what?" demanded Misty Peak.

CHAPTER FOUR
A VIVID IMAGINATION

alling Leaf stared at Misty Peak like she thought the fox woman was particularly slow. She gave Sen a look that, for once, was not that hard to translate. *Why do you put up with this one?* The ghost panther adopted an expression of patience that bordered on patronizing.

Falling Leaf spoke very slowly as she repeated her words. "Sen has taken in a lost human kit."

Based on the way his features seemed to go tight, Sen guessed that it took an act of supreme self-control for Laughing River to keep a straight face. Not that it was much of a guess, since Sen was in the exact same position. It was not helped by the petulant annoyance that crossed the fox woman's face. Realizing that his self-control was a tenuous shield against making the situation worse, Sen made a swift decision. He stood up before anyone could do or say anything else that might make him burst into laughter.

"Well, it seems like you all have this under control. I'll be back in three days," said Sen before turning his eyes on Falling Leaf. "Do you need money for a room?"

Falling Leaf looked at him fondly before she stared death at something beyond him.

"Do I need money for a room?" she asked.

Sen turned to see the inn owner standing behind the bar again. The man stood absolutely straight and visibly trembled.

"N— n— no, Mistress Cultivator," said the owner.

"That's a good decision," said Sen.

With a quick nod in the general direction of the foxes, Sen headed for, well, the open space where a door used to be. He frowned down at the still limp form that was sprawled across the remains of the displaced door. *He's still breathing*, thought Sen. *I guess that's as good as it gets for these idiots.* Stepping over the unconscious man, Sen started toward the northern edge of the town. While he didn't burst into laughter over that last interaction between Falling Leaf and Misty Peak, chuckles kept slipping free. Chuckles he had to suppress when he felt a familiar presence close in on him. Rolling his eyes, he said something that rang familiar in his ears.

"What can I do for you, Misty Peak?"

The fox woman caught up and fell into step beside him. Her expression was fixed in mild anger.

"That ghost panther is insufferable."

Sen stopped walking. Misty Peak took a couple more steps before she turned to look at him.

"That ghost panther is my closest friend," said Sen. "She saved my life. She sacrificed for me. You don't have to like her. But if you speak about her in my presence, I suggest you choose your words with exceptional care."

The fox woman went very still. She seemed to realize that she had come within a hair of crossing a line that might well prove lethal. Sen decided that he might have turned up the intensity just a bit much in his desire to convey how much he did not appreciate negative comments about Falling Leaf.

"You can think all the nasty things about her that you want. You can even say them. Just not to me."

Misty Peak relaxed a bit when it became clear that Sen was making an effort to reduce how much threat he was projecting. She nodded slowly.

"I understand. I'll keep my commentary to a minimum."

"Appreciated," said Sen as he resumed walking.

The fox fell into step beside him again but remained quiet. As they approached the edge of town, Sen broke the silence.

"Was there something you needed? I assume there was since you came after me."

After a much too lengthy pause, the fox woman spoke. "You don't particularly care for my company, do you?"

Sen almost fired off a sarcastic comment, but he caught himself. He had the nagging feeling that the fox was being unusually sincere. He waited until they cleared the gates of the town before he answered.

"Are you looking for an honest answer here?"

"Yes."

Sen gave the question more consideration than it probably deserved.

"I don't care for the kind of games that you and your grandfather play. And, as near as I can tell, nine-tail foxes are only about their games. I don't think I'm any closer to knowing you today than on the first day we met. So, if there is a truthful answer to your question, it's this. I don't know if I care for your company or not because I have no idea who you actually are. Of course, there is an argument that you are what you do. If you're nothing more than the games you play, then, no, I don't particularly care for your company."

Sen found it interesting to watch Misty Peak's expression morph as he spoke. It started out as vaguely offended, changed to shocked, then moved on to hurt, and finally landed on thoughtful. He thought that there were a few others in there, but they came and went so fast he didn't get a chance to identify them. The problem was that he didn't know if he could trust anything he had just seen. He couldn't even be entirely certain that the face he was looking at was the fox woman's actual face. He thought it was, having stripped away at least one illusion, but that was the challenge with very good illusions. You never recognized the really good ones as fake. Misty Peak eventually nodded.

"I think I understand," she said.

Sen lifted an eyebrow in surprise. "Not going to defend your honor or the honor of all nine-tail foxes?"

"Would it make a difference to you if I did?"

She had him there. Sen inclined his head in acknowledgment of the point.

"No, I don't imagine it would."

"Then, I think I'll save my energy for things that might make a difference."

"Such as?"

A bit of the amusement at the world, which he'd come to expect from the woman, glittered in her eyes. "Oh, now that would be telling. I can't ruin the surprise."

That drew a deep frown from Sen, which just made the fox laugh.

"I'm going to hate this surprise, aren't I?" asked Sen.

"I get the feeling that you hate every surprise."

"Oh, that's patently untrue. I'm surprised every single time that things don't go horribly wrong at the worst possible moment to get me killed by a rampaging spirit beast that looks like the unholy union of a bear and a large cat. It's also great when I'm not forced to negotiate with a nascent soul cultivator under threat of death because some half-wit sect elder in the capital has an overinflated sense of her own importance. I *love* those surprises."

"Those are remarkably specific," observed Misty Peak.

"Yeah, well, I guess I just have a vivid imagination."

The fox woman sniffed. "Imagination. Right. Those were totally made-up examples."

"Completely made up. Every word of it."

An awkward pause fell over the two as Sen waited for the fox woman to either find something else she wanted to discuss or go away. It seemed that her ability to imagine things to talk about wasn't quite as vivid as Sen's. The fox eventually sighed.

"I suppose that this is the last I'll see of you for a while," she offered.

Sen nodded. "I expect that's true. I'll certainly be busy for the foreseeable future."

"Raising a mortal child?"

"I'm just providing her a safe haven for now. I'll leave raising her to someone equipped for the job."

Misty Peak gave Sen a strange look before she shook her head a little. "Goodbye, for now, Judgment's Gale."

"Goodbye, for now, nine-tailed fox."

Sen turned to walk down the road and even managed to get a half-dozen steps before Misty Peak called after him.

"There's something you should know."

Sen turned to look at the fox. "What is that?"

"No one is equipped for that job. Parents just do what they can. Try their best. It's all anyone can do. That and hope it's enough."

Sen gave Misty Peak a sharp look that seemed to make the fox woman very nervous. She shuffled her feet in a way he'd never seen her do before.

"That sounds like the voice of experience talking," said Sen.

The fox regained some of her composure and offered him an amused smile. "Does it, now? How interesting."

With that, she turned and sauntered away. Sen might have appreciated the sway of her hips a little more than was strictly necessary. A fact that became apparent when the fox woman glanced over her shoulder and caught him watching. She smirked at him and swayed her hips even more, just to let him know that she knew. *Damn it*, thought Sen. *That's just going to encourage her.* Rolling his eyes at his own folly, he turned and headed back toward Fu Ruolan's. Regardless of anything else, he'd left poor Glimmer of Night to babysit a toddler with questionable behavior. That was to say nothing of Liu Ai. He should at least have the decency to relieve the spider of Fu Ruolan.

CHAPTER FIVE

SLEEP AND SHADOW

Despite his misgivings about what he might find when he got back, Sen was surprised to discover relative tranquility. Fu Ruolan had decided that the best thing for a young child was to have something to chase. So, she had conjured qi constructs for Liu Ai to run around with under the unblinking gaze of Glimmer of Night. By the time he got back, he found the little girl peacefully sleeping on a bed that had been incongruously summoned in a small grove of trees. That had apparently been a sign to Glimmer of Night that the best thing that he could do was construct an almost incomprehensibly complicated web of qi throughout the trees around the bed. Sen had spent nearly ten full minutes studying that web, certain that there was a pattern hidden in it. Before he could glean any true meaning from it, though, the spider had come walking up.

"Did she behave?" asked Sen.

The spider glanced over to the bed before offering Sen a shrug. "She didn't do anything obviously harmful to herself."

After a pause, Sen nodded. He supposed it had been an absurd question to ask the spider. Glimmer of Night was likely only marginally less knowledgeable than Sen himself about what was or was not good behavior in a human child. Give the spider some obvious threat, and Sen had no doubt he would identify it immediately. Something as vague as what a mortal child should or shouldn't be doing, well, that was probably asking a bit much. Sen wasn't even sure if they should let the girl keep sleeping or not. He'd made those kinds of decisions for himself back on the streets of Orchard's Reach and even on Uncle Kho's mountain now that he thought about it. Of course, he wasn't living what anyone would describe as a good life on the streets and the expectations were very different once he got on the mountain.

The problem was that he wasn't trying to make himself a disciple. He just wanted the little girl to be healthy and feel safe. Beyond that, he hadn't thought it through. *She'll need to eat*, he realized, *and not just occasionally*. While he and Falling Leaf ate semiregular meals, it wasn't unusual for either of them to go a few days without bothering with it. He knew from personal experience that children could survive that, but it wasn't a good thing. Once he started thinking about it, though, he started realizing that she was going to need all kinds of things. She'd need clothes, a room of her own, toys, and she would have to start learning things. *Uncle Kho might actually murder me if I don't make sure that she learns to read and write*, thought Sen. That thought brought Sen up short, and he turned to look at Glimmer of Night.

"Do you know how to read?" asked Sen.

"Read? What's that?" asked the spider.

"It's, well—" Sen mentally cast around for the right description.

He'd literally never had to explain reading to anyone before, so he didn't have a good answer at his fingertips. He finally had a minor epiphany and summoned a scroll from his storage ring. He unrolled it and showed the spider the writing.

"All of those symbols are called writing. Each character means something, and you string them together to explain or describe things. If you can look at them and understand it, that's called reading."

The spider tilted his head back and forth as he looked at the scroll. Eventually, he shook his head.

"I think I've heard of this writing before, but spiders don't do this thing."

"Of course they don't," said Sen, pinching the bridge of his nose. "Well, Ai needs to learn, so I guess I'll add teaching you to the list of things that need to be done."

"Why?" asked the spider.

Sen felt a surge of empathy for Uncle Kho's reaction to learning that he couldn't read. It didn't seem important when you couldn't do it. Once you could, you realized just how many things in life were made better, easier, or simply possible by reading. Sen gave it a moment of thought before he answered.

"If you're going to be moving through the human world, it's an essential skill."

Glimmer of Night's expression didn't change exactly, but Sen got the impression that the spider had just accepted his words at face value. *Thank the heavens*, thought Sen. That was a fight he didn't want to have.

"If you say it is necessary, I will learn it."

"Good," said Sen, turning his mind back to everything Ai would need.

As the full scope of the responsibility he'd taken on settled over Sen, he felt a tightness in his chest that he was pretty sure didn't have anything to do with his body. He wondered if he might not have done Ai any favors bringing her with him. Then, he remembered the way the other people from her village had simply not paid any attention when the girl had gone missing. That still made him angry enough that he had to suppress an urge to go back and do... He wasn't sure what. Do *something* to them. He had no idea if that's how all villagers were about other people's children, although he sincerely hoped not. If that was the standard, though, he doubted he would do worse than that. At least, he hoped he wouldn't. A soft snicker brought Sen out of his mental world. He turned to see Fu Ruolan standing a few feet away.

"What?" he asked.

"You have that look," she said.

"What look?"

"The look of a man who just realized that something is going to be much harder than he thought it would. Tell me, have you figured out how you'll handle bathing the child?"

Sen's eyes went a little wide. He *had not* considered that problem. The mild anxiety he'd been experiencing exploded into full-blown panic. That went on for nearly ten seconds before Fu Ruolan had finished having her fun.

"I'll deal with it," she said. "Or your wife can."

Glimmer of Night looked at Sen. "You have a mate?"

"I don't," said Sen. "She means Falling Leaf."

"Aren't you worried that the ghost panther might eat the child?" asked the spider.

That sent Fu Ruolan off into a fit of laughter that Sen thought was a little inappropriate.

He eyed the spider and said, "Not really. Should I be worried that you'll eat the child?"

"No," said Glimmer of Night. "Humans don't taste good. Also, she is very small. I prefer spirit boar. That is a true meal."

Sen couldn't decide if that answer was comforting in its pragmatism or not. After all, he had said he wouldn't eat her, but he also knew what humans tasted like. Sen gave the spider a thoughtful look and smirked a little.

"And you like her," said Sen.

"She is not objectionable. Not like the always talking one."

Sen wasn't sure if the spider meant Li Yi Nuo or Misty Peak. *Probably both*, thought Sen. Shaking off that line of thought, Sen turned his attention back to Fu Ruolan.

"I assume you didn't come over here just to taunt me."

"Isn't that a good enough reason?" asked Fu Ruolan. "Your expression was priceless."

"So glad I can entertain you," muttered Sen.

"It's one of the small compensations for being a teacher," said the nascent soul cultivator. "You get to make your students squirm."

"That sounds productive."

"It's not productive at all, but it is funny. Sometimes, you just have to sacrifice efficiency in the good cause of personal amusement."

"You remind me of a couple of nine-tail foxes I know," said Sen.

"Well, they can be frustrating, but that doesn't mean they're wrong about everything."

"Seriously, did you just come over here to make me squirm?"

Fu Ruolan tapped her chin for a moment before shaking her head. "You got to go off and have fun, but it's time to get back to work. I've decided what you're going to learn next."

"Fun? I don't remember having any fun," said Sen, turning to Glimmer of Night. "Do you remember having any fun?"

"It was fun watching you fight that horde of devilish beasts. I liked it when you made tribulation lightning," said the spider.

"What?" demanded Fu Ruolan. "You made tribulation lightning?"

Sen sighed. "It wasn't real tribulation lightning."

"It looked real," Glimmer of Night helpfully added.

"It *wasn't*."

"We are clearly going to need to have a longer talk about that at some point," said Fu Ruolan.

"If we must," said Sen.

"In the meantime, come along Sen. I'm sure your spider friend can keep watch on little Ai until we're done."

"Do you mind watching her?" Sen asked the spider.

"I can watch her. I'll practice my webs while she sleeps," said Glimmer of Night.

"Thank you," said Sen, before trailing after Fu Ruolan.

They walked to her strange wooden house before the woman detoured over to her garden. It had surged back to life while he was gone, and he heard a few bees flying around it. The nascent soul cultivator took a moment to poke and prod a few of the plants and even picked a few ripe vegetables before she led Sen inside. She waved a hand at a teapot while disappearing into another room. Sen dutifully prepared the tea and poured a cup for each of them when she returned. She studied him while sipping at the tea.

"You've advanced again," she noted. "I'd say you did it a couple of times if I didn't know that was impossible."

"I did advance. It was not what you'd call a normal advancement."

"In what way?"

Sen released the suppression he maintained on the divine qi in his skin. One of Fu Ruolan's eyebrows shot up when the glow from his skin added another layer of illumination to the room. He felt her spiritual sense wash over him and didn't try to resist it. He might be able to stop her but couldn't see the point of it. He simply endured the poking and prodding until it was over, at which point he suppressed the visual evidence of his changes.

"Well, that is certainly interesting. I'd be curious how such a change came about."

"The heavens like to play games with me. At least, that's the best answer I have."

"Explain," said Fu Ruolan.

Sen took a second to organize his experiences into something that another person might understand. Then, he walked her through that particularly unpleasant advancement. He did leave out the bit of opening some kind of gate inside himself where a bunch of divine qi drained away. He had the feeling that it was something he needed to keep to himself, at least until he understood it better. When he was done, Fu Ruolan shook her head.

"You are either the luckiest or unluckiest core cultivator alive. I'm honestly not sure which."

"Any thoughts other than that?" asked Sen.

"A lot, but I need to consider it more. Plus, that's not what we're here for. We're here about that shadow qi affinity that you have shamefully neglected in its entirety."

Sen thought that he could argue that he hadn't neglected it, but he hadn't put it to a lot of good use recently either. He waited. Fu Ruolan set down her teacup, stood from the chair, and walked over to a corner.

"This is the first thing you'll learn," she said.

With that, she took a step backward and vanished into a shadow. Sen shot to his feet as the other cultivator simply winked out of his senses. It was abrupt, jarring, and complete. She was there one moment, gone the next. He strode over to the corner to see if there was a formation in place to hide the woman only to discover nothing. He examined the corner with his spiritual sense and his qi, but there was nothing special about the space itself. Just when confusion and curiosity were about to give way to annoyance, there was a strange rippling sensation that made Sen spin around. He watched in surprise and a bit of awe as Fu Ruolan stepped out of a shadow on the other side of the room. She gave Sen a self-satisfied little smile.

"It's got a lot of names," said Fu Ruolan. "Most people just call it shadow travel or shadow jumping. With your affinity for shadow qi, it's just appalling that you don't know how to do this yet. So, I intend to fix that."

CHAPTER SIX

INACCURATE ANALOGY

S en turned his gaze back and forth from the corner to where Fu Ruolan now stood. His teachers had told him about things that were *like* what he'd just seen, but this was different. The techniques he'd been told about were just advanced movement skills. They seemed to make someone disappear and reappear, but it was just magnified speed. There was also something called teleportation, where someone literally disappeared and then reappeared somewhere else. That had something to do with having a space qi affinity and remained firmly beyond Sen's understanding. Yet, that was supposed to be instantaneous, and with Sen's spiritual sense, he would have been immediately aware of their new location if they were close enough to be a threat. Fu Ruolan had vanished from his senses and been gone for long enough that he'd had the time to stand up and examine the corner. In fact, it had been about as long as it might have taken someone to casually walk across the room.

Master Feng had also told him about shadow travel techniques, but the way they had been described it sounded more like a hiding technique than a true travel technique. The cultivators used shadow to obscure themselves, and some even managed to briefly take on the insubstantial nature of shadows. It made them harder to sense, find, and track, but that didn't seem to be what Fu Ruolan had done either. She hadn't been obscured. She had been gone. Like she stepped outside of reality altogether and then stepped back into reality somewhere else. Sen frowned. He wondered if that was exactly what she had done. The very idea would have seemed impossible to Sen back in his mortal days, but he'd been a cultivator long enough to only ever put things into categories like probable and improbable. Stepping out of reality sounded more like an improbable technique than a probable one, but he had to keep in mind that he was dealing with a nascent soul cultivator. Sen frowned.

"It looks like you aren't happy with the potential explanations. Good. That means you're likely on the right track," said Fu Ruolan. "So, tell me. What do you think I just did?"

"I don't know," answered Sen. "You say it's something to do with shadow affinity, but I don't see the connection. To me, it felt like you stepped right out of tangible reality and stepped back in again, somehow."

Fu Ruolan lifted an eyebrow at Sen. "Well, that was annoyingly accurate. I guess Feng Ming and his cohorts wouldn't have put up with you if you weren't quick."

"I don't know about that. Besides, it's not like I know how you did it or where you went."

"True enough," conceded Fu Ruolan. "So, let's start with the where since that's probably the more interesting part. Where do you think I went?"

Sen thought hard about it. No matter what he came up with, though, it just sounded absurd. Eventually, he just gave up and went with the stupidest idea that passed through his head.

Laughing a little, he answered, "I think you stepped through that shadow into some separate realm where all the shadows dance and play."

His amusement faded as Fu Ruolan glared at him. He swallowed hard to clear the sudden lump of concern in his throat.

"Did someone explain this technique to you?" asked Fu Ruolan.

"No," said Sen before hurriedly adding, "I didn't think that was the *actual* answer."

"No? You just picked that out of the air and happened to be right?"

Sen reached up and rubbed at the back of his neck, where all the hairs had suddenly stood up on end.

"Yeah," said Sen, his voice a little weak.

A part of him wanted to explain, except that there was nothing to explain. He'd guessed. No, he hadn't even guessed. He'd picked the answer that he was certain was wrong. Yet, Fu Ruolan seemed convinced that he'd pulled some kind of trick on her, and Sen couldn't figure out how to convince the woman that it had just been a stupid coincidence. Fu Ruolan eyed him suspiciously for an uncomfortably long time before she sniffed in a decidedly unimpressed way.

"Well, now that you sucked all of the fun out of the answer, that's what the technique does. Well except for that part about the dancing and playing," she said.

"How does that even work?" asked Sen.

"I'm going to go ahead and assume that your working knowledge of space qi techniques is limited."

Sen frowned at that. "I know a bit about how time acceleration chambers work. Same for storage treasures. Beyond that, though, not really."

"Why in the world would you know about time acceleration chambers?"

"There was a copy of the Five-Fold Body Transformation manual stuck inside of one. I was trying to figure out how to get into the chamber to retrieve it."

"You obviously didn't succeed," said Fu Ruolan.

"The chamber had been sealed from the inside," said Sen.

"Oh, well, that would do it. And you thought you were just going to master space qi and get in there?"

"Nothing so grand. I wasn't really trying to figure out the chamber, just the seal. But it was hard to understand one without the other. I learned enough to know that I didn't have the time to learn what I needed to know."

"Well, that might make for interesting discussion at some point, but it also means you don't really have the background to understand how the shadow realm works," said Fu Ruolan. "So, I'm going to give you a very inaccurate analogy that gets the basic idea across. You know how a manual is just a bunch of pages stacked together?"

"Sure."

"Well, you can imagine that reality is like a bunch of realms stacked up together the same way. The everyday world or realm that we deal with is on one page. The shadow realm is the next page over. Or, if you like, it's the space between this page and the next. If you know what you're doing, you can move between this page and the next page. Does that make sense?"

Given that she'd said it was a very inaccurate description, Sen was certain that it was a lot more complicated than that. On the other hand, he supposed that it wasn't crucial for him to fully understand the nuances. After all, he didn't really know what lightning was but that didn't stop him from using it. He decided that this was the same thing. Until it became an issue, he'd take it at face value.

"Yes, that makes sense."

"The shadows in our realm can act as access points between those pages. So, I stepped through the shadow in that corner to get to that other realm. Then, I used this shadow," she gestured at the shadow she was standing in, "to get back here."

"So, you can just walk around in that other realm like you would here?" asked Sen.

Fu Ruolan waggled a hand in the air. "Not exactly, but that's close enough for right now. With a technique like this, you can pass by enemies to escape or even attack them directly out of their shadow. That's to say nothing of walking through walls right into their very homes and strongholds."

"I can certainly see the advantages to something like that," said Sen.

"I expected you would. Now, can you think of any potential disadvantages to a technique like that?"

Sen thought about how he might deal with someone who could do that.

"Well, with enough light, you could simply erase every nearby shadow. It wouldn't be easy to do, but it could be done. It seems like that would be potentially catastrophic if you were halfway through to that other realm. I have to imagine that there are formations that prevent people from using the technique to pass through walls."

Fu Ruolan nodded. "Both are legitimate concerns. Anything else?"

"You didn't stay in that other realm for very long. Is there a limit on how long you can stay there?"

"For practical purposes, let's say yes. It varies from person to person based on a lot of things we won't get into right now, but there is a hard limit for everyone. Stay in that other realm for too long, and you don't come back."

"Because you die?"

"No one knows. People have their theories, but theories are all they are. Well, I suppose someone might know, but they aren't spreading the information. The only solid fact we have is that, beyond some threshold, you don't return. Maybe you die. Maybe you get transformed into something. As you might imagine, it's not a subject that anyone is eager is study firsthand."

"You can add me to the list of people who don't want to discover the truth for themselves," said Sen.

Fu Ruolan snorted. "So, there is a tiny shred of caution buried deep inside of you. I was starting to wonder."

Sen considered everything he'd just learned and noticed a bit of a logical disconnect.

"Are you saying that anyone with a shadow qi affinity can do this? If they could, it seems like something that Master Feng would have warned me about."

"A shadow qi affinity isn't that common," admitted Fu Ruolan. "In fact, it's one of the rarer affinities out there. As to your question, no, not every cultivator with a shadow qi affinity can do it. You need a strong affinity to use this particular technique."

Sen's eyes narrowed. "How strong?"

"Quite strong," said Fu Ruolan without quite meeting his eyes.

A suspicion formed in Sen's mind.

"How many people have a strong enough affinity? Ten percent of cultivators? Five percent?"

"Four," said Fu Ruolan.

"Four percent?"

"Four people that I'm aware of, including you."

The value of the technique that he was going to learn went way, way up in Sen's mind. If it was that rare, it meant that it was something that most cultivators wouldn't be protecting against. *Hells*, he thought, *most sects probably wouldn't bother with it either. Why would they*? It was one thing for sects to protect themselves against threats that were likely. But only the most paranoid of sects or one with a reason to think someone with that skill would target them would bother defending against it. If nothing else, it meant that most sects would have a hard time holding him if he got even a brief window of opportunity to act. Sen smiled.

"In that case, what's next?"

CHAPTER SEVEN

SAFE?

Sen stepped out of Fu Ruolan's home with a mildly perplexed expression on his face. It turned out that what came next was not even remotely what he thought would come next. Sen had fully expected the woman to go into a full-blown explanation of the technique. Instead, she had instructed him to do something he thought was absurdly simple. It was something that he'd figured out how to do years before.

"I'll need you to practice isolating the shadow qi in your core," she said. "It's an essential step—"

"Done," said Sen, having carried out the order.

Fu Ruolan's face scrunched up in confusion. "What's done?"

"I isolated the shadow qi in my core."

"Just like that?" asked the nascent soul cultivator.

Sen got the distinct impression that Fu Ruolan was aggravated with him, although he couldn't quite imagine why.

"Um, yes."

Fu Ruolan closed her eyes and took several deep breaths. Then, she opened them and gave Sen a very strained-looking smile.

"Has anyone ever told you how utterly ridiculous you are?"

It was Sen's turn to close his eyes and take a couple of breaths.

"It might have come up once or twice," he answered.

"Well, you should sleep soundly in the knowledge that it's still true."

"Terrific," said Sen in an extra-dry tone. "So, what's next?"

"Now, you go away from me for a couple of weeks and play with shadow qi. Figure out what it can really do. Something I must assume you haven't bothered with, given what I've seen and the stories about you."

"What does that mean?"

"Fire and lightning, isn't it? Those are your preferred tools. No one ever talks about the things you do with shadows."

"Just because they don't talk about it, that doesn't mean it never happens."

"Alright," said Fu Ruolan. "When did you last use shadow qi in a battle?"

"It's been," Sen paused and thought hard, "a while."

"And did you use it to do anything but blanket the area in darkness?"

"I have used it to do other things," hedged Sen.

"Recently?"

"No," he admitted.

"It's hard to estimate these things with certainty, but shadow is possibly your strongest affinity. Yet, as near as I can tell, you don't even bother with it. I blame Feng Ming and Kho Jaw-Long for that. You got most of your combat training from them, didn't you?"

"I did," said Sen, feeling protectively defensive about his teachers. "But what does that have to do with it?"

"They both favor direct confrontation. Victory through pure, overwhelming strength. That's fine if you can back it up, which they can," she said before giving Sen an appraising look. "Granted, it seems you can as well, most of the time, but it's foolish to leave such a useful tool untrained. Shadow qi gives you more options. I've never had a moment where I believed that having more options for ending my enemies was a bad thing."

Sen was hard-pressed to disagree with her without sounding like a complete fool. In his experience, victory was the goal. Any path he could stomach that would get him there was a good path. Plus, she had a point. He'd always known he had a strong shadow affinity. He'd used it pretty regularly in the early days away from the mountain. Hells, Auntie Caihong had even made him that pill that seemed to enhance that affinity in some way. That he had neglected it in recent years was an oversight on his part. Any affinity could be a very useful tool in the right circumstances, but only if you knew what it could do.

On the other hand, he had been rather busy these last few years with trying to escape demonic cultivators and not die. He hadn't been overwhelmed with time to explore affinities that didn't seem to contribute to his immediate survival. Fire, lightning, and earth had become his go-to options because they did just that. Now, though, he *did* have the time. More importantly, he was being outright told to take that time. To fight against that because she had made a slightly disparaging but ultimately accurate observation about his other teachers would be... Well, it would just be stupid on his part. A stupidity born of ego and misplaced loyalty. He had learned a great deal from Master Feng and Uncle Kho. Yet, their way wasn't the only way or even the best way in every situation.

He expected that they would probably *agree* that he shouldn't ignore a practical tool. The fact that they had overlooked it probably had more to do with them trying to cram as much as they could teach him into his mind in the time they had. Looking back on it, he wished he had been less impatient. He wished he had been much less impatient. Given how much he had learned, how much more could he have learned if he had stayed for another five years or ten years? Part of him thought that he could go back, but it wouldn't be the same. *He* wasn't the same as he had been. They would welcome him with open arms, no doubt, and teach him if he asked them to. However, Sen intuitively understood that some window of opportunity had closed when he left the mountain. It took Fu Ruolan making an impatient noise to bring Sen out of his ruminations.

Sen offered Fu Ruolan a bow. "As you say."

She had gestured toward the door, and Sen took his cue to leave. Once he was outside, though, he found himself a bit at loose ends. He understood, in general, what she expected him to do. It was the details that eluded him. He wondered if he had become a little narrow of vision in his relentless pursuit of survival. He didn't think that his younger self would have found this task difficult to understand. Now that he thought about it, his younger self probably would have reveled in the freedom of the opportunity. He would have let his imagination run wild with possibilities. *I need to recapture a bit of that mindset*, he thought.

It was sobering to realize that he had sacrificed some piece of himself in the drive to live. He'd done it and not even realized it. He wasn't even certain what it was, just that it was gone or so deeply buried that he was having a very hard time finding it again. He supposed some of that was down to having done a lot of difficult living in a relatively short period of time. He'd made a lot of hard choices in that time. So much of what had seemed so bright and wondrous about the world had lost its shine for him. Instead, Sen had started simplifying the world around him to make it easier to deal with. He'd started dividing everything into opposing camps. Things that help me, and things that don't. People I trust, and people I don't.

As with so many things, he'd taken it too far. The world was more complicated than that. Someone who wasn't a trusted friend needn't be an enemy. Just because something didn't have immediate survival value didn't make it worthless. He could understand how he'd gotten there. That mindset had even been necessary for him when everything was on the line and absolutely every second counted, but was everything on the line anymore? Sen still needed to complete the Five-Fold Body Transformation, but that was a perfectly achievable goal now. He wasn't being actively hunted by anyone that he knew about. In fact, his only real obligation was to Fu Ruolan. It hit him all at once that he was, for all intents and purposes, safe. It was okay to relax, even if it was only a little bit.

Sure, there were probably people out there still trying to work out a way to use him or his reputation to their advantage. But he didn't really care about those people. He had passed through worse trials than telling people *no*. Beyond that, at the pace he was advancing, he would soon grow beyond the reach of almost anyone to force him into doing what they wanted. The people he cared about were largely beyond reach or swiftly growing powerful enough that it would take true powerhouses to threaten them. It was true. It was actually true. He wasn't in any real danger anymore. He had simply been in the crucible for so long that he hadn't recognized it when he came out the other side. He hadn't come out unscathed. Far from it. Yet, he had come through it. As Sen walked away from Fu Ruolan's home, he started to laugh. If that laugh sounded a little manic or hysterical, he was alright with it.

Sen choked off that laughter as he approached the little grove of trees where he'd left Liu Ai sleeping. She'd apparently grown bored with her nap because he could hear her giggling. Sen came to an abrupt stop at what he saw. It seemed that Glimmer of Night had created a large, flat, tightly woven web of qi between several trees. Liu Ai was jumping up and down on the web. It seemed to flex slightly and rebound to send the girl higher into the air than it ought to. If the web hadn't been so big that the girl could only fall off of it if she tried, Sen might have been concerned. Plus, the spider was nearby, attentively watching the girl with his reflective black eyes. Again, it might have concerned Sen if the spider hadn't already proven several times that he wasn't going to hurt the child.

The glee on Liu Ai's face was uncomplicated. Even if Sen knew that there would be more nightmares to come, and a shadow that would hang over the girl for a time, there was none of that now. All that existed for her was the simple joy of jumping up and down on that absurd web. She didn't need anything else in that moment. It was enough to be alive and having that experience, to simply be, and have it fill her world with happiness. Sen eventually walked over to Glimmer of Night, and they stood side by side, a pair of deadly sentinels to keep the uncaring world at bay for however long a little girl wanted to jump and laugh.

CHAPTER EIGHT

BREAKFAST AND A CHECKUP

Sen opened his eyes and looked down. A mop of disheveled black hair met his gaze. Liu Ai was using his chest as her bed, having come looking for him after another bad dream. He had still been awake, idly trying to make shapes out of shadow qi. He was taking Fu Ruolan's instruction to play with shadow qi quite literally. It wasn't coming as easily as he might like, but it felt like old instincts were stirring inside of him. He had heard Ai calling out in half-formed words for parents that would never come. That had been painful to hear. He remembered his time as a child and waking up on the edge of calling out for help, for parents he couldn't remember, for safety, only to bite back the words lest he draw attention. His initial reaction had been to go to her, but he forced himself not to. She hadn't been calling for him. He didn't want to wake her up from the dream, only to be the source of heartbreaking disappointment when she realized he wasn't her father.

When she had stumbled out of the room he had made for her, though, he abandoned his shadow play. She'd climbed into his lap and told him a disjointed tale of fear and death. He'd gently rocked her, stroked her hair, and made soothing noises until she'd quietly cried herself back to sleep. It was all he could think to do. Now, though, her breathing was calm and steady. Sen took that as a good sign that, for the moment, her sleep was untroubled. He could hear the sounds of the world waking up outside. His superhuman senses alerted him to the shift from night to day even through the thick walls of the galehouse. Sen carried Ai back to her room and gently settled her on the pile of blankets he'd assembled in lieu of a traditional bed, something else he'd added to the list of things she'd need. She stirred briefly as he placed a blanket over her before settling down again.

He let his mind go over what he needed to do that day as he started making breakfast. He needed to venture back to the town for several reasons. First of all, he needed to check on Falling Leaf and Laughing River. He didn't know if three days was enough for them to have made any progress, or even if the fox could help Falling Leaf transform back into her panther form, but it seemed like a bad idea to leave the fox unattended for any length of time. Then, there were all the things he needed to buy for Ai. He'd made a list, and Fu Ruolan had added several things to it. He didn't question her additions. Sen was all too well aware that he didn't have the right personal experience to second guess what a child did or did not need. He'd worn the same tattered robes for years, after all. It had been a relief to get a second opinion, even if he questioned whether Fu Ruolan was really in a better position to know.

Finally, he needed to check on that man who had the tree fall on him. Sen was fairly confident that his elixirs would do the trick, but he hadn't made those elixirs specifically for the man. He also worried that he might have missed something. His senses were sharp, but injuries were tricky things. They could hide, just to kill someone who seemed like they should be fine. It was a small but real worry for anyone who dealt in healing. Plus, he was out of practice. He hadn't done much in the way of healing others since after that battle back in Inferno's Vale. While his alchemy skills had advanced by leaps and bounds, that wasn't a replacement for practice and experience. He pushed that thought aside. He'd find out soon enough. There was no use in worrying over a problem that might not even exist.

Sen felt Glimmer of Night walking toward the galehouse. Not caring to walk to the door, he opened it with a gesture and a rather complicated application of wind qi. He paused to consider what he'd just done for a moment. A part of him was amused that he'd used qi for something so utterly mundane. Yet, the complexity of what he'd done and how much he'd taken it for granted was telling. Using qi that way would have seemed very difficult not so many years ago. While he had become adept at using multiple kinds of qi, even using them at the same time, those had largely been big, destructive uses. Fine control was something that, according to Master Feng, was almost always the last thing to come to a cultivator. That was if it ever did. While Sen took subtle uses for granted in alchemy, that was something that he'd never understood. It certainly wasn't under his full control. Shaking his head, he went back to setting out food on the table.

The spider came in, eyed the door for a moment, then closed it behind him. He sat down at the table and just watched Sen. It probably would have unnerved most people to have the human-form spider study them so intently. Except, Sen had seen the spider study rocks, trees, and blades of grass with the same unwavering intensity. It was just how Glimmer of Night approached the world. He had also agreed to keep Ai entertained for the day while Sen took care of his various tasks in town. Sen had considered taking the girl with him, but he wasn't eager to expose her to Laughing River. He didn't think the fox would do anything to her, just that the fox would be himself and that was probably something the girl could do without. With the food ready, Sen turned to go get Ai, but she trudged out of her room with sleepy eyes and dragged a blanket along with her. She brightened up when she saw the spider. The blanket was abandoned as she ran over to the table and hopped up onto her chair. It was hers by virtue of Sen putting it on a raised section of the floor so she could reach the table more easily.

"Good morning, Ai," said Sen.

"Morning, Sen. Morning, Glimmerite," said the girl around a sudden yawn.

Sen was still working out what kind of food the girl liked, so he served her a bit of rice porridge, some fruit, and a few other things. She ate like she hadn't seen food in a week, and filled in the silence with a story about a pretty bird she'd seen the day before. Sen nodded along like it was new information, despite the fact that he'd been the one to point out the bird to her. In the middle of her story, she gave Glimmer of Night a strange look.

"You're not hungry?"

The spider seemed startled by the question. He glanced at Sen as if looking for help. Sen took pity on the spider.

"Glimmer of Night eats different things than we do," said Sen. "Of course, he can eat some of this too if he wants."

Seeming to take that as encouragement, Ai picked a piece of dragon fruit off her plate and held it out to the spider. Sen had to resist the urge to laugh as the spider hesitantly took the proffered food and then cautiously chewed on it. It was like he expected the mild fruit to taste terrible. That turned into a new game for Ai, as she grabbed one thing after another and handed them to the spider. Sen kept his mouth shut. The spider was going to have to learn how to say *no* all by himself. After breakfast, though, a mild crisis arose when Sen said he was going to be gone for the day. Ai immediately got teary-eyed and demanded to know where he was going. Then, of course, she wanted to go. Sen finally had to promise to take her next time before she would let go of his leg. He wondered if that had been karma coming back on him extra fast for laughing at Glimmer of Night in his head.

When he got to town, he peeked into the common room of the inn. He frowned when he didn't see Laughing River or Falling Leaf. He almost searched the inn with his spiritual sense before deciding that might be taking things a bit too far. Instead, he went to the house of the injured man and knocked. He waited patiently until Du Fen opened the door. Her eyes went comically wide, then she went into a ridiculously deep bow.

"This Du Fen greets the honored cultivator," said the woman.

Sen heard a choked sound from inside the house and rushed steps as Wang Bo appeared next to his mother. He went into a deep bow.

"This Wang Bo greets the honored cultivator," said the young man.

"Mistress Du Fen. Wang Bo," said Sen. "I have come to see the results of my elixirs."

"Of course!" cried Wang Bo. "Come in! Come in!"

The young man gently urged his mother back into the house and waved Sen to enter. The fearful formality was already grating on Sen. Yet, he understood it, and so he endured it. Sen was a little surprised to find that the young man's father was still on the pallet by the stove. He'd have expected the man to be up and about. Sen pondered it before realization hit him. *No*, he thought, *he'd be up now if he was a cultivator*. Healing took a lot out of mortals. He could feel Du Fen and Wang Bo studying him with worried eyes. *I should do something*, he thought. He walked over to where the man was on the floor and crouched down. Sen made an overly dramatic flourish with a hand and laid it on the man's head. It was entirely unnecessary. He could probably have learned everything he needed to learn standing at the door. Yet, the playacting seemed to relieve the woman and her son.

Sen was relieved to find that he had, indeed, been worrying about nothing. The elixirs had done their work. The man was essentially healed. At this point, rest was the best medicine. As long they kept feeding the man, he'd probably be up and around in another day or two. Sen put on a thoughtful expression and nodded to himself before standing. He looked at the nervous pair who hovered a few feet away, their expressions shifting between apprehension and cautious hope.

"My elixirs have worked well. Give him another day or two of rest and food. I expect he'll be back to cutting down trees."

Du Fen slumped in relief as she gazed down at her husband. Wang Bo, on the other hand, stared at Sen warily. It was as though he expected something. Sen lifted an eyebrow at the young man, who immediately averted his gaze. Finally, after a very awkward pause, the young man spoke.

"What payment can this humble Wang Bo provide the honored cultivator?"

Oh, thought Sen. *He's still worried about that.*

"I require no payment. This was—" Sen forced himself to bite back the word that sprang to mind.

No matter how trivial it might have seemed to him, Sen knew that it wasn't trivial to them. If the injured man had died, the young man might have been able to support his mother. On the other hand, he might not have been able to support her. All of that was before considering how hard the loss of a loved one might strike. He knew nothing of their circumstances. To say it was trivial would have been condescending. He could just imagine how it would look to them for him to treat it dismissively. He would be the image of the worst kind of young master. He chose his next words with great care.

"This was an excellent opportunity to see how well my elixirs work for a mortal. I am grateful that you allowed it," he said, giving the pair a shallow bow.

Wang Bo and Du Fen gave him stunned looks of incomprehension. Sen supposed it was better than the alternatives. He did his best to make excuses to leave, his work there done, but still found himself having tea with the grateful family. He reasoned that letting them show him hospitality would make them feel better about all of it like face had been saved. Plus, the tea wasn't bad.

CHAPTER NINE

OR I WILL DO IT FOR YOU

It only took about an hour of wandering through the town for Sen to yearn for a place like Grandmother Lu's shop. A place where you could find a bit of everything, as long as it was meant for mortals to use. Instead, he had to ask where to find a tailor shop, only to be directed to the home of a very terse, very stern woman who told him in no uncertain terms that if she was going to make clothes for a child, she had to actually *see* the child. At which point, he was summarily dismissed with an admonition to acquire cloth for the clothes. It was sort of refreshing, if abrupt. From there, he had to track down a carpenter to make the bed, just to discover that man didn't deal with things like pads. On and on it went, with Sen crossing back and forth across the town a dozen times, only to get about a third of the things he had on his list.

With the afternoon sun dipping toward the horizon, Sen finally went back to the inn. When Sen once more didn't find either Falling Leaf or Laughing River there, he walked toward the bar. The inn owner took one look at Sen and went very pale. Sen stepped up to the bar and placed his hand flat on top of it. He stared at the inn owner as he started putting pressure on the bar.

The wood creaked ominously, which made the inn owner's eyes go very wide.

"Where is my friend?" asked Sen in a tone that he would never describe as murderous.

"She... She left."

"She left," repeated Sen, putting a little more pressure on the wood beneath his hand. "When did she leave?"

"Yesterday, honored cultivator."

"Did she leave me a message?"

The inn owner shook his head back and forth while his eyes never left Sen's hand.

"Did she say where she was going?"

"No, honored cultivator," said the man, sweat streaming freely down his face.

"Did she leave *with* someone?"

The inn owner nodded vigorously. "She did! She left with that older man you were sitting with the day that... The other day."

"I see," said Sen, lifting his hand from the bar.

The inn owner sagged in relief. Sen didn't say anything else. He simply turned and walked out of the inn. As soon as he stepped outside, his spiritual sense crashed down on the town like a force of nature. Nothing was hidden from him, which was how he knew that Falling Leaf was nowhere to be found. While he normally made a point not to do anything that made it too obvious he was a cultivator, all he could think about right then was that Falling Leaf had gone somewhere with the elder fox. A being with countless centuries of crafting illusions behind him. While Sen couldn't imagine *why* the fox had taken Falling Leaf and left, he had done it. With a burst of qi so powerful that all of the mortals in the town felt it, Sen vanished heading south at qinggong speeds.

He let his spiritual sense expand around him to its full extent, spreading out miles in every direction. He could tell that it was infused with his anger by the way that every living thing within range froze as soon as it landed on them, only for those same things to flee blindly in terror before it. He'd assumed that they went south because there was very little to the north of them. Yet, as the miles fell away in a blur, he became less and less certain. He didn't even notice that the sun had gone down until he finally stopped. Frustrated by the failure he turned around and headed back. His anger was an almost physical thing writhing around him and barely under control.

He wondered what the hell Laughing River was playing at. What could the fox possibly hope to accomplish with this act? If it was just to infuriate Sen, then the fox had gotten that much done. It was all that Sen could do not to take the spatial treasure out of his storage ring and destroy it as a preemptive act of punishment. Even that was only forestalled by Sen's uncertainty about what destroying such a powerful treasure might do to the surrounding area. *I could go to the sea and hurl it as far as my strength with allow*, he thought. That would be a very long way indeed, and even Sen wouldn't truly know where it was after that, likely putting it beyond the fox's reach forever. The appeal of that idea almost made him turn east immediately.

With the temper he was in and the thousands of spirit beasts he'd slaughtered over the years, he expected that crossing through the wilds would likely prove as safe for him as simply traveling the roads. After all, what spirit beasts would dare to challenge him when he was in such an obviously wrathful state of mind? Spirit beasts could be brave, but they generally weren't suicidal unless they were worked up into a frenzy during a beast tide. As much as he might welcome such a challenge at the moment, and as much as he wanted to do something that would damage Laughing River, a tenuous thread of reason held him back. He didn't know what had happened yet. It was possible, *maybe*, that it was all innocent. It was also possible that the fox intended to leverage Falling Leaf's location to force the treasure out of Sen's hands. And he couldn't trade the treasure if he sank it to the bottom of the ocean miles from shore or smashed it to pieces. Those fragile threads of sanity left him with no other course than to return to the galehouse and wait.

Even as fast as he was moving, it still took time for him to get back. It was deep into the night when he was finally approaching Fu Ruolan's domain. Yet, before he could sense it, a presence rose up out of the darkness to hold him back. He jerked to a halt, hand dropping to his jian, and cycling for lightning. After a moment, though, he released his cycling pattern and loosened his grip on the weapon. He'd been so startled by the appearance of the other presence that it took him a moment to recognize it as Fu Ruolan's. She rarely deployed it so aggressively. When she stepped out of a shadow, her face was as hard as Sen had ever seen it. Sen had witnessed the woman being erratic, frivolous, focused, contemplative, and studious. However, this was the first time that he truly saw her as the nascent soul cultivator that she was. The woman was imperious, commanding, and there was not so much as a hint of the eccentric in her. She fixed him in place with eyes that looked impossibly ancient and utterly without mercy.

"Calm your mind," she ordered, the words slamming against his body and spirit like hammer blows. "Or I will do it *for* you."

Sen was so stunned by the transformation in Fu Ruolan's demeanor that his mind went blank for several seconds as he tried to catch up. He did his best to shake off his shock and confusion. He gave her a quizzical look.

"What do you care?" he asked.

"I will not have you disrupt everything I have built here with an infantile temper tantrum," she said, her expression not softening in the slightest. "Then, there is the minor matter of the child. Would you prefer that I let you kill her with this outburst of yours?"

Sen went rigid as he felt like someone had just poured ice into his soul. He hadn't even thought about Liu Ai. Someone that young would be utterly without defense against something like his anger-suffused presence. Fu Ruolan hadn't been hyperbolic in her assertion that he could kill a mortal child that way. It wasn't just possible but nearly certain that the combination of pressure and fear would simply stop the girl's heart in her chest. For all her chill imperiousness, Fu Ruolan had just saved him from the kind of mistake that Sen recognized that he would not have recovered from. It might not have shown immediately. If he had accidentally killed Ai, though, carrying that burden would have *broken* him. Utterly. Some people might have been able to live with it, but there would have been no coming back from that for him.

Reining in his anger was beyond difficult. It had been growing since he discovered that the damn nine-tail fox had taken his friend and gone off the gods knew where. Bit by bit, he clawed that nearly boundless fury back and compressed it until it was a white-hot coal in his chest. It wasn't gone. No, it most certainly wasn't gone. He had just tucked it away where it wouldn't hurt the wrong people. It could stay there until the right moment presented itself. Taking a deep breath, he gave Fu Ruolan a deep bow.

"I am indebted to you, Fu Ruolan."

He felt her presence recede into the background, and she sniffed in a way that was much more characteristic of her.

"Well, obviously. Now, explain yourself. You're usually much more self-contained. What brought this on?"

"It seems that Laughing River decided to wander off and take Falling Leaf with him."

Fu Ruolan lifted an eyebrow. "That's a remarkably stupid thing for him to do. Which is strange, because he isn't usually stupid. Well, setting aside the whole ignoring his entire species thing. Doesn't he know you're Feng Ming's disciple? Does he *want* someone hunting him until the end of time?"

"I have no idea," said Sen. "All I can think of is that he's going to use her to blackmail me for the spatial treasure."

"Weren't you going to give it to him anyway?"

"Yes!" said an exasperated Sen. "Which is what makes all of this so bizarre."

The nascent soul cultivator gave him a dubious look.

"You didn't do anything drastic with that treasure, did you?

"Like what?"

"I don't know," said Fu Ruolan. "Hurl it into space? Drop it into a volcano?"

Sen felt a mild inclination to act offended that she'd even suggest such a thing, but he couldn't bring himself to do it. He had been contemplating exactly such a thing. Instead, he just shook his head.

"I didn't. It was a close thing, but I didn't."

"Let's call that a victory for sanity. Come along. We can discuss the rest of this tomorrow. You should at least be there when the little one wakes up. She was all but inconsolable when you didn't come back. I think she thinks that you're dead."

Sen winced. It was hard to hear clear evidence that he hadn't done *nearly* enough thinking all day. But he could take a tiny bit of comfort in the knowledge that he hadn't done anything truly irrevocable.

CHAPTER TEN
WISDOM

Mindful of Fu Ruolan's words, Sen relieved Glimmer of Night from watching over Liu Ai. Granted, it mostly involved telling the spider he didn't need to stand at the girl's door, but Sen found it relieving that she hadn't been left entirely alone. That thought sparked more than a little guilt. He was so used to being responsible only for himself, that he'd fallen into that mindset immediately when he went searching for Falling Leaf and the damned nine-tailed fox. Unlike Falling Leaf, Liu Ai couldn't take care of herself. He hadn't given it a single thought. He hadn't truly left her alone, but he couldn't simply expect Glimmer of Night to watch her all the time. The spider hadn't taken responsibility for her, after all. *I can't run off like that anymore*, thought Sen as he watched the little girl sleeping for a moment. He was once more struck by how much bigger the scope of what he'd taken on really was compared to what he'd imagined.

"How was she?" Sen asked, turning his eyes away from the partially open door to the spider.

The spider looked at him with that unreadable expression. "Upset. Afraid."

Sen nodded. "I owe you an apology. I shouldn't have left you here with her like that. It wasn't fair to either of you. I won't let it happen again."

The spider shrugged. "The child is not offensive. Also, the nascent soul cultivator helped. She made food. Told stories."

That surprised Sen. He tried to imagine Fu Ruolan being comforting and found it more than a little difficult to picture. However, the spider's complete lack of incentive to lie gave the whole thing a certain air of truth. That meant Sen was doubly indebted to the woman for stepping in when he'd failed so spectacularly. It wasn't a comfortable feeling. Sen eyed Glimmer of Night and wished he had a better sense of the spider. It wasn't as though they had made any kind of formal agreement or spent a lot of time together. Truth be told, Sen had thought the transformed spider would just wander off one day.

"I can't imagine this is what you expected when you came with me," said Sen. "I doubt it's what your Great Matriarch had in mind either. If you want to leave, I certainly won't hold it against you."

Glimmer of Night didn't respond immediately. He looked at Sen for a time. Then, he looked through the door at Ai.

"I will stay," said the spider.

Sen waited for some kind of elaboration that it became increasingly clear that the spider wasn't going to provide.

"Any particular reason why?" prompted Sen.

That question was met with another protracted pause before Glimmer of Night finally said, "I was sent to learn. I am learning."

"About what?" asked Sen.

"Humans. Cultivation. You."

"And that's enough?"

"The Great Matriarch must believe it is, so I believe it is."

Sen thought that the spiders must have a very different relationship with their matriarch divine being than the one that humans had with their divine beings. He would have many doubts about the project if he'd found himself in Glimmer of Night's position. He probably would have thought that some transcendent being was having a joke at his expense. The spider seemed perfectly content with his vague mission to seemingly tag along for Sen's misadventures. Given that spiders were hunters by nature, he'd expected more aggression from his new companion. Yet, by all appearances, Glimmer of Night was at peace with the universe. *I wish I was that comfortable with the state of things*, thought Sen with more than a touch of envy.

"The Great Matriarch didn't explain what she expected you to learn?" asked Sen, his curiosity piqued.

"She did not."

"And that doesn't bother you? You didn't want to know why she told you to come with me?"

Glimmer of Night tilted his head a little to one side in a gesture that Sen wanted to believe was confusion or thoughtfulness, but he just couldn't tell. The spider's answer didn't particularly shed any light on the subject either.

"You ask many questions."

"I'm sorry. I didn't mean to pry."

"I mean humans. You ask many questions. The child asks many questions. The nascent soul cultivator asks many questions. It is as if you received no wisdom from your elders, as though you do not understand what you are. Spiders do not ask many questions. We know what we are. We receive wisdom from our elders. We trust that wisdom. The Great Matriarch says I am to learn. I don't ask why she wishes me to learn. Even if she told me, I have no faith that I would understand her reasons. I am untempered by time," said the spider, before shaking his head. "Young. You would say I am young. It is not for me to question the Great Matriarch. I simply trust that there is wisdom in what she asks of me. Before, you fought the corrupted beasts and angry spirits. You called down lightning touched by the heavens. Now, you learn of cultivation. You care for the child. I don't ask why you do these things. I simply trust that there is wisdom to be gleaned from it."

Sen had to work to keep his jaw from dropping. That was the most words he had ever heard come out of the spider's mouth at one time. There was also a lot in those words. More than Sen could hope to understand without taking some time and really thinking them through. It was clear that Glimmer of Night enjoyed a *profoundly* different view of things than Sen. Elder Bo had thoroughly shattered any ideas that Sen possessed of simply trusting that "divine" guidance was a good thing. Then again, maybe the Great Matriarch was a more reliable source of advice and guidance than the turtle. Beyond that, even if Sen did trust divine guidance, he wasn't sure he could take that advice as unquestioningly as the spider. The problem in front of Sen was that he didn't know why the spider accepted things as they were. Was it a lack of curiosity? A lack of imagination? Or did the spider truly have such an unbreakable faith? Without that insight, he couldn't put most of what he'd just heard into the proper context.

"I see," said Sen when he felt the silence had dragged out for too long. "I suppose we, humans, do struggle with knowing what we are. Although, I don't think you can blame our elders for that. It seems to me that most elders try to impart their wisdom. We just aren't always very good at listening to it."

"That seems a sure path to destruction."

Sen nodded. "I expect that's exactly what it is for many."

"Then, why ignore wisdom that is freely offered?"

What a question, thought Sen. *Like I have any real idea*. Still, he thought he should take a stab at it. If the Great Matriarch had sent the spider to learn from him, Sen supposed she must think he had something worthwhile to offer.

"Pride, I guess. It's easier to think that you're right than accept that someone else knows better. It's also in our nature to question and confront. Asking questions is a way to get information, but it's also a way to test our thoughts and ideas. The things other people tell us can shape how we see the world and how we understand truths. Not every person rejects the wisdom they receive. Of course, not every elder is truly wise. Everyone can be blind in some way."

"Is that true of you? Are you blinded in some way?" asked Glimmer of Night, seeming truly curious for the first time.

"Me? Very much so. It happened today. I was blinded by anger at Laughing River. It made me forget that I had other responsibilities."

"Will knowing this change what you do?"

Sen actually let out a tired laugh at that question. "If people were reasonable, it should and would change what I do. But people aren't always reasonable. Changing things about yourself is hard for humans. Emotions are... Well, for humans, they're powerful and unpredictable. It's hard to see past them to the best course of action sometimes. Is that not the case for spiders?"

The spider considered that question for a long time before shaking his head. "We don't feel things this way. We have anger, fear, and even affection, but they rarely overwhelm us. To survive, to hunt, one must be calm and patient. When emotions overwhelm us, we become the prey of others instead of the hunters."

"I guess that makes sense. Humans do tend to band together. It makes things a bit safer. It certainly lets us indulge our emotions more," said Sen before hauling in his curiosity. "You don't need to stay and talk with me if you'd like to be alone or to sleep."

The spider didn't hesitate. "I'll go. I wish to rest."

"Thank you for watching over Ai for me. I appreciate it."

Glimmer of Night just nodded before disappearing out the door to return to his own little dwelling. Sen had helped him set it up when they first arrived. Sen would have just made another gale-house, but the spider wanted something smaller, round, and without rooms in it. It struck Sen as odd, but he raised it to match the requests. At some point, he might even ask the spider about it. In the meantime, he pulled a chair out of his storage ring and put it down near Liu Ai's door. That way, he'd be one of the first things she saw when she got up in the morning.

CHAPTER ELEVEN

SETTLING IN

L iu Ai was ecstatic when she saw Sen, jumping up into the chair to hug him as hard as her little arms would let her. That held up for about five minutes. Then, she remembered she was angry with him.

"You weren't here!" she accused, her eyes huge and brimming with unshed tears.

Sen did his best to keep a straight face. It wasn't funny, exactly, but her unhappiness was so unfiltered and turned up so high that it almost became a parody of itself. The vague humor of the moment was neatly offset by Sen's stab of guilt. He nodded.

"I know. I should have come back sooner than I did. That was wrong of me, and I am sorry about that. I'll do my best to make sure it doesn't happen again."

Sen knew for a fact that he couldn't promise it would never happen again. A cultivator's life was too unpredictable for those kinds of vows, so he didn't make that mistake. The girl's face scrunched up a little in suspicion, as though she wasn't really convinced he meant it. She reluctantly nodded.

"Okay," she said.

Figuring that was as close to forgiveness as he was going to get,

Sen set about making breakfast. Liu Ai followed him around and kept up a stream-of-consciousness commentary about what he was doing that was interspersed with stories about what she had done the day before. He nodded along and made an encouraging noise or exclamation of shock and wonder from time to time to let her know he was listening. He was genuinely startled the first time she said something about someone called Auntie Ru. The hand he was using to stir the rice porridge stopped moving for a second when he realized that she was talking about Fu Ruolan. *Auntie Ru*? He wondered if Ai simply couldn't say *Ruolan* or if the diminutive was what the nascent soul cultivator had told the girl to call her.

Sen briefly considered using the name himself the next time he saw her. He imagined the stunned look on her face and smiled. A brief mental flash of the imperious version of the woman who had met him in the forest killed that idea in a hurry, though. The adorable little girl might get to call Fu Ruolan that, but Sen didn't think that the woman would find it nearly as charming if he did it. Not that she'd necessarily do anything overt to him for it, but he expected she'd find some more subtle way to punish him for overstepping those social bounds. *No*, he decided, *better to not intentionally aggravate the teacher I'm stuck with for years.* Putting his attention back on Ai, he watched in fond amusement as she pretended a slice of orange was a bird that flew into her mouth.

The rest of the morning passed in a strange state of distraction for Sen, which wasn't to say that it was entirely useless. His thoughts kept drifting back to where Falling Leaf might be and trying to figure out some explanation for Laughing River's behavior. He didn't get anywhere with those thoughts, but keeping Liu Ai entertained soaked up a lot of the mental energy he'd normally use for brooding. They went for a walk, and Sen used the opportunity to make things out of shadows for her to chase after. They didn't look like anything real. Instead, they were just vaguely animal-shaped blobs of darkness. But she seemed delighted by them. Laughing and running after them until she "caught" and popped them like soap bubbles, which brought on more gales of laughter.

When she seemed like she was getting tired, Sen decided she needed something more tangible to play with. It took a while to work it out, but Sen already knew he could fuse shadow with other things. He eventually managed to fuse shadow and air to make a ball that Ai could carry around, throw, or kick. It also had the added bonus that she couldn't lose it. Even if it fell into a stream and got carried away, which it did several times, or got kicked out into the forest beyond where Sen told her not to go, he could just call it back to them or make a new one. Sen wasn't sure if that was exactly what Fu Ruolan meant by playing around with shadow or not, but he thought it probably qualified as practice.

They came across Glimmer of Night at one point. He was standing on a rock out in the middle of one of the wider streams, almost wide enough to qualify as a river. There was a web made of gossamer thin strands of qi floating around him. Sen couldn't quite figure out what the spider was up to other than some kind of practice. It certainly took a deft hand to keep something that complex under control. Without any kind of warning, part of the web plunged down into the water. It resurfaced a moment later. Sen's eyes bulged at the preposterously large fish that was caught in the web, its great body thrashing and heaving. Glimmer of Night looked at the fish for a moment before dissolving the web. The fish dropped back into the water with a splash. Little Ai squealed in glee.

"Do it again!"

The spider looked over at the little girl who was still clutching the shadow ball that Sen had made for her. Glimmer of Night hadn't given any sign that he was shocked to see them there and had presumably noticed them in his spiritual sense. He shrugged, and the web reformed around him with startling speed. Less than a minute later, another absurdly large fish was pulled from the water. Sen gave the stream a dubious look. Some fish were carnivorous. Fish as big as the ones the spider was catching could pose a danger to Ai. He'd have to make sure she didn't wander too close to the water when she was alone. The appearance of the second fish brought on just as much joy as the first.

"Again! Again!" shouted Ai, jumping up and down in excitement.

Glimmer of Night repeated the trick several more times before Sen finally put a stop to it.

"That's probably enough, Ai," said Sen.

She gave him a pouty look, then remembered she still had the shadow ball.

"Catch, Glimmerite!" she exclaimed and threw the ball with all her strength.

It flew a mighty three or four feet before it started plunging toward the water, far short of the spider's position. A miniature version of the web burst into existence and captured the ball. The web snapped back to Glimmer of Night, who took hold of the ball and examined it curiously. He looked over at Sen.

"You made this?"

"It was easy enough once I figured out how to do it," said Sen.

Glimmer of Night held the ball up close to his face so he could get a better look at it. He nodded in seeming satisfaction at something he saw in the ball before he casually lobbed it back to Ai.

"Catch," called the spider.

The spider had good aim because Ai didn't really need to catch the ball. It practically dropped into her waiting, outstretched arms. She hugged the ball to her chest with a big smile on her face. Sen stopped her before she could try to engage the spider in an ongoing game. It was close to midday, after all.

"Let's leave Glimmer of Night alone," he said gently. "It's time for lunch."

It took a little cajoling to convince her that lunch was better than more games, but hunger won out in the end. The morning's activities and the food seemed to overwhelm the girl's youthful vigor because she almost fell asleep while she was eating. Sen carried her limp, yawning form to her bed. She was asleep before he even left the room. He stepped outside and took a deep breath. Keeping up with Ai wasn't physically demanding, but it did require a lot more mental engagement than Sen had expected. He'd need to figure out things that she could do that would keep her mind engaged for a while. Sen left the door to the galehouse open so that he'd hear it when Ai got up from her nap and decided to take advantage of the brief lull in his day. Drawing his jian, Sen worked his sword forms. He felt Glimmer of Night approach but didn't let it immediately interrupt his work. When he finished the form he was working through, he stopped and looked over at the spider.

"Is this what you mean to teach me?" asked the spider.

"Among other things," said Sen. "The basics, at least. I can teach you some spear basics as well. We'll cover some of both, and you can decide if you like one of them better."

"Why would I need this?" asked the spider.

"Most cultivators use a weapon of some kind. It's not impossible to fight them without a weapon of your own, but it's much harder."

"And how long did it take you to learn it?"

"Years," said Sen. "But it sounds like you'll be around for years. Might as well take advantage of that."

Glimmer of Night nodded in agreement. "Will you teach the child these things?"

Part of Sen rebelled at the idea of teaching Liu Ai how to fight. *I'll fight anything that threatens her*, thought Sen. *She doesn't need to know how to do this.* He let himself indulge in that blatant falsehood for a few seconds. Falling Leaf had been right, though. Even if Ai might never be a cultivator, she would have to live in the world, and Sen knew what kind of world it was. It didn't matter how much Sen loathed the very thought of Liu Ai ever needing to shed blood. She *did* need to know how to fight, at least against other mortals.

"I expect I will," conceded Sen. "Although, I'm not expecting a lot of violence to find us here. Who would dare? I think teaching you both to read is probably more useful for the immediate future."

"When will you begin this teaching?"

"Soon," said Sen. "I want to give Liu Ai a little while to feel a bit more secure here before I start putting demands on her. I remember how unsettled I felt when my master took me away from my home. I was a lot older than her when it happened. I understood what was being asked of me, and it was still overwhelming. Speaking of which, how are you finding it here?"

"I do not mind this place. I have a nest. There is plenty to eat in the forest. What more could I need?"

"I suppose that's true. Well, if you do need anything—"

Sen's words evaporated as his spiritual sense detected a familiar presence at the very outer limits of his range. Everything in him demanded that he leave immediately and race toward Falling Leaf. He resisted the insistent demand by looking at the galehouse and reminding himself that Ai could wake up at any time. He'd said he wouldn't just vanish again. It hadn't been an absolute commitment, but leaving now wasn't a necessary act. It was just what he wanted to do. *She'll be here soon enough*, he told himself. *I can get answers then*. He made himself focus on what he'd been doing.

"Sorry," said Sen. "Like I was saying, if you do need anything let me know."

CHAPTER TWELVE

FOX DEAL

Laughing River frowned as he thought about the ghost panther kit. While his transformation skills weren't the same as those used by other spirit beasts, he would have been willing to bet that he knew as much about the process as any spirit beast or cultivator alive. Yet, he hadn't been able to crack the mystery of why she couldn't change back into her original form. It was equal parts frustrating and intriguing. Every piece of knowledge he had gathered said she should be able to move back and forth freely with her beast core as advanced as it was. When she attempted the transformation with his guidance, it had certainly felt like the process started. However, it also felt like something intervened directly to prevent it from taking hold. Whatever that something was, he'd never seen the likes before. He couldn't figure out if she had employed some variant path to accomplish her original shift or if, as unlikely as it seemed, some power had helped it along but at a price.

The kit had seemed disappointed by the failure. He couldn't rightly blame her. Being in a human form had its advantages. There was no question about that. It was hard to put a value on something like thumbs or passing unnoticed through cities.

Despite those advantages, there was a deep comfort to be found in resuming one's original form. Laughing River rarely did it around others because he knew the effect it had, but even he would change back sometimes. It just felt right to have dirt, grass, and snow beneath one's paws. For all her understandable disappointment, Falling Leaf had come across as wholly unsurprised by the turn of events. It was as if she had known all along that it was a hopeless endeavor and went along only to humor that human boy.

Laughing River paused at the word *boy* and shook his head. *No*, he thought. *Boy is definitely not the right word for that being.* After what he'd seen Sen do, what he'd seen him endure, he wasn't sure what word would be the right word to apply to him. He just knew that *boy* was a word that fundamentally failed to capture the reality. However, he knew that the ghost panther's transformation problem was going to vex him and vex him until he figured it out. He just feared that he wouldn't find the answer until after he ascended, at which point it wouldn't be any use to the kit. If there were any hard and fast rules to ascension, the only one he knew was that there was no coming back. Having waited far longer than he should to pursue his own ascension, he was uniquely qualified to understand just how unforgiving the world became to those who overstayed their welcome. He couldn't imagine that the situation would be *more* friendly to anyone who came back.

There was still a little time left to him before things turned utterly catastrophic, though. At the very least, he needed to go and pay his people a visit. Set the history straight. There might also be a bit of ruthless assassination in there somewhere, given the lies that people had been telling about him. He supposed that was his own fault. He'd just felt so guilty after the slaughter of all those nine-tail foxes who followed him to that cursed gathering. The idea of facing his people after that failure had seemed like too much. He could admit now that it had been a mistake. It would have been hard to do but not impossible. He'd given himself the gift of a little bit of cowardice just to discover now that it was a gift covered in poison. At least he'd learned about it soon enough to put some small pieces of it right.

All he needed to do was collect that spatial treasure from Sen. He didn't expect that it would be too much trouble. He had held up his end of the agreement. He did wish he'd been able to do more for the ghost panther, though. She wasn't happy in her human body, even if she'd resigned herself to it. It was too bad, really. She was terribly fetching as a human. His granddaughter could learn a thing or two about shaping a human body from her. He had been harboring some vague hopes that she'd succeed in capturing Sen's attention. Securing even a little bit of whatever freakish luck he had would be a profound boon for the nine-tail bloodlines as a whole. Unfortunately, she'd misread him. They both had. He had been too manipulative with Sen, while she had been too aggressive. Sen did appear less overtly hostile to Misty Peak. He seemed to regard her more as a nuisance than anything else. Not the most auspicious start but something that she could recover from if she worked at it.

He looked up to see the serving girl setting food down at his table. He directed a smile at her that made the girl's ears go pink. Not that he'd do anything about it. Some prey was simply too easy to catch. One had to maintain standards after all. He glanced around the common room. The inn owner had replaced most of the broken furniture from the fight, even if much of it was mismatched. Laughing River wondered if the man had gone from house to house buying whatever he could from the townspeople. He supposed that was a viable short-term solution. The motley assortment simply offended Laughing River's aesthetic sensibilities. He reminded himself again that this was a small, rural town, not a major city where nearly anything could be had at a moment's notice if you had the money. *I cannot fathom why anyone would choose to live here*, he thought. *Fu Ruolan must have chosen this spot.* It was the only explanation he could come up with for why they were there at all.

He'd eaten most of his food when he saw the door open. Sen walked in holding a darling little girl in one arm. She looked around with open curiosity and zero fear. Not that she needed to fear much with a protector like Judgment's Gale keeping an eye on her. Sen put the girl down, and she immediately walked over to the biggest, most grizzled man in the common room. She stared up at the man who gave her a startled glower.

"What's your name?" she asked with a bright smile.

Laughing River watched in rapt fascination as the little girl innocently leveraged the power of cuteness to charm a man who looked like life had beaten him mercilessly with the stick of hardship. The man remained silent and still for a few seconds before the hard lines in his face softened into a gruff smile.

"I'm Dai Bao. What's your name, little one?"

"Liu Ai," she said suddenly looking shy.

Awe. That was what Laughing River was feeling right at that moment. It was undiluted awe at how effortlessly that little girl achieved what a nine-tail fox had to work so hard to accomplish. Sen walked over and gave the girl a fond smile.

"Don't bother the man, Ai," he told her.

"Oh, she's no bother at all," said Dai Bao, casting a dark look around the room that promised dire consequences if he didn't like what he heard next. "Is she?"

There were hasty head shakes and a general exclamation that the little girl was joyously welcomed by all. The little girl, Liu Ai, giggled and then clambered up onto a chair at Dai Bao's table, earning another gruff smile from the man. Sen gave the scene a skeptical look before he seemed to decide, correctly in Laughing River's opinion, that Dai Bao would casually murder anyone who decided to bother his new friend.

"Are you hungry?" Sen asked the girl.

She nodded enthusiastically at him.

Sen turned an inquiring look at the gruff man. "Do you mind if she sits here? I don't want her to trouble you."

"No trouble at all," said the man.

Sen retrieved a snack for the girl from the very nervous inn owner and set it down in front of her.

"I'll be right over there if you need me for anything, okay?" Sen asked the girl.

She nodded at him before turning her attention to Dai Bao.

"You want one?" she asked, holding out a piece of fruit.

That's it, thought Laughing River as the gruff man took the fruit with a grandfatherly smile. *She owns that man for life, now.* Laughing River forgot all about the little girl right then because that was the moment when Sen focused on him. Every finely honed instinct for danger that the fox had ever developed suddenly started screaming at him that bad things were incoming. He met Sen's eyes as the cultivator approached and started scrambling to understand what had changed. Laughing River had seen more warmth in a frozen lake. Not that he thought that Sen could actually beat him in a fight, but he was pretty sure the cultivator could injure him after that display against the horde. The only thing that kept the fox from deciding he was needed elsewhere was the conviction that Sen wouldn't start a violent confrontation with a child so close at hand.

Sen sat down across from Laughing River and just stared with those cold, cold eyes for an uncomfortable number of heartbeats. Then, in an act that seemed to be happening almost against his will, Sen summoned a box from a storage ring and pushed it across the table. Laughing River eyed the box with more than usual caution. He didn't need to open the box to know that it was the treasure he needed. He didn't reach for it. Instead, he lifted an eyebrow at Sen.

"You seem rather out of sorts with me."

Sen's expression didn't change at all. "What gave it away?"

"The overwhelming impression I get that you'd like to bury your jian in my eye. Dare I ask what prompted this change of heart?"

"You really don't know?" asked Sen.

"I really don't."

"You took my friend and left."

"Yes, I took her away from the humans to practice."

"You took my friend and left without bothering to provide so much as a clue about where you were going or when you might be back," said Sen through clenched teeth.

Laughing River realized, yet again, that he had misread Sen. He'd assumed since they had an agreement in place, Sen would understand that he wouldn't do anything to jeopardize that deal. If nothing else, Laughing River had too much to lose if things went wrong. Of course, that all hinged on Sen trusting him to keep his word. That all fell apart if he assumed that Sen didn't trust him. Under those conditions, it would look incredibly suspect to just leave with his friend without providing a note or message of some kind.

"You clearly know I did everything I could to help your ghost panther friend."

"I do know that, which is why I'm giving you the spatial treasure as agreed. But that's not really the point, is it? You could have done anything to her. You could have taken her somewhere dangerous or somewhere she couldn't escape. You could have tricked her into thinking that you were me, for a while at least."

"I wouldn't do that," said Laughing River.

"You didn't do that. Given your history with me, I think saying *wouldn't* stretches credulity."

The fox almost fell into the trap of trying to defend himself, but he'd been dealing with humans for a long, long time. The anger Sen was feeling was driven by very real fears, even if Laughing River didn't know the exact nature or source of those fears. Both anger and fear would fade with time as better sense eventually took hold. He had made a mistake. He just had to trust time to make that clear to Sen. Trying to convince him of anything now was a lost cause. Instead, he just nodded and took the spatial treasure.

"I'll leave you to your business," said Laughing River.

"It would probably be best if we don't see each other for a while," said Sen. "Give my temper and my nerves some time to settle."

"I expect the townspeople would appreciate us not destroying everything they've worked to build here."

"My thoughts as well. They don't deserve that."

"Until I see you again," said Laughing River.

The fox left the inn immediately, not wanting to compound the problem he had inadvertently created. He'd hoped that trying to help Falling Leaf would mend things a little, but it seemed that had been too much to hope for. Even so, Sen had handed over the treasure with no fuss. There would likely be time to fix things later. If there was one thing that ascended spirit beasts and cultivators had, it was time. Until the day arrived to have a more rational exchange, Laughing River would deal with his own people. There was plenty of work to be done on that front.

CHAPTER THIRTEEN
I AM NOT WEAK

"You're angry with me," said Falling Leaf.

Sen glanced over at the ghost panther, noting the unusually intense look in her eyes. He'd known this conversation was coming. He just wished she'd picked a more convenient time for it. Waiting until he was three feet in the air and balancing on a shaft of hardened shadow no wider than a finger was not, in his opinion, the ideal moment. Not that balancing was particularly difficult or that the fall would mean anything to him. The challenge was that he'd just barely figured out how to make something out of pure shadow that was sturdy enough to support his weight and would last longer than a few seconds. It took nearly all of his concentration to maintain it. His slight glance and momentary loss of focus were enough to destabilize the whole thing. The construct burst into a puff of dispersing shadow qi, and Sen dropped lightly to the ground. He frowned down at a depression in the soil where the construct had been.

It had been a week since Laughing River had gone off to wherever it was that nine-tail foxes lived. Sen never bothered to ask where mostly because he was sure the elder fox would provide either no answer or would simply lie. He wasn't even sure he'd blame the fox for lying about it. Sen had something of an earned, if somewhat unfair, reputation for killing spirit beasts in truly staggering numbers. He couldn't deny that he'd done such things, but he could say that he'd rarely gone looking for it. Laughing River couldn't be sure about any of that, though, and his people had already suffered one mass slaughter. It would be foolish to risk even the possibility of a second such occurrence.

Sen turned his full attention toward Falling Leaf. He had worked hard to stay clear of the ghost panther since the elder fox's departure, and she knew it. It was equally clear that she didn't understand why he was staying away beyond the simple observation that he was angry.

"I am," said Sen, "but I'm not. It's complicated."

"Then, explain it to me."

"I didn't know where you were."

She shrugged. "You often don't know where I am. It's never been a problem before."

That much was true. Sen had always possessed a lot of faith in her ability to take care of herself either by eliminating problems or escaping them. She'd often left for weeks at a time while he'd been feverishly trying to master pill refining. He'd never had so much as a moment of pause over that. This had been different. At least, it had felt different.

"Laughing River comes off as this nice old man, but he's dangerous."

"Yes," agreed Falling Leaf with a definitive nod. "Of course, all nine tail are dangerous in their way. It has always been so."

"But you aren't always with a very old, very powerful, very dangerous nine tail when I don't know where you are. Or where you went. Or when you'd be back. I'm angry because you didn't leave me any way to know if you were overdue, or in trouble, or even which direction to search in if you disappeared."

Falling Leaf studied Sen without saying anything for a long time. When she did finally speak, there was no malice or judgment in her words, but they landed like she'd kicked him in the stomach.

"You mean like when you went to have sex with that sect matriarch in the capital and didn't bother to tell any of us where you were?"

Sen opened his mouth but discovered he didn't have any words. He wanted to deny the comparison. He wanted to say that situation had been different. Except, he couldn't deny it. It hadn't been different. It *felt* different to him, but that was only because he'd known the whole time that he was safe. Falling Leaf, Lo Meifeng, and Shi Ping hadn't known it. They'd all been under threat then, and he'd just up and vanished for days. He might have been dead, or captured, and they wouldn't have known. Sen's eyes narrowed. Had she set all of this up as some kind of lesson? Was this some bizarre, long-deferred act of petty revenge? That didn't seem like something Falling Leaf would do, but her words made it hard to judge.

"Did you do this on purpose? Was this meant to show me what it was like?"

"No," said Falling Leaf. "I was clear about my thoughts then. Trying to teach a lesson now would be pointless. There is a certain similarity, though."

Sen cast about for some appropriate response and only came up with, "I see that."

Falling Leaf waited to see if Sen had more to offer before she continued.

"I thought the nine tail sincere in his efforts. I didn't see a reason to leave word. If I thought he was a danger to me, I never would have gone with him. Not willingly."

Sen had known all of this if he was being honest with himself. Falling Leaf might have only been a human for a few years, but she had lived for centuries as a ghost panther without him looking over her shoulder. She'd survived the near-total destruction of her species. She had survived on Uncle Kho's mountain, and that was before Master Feng had *pacified* the most dangerous spirit beasts on it. Sen could dress his reactions up any way he wanted, but the source of his anger wasn't that mysterious. That only made him feel worse about how he'd treated Laughing River, who had taken the brunt of Sen's misplaced emotions. It was just easier to be angry than to admit the facts to himself.

"I was afraid for you," admitted Sen.

There it is, he thought. That unvarnished truth hung in the air between them, and Sen couldn't decide if he should have just kept his mouth shut. He hated feeling so exposed, even in front of Falling Leaf who had watched him crawling toward death more than once. Someone who had seen him nearly collapse from exhaustion after training too hard and too long. Someone who had watched him take enough blows from his teachers to bring an entire mortal army to its knees. Hate it or not, she deserved the truth from him. She'd earned that a thousand times and more. Falling Leaf tilted her head a little to one side.

"Sometimes, I think you are mad. Other times, I think that you are without fear. That you somehow seared your soul clean of it. The way you stand defiant before nascent soul cultivators, before tides of enemies, and even before death. Like nothing can truly touch you. Kill you, maybe, but never touch the things that define you," said Falling Leaf. "But that's only true when it comes to fear for yourself, isn't it? That is something you can face without flinching. Fear for others? That is something you have not mastered."

Something icy passed through Sen at her last words that made him shiver. He stared at her and felt translucent, like a pane of glass that she was peering through. His voice was quiet and tight when he finally mustered something to say.

"No," he said. "No, I have not."

"You can't protect us all the time," said Falling Leaf with affection and sympathy. "You want to. You think you can, even though this is foolishness. Danger *will* find us all."

"I understand that," said Sen. "You of all people know that I understand danger is an inescapable truth of life."

"You understand this, but you refuse to accept it. Regardless of your wishes, the world isn't made for the weak," said Falling Leaf, before her voice went as hard as stone, "and I am not weak."

"I know that," said Sen, finding a bit of fire inside himself.

"Do you?" asked Falling Leaf.

She was on him before Sen could say a word, and it was no friendly sparring match. He was so shocked that he didn't even try to block her first blow. He discovered what a colossal error that was when her fist crashed into his chest. He felt like he'd been struck by a stone battering ram. The blow lifted him off his feet and sent him hurtling through the air. Just about the time he was getting his wits about him, he plowed into a rock that was jutting out of the ground. A few years earlier, that impact would have shattered bones and probably left him unconscious. Now, it was just miserably painful as the stone cracked beneath the impact. All of that training under the unyielding expectations of Master Feng kicked in. *You can't stay down*, thought Sen. *That way lies death*. He pushed himself up to his feet, ignoring the pain, the shock of the attack, and his own wild emotions.

It seemed that Falling Leaf had not wasted time because she was there practically the moment he was upright. He had to lean out of the way as she swiped for his throat with claws made of shadow encasing the ends of her fingers. Those claws looked more solid and dense than anything Sen could currently make. Even as he felt a brief stab of envy at the sight of them, he also realized that she would have torn out his throat if he'd been a second slower. The distraction of that realization cost him again as she landed a brutal knee strike to his ribs that sent him stumbling away. He didn't regain his feet. Instead, something wrapped around his ankle and jerked his leg out from beneath him. He landed facedown. Battle instincts started kicking in then, and Sen rolled to the side. Falling Leaf's foot slammed into the ground where his head had been, so close he felt the air move. He cycled for wind and used a burst of it to send himself sliding away from the seemingly enraged Falling Leaf.

It wasn't a lot of breathing room, but it gave him the chance to regain his feet and set a stance. *Fine*, thought Sen. *If she doesn't want to play nice, then we won't play nice.* Yet, he discovered that was easier said than done. As fast and experienced as Sen was, Falling Leaf seemed to have no trouble anticipating his blows. She moved like, well, like a ghost. Every time Sen thought that he had her, she slipped out of the way and punished his hubris with a blow of her own or by raking shadow claws across whatever was convenient. Before he knew it, Sen was covered in blood that was leaking from dozens of shallow and not-so-shallow cuts. He could feel genuine anger bubbling away inside him, rising closer and closer to the surface, and threatening to erupt. He wasn't sure what he would do if that eruption arrived.

"Enough," said Sen.

Falling Leaf paused for a moment to look at him. With an almost sad look on her face, she shook her head.

"Not yet."

She resumed the assault instantly. Sen found himself paying less attention to the fight with Falling Leaf than to the fight going on inside of him. He fought to keep that anger pushed down. Yet, that split focus just meant that Falling Leaf savaged him even more brutally. When those shadow claws left five deep gouges across one of his cheeks, Sen lost the internal fight. A hundred restraints he'd imposed on himself without even realizing it fell away. He slapped away two fast strikes on her part without even thinking about it before he landed a blow to her chest that sent her bouncing and tumbling across the ground. Sen stormed after her. He saw her shake her head a little, spit out a mouthful of blood, and then fix her gaze on him. There was something feral in her eyes and her expression.

"There you are," she snarled.

The dynamic of the fight changed after that. This time, it was Falling Leaf on the defensive, dodging, weaving, and occasionally diving out of the way of Sen's unrestrained strikes. It wasn't entirely one-sided either. With his anger largely unchecked, Sen made mistakes he wouldn't normally make. Falling Leaf punished every one of them without mercy. When his anger started to die down again and the insanity of what they were doing finally started to sink in, Sen drew back.

"Enough!" he roared, unconsciously infusing the word with qi.

The world around them shuddered, and Falling Leaf stumbled back. She blinked several times and seemed to come back to herself from some other place. She spit out another mouthful of blood that landed on the ground with a bright red splash. She wiped her mouth with the back of a hand, winced, and then gave him an even look.

"I do not need your protection," she said. "Do you understand?"

Sen nodded. He did understand.

"Good. Now, while I don't need your protection, I do need one of your healing elixirs," said Falling Leaf and pressed a hand to her ribs. "You hit very hard."

CHAPTER FOURTEEN
A BEAUTIFUL ORCHID

Sen had a lot to think about when he took Liu Ai back to the town to get her new clothes. He was so caught up in his own thoughts that Ai had to poke his cheek to get his attention. He blinked and looked at her. He had a dim recollection that she might have asked him something.

"I'm sorry," said Sen. "What did you ask me?"

"Can I see Dai Bao?" asked Liu Ai.

Sen had to rack his memory. *Dai Bao*? Then, he remembered the grizzled man at the inn that the little girl had somehow befriended. Sen had mixed feelings about her spending time with the man. He was quite sure that Dai Bao had decided that Ai was part of his extended family and wouldn't do anything to hurt her. On the other hand, he thought that she'd be better served by spending more time with other children and less time with yet another adult. She was already getting plenty of time with adults of varying species. That was to say nothing of the abnormality of spending all of her time with cultivators and spirit beasts. He wanted her to at least get a few glimpses of normalcy. The thing that gave him pause was the question of whether or not *he* would recognize normalcy if he saw it. Sen ultimately caved. In the end, what was one more adult in the mix?

"After we get your clothes, we'll see if we can find him."

She beamed at him and hugged his neck, which made him feel decidedly warm and loved. *Yeah*, he thought, *I'm not a pushover. Not at all.* He kept his focus on what he was doing until they got into town and knocked on the door of the stern woman who made clothes. She opened the door, gave Sen a decidedly neutral look, and then smiled at Ai. The woman ushered the little girl inside, leaving Sen to follow on his own and close the door behind them. Sen settled in a corner out of the way and summoned what he needed to make tea from a storage ring. He kept half an eye on what was happening, but his thoughts drifted back to the... He wasn't sure if he wanted to call it a fight, a confrontation, or a very indirect discussion with Falling Leaf. There had been some surface talk, but that hadn't been the point she was trying to make. The discussion had never really been about protection. It had been about behavior and hypocrisy.

He'd been angry and frustrated that Falling Leaf had gone off into what he had assumed was a dangerous situation without telling him anything about it. He'd expected to be informed, but mostly because he'd concluded that she was no match for Laughing River. And she wasn't. Of course, neither was he. All of which painted his reaction in a not particularly good light, because he'd done similar things over and over and over again. He'd gone off into the world and just expected everyone to accept that he would be fine. Even when he was traveling with others, he routinely went off by himself without a word to do things that could *only* be described as monumentally stupid and dangerous.

He did those things and just expected people to go along with it because... And that's where it all fell apart. Sure, he'd survived those experiences but not because he was just that good. He might be just that lucky, but definitely not just that good. The cold truth was that he applied two sets of expectations to the world. He expected everyone else to treat him as though he was capable enough to handle *any* situation he might find himself in. An expectation that even he could recognize was patently absurd because it was patently untrue. However, he expected everyone else to recognize their limitations and keep him in the know when they exceeded them. All in the service of him being around to intervene if things went terribly wrong. Except, the people around him weren't incompetent. There might be a bit of power gap now between him and most of the people he'd traveled with, but not enough of one that he could serve as a one-man rescue service in any situation. That was more in line with what Master Feng could bring to the table.

The point Falling Leaf had been making wasn't that she never wanted his help or protection, but that she didn't want it on those terms. *And I can't really blame her for that*, thought Sen. It was condescending, and doubly so because of the kinds of out-of-his-depth solo risks he made a habit of taking. He couldn't have it both ways. He either needed to tell people what was going on the way he expected to be told, or he needed to assume that his companions were capable of handling any situation in which they found themselves. Since option two was so wildly impractical, because almost no one was capable of that, he needed to stop treating his entire life like it was a solo venture. When he actually was off on his own or traveling with relative strangers, it was fine to behave that way because he owed them nothing. When with people he loved and respected, he owed them better than that. A woman's voice jarred him from his thoughts.

"Your daughter is very well-behaved," said the stern woman.

Sen's eyes shot up to the woman from where he was sitting on the floor with the tea set. He gestured at an empty cup he'd set out and the woman nodded. Sen poured her a cup of tea and rose to hand it to her.

"She's not my daughter," said Sen.

"No?" asked the woman, her eyes narrowing a little. "Sister?"

"Her parents were killed by bandits in a raid. I'm just," Sen hesitated, "looking after her for now."

"And why would you, a mighty cultivator, deign to look after a mortal child?" asked the woman.

Sen did his best to push thoughts of the burned-out village from his mind.

"No one is born a cultivator," said Sen. "We all start out as mortals, and I happen to know from experience that life is very hard for an orphan child. I would spare her that."

Some complicated things happened to the woman's expression that Sen had trouble sorting out, but she finally settled on something that looked almost friendly.

"I suppose there are worse motives than that," she said. "I guess you wandering cultivators are a different breed."

"Out of idle curiosity, how did you know I was a cultivator, and a wandering cultivator at that?"

"Everyone in the town knows. After you lifted a tree off a man and gave him elixirs, it was pretty obvious. To say nothing of what your wife did at the inn."

Sen reached up and rubbed at his eyes with his fingers. "Why does everyone think she's my wife?"

"She isn't?" asked the surprised woman. "I'm sorry. That was just how everyone described her."

Sen waved it off. "It's fine. It's not like that's the first time someone made the assumption."

The woman sipped her tea, although Sen got the impression that it was mostly meant to buy her some time to think. He didn't press the issue.

"Well, all of that aside, she's a well-behaved girl. You should encourage that," said the woman.

"I'll do my best," said Sen.

Liu Ai spared Sen more awkward conversation by coming out from behind some folding panels. She was happily trying to adjust a robe and not doing a terribly good job of it. Sen set his cup down and went over to help her, gently tying the knots and settling the folds of blue and black fabric around her. She held out her arms to each side.

"I'm a flower," she announced.

"You certainly are," agreed Sen. "A beautiful orchid."

A look of hesitant uncertainty crossed the little girl's face. "What's an orchid?"

"It's a very lovely flower," said the woman from behind Sen.

Reassured, Ai smiled at Sen. "I'm an orchid!"

Before Sen could reply, he heard a dull roar from some kind of beast. Based on the way that Ai's head jerked and started swinging around, she heard it too. Sen had been keeping his spiritual sense reined in, mostly to limit the distractions in his world for a little while. At that noise, though, he let it spread out over the whole town. He heard several more roars at about the same time that he sensed the small pack of beasts on the far side of town. Not far from the home of that man he'd helped before because, naturally, they would be there. Sen looked back at Ai and his first instinct was to sweep her up into his arms and carry her far away from those beasts. He didn't get a chance to act on that instinct. The woman who had made Ai's new clothes grabbed his arm.

"You're a cultivator. Will you help us?" she pleaded.

Sen wanted to slap her hand away and get on with taking Ai to safety, but he forced himself to calm down. This close to town, on a road, any spirit beasts were likely things he could handle without even really trying. He could keep Ai safe by simply going to where the spirit beasts were and cutting them down. It likely wouldn't even take that long if he put a little effort into it. However, he couldn't take her with him for that. No matter how confident he might be that he could win, anything could happen in the heat of a fight. She could get hit by a stray bit of qi or die from a glancing blow that wouldn't even disrupt one of his punches. That meant leaving her somewhere with people he barely knew. More importantly, it meant leaving her with people he didn't trust could protect her if the worst happened. *No*, he thought, *my priority has to be getting Ai somewhere safe.* The woman clearly saw the decision in his eyes because she took hold of his arm with her other hand.

"Please," she begged and looked at Ai. "She isn't the only child here."

Damn it, thought Sen. *Way to hit me where I'm weak.*

"What's that noise?" asked Ai, her eyes wide and glistening with unshed tears.

"There are some bad things outside the town," said Sen.

Ai's lip started to quiver and a tear slid down her cheek. Sen knew he'd probably said the wrong thing. Sadly, he didn't know the right thing to say, so he just took a guess and went with it. He wiped the tear from her cheek and gave her a confident smile.

"Don't worry. They won't get you."

"Are you sure?" she asked.

"I am because I won't let them get you. I'm an expert at dealing with monsters. But I need you to do something for me. I need you to help," Sen glanced at the woman and tried to remember if he'd ever asked her name, "the pretty lady here to be brave. Can you do that? Can you help her be brave?"

Ai looked from Sen to the woman. He could see that she wasn't sure about this whole thing, but she nodded at him. He put his hand on her shoulder and tried to ignore the roars that were growing louder and fiercer.

"That's my brave girl. You help her, and I'll go send those monsters running."

Sen shot the woman a look that communicated with utter clarity how violently upset he was going to be if anything *at all* happened to Ai. Then he was out the door, activating his qinggong technique, and all but flying through town.

CHAPTER FIFTEEN

GROUP TACTICS

I t took longer than Sen would have liked to get to the battle because he had to keep dodging around panicked townspeople. Granted, it only added a few seconds to his journey, but he knew as well as any warrior that seconds could cost lives. However, when he arrived at the scene of the fight by the simple expedient of jumping over the town wall, he couldn't help but pause. He wondered, *what in the hells are they doing?* Some of the men from the town were out... Sen thought the right phrase was probably *defending their homes*, but it only applied in the loosest sense. They weren't working together, except for one or two pairs of men. It was just a loose collection of people armed with shovels and pitchforks. Plus, they weren't even putting those farm implements to good use. They were just waving them at the spirit beasts, or occasionally thrusting them at the creatures. This had all the makings of a slaughter, and not one that favored the humans.

Sen turned his attention to the spirit beasts. He didn't recognize them, but the wilds always seemed to be throwing some new thing at humanity. They were long and thin, slung low to the ground, but they moved fast. They had the kind of liquid black eyes that were more common to rodents than other beasts. Their bodies were covered in soft brown fur. It was also clear that their teeth and claws were as sharp as one might expect from the number of bleeding wounds that Sen could see on the men. He also saw two limp, lifeless bodies that had been dragged back. It was yet another reminder, not that Sen particularly needed one, that life was precarious for the mortals. He eyed the spirit beasts. If the men out here fell, those things could probably go right over the wall. Once they got into the town, it would get very ugly, very fast.

For all the threat that the spirit beasts posed to the townspeople, Sen was pretty sure he could wipe them out with one volley of wind blades. That would solve his problem, but it wouldn't do much to help the townspeople the next time something came looking to eat them all. He considered whether that was his problem. He had only agreed to help deal with the problem. He hadn't agreed to teach the people here basic group tactics. Of course, these people were also his neighbors for all intents and purposes. He got things here for Ai, and Falling Leaf had even bought some furniture here. Helping these people learn to defend themselves better was probably the neighborly thing to do. Sighing to himself a little, Sen strode forward and sent a half dozen small fireballs to drop between the humans and the spirit beasts. It was enough to make the spirit beasts back off slightly but not enough to send them running. Sen took advantage of the pause in the fight to start barking orders the way he'd seen some older city guards do when dealing with younger guards.

"Get into groups of three!" he bellowed. "Two pitchforks, one shovel."

The men all stared at him in bewilderment. It wasn't until Dai Bao got involved that anything useful happened. The man glared around for a moment before he started bellowing.

"You heard the cultivator! Do it now!"

Sen sent out another wave of small fireballs to keep the spirit beasts wary while the men shuffled and bumbled their way into small groups. He strode up to the group with Dai Bao and gave the man a nod. Then, he addressed the group.

"Use the pitchforks to harass and distract. Spirit beasts are living creatures. They don't like pain any more than you do," he said holding out a hand toward a young man with a pitchfork.

The young man, practically still a boy, stared at Sen until Dai Bao rolled his eyes.

"Give him the pitchfork, idiot."

The young man flushed in embarrassment but promptly handed over the pitchfork. Sen swiftly showed them how to hold it.

"One hand high up. You use this for force. The other hand lower down to guide the blow. Stab, don't shake," he said demonstrating the motion. "You're there to keep the keep the beasts off balance. Stab, then back off a step or two. Let the other people take their turns."

Sen handed the pitchfork back, sent a few more fireballs, and then held a hand out toward a man holding a shovel. The man handed it over without any prompting. Sen simply swung the shovel in a short arc.

"Blunt force. Hit them in the head. Nothing fancy. Wait until they're distracted, then make your move. Work together!"

Sen knew he was taking a risk with these men's lives by not simply killing the spirit beasts, but he wouldn't always be there to protect them. They *had* to learn or this town wouldn't survive. The groups moved forward, spaced a little too loosely, but it was the best Sen could do on short notice. The spirit beasts seemed to sense that Sen wasn't planning on taking an active hand, and they charged forward. The strategy almost fell apart immediately. The groups had no experience working together, so the men with the pitchforks frequently tried to distract the spirit beasts at the same time. Sen would surreptitiously send small wind blades as distractions when it looked like someone was about to get themselves killed. After a few back-and-forth exchanges with the huge rodent creatures, though, the townspeople started to figure out their timing. There was the metallic smell of blood in the air. Some of it human, some of it from the beasts, and all of it unpleasant.

Sen heard a mild cheer from one group and focused there for a moment. The creature was lying still on the ground, but Sen's spiritual sense told him it was still alive. He flashed over with his qing-gong technique. He glared at the men, who shrank back from that look.

"It's not over until you take off its head," he growled. "That thing is still alive."

The stunned men turned back to the creature that was starting to stir. They looked scared and wholly uncertain about what they should do. Sen decided that this was a teaching moment. He held out a hand to a bearded man with a shovel. The man gave it to him. Sen walked over to the beast, raised the shovel up over the beast's neck, and drove the sharpened edge of the shovel straight down. The creature's head flopped free in a spray of blood. One of the men with a pitchfork stumbled away and retched. The bearded man's lips thinned into a line, but he nodded in understanding. Sen gave him back the shovel. He hung back after that. In part, he wanted the townspeople to get some experience. In part, he was scanning the nearby forest with his spiritual sense. These creatures weren't acting the way he'd expect experienced spirit beasts to act. They were more like, well, like that young man who hadn't realized he should give Sen the pitchfork.

Sen was waiting for whatever had sent them this way to make an appearance. He didn't have to wait long before an ear-splitting roar shook the air and a similar spirit beast that was three times the size of the rest crashed out of the trees. The humans and the younger rodent creatures were all stunned motionless by the power of that roar. But Sen charged at it while sending red-tinged wind blades, the vermilion blades he'd seen Li Yi Nuo use, flying out before him. The massive rodent beast roared again in anger and pain as those blades tore deep gouges into its long body. There was a swell of qi from the beast and vines shot out of the ground. Sen dodged, but three of the vines managed to bury themselves in his left leg. The sheer power of his momentum ripped the vines free from the ground, but he was stunned that they had managed to pierce his skin. He'd caught blades swung by cultivators without getting a scratch.

Worse, he could feel the vines still wriggling in his flesh, trying to find purchase. Under normal circumstances, it wouldn't be a problem. However, there was still a massive rodent bearing down on him. He was shocked that anything this powerful had come near both civilization and Fu Ruolan's domain. He did his best to ignore the injured leg, although the vines were making it difficult to run. He hadn't planned on meeting the creature's charge head-on, but he'd had an idea for a new blade technique in the back of his head for a while now. He supposed this was as good an opportunity as any to test it. If it failed, he could always just fall back on Heavens' Rebuke. Sen grasped the hilt of his jian and began channeling for earth qi, swiftly infusing the blade with it. He took a breath, focused, and drew the blade in a smooth motion. The blade followed an arc up toward the sky. As it went, the earth qi he'd gathered was unleashed. A wall of stone as thin and sharp as a jian blade shot out of the ground. The massive spirit beast was split cleanly down the middle.

The vines still embedded in Sen's leg stopped writhing, which was a relief because it was painful and more than a little creepy to have something alive moving inside of him. He formed a qi platform beneath his feet and used it to lift himself out of the way of the two pieces of the spirit beast that were sliding toward him. The two parts fell away to each side, exposing the interior of the beast. It was a bit much even for Sen's hardened stomach to see the organs and blood spilling out onto the ground. Instead, he turned back to the men who had been fighting the smaller beasts. The bearded man he'd been with before had a stoic look on his face as he decapitated the last of the smaller beasts. Satisfied that the threat was over for now, Sen reached down and started ripping the vines out of his leg. He grimaced and told himself that he needed to change before Ai saw him again. He wasn't as covered in blood as he had been on many prior occasions, but there was more than enough on him to scare a small child.

While he had the platform carry him back toward the men, he summoned a healing elixir and drank it. He let the platform drop to the ground and dismissed it before he looked around at the exhausted and injured men. He nodded at them.

"You did well," he said. "You should collect the beast cores and sell them. I'd recommend investing some of that money in spears and halberds. They'll be more effective than farm implements the next time spirit beasts attack. Now, bring the wounded to me, and I'll see what I can do about speeding along your recoveries."

CHAPTER SIXTEEN
RETRIEVE AND ESCAPE

Sen tried to work as quickly as he could to help the injured, but things only grew more chaotic as people poured out of the gates. Some came looking to find loved ones, while others simply wanted to see what had happened. There were wails of grief over the two men who had died, but Sen had to steel himself against them. There was nothing he could do for those people except offer empty words he was certain they wouldn't want to hear. By the time he'd finished dispensing what immediate aid he could, nearly two full hours had passed since he'd left Liu Ai in the care of the seamstress. Despite the injuries and the grief, most of the townspeople were jubilant that the spirit beasts had been killed and so few had died. Sen waited until no one was paying him any particular attention to quite literally slip away in the shadows. He still wasn't anywhere close to performing whatever technique it was Fu Ruolan had demonstrated, but he'd become rapidly more proficient at manipulating shadows, both the ones he made and the ones around him.

He made a point to stop, wreathe himself in darkness, and change out of his bloodied robes. He even took a few minutes to wash his face, hands, and arms. Satisfied that he'd done what he could to not scare Ai, he started walking back. There was happy confusion in the town as everyone realized that the threat had passed, but the details hadn't spread yet. Sen wanted to be well away before they did. Not that he expected that this incident would particularly add to the legend of Judgment's Gale, but he didn't want to announce to the world that he was in the area. Even if there weren't ruthless, murderous cultivators actively searching for him, it didn't mean that there weren't cultivators and sects passively monitoring for news of his whereabouts. He didn't want those cultivators descending on these people and throwing their weight around like the bunch of arrogant, entitled cultivators they would no doubt be. No, it was better if he slipped away in the confusion. Besides, he hadn't done that much, except right at the very end.

Let the townspeople claim this victory as their own and leave him out of it. Just some wandering cultivator who helped out a little and then went on his way. No reason for anyone to pay special attention to this place or these people. As Sen approached his destination, he came up short when he saw Ai happily talking with another little girl as the pair of them drew on the ground with sticks of chalk under the watchful eye of the seamstress. His cultivation-enhanced eyes let him see crude drawings of flowers and birds. He released a gentle sigh of relief. She'd gotten a touch of normalcy after all. Sen just watched the girls for a few minutes before he walked over to the woman. She glanced at him, her eyes lingering on his robes.

"You changed," she observed.

"The other robes weren't really fit for the eyes of children anymore," he said.

"Oh?"

"Too much blood."

"Yours or the spirit beasts'?"

"Some of both. Who is that other girl Ai is playing with?"

"My daughter," said the seamstress.

Sen gave the woman a longer look. There was love in her eyes as she watched her daughter. There was also pain there. There had been some kind of loss, not recently perhaps, but it still lingered. *No wonder she'd been so desperate to get me to help*, thought Sen. She noticed his scrutiny and drew herself up a little. It was a subtle thing like she was wrapping a cloak of dignity around herself.

"What?" she asked, her stern sharpness returning.

Sen very deliberately looked away and, rather than answer the question, he changed the subject.

"I don't believe I ever asked your name," he said.

He could feel the look she directed at him, but he kept his eyes on the girls.

"Li Hua," she answered in an almost reluctant tone.

"Lu Sen."

"Is that the name you use when you don't want to use the name Judgment's Gale?"

Sen closed his eyes and sighed. He hadn't been doing a lot to hide that he was that increasingly well-known folk hero. He'd just hoped that no one in the town would figure it out quite this soon. It could make things inconvenient, or at least aggravating, if people started treating him like some kind of hero. The way most people already treated him as a cultivator was uncomfortable at best. Adding some kind of misplaced hero worship or heroic expectations on him would only lead to a lot of disappointment for them. As for the name, well, he had a simple enough answer to that.

"No. It's just my name. That other person doesn't really exist."

"You look real to me," she said.

He couldn't be sure, but Sen thought he caught the slightest trace of amusement in her tone.

"Don't be fooled. I'm entirely made up. Turn your back, and I'll vanish like smoke in a dream."

"Can you—" Li Hua hesitated. "Can you really do that?"

Sen went to deny the silly idea and then thought a little harder about it. *Could I?*

"Maybe," he said. "Probably not if anyone was paying close attention."

"So, not all-powerful?"

"Not even remotely. Any cultivator who says otherwise is lying," answered Sen. "I think it's probably time for a quiet departure. Things are calming down at the gate."

"How do you know that?"

"I can hear them," said Sen as he walked over to collect Liu Ai.

She noticed him and ran over, her eyes wide.

"Did you chase the monsters away?" she asked.

"I did, with some help," said Sen, not feeling the tiniest bit guilty about the half-lie. "But it is about time for us to head home. Otherwise, we'll never get there before dark."

The girl got a pouty look on her face. Ai wasn't generally a willful girl, but Sen had learned that she could get tired or cranky like anyone else. He wanted to cut that off before it turned into something ugly.

"Why don't you show me what you were drawing?"

Distracted by the task, she reached out, seized one of Sen's fingers in her hand, and pulled him over. She proudly pointed to a misshapen, vaguely flower-shaped creation and proclaimed it a beautiful orchid. Sen nodded gravely while the other girl awkwardly stared up at him, seemingly unsure what to do. He crouched down and spoke to Ai in a very loud whisper.

"Who is your friend?"

"Zhi," said Ai. "She drew birds."

Sen smiled at the other girl and made impressed noises at her bird drawings. They did at least have wings. That was close enough. Taking the opportunity, Sen scooped Ai up into his arms, making her giggle.

"Okay, we really do need to go now. Say goodbye to Zhi."

"Bye!" shouted Ai as she waved furiously at the other girl.

The other girl gave Sen a shy look before she waved back and said, "Bye!"

"It was very nice to meet you, Zhi," said Sen and glanced over at the seamstress. "And you, Li Hua."

She lifted an eyebrow at him but offered a shallow bow. "It was nice to meet you, honored cultivator."

Sen again thought that he caught the edges of amusement in the woman's voice, but it was just subtle enough that he couldn't be sure. He gave the woman a casual wave before he set out for the gate that didn't have half the town crowding around it. Once they cleared the town, Sen activated his qinggong technique and wrapped Ai up in protective layers of air. He'd done it instinctively the other times he'd carried her, and he assumed that Glimmer of Night must have done the same. Traveling at those speeds would normally be dangerous in the extreme for any mortal. Once he realized he was doing it, though, he'd decided to take a more active hand in the process. Ai remained blissfully unaware of the situation, talking excitedly about her new friend and how much fun drawing was for the better part of an hour. After the excitement wore off, though, she grew quiet. Sen felt her head settle onto his shoulder and quiet snoring soon filled his ear.

He let his mind drift back to that spirit beast attack. Something about it didn't sit well with him. After sorting through the experiences, he settled on the simple answer that the last spirit beast had been too powerful. The town was quite rural, but not so rural that spirit beasts powerful enough to injure *him* should be attacking. Sen was starting to think that Master Feng's ongoing interest in the odd spirit beast behavior over the last few years was worth investigating. Not that Sen himself shared a yearning to investigate the issue. He had more than enough to shoulder for the moment, and it had been a long time since he wasn't surrounded by deadly threats. A bit of time focusing was just what he needed. Not that Fu Ruolan would let him slack off. She might have told him to go and play around with shadow qi, but he had also sensed her lurking on occasion. Since he was relatively certain she could hide from him completely if she wished to, letting him sense her was a quiet reminder that he was there with a purpose.

Of course, that didn't prevent him from contacting his master. *I should write to him about the spirit beasts*, thought Sen. *In fact, I should write to all of them.* He tried to remember how long it had been since he last spoke or wrote to Grandmother Lu and couldn't come up with an answer. That made the answer all too clear. *It's been too long*, he decided. He had acceptable reasons for the long silences, but he knew that particular missive was long, long over-due. Given all of his advancements and experiences since they last saw each other, he wondered if she'd even recognize the person he'd become. Then again, she'd probably heard the stories. She'd have some sense, however distorted, of what he had gone through. She was also a practical woman. She'd probably had a far better idea of what he'd face and what it would mean for him than he had the day he left Orchard's Reach. While a small part of him feared that she'd be disappointed in him, the sensible part of him knew that wasn't likely. She'd just be happy he was alive and not obvi-ously evil. It was a low bar, perhaps, but not one he felt it wise to complain about.

He nodded to himself. He'd prepare letters and send them out the next time he had a reason to visit the town. It would start to get cold in a few months, so Ai would need warmer clothes before too long if nothing else. That would be the perfect opportunity.

CHAPTER SEVENTEEN

WEB LESSON

"How in the world do you maintain this?" asked Sen.

He was staring at the qi web that stretched for hundreds of feet between widely spaced trees. Sen wasn't sure exactly why the spider had constructed such a thing, but that question took a distant second position to the how of it. Sen was no stranger to large-scale techniques. The difference was that he often relied on the internal momentum of the techniques to keep them active. After all, once a storm got moving, it didn't usually need much help to keep going. What Glimmer of Night had done was a completely different animal. There were thousands of individual qi strands involved. To rub a bit of salt in the wound, the spider was frowning at the web like he was more worried about some imperceptible flaw in the pattern than the impossible mental strain of keeping all those strands active and stable. Sen was used to doing difficult things. This beggared his imagination, though. The spider turned his attention away from the web to look at Sen.

"What do you mean?" asked Glimmer of Night.

"I mean how can you possibly divide your attention so many ways? All those strands. How does your mind hold up under the pressure?"

The spider regarded Sen in contemplative silence before repeating himself. "What do you mean?"

"I mean that I couldn't maintain a web a fraction this large, and it would take every last bit of my concentration to do it."

"Why?"

Sen briefly thought that the spider was having a joke at his expense but dismissed the idea. Glimmer of Night sounded genuinely perplexed by what Sen was saying. He tried to think of a better way to explain it.

"I mean, assembling all of those individual strands and keeping them in place would be a huge task."

The spider tilted his head a little to one side. "What kind of human madness would possess you to do it like that?"

Sen wasn't entirely sure how to respond to that question. He was sure that Glimmer of Night wasn't trying to insult him. There had been an almost horrified quality to the spider's voice, like he couldn't comprehend why anyone, not just Sen, would do things that way. On the other hand, it also seemed like the spider took it for granted that there was a better way and that everyone should know it. Sen didn't know *how* everyone was supposed to possess that knowledge, though.

"What other way is there?" Sen asked, still half-waiting for the spider to let him in on the joke.

While he had gotten better at reading Glimmer of Night since the spider's transformation, it was by no means a perfected skill. There were moments, like the one Sen found himself stuck in right then, where the spider remained a wholly alien being. Again, Sen didn't believe that Glimmer of Night was intentionally being unreadable. It was just that whatever spiders normally did to convey their emotions didn't convert terribly well to the vaguely human form that the spider now inhabited. Sen's automatic response for gauging people's state of mind was to look at their faces and eyes. Glimmer of Night's face was usually an impassive mask. The spider's eyes were just black, liquid pools that conveyed nothing. After a moment of reflection, Sen reasoned that they'd probably be downright unnerving for a mortal. He'd simply faced down too many people and things that posed a literal threat to his survival to find strange eyes anything more than a curiosity. The spider must have come to the conclusion that Sen wasn't trying to be difficult.

"You hold the pattern in your mind and fill it with qi," said Glimmer of Night. "The web manifests from that mental pattern and largely sustains itself, as long as you maintain the mental image."

It was a remarkably concise answer to have left Sen with so many uncertainties. Sen gestured at the massive web.

"You're holding *that* pattern in your mind, right now?" he asked.

"Yes," said the spider, as though it were self-evident.

"You thought that up and can keep all the details straight?"

"Of course not," said the spider. "I didn't think this up in its entirety. I modified one of the inherited patterns, although this one is a failure."

Glimmer of Night glanced at the web, and the qi that made it up dispersed into the environment.

"Inherited patterns?" asked Sen, certain that he was missing something crucial.

The spider looked back at Sen and drew the obvious conclusion. "You don't have those?"

"If I do, no one has ever made me aware of them."

"That is unfortunate."

Sen waited for more information, but the spider just stood there looking at him.

"What are the inherited patterns? I mean, I get that they're web patterns that you somehow automatically know, but what are they for? What do they do other than let you make webs?"

"They let us understand, interpret, and influence the layers of reality," said Glimmer of Night in such an offhand tone that the magnitude of the statement didn't fully sink in before the spider continued. "They are, of course, simplified mechanisms based on the pure perfection that is the web of the Great Matriarch. Her web intersects with all truths and all universes. We, her children, are lesser beings. We cannot hope to withstand the knowledge and inherent power contained in the full reach and breadth of her web. In her benevolence, she gave us the inherited patterns, each of which touches on a single, lesser truth. By mastering each of the inherited patterns, we gain insight and grow in strength. Master them all, and we can begin to touch upon the greater truths and even, perhaps, receive instruction directly from the Great Matriarch."

Sen felt like he'd taken a very hard blow to the head. He was dizzy and didn't trust that he had full control over his body. He was dimly aware that his mouth was hanging slightly open, which was probably making him look like an idiot. Yet, it was hard to focus on such mundane concerns with so many revelations landing on him in short order. Laughing River had implied that there were other realities and dropped some hints about it, but Sen had sent him away before they ever really discussed it. Of course, he'd also assumed that the elder nine tail was simply having fun at the expense of a young human cultivator because, after all, that's what nine-tail foxes did. It seemed that all sapient spider spirit beasts took this piece of information for granted and even got knowledge imparted to them to help them understand and navigate that truth.

Beyond that, it seemed that the Great Matriarch, a being that Sen was increasingly frightened of, had given her children the means to manipulate reality. That wasn't quite as mind-numbing, as Sen himself manipulated reality in some ways with qi. He was also aware of the fact that layers of reality existed. Fu Ruolan had made that much clear with her explanation of how the shadow walking technique worked. Yet, it seemed that manipulating those layers was a normal and expected part of a spider spirit beast's life.

The implications of that left Sen feeling a little cold, given how many of the spiders he had butchered back on Mt. Solace. Was the Great Matriarch the kind of ascended being that took those kinds of slights personally? Would she hold a grudge? If she could manipulate the layers of reality, would Sen find himself stepping through a hole in the world to some terrible and lethal place? *Oh, this is bad*, thought Sen.

Glimmer of Night continued. "You truly don't have the inherited patterns?"

"No," murmured Sen, his mind still back on all of the other things that the spider had said.

"A pity," said the spider. "How are you ever to understand reality without such insights? The gap in your knowledge will only grow more profound if you ascend."

Sen didn't even begin to have the context to understand what the spider was getting at. So, he just tossed out the first thing that came to mind.

"I'll just have to stumble through. I wouldn't be the first to do so."

"I wonder why the Great Matriarch withheld them from you. Perhaps it is because you are not her children."

Sen shrugged at that. "Perhaps she couldn't. It might have been forbidden."

He could feel the skepticism radiating off of the spider, which gave Sen a bit of insight into the spider's view of the world. As far as Glimmer of Night was concerned, the Great Matriarch sat at the pinnacle of power in the universe. Sen had doubts about that but didn't feel any pressing need to express those doubts. He didn't have any proof that the spider was wrong. It was just an intuition that things were more complicated than that. With his equilibrium returning, Sen recognized that most of what he'd just learned wasn't something he had to explore immediately. He'd need to think about it and ask more questions later, but he'd had a purpose when he came over.

"So, you said that you infuse the pattern in your mind with qi to make it manifest?"

"Yes," agreed Glimmer of Night.

"How do you infuse something that only exists in your mind? I infuse objects with qi all the time, but I don't think I've ever infused an idea with qi before."

"You do it all the time," said the spider.

"I really don't."

"You do," insisted Glimmer of Night. "Every time you shape a technique. You structure the technique in your mind and fill it with qi."

Sen frowned. It was sort of true, but it also wasn't. Those things didn't happen in his mind. At least, he didn't see it that way. He fashioned his techniques out in the world. It was a complicated interplay of his qi, environmental qi, and mental manipulation of both. Granted, he could build techniques using nothing but his own qi if he ever found himself in a place devoid of environmental qi. Even then, he didn't think he'd be doing what Glimmer of Night was describing. Maybe the spider was doing what Sen did and just didn't talk about it the same way.

"Could you show me?" asked Sen. "Could you make a web? Just do it slowly so I can observe."

The spider nodded enthusiastically. Sen paid close attention to what happened with his spiritual sense. He felt Glimmer of Night's qi stirring, and then a web appeared. Sen frowned. The spider had definitely done something. Whatever he'd done, though, it didn't involve constructing a technique that interacted with the environmental qi. Sen resigned himself to spending a long afternoon feeling like a novice again.

"Could you show me again?" asked Sen.

CHAPTER EIGHTEEN
FOCUSED CONSIDERATION

I t was both fortunate and unfortunate that Glimmer of Night *loved* making webs, at least in Sen's opinion. The spider had made dozens of them at Sen's request without a single complaint. If anything, he had seemed quite pleased with Sen's focused attention on the process. That meant there were ample opportunities to see how the webs were constructed. It also meant that there were ample opportunities for Sen to experience the true and magnificent depths of his failure to understand what the spider was doing. Glimmer of Night had tried to find other ways of explaining what he was doing, but even Sen could recognize that the problem was with his comprehension and not the explanation itself. He did consider the possibility that the sapient spiders as a whole were simply interacting with qi in a fundamentally different way than human cultivators.

While they might use different methods, those methods shouldn't be out of reach for him. Spirit beasts still relied on cores and qi channels. Qi could come in lots of different types, but no one could make qi operate in ways that violated its basic nature. So, despite the fact that Sen couldn't immediately see how it was done, the qi in the webs acted the way that he expected qi to act.

Even if he couldn't quite pin down what type of qi it was, he assumed that was a temporary problem.

It had qualities that reminded him of air qi, but there were other things mixed in with it. Types of qi that Sen was confident that he hadn't seen before. When he'd asked Glimmer of Night about it, the spider had just shrugged and called it *web qi*. That struck Sen as a terribly specific and complex concept for qi, which was usually attuned to simpler and broader concepts, like air, fire, and shadow. Since he lacked a better name for it, Sen was left with little choice but to accept the one the spider had given for it.

More importantly, he wasn't focused on the web qi itself. That was little more than an interesting cultivation puzzle that he'd think about in spare moments for months or even years to come. He was intent on finding a way of manifesting shadow techniques like Glimmer of Night did with webs. Sen could solidify shadow qi. He could already imagine the disruption to entire groups of enemies if he hit them with a solidified shadow web. The technique wouldn't even need to last more than a few seconds to do its work. That kind of shadow web would have caused havoc with the horde of devilish spirit beasts back at the ruins. *It's a good idea*, thought Sen, *if I can make it work*. The problem was that he couldn't take the time to brute force it during a battle. If he could co-opt whatever method the spider used for the webs, though, near instant manifestation of shadow webs would prove hard to defend against in the middle of a fight.

Good idea or not, though, he couldn't seem to make it work. Falling Leaf could tell he was fixating hard on something and offered to keep watch over Ai while he tried to sort it out. He'd spent the last two days away from the galehouse in deep meditation that was only occasionally broken when he tried out some new idea to make it work. He'd felt Fu Ruolan keeping an eye on him from a distance, but she didn't interrupt. It seemed that she was satisfied that he was putting full effort into the task. Sen was coming to the unhappy conclusion that full effort wasn't going to be the key to solving the problem. He needed some kind of nudge or insight that was eluding him. Frustrated with himself and the overall lack of progress, Sen turned his mind to the more obscure but equally compelling bit of information that Glimmer of Night had provided. That the inherited web patterns that the Great Matriarch had provided to all spider kind were some manner of roadmap to modifying reality or possibly accessing the layers of reality.

There was more than a little overlap between that and what Fu Ruolan wanted him to do with shadow walking. Except, the spiders were taking it a lot further than mere shadow walking. What Sen couldn't figure out was why spiders didn't rule the universe if they could somehow change reality to suit their whims or needs. He'd hesitated to press Glimmer of Night for more information because he had a few suspicions of his own. The simplest explanation was that the other gods, goddesses, and ascended beings had made it clear that they wouldn't tolerate such a situation. Another possibility was that there had already been a war of some kind over the matter and the Great Matriarch had come out on the losing side. Of course, it was equally possible that the spider divinity was working toward wholly inscrutable goals from utterly unfathomable principles that were well beyond the comprehension of a lowly core cultivator like Sen. Without a better sense of which explanation was true, Sen didn't see many advantages to asking the questions.

What he did wonder about was how those inherited patterns conferred knowledge and truths. Glimmer of Night was absolutely certain they did, so Sen believed they did as well. Sen considered that the inherited patterns might function as a kind of spider code that served in the place of written language. The longer he thought about it, though, the less that felt right. No, whatever was happening there was touching on some deeper truths. He could feel it, the way he could feel vast powers moving behind the world if he concentrated just the right way. Not that he did that very often. There was insight to be gleaned by observing that world behind the world, but the risks to mind and soul were enormous while the benefits were in no way guaranteed. None of that stopped Sen from speculating about whether he could access the knowledge and truths in those patterns if he could see them. He doubted it, but he wasn't eager to neglect anything that would help him master shadow walking.

He'd have to broach the subject with Glimmer of Night. The good news was the spider was so direct that he'd just tell Sen if it was forbidden. It seemed like there was a solid chance that was the situation given that the patterns seemed to form the central core of spider cultivation. Even so, just asking about it probably wouldn't cause any meaningful problems as long as he accepted whatever answer he got with good grace. While some people wouldn't believe it was so, Sen was capable of acting with some decorum. He just didn't meet a lot of people who warranted expending that kind of effort. With a start, Sen realized that he was rapidly drifting away from the reason he had taken up station away from everyone else. That probably meant it was time to head back or at least take a break and do something else.

It was still a couple of hours until Ai would need her evening meal judging by the sun. Sen made one of the shadow balls that he used to help distract the little girl. He tossed it back and forth between his hands as he idly examined the trees around him. Most of them were old. Very old. So old that the lowest branches were dozens of feet above him. With nothing but bark on the trees down at ground level with him, Sen got an idea. He drew his arm back and threw the ball at one of the trees. It hit the trunk and bounced off at an angle. Sen let it dissipate and formed a new ball rather than chase the other one down. He spent a few minutes figuring out how to make the ball bounce back to him, but then it got boring. Thinking about how the first ball had bounced away, Sen started trying to work out how to make the ball bounce between two trees and come back to him. It took close to half an hour to make that happen. Sen felt it as Glimmer of Night approached, but he kept at his game.

"What are you doing?" asked the spider.

"Taking a break. Having fun."

"Alright, but what are you doing?"

"I'm trying to make the ball bounce between several trees and then come back to me without actively influencing it."

"I see," said Glimmer of Night.

The spider watched Sen's game for a while before he spoke up again.

"Can I try?" asked the spider.

Sen gave Glimmer of Night a surprised look. He wouldn't have thought the spider went in for such trivial things, but maybe spiders had their own games. Sen handed over the ball and went to stand where the spider had been. Glimmer of Night took maybe six practice throws before he threw it hard enough to make the construct pop. Sen winced as the minor technique was broken, but the backlash was minimal. He gave his head a little shake, made another ball, and tossed it to the spider. The spider nodded, turned, and threw the ball. Sen was torn between outrage and amazement as the ball bounced between six trees before flying back to the spider's outstretched hand. Glimmer of Night paused for a moment before he adjusted his position slightly. Another throw resulted in the ball bouncing between eight trees before flying back to the spider.

"This *is* entertaining," said the spider. "The geometries are fascinating."

"I think I'm starting to understand why so many people don't like me," said Sen.

"Why is that?" asked the spider in a tone of completely unfeigned innocence.

"I—" Sen didn't have the heart to explain. "It doesn't matter. Okay, so explain to me how you just did that."

CHAPTER NINETEEN

SAGE ADVICE

"Finally got tired of lurking?" asked Sen.

Fu Ruolan's eyes went wide with outrage. "I was not *lurking*!"

"Really? Because it looked a lot like lurking. Hovering just out of sight all of the time while watching me," said Sen as he made a stupendous effort to keep a straight face.

The nascent soul cultivator pointed at him and started to say something before her eyes narrowed. She slowly lowered her pointing finger and fixed him with a glare that promised vengeance.

"You aren't funny," said Fu Ruolan in a very even tone.

Sen couldn't help the smile that cracked his lips.

"I'm a little funny."

"Do you make a habit of taunting nascent soul cultivators? You know, that select group of individuals who actually *can* kill you."

Sen thought it over. "On the whole, I'm probably going to have to go with yes. It's not always taunting, but I definitely make a habit of defying them."

"Didn't anyone ever teach you manners? Or the basic order of things?"

It was Sen's turn to give her a look. A look that said, are you really asking *me*, of all people, the orphaned street rat raised by three old monsters, those questions? They locked gazes for a moment before Fu Ruolan shook her head.

"Right," she said. "I forgot who I was talking to there for a second. Your master never knew his place either."

"I get the impression that holds true for most people who make it to the nascent soul stage."

Fu Ruolan pursed her lips. "That's true for wandering cultivators, as far as it goes. The part no one talks about is how many core cultivators get killed trying the same thing. Don't delude yourself. There is a real element of luck involved. Meet the wrong old monster, and they will kill you out of hand for too much insolence."

Sen couldn't really argue that point. First, he thought she was almost certainly right. Second, there was no advantage in thinking she was wrong. If anything, he'd probably be well served to at least keep that warning in mind when dealing with nascent soul cultivators. He didn't tell himself that he'd follow that advice because he knew himself too well by now. There was something in him that just couldn't accept it when someone assumed he owed them obedience because they'd started out on the path of cultivation a little earlier than him. He could respect that someone was more powerful than him, be wary of it, but never subservient. It just *wasn't* in him. And there was the distinct possibility that sooner or later he'd come across someone who wouldn't tolerate some lesser cultivator not being impressed with them and all they said. He'd just have to hope that on that day, the gap between him and that person would prove smaller than they assumed. Sen nodded at Fu Ruolan to at least acknowledge that he'd heard her words. She rolled her eyes.

"Not everyone is afraid of Feng Ming," pressed Fu Ruolan.

"You can't assume that his reputation will get you out of every bad situation."

"These days, I find that my reputation is often sufficient. I'll grant you that I'm not sure that's a *good* thing, but it is definitely *a* thing. Besides, I try to avoid leaning on his reputation whenever humanly possible. I'm not looking to bring trouble to his door," said Sen before he directed a quizzical look at Fu Ruolan. "Are there really people who aren't afraid of him?"

"There are."

"Are their minds functioning properly?"

Fu Ruolan hesitated at that before she said, "Probably not, which is my point in a roundabout way. The kinds of people who don't fear him are also the kinds of people who will find your particular brand of disregard for them intolerable."

"I can't control that," said Sen. "But I won't fake respect or obedience because someone else never developed a sense of self-worth."

"How about self-preservation? A failure to develop that is an excellent way to die young."

"I get the sense that you're worried about me for some reason. Are you expecting a visitor? Someone with no sense of humor and a terribly fragile ego?"

"No," said Fu Ruolan with a visible shudder. "I hate people. Especially visitors. But you will leave here very soon and once more inflict yourself on the wider world."

"I still have a few years."

"Like I said, very soon. I don't want to see my investment in you wasted because you never learned how to just do what you're told."

"If I'd learned how to just do what I was told, I'd have long since ended up the whipping boy in some crappy sect or been sucked into a particularly creepy cult."

"Oh please. That might have been the case when you first started out. Now, sects would fall all over themselves to have you join. They'd bury you in resources, training, and probably all the sect princesses you wanted if they thought there was even a remote chance of getting you into the fold."

"That would only last until they had a conversation with me and realized exactly how little I care about things like sect hierarchy and their absurd notions of honor," said Sen.

"Well, yes, obviously, but you could milk them for resources before they figured that out."

Sen gaped at the nascent soul cultivator. "Are you suggesting that I play some kind of game with the sects to get natural treasures and cultivation manuals? Isn't that, I don't know, sort of dishonest if I know for sure that I'm never going to actually join their sect?"

Sen gaped even more when Fu Ruolan gave a disinterested shrug to his words.

"Do you really care about that?" she asked. "I'm not saying you should do that to every sect. Just ones that you don't particularly like. It's not like every sect is evil. There are some that you might not hate. There are even a few that you might benefit from joining. For a while at least."

"No thanks," said Sen.

"Don't dismiss the possibility out of hand. Sects serve a function."

"Auntie Caihong said the same thing. I don't see it, though. As near as I can tell, all sects do is breed unearned arrogance."

Fu Ruolan barked out a short laugh. "Well, you're not entirely wrong on that score. Sects do excel at that. That isn't what I meant, though. The other thing that sects excel at is concentrating information and talent. For all that garbage about facing the heavens alone, most cultivators who reach the point of ascension get a lot of help along the way. Even your master, who has always charted his own course, benefited from lucky encounters and occasionally interacting with some sects. Joining the right sect as a visiting elder, which is what most sects would consider you at this point, gives you access to both of those things. It's worth exploring."

Sen did his best to push against his near-instantaneous rejection of the idea. He'd had so many bad experiences with sects or at least their members that he struggled not to lump them all together in a big pile. Of course, he was fast-approaching if not already beyond the level of power where most sect members would willingly bother him. Even without his body cultivation, his spirit cultivation had evolved to somewhere around the late stage of core formation. He didn't think he was peak yet, but that extra-thick layer he'd made during his last advancement had muddied the waters for him. Either way, only someone supremely skilled, supremely confident, or supremely stupid was likely to accost him now.

That didn't exclude the potential situation of several core formation sect lackeys coming after him at the same time, but the odds of that kind of trouble had gone down a lot. His rapid advancements had simply outpaced the kinds of trouble that most wandering cultivators dealt with for centuries. Of course, he was still harboring a lot of mixed feelings about that rapid advancement. Every attempt to slow it down had met with dismal failure. Still, he did have a nascent soul cultivator right at hand to clear up at least one minor mystery in his life.

"In terms of core cultivators," said Sen, "where would you place my advancement? Late-stage core formation?"

There was an uncomfortably long pause as Fu Ruolan studied him. "Assuming that I knew absolutely nothing else *at all* about you, that is approximately where I would judge your advancement. Not that you have any business being at that stage of advancement given where you were when you left to see Elder Bo. You should have had to toil for decades to make that kind of jump. I'm honestly still trying to decide whether it's hideously unfair that the heavens just heap divine qi on you the way you described, or if it's something that I should be deliriously happy isn't happening to me."

"You should be happy," replied Sen in a tone of abject weariness.

Remembering all of that divine qi pouring into him and not being able to funnel it off to somewhere else, the sense that he might be ripped apart by it, was one of the things that woke him in cold sweats. He knew that other cultivators would kill and die for chances like that but only because they didn't truly grasp what it entailed. It was impossible to convey the overwhelming helplessness that came along with the heavens doing what they wanted to him and offering no chance of escaping it. He didn't have the words to explain how profoundly desperate he became in his attempts to find a path to survival only for them to be closed off one after the next. Sure, he'd come out the other side of it stronger, arguably better, but it was just the latest in a long string of experiences that had scarred him in ways that didn't show on his skin. He would have immediately, unquestioningly, joyously traded that experience for decades of toiling toward advancement the way others did it. Sen did his best to mentally shrug off those memories and focus on the now.

"As for your advice about sects, I'll try to keep it in mind. Although, I like the idea of tricking them into giving me resources a lot better than the idea of joining one."

"Do both," said Fu Ruolan. "I did."

"You did?!"

"Of course. You didn't think I filled that storage treasure with nothing but my own hard work, did you?"

Sen gave her a sheepish look. "Yes. I did think that."

"There is such a thing as being too straightforward, Sen. A little subterfuge can go a long way in life. Now, you've been distracting me into giving you sage advice for almost half an hour. It's time to get down to the actual business I came over here for. Tell me what you've learned about shadows."

CHAPTER TWENTY

THAT ISN'T HOW LEARNING WORKS

The order seemed odd to Sen. There was certainly a place for discussing things, but he'd generally found it more effective to simply demonstrate his understanding rather than fumble through verbal explanations that only partially captured the true meaning of something. For him, cultivation was at least equal parts clear understanding and intuition. Much of what he did he accomplished because it felt right, not because he possessed some deep theoretical understanding of the topic. Adding to the oddness of Fu Ruolan's order for him to explain was that she knew this about him.

"Wouldn't it be easier for me to just show you?" asked Sen.

"I don't need you to show me what you can do with shadows. I've seen that already. Just as importantly, there is often a rather steep imbalance between what someone can do and what they know."

Sen had worried she would say something like that. He summoned a chair from a storage ring and sat down in it. He could feel his eyebrows trying to meet each other as he thought hard about how to answer the question. However, no amount of hard thinking was going to turn intuitions into information, at least not in the space of a conversation. He finally said the only thing he really felt he knew about shadows.

"They're fuzzy. So, they're malleable."

After ten seconds of waiting, during which the nascent soul cultivator grew visibly and increasingly impatient, she said, "And?"

"That's it," answered Sen.

"After weeks of focused study of shadows, the best you've got is that they're fuzzy, so they're malleable?"

Sen nodded. "That's what I've got."

"But I know that you know more than that. You couldn't have done things like make those shadow balls you, the spider, and Liu Ai play with all the time if you didn't know more."

"No. *You* would know more. I expect Auntie Caihong, Uncle Kho, and Master Feng would know more. In fact, I bet almost any other cultivator would know more. All I really know is that shadows are less fixed than other things, which makes shadow qi less fixed than other kinds of qi. Hence, they're more malleable. Everything beyond that, it's just intuitions and experimentation. Even when things do work, I don't know why they work most of the time. For example, I know that I can harden shadow to the point of physicality. But that's all I know. I only knew that much because I've seen Falling Leaf do it. Even having done it, I couldn't explain why it works. I certainly couldn't teach someone else to do it."

"So, you didn't condense and layer the intrinsic matrix?"

Sen blinked. "What's an intrinsic matr—"

The words trailed off as a flood of connections formed inside of Sen's mind. Disparate pieces of knowledge, information, and intuition were forged into a moment of clarity and understanding. Sen shot up out of his chair, spun away from Fu Ruolan, and threw out his hand in a gesture that was wholly unnecessary, yet felt right to him. A narrow tower of shadow slowly rose out of the ground. Over the course of a minute, it rose to nearly thirty feet tall. Sen felt a swell of pride as it loomed over them in all of its pitch-black glory. As he withdrew his active control of the qi, Sen crossed his arms and waited. The seconds felt like they were dragging by at one-tenth their normal speed, but he never let his eyes wander from the hasty construction.

"What are you doing?" asked Fu Ruolan.

"I'm waiting," said Sen.

"For what? My patience to run out?"

"Just give it another ten seconds. Then, I'll know."

"Fine."

Ten seconds later, Sen beamed at the tower that was still just sitting there. It didn't crumble or dissipate under the fury of daylight. It just endured. Still smiling, Sen returned to his chair and snapped his fingers. The tower puffed out of existence.

"Yes," said Sen, "I condensed and layered the intrinsic matrix."

Instead of saying anything, Fu Ruolan closed her hand into a fist and started pounding it against her forehead. Sen watched this display for a while before he couldn't take it anymore.

"Why are you doing that?" he demanded.

"I'm trying to dislodge the memory of what I just saw."

Sen wasn't sure how seriously he should take that statement.

"Okay. Why?"

"Why?" asked Fu Ruolan, letting the fist drop away from her forehead. "Because that isn't how learning works. You don't just hear a phrase and attain instant understanding."

"That isn't what happened," objected Sen.

"It's funny you should say that because it looked an awful lot like that's exactly what happened from over here."

"It really didn't happen like that, though. I had some things half figured out, a few background guesses, but when you said intrinsic matrix, it brought it all together for me. But that wouldn't have happened if I hadn't spent the last few weeks trying things and failing at them a few hundred times. I never would have thought of it like that if you hadn't said something. Hey, do the other kinds of qi work like that as well?"

Fu Ruolan immediately started pounding her own forehead again. Sen thought he should intervene, but he wasn't sure how.

"You should probably stop that. It can't be good for your brain. Plus, what if you knock some of that alchemy knowledge away?"

While that brought the nascent soul cultivator's self-abuse to an immediate end, she still didn't look happy. Sen kind of felt like it was his fault, but he didn't see anything he'd actually done wrong. He'd just had an insight. That seemed like something that most teachers ought to be happy about triggering. Minimally, she should be happy about it because he was confident that he'd just taken a big step toward being able to do the shadow walking technique. Having thought it over, Sen concluded that this was a *her* problem and not a *him* problem. If she didn't like the way he achieved his understanding, there was basically nothing he could do about that. While Fu Ruolan dealt with her... Sen didn't know what exactly it was she was dealing with. While she dealt with her issue, Sen had fun making stable objects out of shadow.

He started with another chair. It felt strange when he sat down in it like it was there but not really there. Either way, it held his weight, which was all he really asked from a chair. Next, he made a rope that was stretched taut between two trees. He made it so that it was high enough that he had to jump up and catch it. He dangled there from the shadow rope for a while, just to see if it would maintain integrity. It felt like it would, but he dug a little deeper into what he now knew was called the intrinsic matrix. Even as he looked at it, Sen could tell that the rope was slowly breaking down. It might not evaporate in the next two minutes, but it wouldn't last for more than ten minutes. It was also getting progressively weaker as time went by. It seemed that even with the condensing and layering that shadow qi had firm limits on how long it could remain solid. He might be able to get a little more life out of it if he could condense the matrix a bit more or add additional layers, but only testing would answer that question.

He was far more certain that adding layers of other kinds of stable qi would vastly improve the total life of the shadow objects. He expected that earth would work the best since it was the most stable qi type or the most stable he had any direct experience using. Plus, earth qi was simply less hostile to shadow qi than metal qi. It seemed entirely possible to make temporary structures that were nearly as strong as a galehouse, but that would break down naturally after a day or three. He could capture most of the benefits of a galehouse but leave minimal evidence behind. That could prove quite useful if he found himself in hostile territory. Given the heavens seemed to both love and hate him, that situation seemed like an almost foregone conclusion.

For fast and dirty work, though, Sen thought that metal qi would still work the best. He could already see much-improved versions of his shadow-metal qi spears. Ones that might well last for hours, even as much as half a day, and would survive multiple uses. Something like that would have been extremely helpful when facing that horde. Even better, he could dissipate them right out of enemy hands if they grabbed them. As he considered the options, , he knew that air qi and shadow qi were the most natural pairing. He could probably make one of those shadow balls for Ai that would hold up for a week or two. Maybe longer if he put it together the right way.

"What are you doing?" asked Fu Ruolan.

He'd been so lost in his own thoughts that Sen hadn't even noticed that he was still hanging from the shadow rope. He released his grip and dropped to the ground. He made a conscious effort to dispel the rope before addressing Fu Ruolan.

"I was just testing something."

"Did you at least learn something useful?"

"I did."

"Care to share?"

"I think I can make a ball for Ai that will hold up better."

Fu Ruolan's lips twitched a few times like words were trying to force their way out. Then, she turned on her heel and stalked away. Sen stared at her retreating form in confusion.

"What?" Sen called out after her. "She likes them!"

CHAPTER TWENTY-ONE

WRITING LESSON

S en got the distinct impression over the next week or two that Fu Ruolan was actively avoiding him. Not that he necessarily minded that. It let him keep playing around with shadow qi and locking in his new understanding of the intrinsic matrix. He confirmed that all of the qi types he could access relied on the structure. He also learned that his approach to combining qi types was horrifyingly crude. Layering the different qi types provided an incredibly stable fusion. It also made doing things like crafting his shadow-metal spears feel almost effortless compared with how he used to do it. Knowing what he knew now, it wasn't shocking that his approach of simply mashing the qi types together and binding them through brute force and willpower was so strenuous. He'd been working against the natural order of things, rather than with them.

Of course, just because something was easier didn't make it automatic. He was quite certain that it was going to take time to make layering the qi types an instinctive action. He'd probably fall back on mashing things together for quite some time. He also hadn't tested how this newfound insight did or did not impact techniques like Heavens' Rebuke and Heavens' Shadow. The former was too wildly destructive to the material world to test near anything he cared about. The latter was so dangerous to the mind and soul that he didn't plan on using it within miles of another human being that he didn't know, without doubt, was irredeemably evil. He damn sure wasn't going to mess around with something that caused such instinctive revulsion in him near Liu Ai.

Fu Ruolan avoiding him also came with the side benefit that Sen could take more breaks than he should to go and play with Ai. She had been overjoyed to discover that the balls he made her now would last overnight. She'd been taking one to sleep with her every night. He'd had some doubts about how good an idea that was, but he couldn't actually think of a specific reason other than it had been on the ground. Its basic nature meant that nothing stuck to it, so it wasn't as though she was dragging dirt to bed with her. She also seemed to have fewer bad dreams when she had the ball with her. Sen didn't understand minds especially well, but he had a hard time seeing fewer violent nightmares as a bad thing. If the ball gave her comfort, he was willing to let the minor oddness of it pass without comment. Falling Leaf hadn't batted an eye at it, but she probably wouldn't have batted an eye if the little girl wanted to take a sword to bed with her at night.

However, as much as he was enjoying being more or less unwatched by his strange and occasionally unsettling teacher, he wondered about her absence. The woman seemed very restrained around Ai, and her interactions with Falling Leaf were primarily combat instruction. When she had to interact with Sen on something like a personal level, though, he often got the feeling that she was forcing herself to do it. Almost like the action taxed her mind in some way. He wondered if that was why she'd taken to lurking in the first place. She could keep an eye on him and his progress but avoid those conversations she didn't like. Sen shook his head.

He was just guessing and had no plans to ask her about it. If he was wrong, he'd look like a fool and run the risk of truly offending her. If he was right, then that conversation would just be a mental and emotional strain for Fu Ruolan. In short, there was no benefit to pressing the issue. She'd come back around when she did. In the meantime, he would do something that he'd been meaning to do for a while.

He sat down at the table where they all usually ate and pulled out the writing kit that Auntie Caihong had given him. It had gotten a lot less use than either he or she probably thought it would over the years. He finished with the inkstone and opened a clean scroll. He dipped the brush into the ink, gathered his thoughts for a moment, and started writing.

Auntie Caihong,

You'll be pleased to know that I'm using the writing kit you gave me. I'm sure you're aware by now that I found Fu Ruolan and accessed the manual I needed.

While Sen provided a brief overview of the events that had transpired since they last saw each other, Ai and Glimmer of Night came into the galehouse. She had convinced him to make webs for her to jump on, and they had been at that for hours. It seemed that she'd grown tired of the game, but was immediately intrigued by what Sen was doing. She rushed to the table and peeked over the edge at the scroll.

"What are you doing?" she asked, transfixed by the motion of the brush.

"I'm writing to my auntie," said Sen.

"You have an auntie?" she asked, momentarily shifting her eyes to him.

"I do, but she lives very far away. So, I'm writing this to tell her about what I've been doing. I'm writing about you right now."

Ai looked at him with big, curious eyes, before she climbed up into his lap to get a better look at the scroll.

"Where?" she asked, leaning forward to stare at the scroll from mere inches away.

Sen carefully put down the brush and pointed to the characters for her name. "That right there is your name."

"Really?"

"Yes," said Sen, and pointed to another part of the scroll. "That's how you write Glimmer of Night's name."

"Glimmerite!" she shouted, almost vibrating with excitement. "Come look! Come look! Come look!"

The spider, who had been hovering nearby, quickly closed the distance. His gaze locked onto the spot where Sen was pointing.

"That's your name!" she said, pointing at where Sen was pointing before moving her finger. "That's my name!"

"Would you like to learn how to write your name?" Sen asked.

The little girl's eyes went huge. "Yes."

"Well then, I'll teach you."

Sen carefully set aside the nearly complete letter he'd written to spare it from any accidents. He summoned another blank scroll from his ring and unrolled it.

"Okay, watch closely while I write your name," said Sen.

She nodded and barely blinked as Sen picked up the brush and dipped it. He made a point to exaggerate the characters and make them much bigger than he ordinarily would in a scroll. He figured that just getting the basic shapes down would be more than enough for this first, impromptu lesson. Sen dipped the brush again and then showed Ai how to hold it. The brush was really too big for her small hands. Sen made a mental note to ask around and see if everyone learned with the full-size brush or if they had smaller ones for children. He watched as she applied the brush to the scroll and the inevitable disaster of smeared ink occurred. Sen let her try a few more times but intervened before mild frustration escalated into angry frustration and turned her against the idea of writing altogether.

"Is it okay if I help a little?" asked Sen.

Ai looked up at him, her eyes filled with absolute trust, and nodded. It took Sen a moment to slow his racing heart. No one had ever looked at him that way before. He'd seen trust before, of course, but never that kind of blind certainty that someone was safe with him. It was a kind of trust that couldn't be failed because it could never, ever be regained once lost. Sen didn't know how he knew it, but he knew it to his bones. He reached out and had to take a moment to still his shaking hand. Only after he'd reclaimed control did he gently wrap his hand around Ai's. He remembered the way that Uncle Kho had guided his hand when Sen was trying to learn how to read and write. He did his best to mimic that gentle teaching. It wasn't any kind of automatic success, nor did he expect it to be. But Ai picked up fast on the big things, like not putting too much pressure on the brush.

It took a while, but she eventually managed to write something that could charitably be described as her name. Sen congratulated her for writing her name, but he praised her outrageously for not giving up. Sen had learned a lot about cultivation, but he'd learned a lot of hard lessons about life before that. Possibly the most important lesson he'd taken away from both things was that enough perseverance could carry you through most challenges. If she never learned anything else from him, that was something he wanted to give her. She smiled and covered her face in something that wasn't quite embarrassment. She stayed in his lap and watched him finish writing his letter to Auntie Caihong.

"Do you want to put your name on it, too?" asked Sen.

She gave him a shy smile and nodded. Sen dipped the brush and handed it to her. He worked hard to keep a serious expression as her little face scrunched up into a look of fierce concentration. Her tongue was sticking out a little and caught between her teeth. She worked with agonizing slowness. When she was done, though, a shaky, wobbly version of her name was on the scroll. Sen gently took the brush and then gave the girl a hug. She laughed and giggled before hopping down to the floor. Sen looked over to Glimmer of Night. The spider had stood and watched silently.

"Were you paying attention?" Sen asked.

"I was."

"Good. Because you get to try tomorrow."

CHAPTER TWENTY-TWO
IT HURTS MY SOUL

S en stared at the eager face of the young man. While only a handful of years separated them, Sen couldn't help the question that sprang to his mind. *Was I ever that young?* Whatever a calendar might say, Sen was quite certain that a massive canyon filled with experience stood between them. It was only the fact that he was acquainted with Wang Bo that had kept him from simply ordering the young man to go away and leave him alone. Sen had barely set foot in town before people started accosting him. They were kind enough about it. Coming up and thanking him for helping them with the spirit beasts. But Sen was getting tired of smiling and nodding and assuring everyone that he didn't need tea... Or food... Or a wife. He had been particularly gentle with that last refusal since he could see the young woman in question hovering nervously in the background behind her father. No need to make her feel bad. Still, it all grew very tiresome, very quickly. When Wang Bo had come sprinting up to him, though, Sen was starting to wonder if he'd ever actually get to the shops.

"Please, master cultivator," said Wang Bo. "You must come and see."

Taking a steadying breath, Sen gestured for the young man to lead the way. It would, no doubt, prove easier and faster to just go and look at whatever had the young man in such an excitable mood. Perhaps there was some other threat that required immediate action or an injured person beyond the aid of the local healers. Sen was feeling impatient with the situation, but he didn't want to let his impatience make a bad choice for him. So, he followed and made a noise now and then while the young man filled the air with words. So. Many. Words. He retreated into a semi-meditative state to withstand the verbal deluge, already wishing that he had gone somewhere else or simply stayed home. Ai could be noisy. There was no denying it, but that was noise he didn't mind. Wang Bo finally led them past the inn, where the grizzled Dai Bao caught sight of them. He shook his head and walked over to meet them.

"Quiet, boy," barked the older man. "Can't you see the man's had enough?"

Wang Bo's mouth snapped shut as he cast a furtive, cautious look at Sen. He quickly turned his face away, apparently mistaking the distant, abstracted expression on Sen's face for some kind of anger. *At least, he's quiet now*, thought Sen and focused on the older man.

"Wang Bo seemed very insistent that there was something I needed to see," offered Sen.

"Oh," said Dai Bao, burying his face in his hand. "By the thousand hells, boy, don't you have any sense?"

Wang Bo turned bright red at the, in Sen's opinion, light chastisement. The older man gave Sen an apologetic look.

"Well, he brought you this far. I guess there's no reason not to finish what he started."

Sen drifted in the wake of the other two, not making an effort to listen in while Dai Bao gave the much younger Wang Bo a stern lecture on not rushing things that didn't need to be rushed for no good reason. Eventually, they passed out the other side of town and stopped at a building that didn't look like it was attached to any particular property. Dai Bao picked up on Sen's confusion and interpreted it correctly.

"It's a community building," said the gruff man. "We use it to store things when there isn't a better place."

Sen nodded in understanding but didn't comment. There had been a few buildings like that back in Orchard's Reach. He'd even sheltered in them on rare occasions, but it was risky. There were always a lot of people coming and going, and the town guards had checked in the buildings regularly. Dai Bao pushed open the door and the trio stepped inside. Unable or unwilling to restrain his excitement any longer, Wang Bo rushed over to a pair of long, deep crates. He grabbed the top of one of the crates and shoved it out of the way.

Dai Bao muttered something about damn children, while Sen stepped closer to the crate. Wang Bo was smiling like he'd just discovered that his well produced silver tael instead of water. Sen peered down into the crate and saw that it was filled with tightly packed spears. He blinked at them a few times, but before he could ask anything, Wang Bo exploded into speech again.

"We did what you said. We sold the cores. Well, we bartered the cores for these spears, and for these," he said, rushing over and pushing the top off the second crate to reveal similarly packed halberds.

Wang Bo was staring at him expectantly, but Sen was still caught on the fact that they thought he told them to do this. Then, he remembered that he had made some offhand suggestion that they buy spears and halberds. They would certainly be more useful against spirit beasts. Sen nodded.

"That's good," he said.

Sen still felt a bit hazy about why he had needed to see it, but the young man was clearly excited. It wouldn't hurt to indulge that excitement a little. Wang Bo was still giving him that expectant look like he was sure that Sen was about to say something very interesting or very important. *Maybe I wasn't enthusiastic enough*, thought Sen. He tried again.

"That's very good."

Wang Bo was shifting back and forth on his feet, his eyes bright and hopeful. Sen knew that he was missing something here, but he just couldn't put his finger on what was escaping his notice. He felt like it must be obvious. He turned to look at Dai Bao. The gruff man had barely opened his mouth to speak when impatience won out over Wang Bo's painfully limited self-control.

"When will you start?" asked the young man.

Sen frowned at him. "Start what?"

"Training us."

"Training you to do what?" asked Sen.

"To use the spears and halberds!"

Now, Sen understood. This kid had taken that offhand statement Sen had made and exaggerated it in his mind into some kind of promise that Sen would become their teacher. He didn't have time for that nonsense. He had his own training to deal with. He had little Ai to take care of and teach how to write. This was not a problem of his making, and he refused to be bound by a promise he never made.

"When did I ever say I would do that?" asked Sen, with a bit too much steel in his words based on how the young man flinched.

"But you said to get spears and halberds," said Wang Bo in a weak, confused voice.

"So you could defend yourselves against spirit beasts. Not so I could become your martial teacher."

"We all warned you not to rush this, boy. We all told you not to assume things," said Dai Bao.

He used a more sympathetic tone than Sen would have expected, all things considered. Even so, the young man looked like a puppy that had just been unexpectedly kicked. Sen added that to a list of things that were not his problem. Instead, he pointed at Dai Bao.

"If you want someone to teach you how to use a spear, ask him," said Sen.

Fresh hope bloomed on Wang Bo's face, while an expression of horror crossed Dai Bao's face.

"What?" demanded the gruff man. "What are you talking about?"

Sen barely even knew the man, and the words still sounded fake.

"Wow," said Sen. "You are a terrible liar."

Dai Bao heaved an enormous sigh. "It's not a lie. I might have known how to use a spear twenty-five years ago. You don't forget everything, even after a couple of decades. But that was a long, long time ago, and I've forgotten most of what I knew. Plus, I was never a teacher. Anything I show that boy is as likely to get him killed as save him from a spirit beast."

Sen shook his head. "I cannot be responsible for training your entire town to defend itself. I already have obligations. I helped out with those spirit beasts because I was here, and because I could. It was also because someone was willing to throw aside any notion of honor and *begged* me to do it. I gave you the basics. You have the tools now. That's as far as I'm willing to go."

Without another word, Sen turned away and left the barn. He pretended not to see the heartbroken look on Wang Bo's face or the resigned look on Dai Bao's face. He also pretended he couldn't hear the two talking.

"I thought he'd teach us," said a crestfallen Wang Bo.

"You don't know cultivators, Bo. That man has a soft heart for a cultivator. He helped your father. He helped us fight those spirit beasts. And he didn't ask for anything. Most cultivators would have laughed at you asking them to teach you anything if they didn't kill you for being insolent."

"Kill me?"

"Cultivators are prideful. Arrogant. You're beneath their notice. You asking a cultivator to teach you something is like an ant asking you to teach them. He could have done anything he wanted to you, and no one could have stopped him. All he did was say no."

Sen forced himself to stop listening before the conversation made him feel sick to his stomach. He didn't feel kind. Maybe compared to other cultivators he'd been kind but that was a pretty low standard to reach in Sen's experience. Dai Bao was right, too. Another cultivator might well have killed that young man for the sheer audacity of asking them to sully themselves by training some mortal to use a weapon. In the end, Sen just didn't want to do it. He had other things, important things, that he needed to spend his time on. Things like finding a better brush for Liu Ai. So, that's what he went to do. He went to the shops and spoke with the owners. It turned out that the children who did learn to write almost always used the brushes made for adults. It wasn't what Sen wanted to hear, but he had to console himself with buying one that was thinner and lighter. While not a perfect solution, it should make things easier for little Ai.

While he did that, he pretended that he wasn't paying attention to Dai Bao and Wang Bo with his spiritual sense. The two had gone a little way off from the town. Not in the true forest, but far enough away that no one would see them. Sen's spiritual sense wasn't quite precise enough for him to see what they were doing, but it gave him a clear enough picture that he kept wincing. Uncle Kho would be horrified. Stowing the brush in his storage ring, Sen found himself walking to where they were, grumbling under his breath, and cursing his own heart. He found them quickly enough and it was just as bad as he'd imagined it was. Dai Bao hadn't been lying when he said he'd forgotten most of what he'd known about using a spear. Worse, he was passing on his incomplete knowledge and bad form to someone else. It was more than Sen could bear to watch people using spears so badly.

"Stop!" he shouted, storming up to the pair. "Stop! For the

love of the gods, please stop. It hurts my soul just to see this display."

Wang Bo looked torn between surprise and uncertainty.

"Um," the young man said.

Dai Bao just looked startled. Sen glared around at the clearing they were in.

"Who owns this land?" he demanded.

Dai Bao and Wang Bo traded a look. Wang Bo shrugged. Dai Bao scratched his cheek and gave the spot a thoughtful frown.

"The king? Maybe," offered the older man.

"So, it doesn't belong to anyone in town?"

"No," said Dai Bao.

"Good," said Sen.

He cycled for earth qi and went to work. Soon, stone formed beneath their feet into something that resembled the courtyard at Uncle Kho's home. The earth heaved and shook in every direction removing trees, undergrowth, and a few spirit beasts that thought they were being sneaky. Soon, a flat square of stone, one hundred and fifty feet on each side, stretched out around them. Sen decided that was big enough for now, and walls started rising out of the ground, largely closing in the area except for a single large opening that faced toward the road. Sen turned to look at the pair of inept, would-be spearmen. Wang Bo was gaping at him with his mouth hanging open. Dai Bao's expression was more subdued, but his eyes were opened as wide as they would go. Sen held a hand out to one side and summoned a spear from his storage ring.

"If you're going to use spears, you should at least get the basics right," said Sen. "Rule one, you always, *always* keep two hands on the spear."

CHAPTER TWENTY-THREE
THAT WAS SECT THINKING

Committed to his promise not to simply disappear because he got distracted, Sen limited his instruction of Dai Bao and Wang Bo to two hours. He drew a few conclusions from those two hours, though. The most important conclusion was that starting with someone who knew *nothing* about using a spear was infinitely better than starting with someone who had learned bad habits so long ago that they were practically instincts. He had to spend much longer working with Dai Bao simply to start correcting a lot of sloppy form. Some of that he was willing to chalk up to the years since the man last held a spear. Some of it, however, was ingrained enough that Sen could only assume that it was a product of some very shoddy instruction. Sen wasn't sure if Uncle Kho would have wept actual blood if he saw the abominations that Dai Bao was committing with a spear, but the elder cultivator would have had some strong thoughts on the matter. With Wang Bo, he was mercifully able to correct the worst habits before they ever got a chance to take root in the young man's form. *So much easier*, thought Sen.

The second conclusion he drew was that neither man was destined for greatness with the spear. Dai Bao was a willing student but willingness could only carry you so far. Training could teach you the techniques and movements, but it couldn't give you a feel for the weapon. It couldn't give you instincts. Wang Bo was an eager student and did everything that was asked of him. But Sen could see in the boy's eyes that he simply didn't have the relentless drive to achieve mastery. He would work hard. He would become competent. He would never do what Sen had done and drive himself to exhaustion with drills. Of course, that was sufficient for Wang Bo. He clearly didn't have any aspirations to become the greatest mortal spearman in the world. He wanted to know how to protect his family from spirit beasts and competence was enough for that.

Sen also concluded that aging as a mortal was awful. Dai Bao had problems that stemmed from his body starting to break down and wear out. Sen had sidestepped that entire process with not one but two cultivation paths, so it took him a while to understand that was what his senses and brief qi inspection were telling him. There wasn't that much he could do about natural aging. A lesson he'd learned some time ago on the Luo farm. More concerning to Sen were the problems that the man was suffering from old injuries that had either never healed properly or never been treated properly. Those injuries reduced the man's range of motion, strength, and probably the length of his life if Sen was interpreting correctly.

Dai Bao had learned to work around some of those problems, but those weren't real solutions. Those problems, Sen was pretty sure he *could* do something about. Auntie Caihong had always told him that treating old wounds was much harder than treating new ones. He hadn't fully grasped her meaning until he took a hard look at Dai Bao. With new injuries, the body was doing everything it could to fix the problem. Any alchemical treatments helped those natural processes along. With the old injuries, the body wasn't trying to fix it anymore. The body treated its current state as normal, based on what Sen was seeing. Any treatment would need to overcome the body's indifference to those old injuries. However, it wasn't impossible to do. Just harder. He'd need to think about it and work out what to address first to maximize the value of any treatment, so he kept those basic plans to himself. Better not to say anything until he had solid information to share.

Still, Sen needed Dai Bao in better condition than he was, because Sen needed someone who could do things like oversee training when he couldn't be around. With his own training ongoing, he expected that was going to be a frequent fact of life for anyone in town who decided that they were going to learn how to use a spear. Dai Bao was ideal for that role. He was young enough that he could do the work. It wasn't easy for him, but he could do it. The man was also old enough and grizzled enough to command some innate respect from just about everyone. However, Sen would need to make sure that the hierarchy was clear. That thought alone left such a sour taste in Sen's mouth that it was enough to make him nearly abandon the whole project. That was sect thinking, right there. It was a short trip from necessary hierarchy to all those things Sen hated about how sect members behaved. He'd have to work hard to ensure that as little as possible of that foolishness infected these people.

Don't borrow trouble, Sen told himself as he flashed through the trees toward Fu Ruolan's domain. *You recognized the potential problem. Take steps to avoid it, and then put the concern away.* He tried to take his own advice, but the idea lingered on the edge of his mind, like a fretful ghost intent on haunting his thoughts. He did his best to keep it at bay by thinking about how to treat Dai Bao's old injuries. The man did have some old bone injuries that had not gotten proper attention. Sen decided that those were probably the best place to start. Bone misalignments and injuries could have a cascading effect of problems for the muscles, nerves, and even organs. Simply correcting those could alleviate some of the obvious pain the man was in. *Yes*, Sen decided. *I'll fix the bones first and then the organs.* There weren't injuries to the organs, exactly, but

Sen had seen some deficiencies there that suggested some kind of damage in the past. Getting those back in proper order would improve things like blood flow, which would make any later healing of the other body tissues more effective and efficient. Sen's mind was still on the treatment plan when a tiny body crashed into his leg and hugged it.

"You're back!" shouted a joyful Ai.

Sen laughed and rested his hand on the top of her head before giving her hair a gentle ruffle. She gave him a little scowl that did nothing to hide the happiness in her eyes.

"I'm back," said Sen. "I even brought something for you."

"You did! What is it?"

Sen crouched down and held out his hand with the palm facing up. He summoned the brush he'd gotten her from a storage ring. She stared at it for a moment before snatching it up and bringing it so close to her eye that it made Sen a little nervous.

"It's for when you practice writing," said Sen, not sure if he was telling her something she knew or not.

She seemed a lot less interested in what she was going to do with the brush than what she could do with it right now. She smiled at Sen.

"Thank you."

Then, she turned around and took off at a sprint. Well, a sprint for her, which was a fast walk for Sen. He meandered after her, curious about what she meant to do. He finally understood when she burst into a clearing where Glimmer of Night was once more practicing one of those massive, hideously complicated webs of his. Ai ran up to the spider, waving the brush over her head.

"Glimmerite. I got a brush."

The spider looked down at the little girl and nodded. "You did."

"It's for writing," she said in a conspiratorial whisper.

"I see," said the spider before he abruptly looked over at Sen. "Do I get my own brush?"

Sen's mind blanked out for a second. He hadn't thought about it. It just hadn't seemed important. He'd only gotten Ai a brush to make the work easier for her. He'd never even considered that Glimmer of Night might *want* his own brush. The spider didn't seem to want anything else. Why would he want a brush? Even as the question occurred to Sen, he realized that it didn't matter why. The spider wanted a brush, and Sen had not gotten him one. As he tried to come up with an answer for the spider, his mouth failed him utterly.

"Um," said Sen.

The spider continued to look at him as Ai, in a wholly unintentional act of taunting, ran around Glimmer of Night's legs with a huge smile on her face and the brush held aloft like some kind of prize. Sen's mind finally lurched back into motion.

"Would you like your own brush?" Sen asked.

"Yes," said the spider. "I would like my own brush."

"I'll get you one."

The spider gave Sen a nod before he looked down at Ai, who was still running in circles around him. Glimmer of Night seemed to be at something of a loss about what, if anything, he was supposed to do. Sen took pity on the spider.

"Ai. Why don't we take your brush inside so it doesn't get broken?"

A look of panic crossed the girl's face. She skidded to a stop, almost fell, was saved by Glimmer of Night's lightning reflexes, and clutched the brush to her chest like it was a fragile baby bird. She hurried over to Sen and grabbed his hand. She started pulling him toward the galehouse. Sen waved a hasty goodbye to Glimmer of Night and let himself be "dragged" along. Once they got inside, Liu Ai peered all around as if trying to find a place that was safe enough to protect her new treasure. Sen smiled to himself.

"I have an idea," he said and walked over to a wall.

He picked a spot that was low enough that Ai could easily get at it, and close to the table where she practiced writing. All it took was a quick application of earth qi to create a small hollow in the wall with a little depression at the bottom. He hardened the stone again.

"There," he said. "It can stay in there, so you'll always know where to find it."

Sen occupied himself making tea while Ai put the brush into the hollow and took it back out, over and over. Falling Leaf came in while this was going on and studied the little girl with a befuddled expression.

"What is she doing?" asked Falling Leaf.

"She's having fun," answered Sen. "Let's leave her to it."

CHAPTER TWENTY-FOUR
RELATIONSHIP MANAGEMENT

A cocoon of shadow surrounded Sen. He had made and sustained it all night while he sat cross-legged on the roof of the galehouse. The hope had been that immersing himself in shadow that way would help provide some insight into the shadow walking technique. That hadn't happened at all. It had mostly just served as a way to sharpen the other skills that let him evaluate the environment around him without recourse to sight. It wasn't a wasted effort since Sen couldn't know when an enemy might deploy a technique that would temporarily blind him. It just hadn't done much to help him understand how one stepped through a shadow into some other place. He felt it when Falling Leaf jumped up to join him on the roof. He relaxed his iron grip on the shadow qi and let it disperse, which revealed the predawn illumination just barely lighting the horizon. Falling Leaf studied Sen for a moment before she sat down next to him.

"Why didn't you offer to teach me to write?" she asked without preamble.

"You didn't seem interested," said Sen, frowning as he thought. "Also, I guess I thought you already could since you can read. People who read can usually write."

Falling Leaf shook her head. "I learned to read by watching the humans in town, and by watching you. The Caihong also helped me learn a bit more."

"But no writing?"

She lifted an eyebrow at him. "Paws are not good for holding objects like brushes. There were other priorities since I got hands."

"Right," said Sen feeling a little foolish for not recognizing the obvious there. "Well, you're certainly welcome to join in when I'm teaching Ai and Glimmer of Night."

Falling Leaf looked away then. "It's not important."

He squinted at the ghost panther in the dim light. *I don't understand what is happening right now*, thought Sen. She'd come outside, jumped up to the roof, and asked the question. Then, when he'd told her that she could join in, she suddenly didn't care anymore. While social signals were often lost on Sen, even he could see that there was something else at work. If it wasn't about the writing... Sen wanted to bury his face in his hands for being so oblivious. He'd been pouring time and energy into taking care of Ai. He'd been spending time with Glimmer of Night, trying to use the spider's insights to generate some of his own. He'd been spending time with Fu Ruolan before she stormed off in a huff. He'd even been spending time with the people in town. He'd been spending time with everyone but *her*.

"I haven't been a very good friend to you at all these last few years, have I?" asked Sen. "You're only here because of me, and I'm gone or training most of the time. That's when I'm not almost dying. I know you've been training with Fu Ruolan, but she's not a friend. Glimmer of Night is basically a stranger. And Ai—"

"She is a kit," said Falling Leaf. "A kit must be tended and protected. All understand this."

"True. Still, I haven't been making much time for you."

"I'm not foolish. I know much is demanded of you. I also know that what happens to me matters to you. You would not have brought the elder fox here if it didn't."

"Not that bringing him here did much good," said Sen.

"Perhaps not, but even the fox *thought* he could help. How could you know that he was wrong? You also could have demanded knowledge or treasures for your own use, but you bartered with him to help me. I do not doubt your care for me, human boy. It is simply that I miss you."

Rarely had Sen felt so damned by such a basic utterance as *I miss you*. When the person saying it shared the same home, he couldn't help but feel that it had gone beyond mere inattention and progressed into flat-out negligence. It hadn't been malicious. Sen wasn't delusional. He had been insanely busy for most of the last few years. There had been long stretches where there just hadn't been *any* time to spend on anything other than surviving. Since he'd gotten back from his little adventure with Laughing River, though, he could have found time. He could have, but he hadn't. For once in his life, though, the problem in front of him was something fixable.

"There's no reason why I can't teach you to write after Ai goes to bed for the night. It's not like we need that much sleep."

Falling Leaf didn't say anything. She just smiled at him and nodded. Then, as fast as she had appeared, she was gone from the roof. Sen didn't know if he'd actually end up teaching her to write, although he might. It was a useful skill, and she'd benefit from it. It was the commitment Falling Leaf cared about. The reassurance that he would make time to spend with her now that madness and looming death weren't infecting every part of their lives. And it was such a small thing to ask for when compared to everything she had given him. If he could find entire days to spend in meditation and travel to town to teach people how to use spears, he would find a couple of hours to spend with her most days.

Sen stayed up on the roof for a little longer. He watched as the sun slowly crested the horizon and considered if he was working hard enough to sustain any of his important relationships. While Master Feng, Auntie Caihong, and Uncle Kho were used to long absences in each other's lives, he doubted the same was true for most of the other people he knew. He supposed it was easy to ignore a five or ten-year gap in communication when centuries were trivial to you. Most people didn't have that perspective. Still, most of that was a problem for another day. His more immediate problem was utterly prosaic but oddly pressing. He needed to make Ai breakfast. It was going to be a busy day. She'd been asking about Dai Bao and the little girl she'd met, Zhi. So, Sen had promised he'd take her with him to town the next time he went.

I should invite Falling Leaf, thought Sen as he prepared some food. As had become her habit, Liu Ai groggily came out of her room, shadow ball clutched protectively in one arm and a blanket dragging from the other. Sen settled the blanket around her shoulders and put her in a chair, where she slowly woke up as he finished making breakfast. Falling Leaf came into the galehouse not too long after, which made Ai stir and hold out her arms. The ghost panther had come to some kind of accommodation with her discomfort regarding human children. She dutifully picked up the girl, who put her head on Falling Leaf's shoulder and started snoring lightly.

"We're going to town today as part of my grand plan for Ai to get glimpses of normalcy," said Sen. "You're welcome to come with us. You'll get to see some mortals fumble around with spears."

"They don't like me," said Falling Leaf. "After what I did at the inn."

"I don't care what *they* like. *I* like you, and they can deal with it."

Falling Leaf still looked uncertain.

"If you don't want to go because you simply don't want to go, I understand that. If you don't want to go because of what those townspeople think, to hells with that. That whole town owes me. If the only thing I ask for is that they behave nicely to my friend, they're getting off cheap."

Falling Leaf's face cleared up at those words. "I'll come along. I can leave if I don't like it."

"Good plan," said Sen. "Plus, you'll get to meet Ai's friends."

"The grumpy man?" asked Falling Leaf.

Sen nodded. "Yes. There's also a little girl there she seems to like."

"Zhi," mumbled Ai around a yawn. "She draws birds."

"Yes, she does," agreed Sen.

"I draw orchids," declared Ai.

Falling Leaf looked to Sen for confirmation. He subtly shook his head in the negative.

"Ai does draw lovely flowers," he added to try to give Falling Leaf some kind of context.

The flower conversation was summarily ended by the appearance of hot food. Then, it was time to get ready to leave, at which point Ai couldn't decide if she should bring along her brush to show off. It was clear she wanted to, and equally clear that she was worried it would get damaged. Sen decided that letting her make the occasional decision would probably be good for her in the long run. She eventually plucked the brush out of its cubby and brought it over to Sen. He could see her trying to formulate the question. Confident that phrases like spatial treasure were beyond her, he didn't make her stumble through it.

"Would you like me to hang on to that for you?" he asked.

She nodded. "Please."

Sen held out his hand, and she gently rested it across his palm. He dropped it into his storage ring. As usual, this disappearing trick delighted the little girl to no end. If he was going to be storing things for her, though, he thought it was time she knew where the stuff went.

"Do you know where things go when I do that?" he asked.

Ai shook her head. Sen held out a hand and pointed to one of the rings he wore.

"It goes in there."

Ai shook her head and smiled at him in a way that said she knew he was trying to trick her.

"No, it doesn't," she declared.

"It does."

"It's too small," she said.

"It's a magic ring," he told her. "And its magic power is to store things and keep them safe."

Clearly doubting Sen, Ai looked over to Falling Leaf.

"It's true," said Falling Leaf. "I have a ring like that, too."

An apple appeared in her hand, making the little girl gasp. Ai immediately ran over and poked at the piece of fruit as if to reassure herself that it wasn't some terrible grownup deception. Falling Leaf handed her the apple. Ai examined it closely before she came back over to Sen and very deliberately touched the apple to the ring he'd pointed at earlier. He smiled.

"I have to use my magic to tell the ring to work," said Sen.

It wasn't exactly true, but he figured it was close enough. She gave him another dubious look.

"Really?" she asked.

"Do it again, and I'll tell the ring to work."

Ai once again pressed the apple against the ring. Sen activated the ring, and the apple disappeared. It was only after Sen made the fruit reappear and re-disappear several times that Ai seemed to accept that he wasn't tricking her. Then, she said something that Sen felt like he should have anticipated.

"Put me in the ring!" she shouted excitedly.

Thank the heavens Lo Meifeng isn't here, thought Sen. *She'd be encouraging the girl.*

CHAPTER TWENTY-FIVE

THEN, LEAVE

Then trip took a bit longer than usual since Sen had to keep his speed down a little to let Falling Leaf keep pace for the entire distance. It was late morning by the time they arrived at the wall. While the guards knew to let Sen pass, they eyed Falling Leaf as if they expected her to burst into violence at a moment's notice. She stared back at them with a bored, mildly impatient expression. The guards traded a look, seemed to realize that there was exactly nothing they could do to stop her if she decided to come in, and just let them pass. Sen was glad the men hadn't made a fuss about it. The ghost panther did get a few nervous, sidelong glances from some of the people in town, but everyone restrained themselves from making comments. It wasn't clear if they did that because Sen was with her, or if they feared to anger Falling Leaf. *Maybe they don't want to start anything because Ai is with us*, thought Sen.

Once the fast part of the ride was over, the little girl had decided that she'd been carried enough. So, Ai kept a firm grip on Sen's hand, well, it was her hand firmly wrapped around two of his fingers. They moved along at the little girl's pace, which wasn't fast at all. Every once in a while, she would release Sen's hand to run

147

over and look at something. He only stopped her a few times, like when she'd made to go inside the smithy. Sen had only ever peeked in on a blacksmith's shop before, but that quick look told him that it was no place for a child. Especially one that nobody would realize was there until something bad happened. She'd made a few sad faces but accepted his word that she might get hurt. It was basically the same reason he'd given her for why she couldn't go inside the storage ring.

Falling Leaf had been to the town a few times before, so she wasn't seeing anything new. Instead, she mostly stuck near to Sen. Occasionally, she'd ask him about something that someone was doing that she didn't quite understand. She'd seen two men sitting on either side of a barrel, their elbows up on top, and their hands locked together. That whole thing had mystified her until he explained that it was a test of strength. She'd perked right up at that and wanted to try it.

"You do realize that you're almost certainly far stronger than every man in the village, right?" asked Sen in a bid to avert disaster before it arrived.

Falling Leaf's face fell at that.

"I forgot," she admitted.

"Well, maybe we'll go to a town a bit closer to one of the big cities and find you some sect members. You can make them feel bad about themselves."

That suggestion seemed to cheer her up. However, Sen suspected that the sect members of the world would be less enthusiastic if they knew about the plan. After a particularly slow walk across the town, they finally arrived at the home of Li Hua. Ai was very excited to show off the spot where she drew orchids to Falling Leaf. Sen left the ghost panther to her confusion while he knocked on the door. When no one answered after a respectable amount of time, Sen knocked again. When the knock went unanswered a second time, Sen gave Ai an apologetic look.

"I don't think Zhi is here right now," he told her.

Ai looked at the house like it was telling lies before she turned sad eyes on Sen.

"Where is she?" asked the little girl.

"I don't know," said Sen. "But we'll watch for her. Plus, we can always come back later. She might be home by then."

Placated by those words if not exactly happy, the trio set out again. Ai seemingly decided that Falling Leaf's hand needed to be held because she grabbed several of the ghost panther's fingers. Sen saw Falling Leaf make herself relax at the unexpected touch. It was a small step, but if any living human being was going to win the ghost panther over, it would be Ai. There was simply no malice in the child that Sen could see. He wasn't sure if all children were born with that kind of temperament or if she was just sweet by nature. After a few minutes, her good humor returned. She started to point out all of the things she found interesting. Some of the things she found interesting were baffling to Sen. He understood it when she was excited by a bright red bird that flew by. He did not understand it when she was just as excited about a weed growing between some stones outside of someone's house. Whether he could see why she thought something was amazing or not, he was determined not to deprive her of wonder. Sen, of all people, knew full well just how good the world was at ripping that right out of people. It didn't need his help to accomplish that particular feat. So, he would dutifully attend whenever she wanted him to look at some new discovery. As they passed through the far gate, Falling Leaf gave him a curious look.

"We're going to go and see how people are doing with the spears," he said. "I might even teach them something if anyone is around."

When it became clear that they were going to enter the forest again, Ai immediately ran over to Sen and held her arms out. It wasn't something he'd told her to do. Somewhere along the line, she had just decided that going through the forest meant that he held her. Since that suited his inclination to make sure she was safe, he didn't intend to discourage it any time soon. He scooped her up, and she looked around like she was a queen surveying her kingdom. *Queen Ai and the Kingdom of Forest*, thought Sen. *It sounds like a legend just waiting to be told*. It didn't take long before the structure Sen had erected came into view. Ai gasped and pointed, while even Falling Leaf looked a little startled at the sheer size of it.

"Yeah," said Sen, "I was a little out of sorts when I made it. It's a bit bigger than it needs to be."

They could hear voices and the sounds of people doing exercises of some kind coming from inside the structure. Sen took that as a good sign. When they came through the opening in the wall, though, he came to an abrupt stop at the sight that greeted him. There were indeed some people practicing with the spear under the eye of Dai Bao. It seemed that all of those people were working very hard to ignore the confrontation that was happening between a big man Sen only vaguely recognized from the day they'd all fought the spirit beasts and Li Hua. The big man was crowding Li Hua and talking in a menacing tone, but the seamstress wasn't backing down an inch. He also saw that Zhi was cowering behind her mother, the confrontation obviously terrifying the little girl. Sen did his best to put on a bright smile when he spoke to Ai.

"I want you to stay with Falling Leaf for a little while, okay?"

Ai was staring at the argument with scared eyes, but she nodded. Sen gently passed her to the ghost panther, who held the little girl protectively while never letting her eyes move from the fight that was looking increasingly likely to turn violent. Sen strode over and heard the man speaking clearly for the first time.

"You don't belong here. Go home, seamstress"

"Who says she doesn't belong here?" asked Sen in a neutral tone.

"I do!" snapped the big man without even looking. "She's a woman."

"I noticed that," agreed Sen. "I expect anyone with eyes notices that. But what in the thousand hells does that have to do with whether or not she belongs here? Are you under the mistaken impression that you're in charge?"

"I don't know what game you're playing at. But women have no place—" started the man as he turned around.

The words simply stopped as the big man saw Sen standing there with death in his eyes.

"Go on," said Sen. "Explain to me why women have no place here."

"It's... It's just... Everyone knows that women don't fight."

"Really?" asked Sen. "Everyone knows that? *Everyone* in the whole world?"

The big man seemed to realize that line of argument wasn't going anywhere as his eyes fell on Falling Leaf, who had casually beaten a dozen men half-to-death by herself.

"It's unnatural. I won't tolerate it," said the big man.

"Then, leave," said Sen in a voice so cold that the big man shivered. "And thank the gods that there were children here to keep me from instructing you in exactly what I think of your opinions."

The big man's face turned bright red and then a shade of purple that looked profoundly unhealthy to Sen. The man went to storm past Sen, who stopped him with a look.

"Before you convince yourself that you'll deal with this later," said Sen in a lethally casual tone, "know that I consider her and her daughter my friends."

From the way the blood drained out of the big man's face, he'd understood precisely what kind of murderous rage would come crashing down on him if anything even remotely untoward befell the seamstress or her daughter. It was equally clear that Sen had predicted the man's intentions with stunning accuracy. The big man did his best to gather up his pride and walked toward the opening in the wall that would let him escape the gaze of Judgment's Gale. It was Falling Leaf who made the man simply run away. She turned the most vicious, hungry, predatory gaze that Sen had seen on her in a long time toward the big man. He had to focus to hear what she whispered to him.

"It will be me."

There was a look of animal panic on the man's face, and the fear broke him. He turned and fled as fast as his legs could carry him away. Sen wiped the Judgment's Gale from his expression and turned a kind smile toward Li Hua, who was staring at him with an expression that Sen couldn't quite figure out.

"It's nice to see you again, Li Hua. It's also nice to see you, Li Zhi. You are, of course, both welcome here."

Li Zhi slowly peeked her head out from behind her mother. When it was clear that the source of her terror was gone, the little girl hugged her mother's leg and began sobbing. Recognizing that he could only get in the way, he turned a glower on Dai Bao. The grizzled man at least had the good grace to look ashamed of himself.

"Dai Bao," said Sen. "Join me, please. I would have words with you."

CHAPTER TWENTY-SIX

THE RIGHT START

Dai Bao trudged toward Sen like a man marching toward his own execution. It was obvious from his expression the man knew that Sen wasn't happy and that he blamed Dai Bao for some of that. Sen did him the courtesy of walking them away from the small collection of townspeople and erecting a wind barrier to keep their voices from carrying. Sen knew that he might have some unkind things to say to the man, but he didn't particularly feel the need to shame Dai Bao publicly. It wasn't as though Sen had provided any guidance about how things were or were not to be handled here. He could see now that had been a failure on his part. He simply hadn't anticipated any of the men in town trying to bully a woman. After he put up the wind barrier, he gave Dai Bao a flat look.

"So, that seemed acceptable to you?"

"No," said Dai Bao with a shake of his head. "But he was just saying what a lot of men think. It could have been what you think."

"You see the company I keep. You really thought I'd object to women training here?"

"The pretty girl of yours is a cultivator. Not a mortal."

Sen waited for more, and then he realized that there wasn't any more coming. Sen forgot sometimes just how stark that divide really was, yet, hadn't he had a conversation with Jing about how cultivators were just visitors? That cultivators walked in a different world. Everyone in the town was, as far as Sen knew, a mortal. On top of that, cultivators weren't known to treat mortals all that well. Dai Bao was probably justified in thinking that Sen might well consider mortal women not worthy of training. Sen hadn't shared his thoughts about almost anything other than wielding spears with the man. *You can't expect him to read your mind*, thought Sen. *It isn't fair to be angry with him for not knowing expectations you never set.* Sen frowned but nodded.

"I can see why that might seem like something that would make a difference," said Sen. "This place is open to anyone who wants to learn how to protect their homes and families. Men, women, and even children, though hopefully things will never be so terrible that children need to take up spears in their own defense."

"All right," said Dai Bao.

The man still looked like he expected some calamity to fall on his head any second. Sen couldn't help but think that the man had dealt with cultivators in some other part of his life. He'd learned to wield a spear somewhere. It had probably been in a mortal army, but kingdoms sometimes hired cultivators to fight with their armies. Judging from the man's expectations of doom, his experiences with cultivators had been about as good as Sen's own experiences. Sen needed to do something to alleviate the man's fears.

"I'm not trying to start a sect here," said Sen slowly. "I'll help teach, but this place shouldn't be about serving my ego or reputation. It needs a mortal face on it. I'd like that to be you."

Dai Bao goggled at him. "What?"

"The people here respect you. You've had some experience with the spear. They'll listen to you."

"I'm too old and broken for that kind of responsibility," said Dai Bao.

They were the kinds of words that Sen would have expected to hold a lot of bitterness, but all he heard in Dai Bao's voice was a kind of sad resignation. He'd moved beyond whatever anger he felt.

"Well, I can't help you with the age part. The broken part is a different matter."

Sen explained to Dai Bao what he thought he could mend in the man's body and that he'd try if the man would take on the daily responsibilities of the place. He had to give the grizzled man some credit. Dai Bao didn't immediately accept the offer.

"You say that you can heal some of these old injuries. What does that mean?"

"In practical terms?" asked Sen.

"Please," answered Dai Bao.

"It'll hurt. It'll hurt a lot. It might even hurt more than the original injuries. I can do some things to ease that pain, but it might mean spreading out the process for longer. Afterward, though, I expect that you'll feel about ten years younger. You should also be mostly without pain."

Caution warred with hope in Dai Bao's eyes.

"You can really do this?" asked the man.

Sen nodded. "I can really do this. You don't need to decide right now."

"I want to do it," said Dai Bao, grabbing Sen's arm in a desperate gesture. "When can we start?"

"You should consider this carefully. I can't emphasize enough how much pain it will cause you."

"I'm already in pain. All the time. Every day. If you can put a stop to even some of that, I'll endure whatever I have to."

Sen nodded. "Then, we'll get started in the next few days. In the meantime, though, I should probably say something to everyone else. They've been watching us for a while now."

Dai Bao let go of Sen's arm. He turned a hard look on the townspeople who weren't doing anything even remotely like practicing. They all hurriedly turned away, some even doing mostly acceptable versions of basic spear thrusts. Sen removed the wind barrier, and Dai Bao walked back to where he had been. A quick glance around showed that Ai had gone over and apparently provided a distraction for Zhi. The two looked like they were playing some kind of made-up game using a rock that one of them had found somewhere. Sen didn't see Falling Leaf right at first, but he finally saw that she had grabbed a few of the townspeople and led them off a little way. She was encouraging them to attack her while she expertly fended off their thrusts with her three-section staff. He was uncertain and mildly concerned by that turn of events. At first, Sen couldn't understand why she had done it until he realized that she wanted to be helpful to him if not the townspeople. His concern was that she'd accidentally hurt one of them, but she'd limited her strength and speed to something a mortal could mostly manage.

"Thank you," said Li Hua, drawing Sen's attention away from Falling Leaf. "It wasn't necessary, but thank you."

Sen eyed the woman's expression. She appeared torn about the whole incident. There was relief on her face, but he saw frustration as well. Some of it was directed at him. He supposed he might have undermined her in some way, but he was hard-pressed to really feel bad about it. That man wasn't going to see reason. He also wasn't going to stop until she was gone. If that meant dragging her out by the hair, he would have done it. Sen was pretty sure that she knew it, too. On the flip side, Sen had to decide how things were going to happen in this place. He might put Dai Bao out as the face of things, but everyone was going to look to Sen to make the rules. He couldn't let what that man was doing go unaddressed. And he was pretty sure that Li Hua also knew that. It was one of the situations where there had only been a handful of options, none of them ideal. Sen had chosen the one that suited him best. Still, he could help the woman save a little face.

"I didn't really do it for you," Sen lied.

"No?" asked Li Hua, lifting an accusatory eyebrow.

"I did it for them," he said, gesturing at Ai and Zhi. "They might want to come here and learn someday. I'd rather threaten one man now than be forced to murder someone later because I didn't send a clear message."

"You think you'll still be here when they're old enough to learn?"

Sen shrugged. "I might not be, but it doesn't mean that this place won't still be here. For all I know, you'll be in charge of it. But only if things get off to the right start."

"Me?" scoffed Li Hua. "In charge of this place?"

Sen gave her a level look. "Why not?"

"I—" she trailed off.

Sen inclined his head to her. "Excuse me. I need to make an announcement. It's that whole getting things off on the right foot thing."

Sen left Li Hua to her thoughts and walked over to where Dai Bao was drilling some younger men. The grizzled man called a halt to the drill and, at a signal from Sen, bellowed out an order.

"Everyone gather around!" roared Dai Bao.

Approximately fifteen people drew close to Sen. Most of them were young men, but there were a few older men and Li Hua. Sen gave them all his best stern face, and everyone straightened a little under his intense gaze.

"As you all saw earlier, there is some confusion about what this place is for. About who it is for. Let me clear up that confusion. This place is for anyone who wants to learn how to defend their homes and families. *Anyone*. Men. Women. Children. All are welcome here. The moment you decide that you know better who should or should not be here, expect to find that *you* are no longer welcome. If you have grudges, you leave them at the town wall. If you have blood feuds, you leave them at home.

"If you bring your grudges and feuds into this place, you make them *my* problems. I will solve those problems for everyone involved, immediately and permanently," said Sen, and he watched more than one face pale. "When you come here, come with an open heart. Do just that much, and I will do what I can to teach you. I will not lie to you. Mastering any weapon is something that takes years. It takes effort. It takes practice. Now, you all know Dai Bao. He will be in charge when I'm not here. Do as he tells you, which will likely be that you need to practice more."

"And I'll be right," growled Dai Bao.

That got a few laughs, which broke the tension. A moment later, Ai snuck between some of the people and rushed over to Sen. He picked her up, and she looked around nervously at all the unfamiliar faces.

"This is Liu Ai," said Sen before he gave her an encouraging smile. "Do you want to say hello to everyone?"

Ai gave everyone a shy smile and whispered, "Hi."

Then, she buried her face in Sen's shoulder. He kissed the top of her head, which elicited a giggle from the girl. Dai Bao stepped up next to Sen and pointed at Ai.

"In case any of you were wondering, now you know who's in charge."

CHAPTER TWENTY-SEVEN
THE VALUE OF A DEMONSTRATION

Sen took a little time to review the basic thrusts he'd taught Wang Bo and Dai Bao with the newcomers, before turning most of the gathered townspeople over to the grizzled man. Sen focused most of his time and attention on the newest or most hopeless people, which included Li Hua. Of course, her main impediment was that her gaze constantly wandered the entire place in search of her daughter. Sen had finally picked a corner, raised a small enclosure that was about a foot and a half high, and all but filled it with shadow balls. Liu Ai and Li Zhi had immediately lost interest in anything the adults were doing. The little girls' screams of delight carried over the townspeople as they practiced. With the question of where her daughter was now firmly answered, Li Hua became much more focused on the task at hand. Unfortunately, whenever Sen's gaze rested on her for more than a few moments, she became self-conscious and fumbled the spear. Suppressing a moment of frustration, he walked over to her. She met his eyes, briefly, and then found something on the ground to focus on.

"I'm going to be looking at you a lot," said Sen. "And yes, I will be judging you. It's the only way to know what kind of help you need. If you can't focus when I'm looking at you, how will you focus when there's a thirty-foot snake closing in on you? Or a storm hawk swooping down on you with lightning on its wings? Or a bear-cat the size of a horse leaping at your child?"

Li Hua's eyes shot up to his face again, and she grimaced. "I haven't been a student in a long time. I forgot how humiliating it is to be terrible at something."

Sen gave her an amused smile. "Do you imagine that I was any better the first time I picked up a spear? Or even the fiftieth time? Everyone starts right where you are now. That's as true for cultivators as it is for mortals. That's why we train. That's why we practice."

"Do you still practice?" she asked.

"I do."

"Will you show us?"

"I hadn't planned on it. I mean that I don't know that it would do any good. I'm trying to teach you to fight spirit beasts, not do what I do."

Sen could see the confusion on the woman's face before she even said the words.

"I don't understand."

"I practice to prepare for fights with other cultivators. I practice to kill people."

Li Hua seemed momentarily lost for words. She just stared at him like she was seeing him for the first time all over again.

She grimaced again and said, "I'm sorry."

"It's a hard world," said Sen absently as he looked around at the townspeople.

They were not inspired. Even the ones working hard wore expressions that told Sen they wouldn't last for long unless something changed. *Perhaps that's for the best*, thought Sen. He had excelled because, at the end of the day, he wanted to excel with the spear. He wanted to be good if not the best. Uncle Kho likely had that position tied down hard for the foreseeable future, much as Master Feng owned jian mastery. It wouldn't be a tragedy if these people didn't want to pursue true mastery. Simply imparting the basics would give them a fighting chance against most spirit beasts if they worked together. *On the other hand*, mused Sen, *maybe Li Hua has a point.* They had only seen Sen fight the one spirit beast using a new, jian-centered qi technique. Seeing that he actually knew what he was doing with the spear might serve a purpose after all. Even if it only instilled a sense of confidence in the people about what they were learning, that had value in and of itself. He gave Li Hua a thoughtful look that seemed to make her very nervous.

"You should stick close. You'll want a good view of this," said Sen.

He didn't make a big show of it. Sen just walked over to Dai Bao and asked to see the spear the man was holding but not currently using. Walking a short distance away from everyone, Sen acted as though he were simply examining the spear for problems and imperfections. In reality, he wanted the spear to force himself to keep things at mortal speeds. If he applied his true strength and speed with a mortal-grade spear, its haft would simply explode under the pressure. He didn't make any announcement or try to draw anyone's attention. He simply began. He had formed this place with Uncle Kho's courtyard in mind, and the floor brought back a flood of memories from that time. All the hours of practice, of course, but also the times when Uncle Kho would start laughing and tell Sen to stop so he could listen to a story. Those stories often involved Uncle Kho being in what sounded like, at the time at least, terrifying situations.

Looking back now, he could understand why Uncle Kho had laughed. Sen smiled as he remembered fleeing from Tide's Rest, hiding in the forest, convinced that an army of cultivators was hunting him down. It had all seemed so dire then. Now, he could see how much he'd overestimated the wrath of the Stormy Ocean Sect. Sure, they wouldn't have been happy about him killing that sect member. If he'd been easy to catch, they would no doubt have punished him. But that lone formation foundation cultivator he'd killed just wouldn't have been valuable enough to justify sending out a dedicated search party to find him. Even as those memories and thoughts washed over him, Sen felt the spear moving in his hands and cutting through the air as he took another tiny, incremental step toward the unreachable peak of perfection.

He had long since passed through the basic moves and been progressing through the increasingly difficult forms that Uncle Kho had imparted to him. Being forced to move through them at what felt like a snail's pace let him spot those tiny flaws in his form that no expert could ever truly seem to eliminate entirely. At the same time, he felt closer than ever to the reverence that Uncle Kho showed for the weapon. There was a simplicity to it, a natural directness of action and intention that wasn't found with the jian. The jian was the weapon of sharp-minded strategists who could often plot out their victory fifty exchanges in advance, depending on the choices of their opponents. The spear was a weapon that shared more in common with farming tools than with most other weapons. It was a weapon used by people who had to meet immediate threats with immediate force. Complexity had been layered on top of it over the countless millennia by geniuses, but it always came back to a simple thrust or slash to end the fight.

Sen's body came to rest at the end of the final form he'd learned. He paused because, for the first time ever, he felt like there should be something more. Another form, perhaps? He wasn't entirely sure. *Another question for Uncle Kho*, he thought to himself. He turned his attention to the spear in his hand. It wasn't an excellent spear, but it wasn't junk either. A craftsman who knew what they were doing had made it, likely to serve as a weapon for caravan guards or town guards. It would be more than serviceable for the townspeople to fend off spirit beasts. Sen walked back over to Dai Bao who was staring hard at Sen. Sen glanced around at the rest of the people there. That inspiration they had lacked was evident in their eyes. Li Hua looked like she'd been given instructions directly from the heavens and meant to drag every bit of spear knowledge and insight from Sen's mind by force if necessary. Sen handed the spear back to Dai Bao, who took it and stared down at it like it was some kind of sacred relic. Even Li Zhi and little Ai had gone silent and were watching him with startled expressions.

The only person who didn't look impressed was Falling Leaf. She looked bored, as well she might, having seen him do far more spectacular things on more than one occasion. She hadn't been the audience, though, even if her boredom did serve to keep him from being too dazzled with his own performance. Remembering all of the ways he had failed to find perfection in the forms, that seemed like a very healthy thing. He could never let himself become satisfied with his progress. There was always a next step to take, a better way, a more efficient or elegant delivery of any technique, blow, or form. He almost said as much to the people who were all still just staring at him but decided that idea was probably best reserved for those who showed both aptitude and perseverance. Dai Bao saved him from needing to say anything.

"If you think you can do that by standing around and not practicing, think again!" bellowed the grizzled man.

The townspeople all jerked as though they were snapped free from a trance. There were some halfhearted attempts by some of them to return to practicing, but more of them seemed to want to talk about what they had just seen. Sen let it go on for a few minutes before he clapped his hands. Empowered by his body cultivator strength, the clap drowned out all other sounds and silenced everyone. They all turned to look at him.

"Continue with your practice," said Sen.

That time, everyone went back to work.

CHAPTER TWENTY-EIGHT

TEACHING

"Again," said Sen, doing his very best to keep the boredom out of his voice.

Of all the things Sen had thought might happen when he agreed to teach the townspeople how to use spears all those months ago, he hadn't really considered tedium as a possibility. Of course, he'd only ever come at the process from the side of the student. As a student, everything was about mastering something new or solidifying a technique you'd already learned. It was a race to keep pace. For the teacher, it consisted of watching people carry out actions that you'd carried out thousands of times. That was a lot less fun. Oh, there were high spots, no doubt about that. He'd seen more than one person bursting with pride when they'd mastered some move that they had thought beyond them or bested someone in the *very tightly controlled* sparring sessions that Sen oversaw.

There had also been moments of fun in changing the building as the warm summer weather gave way to the intense chill of a northern autumn. At first, it had simply been putting a roof on the place to keep out the rain and the loose leaves that the autumn windstorms like to deposit everywhere. That took several failures, multiple experiments, and finally bringing in Glimmer of Night to help him work out a support system that could hold up the roof. The spider's keen understanding of webs had become invaluable in that process, even if looking straight up toward the roof from inside was a bit unsettling. It looked like stone webbing. It also didn't take much imagination to picture a massive stone spider waiting up there to pounce on unwary students. However, Sen had learned quite a bit about supporting roofs in large, open structures that might prove useful someday. Not that Glimmer of Night seemed inclined to part company any time soon. The spider had actually seemed a little sad when the roof adventure had been successfully completed.

Of course, installing the roof had necessitated reshaping the walls to include windows for light. Otherwise, Sen just had a very big, very dark cave. That might have the occasional use in training, but he didn't see it as ideal for daily use. Putting in windows had required him to first figure out how to make glass, and then figure out how to make glass strong enough to withstand any windstorms. That had been really interesting and finally healed the rift of silence that had persisted between him and Fu Ruolan. He'd gone to her and explained the fragility problem with the glass. He knew it wasn't an alchemy problem, at least not exactly, but it was close enough to get the pair talking. The issue had intrigued the nascent soul cultivator so much that she'd actually *left* her domain for nearly two weeks to go and talk with someone she knew about it.

She'd come back with a storage ring full of books, scrolls, and materials that Sen hadn't recognized. It had taken a lot more experimentation, but they had finally cracked the problem with a combination of borrowed wisdom, Fu Ruolan's massive experience with alchemy, and a bit of help from Sen's intuitive improvements to things under pressure and heat. Fu Ruolan had even deigned to come and watch as Sen installed the glass in the building. As the weather grew colder, he'd needed to add doors to the main entrance. Then, he'd had to work out a way to heat the place that wouldn't require turning the forest into fields of stumps for miles in every direction. Not that the townspeople would have objected, at first, but Sen knew that would turn into a catastrophe for the land in a hurry. Falling Leaf solved part of that problem for him.

"Just warm the stone of the floor," she said.

"What?" asked Sen.

"Why do you think I always used to nap on those big rocks? The sun would warm them up, and they'd stay warm for hours and hours. Often, they'd stay warm well into the night."

It worked, as far as it went. If Sen warmed the stone of the floor in the morning, it would radiate heat all day. Naturally, he wasn't there every day, so it wasn't a complete solution. A couple of large fireplaces also helped, but they worked best to keep the place warm rather than make it warm. In the end, it took several trips even deeper into the wilds to find natural treasures that were strongly fire-attributed. He placed several of them into the stone of the floor, which served to keep the interior of the building warm all of the time. Of course, he'd have to take them back out in the spring, and the solution would only work as long as he was around to manipulate the stone of the floor. That was a problem that he could deal with down the road. For the moment, it was a functional solution that drastically reduced the amount of wood they needed to burn.

Sen looked down at the fifty townspeople working their way through a spear form. Long gone were their days of spreading out in the space. Now, they assembled themselves into orderly rows. He had Dai Bao to thank for that particular improvement. The man had eventually shared that he was, indeed, a soldier in a long-ago time. Like many, he had chosen to join the army rather than follow his father into a trade. When he'd discovered that war was little more than brutal violence and the constant threat of death, rather than some pathway to glory, he had gotten out at the very first opportunity. Even so, he had remembered some things, like how having people form up into lines could boost efficiency. Sen had never trained in a group with other people, let alone with a group of mortals. He'd let Dai Bao's wisdom guide him in that. It had mostly been successful. Sen had been forced to step in and decree who could stand at the front of the lines to put a stop to petty squabbling.

For all the tedium of playing instructor, Sen wasn't wasting his time. He was sitting directly above the townspeople on a platform of hardened shadow that was supported by half a dozen lines of hardened shadow that he'd anchored to the walls. He was also controlling a shadow construct that was about the size and shape of a very large dog that Ai and Zhi were, in turns, riding, petting, or chasing around at a safe distance from the practicing townspeople. It was a compromise he'd made with Fu Ruolan, who said he still hadn't learned what he needed to learn about shadow qi yet. He could come to town and instruct the mortals, but he had to practice and experiment with shadow qi while he did it.

"Can't you just tell me what I'm missing?" Sen had asked.

"I could, but I won't," said Fu Ruolan.

"Dare I ask why?"

"Because there are benefits to discovering the answers for yourself. I told you before, the transition into the nascent soul stage depends on understanding. If I give you the answer, what understanding will you gain about shadow qi or yourself?"

"None," Sen grudgingly admitted.

"Just as importantly, the higher you climb as a cultivator, the fewer people there will be who can guide you. Even the advice of your other teachers, to say nothing of my advice, will become less and less valuable the closer you get to ascension. Our paths intersect with yours in some ways but they are not the same. As time goes by, you'll need to rely on yourself more and more for the insights that will push you forward. You might as well start now while the stakes are lower."

Sen had reluctantly accepted that for the wisdom it was and gone back to work. He didn't feel any closer to a new insight about shadow qi, but he had to admit that he'd become increasingly adept at manipulating it. He took that as a small victory, even if it wasn't the victory he was looking for. He had found himself going back to Glimmer of Night to discuss webs. He felt sure that the key to understanding what he was missing could be found there. He just hadn't managed to find the right question to expose the information that could turn his mental flailing into comprehension. Or, if the right information had been provided, Sen simply lacked the necessary foundation to see it for what it was. Recognizing that rehashing that problem in his head wouldn't get him anywhere, he stood and jumped down to the floor. The platform and supporting lines dispersed at his will. The townspeople didn't stop their practice. They had grown used to his odd behavior by now.

He walked a slow circle around them, noting which people needed a little more direct attention. Sen was about to call a few people over to him when one of the heavy main doors swung open and let in a burst of wind and snowflakes. He stared at the open door for a moment before he let his spiritual sense sweep outward. Sen had discovered that while the mortal townspeople didn't know what it was, they could feel that spiritual sense when he had it active. It was a distraction that they didn't need and there was little use for it inside the building where he could simply see everything that was happening. What he felt were two cultivators. One was in core formation if just barely, while the other was still in early or maybe early-middle foundation formation. No threat to Sen, but a lethal threat to the townspeople. The pair stepped through the door, and Sen was standing between them and the children in a furious burst of qinggong speed. He almost let his killing intent loose but caught himself at the last moment. His fine control of it was world's better than it had been when he first set off into the world, but he didn't want the girls to feel so much as a drop of it if his control slipped.

He did let his hand drop to his jian, though, as he fixed the pair with a look that wasn't quite hostile. Between the wind, snow, and the hoods pulled far forward, he couldn't get a clear look at them. One looked around, pausing briefly at the assembled mortals who were openly staring at the intruders. The other turned and closed the door. The one in front raised a hand and pulled back her hood before giving Sen something that was almost a smile, but marred with a substantial amount of uncertainty. Sen just stared at her. Of all the people he'd thought might try to track him down one day, she hadn't even been on the list. She'd seemed very keen to sever any relationship with him the last time they'd seen each other.

"You're not an easy man to find, Judgment's Gale," said Wu Meng Yao.

CHAPTER TWENTY-NINE
UNCERTAIN RECEPTION

Wu Meng Yao did her best not to stare at Lu Sen. It had been a long, long road to find him. She'd been away from the Soaring Skies Sect for years now, dragging poor Shen Mingxia along in her wake. They'd been gone so long, in fact, that she suspected they were members in name only by now. Not that the traveling had been entirely a bad thing. Like most members of her sect, she had rarely traveled far beyond the city walls, and on those rare trips only to deal with a spirit beast that was bothering the local farmers. In the intervening years, she had traveled countless miles, seen wonders and horrors, and even had a lucky encounter or two.

Between the resources she'd been given by the sect, those lucky encounters, and a deeper well of experience than most of her sect brethren, she'd even managed to break into core formation decades ahead of schedule. She had the sneaking suspicion that with that advancement under her belt, she'd be welcomed with open arms and hailed as some kind of minor cultivation genius when she did finally return. Shen Mingxia had even benefited indirectly and pushed her advancement forward. It hadn't been as fast as Wu

Meng Yao's own meteoric ascent, but it was enough that she'd likely get some attention.

Of course, any thought that she'd been harboring that Judgment's Gale would be impressed by her advancement evaporated the moment she sensed his power. He was keeping it tightly contained, no doubt for the benefit of all the mortals who were staring at her in a mixture of curiosity, fear, and hostility. Even with that power suppressed, she couldn't believe what she was sensing. He was late core formation, maybe even verging onto peak core formation. She'd heard the stories. *Everyone* had heard the stories of the deranged wandering cultivator who challenged sects and criminal empires, the man who walked the deep wilds without fear, the man who cast down beast tides, and the cultivator who toppled kings. She had assumed those stories were exaggerations built up around real but humbler exploits. Looking at him now, sensing that impossible power, power that had come centuries if not millennia before its time, she wondered how many of those tales were completely accurate or, an even more chilling thought, underselling the reality.

Just as importantly, the man was obviously not happy to see her. He had positioned himself between her and the mortals like she was one of those savage young mistresses who took no account of mortal lives. His hand was resting on the hilt of his jian. That casual gesture was enough to send icy waves coursing through her veins. She remembered him wielding that weapon with terrifying skill when he had been nothing but a foundation formation cultivator. She couldn't imagine what it would be like if he turned that blade against her now backed with all of that newfound power and whatever experience he had accumulated in the intervening years. Part of her realized that it might be a profound experience that could push her cultivation forward. What made that problematic was that it would also certainly mean her near-immediate and dishonorable death. She realized that it was on her to start the conversation since she had come to find him.

"You're not an easy man to find, Judgment's Gale," she offered.

She desperately hoped that her tone had come off as light and friendly. Not that it seemed to make even the tiniest impression on the man. His expression didn't move at all from the inhumanly cold neutrality that he'd fixed in place. Wu Meng Yao found herself abruptly wondering how many people had died after seeing that exact expression on that face. She could almost feel him making a decision about whether or not he should simply end her life and be done with it. The tension grew as the silence stretched out until it reached a point that made her want to scream. Then, as if sent by the heavens, one of the most adorable little girls that Wu Meng Yao had ever seen walked up to the pillar of destructive power that was Judgment's Gale. There was absolutely no fear in the child at all as she reached up, grabbed two of the fingers on his free hand, and peered across the intervening space with curious eyes.

"Who's that?" asked the little girl.

As if that child's touch had turned restored something inside of Lu Sen, humanity bled back into his face. He smiled down at the little girl with so much tender affection that Wu Meng Yao felt a brief stab of envy. Not so much that Lu Sen was looking at the little girl that way, but that she couldn't recall anyone ever looking at her that way, not even her own parents. She also felt like the shadow of certain death had fallen across her and that only a quirk of fortune had allowed her to escape it. Once that wave of relief passed, though, she found herself looking back and forth from Lu Sen to the little girl. She couldn't help but wonder. *Is that his daughter?* The girl didn't look too old. Enough time had passed that he could have a daughter that age, but she couldn't imagine when he would have found the time. By all accounts, Judgment's Gale had spent most of the last ten years moving around in the kingdom. By the way he was looking at the little girl and the pure trust she had in the man, though, Wu Meng Yao struggled to imagine that she could be anything but his daughter. Lu Sen turned his gaze from the girl back to her.

"Her name if Wu Meng Yao. We," he paused, "met a long time ago."

"She is so cute!" cried Shen Mingxia.

Wu Meng Yao wanted to shout at the other woman for undermining whatever scraps of dignity they had left. However, it seemed that the path into Lu Sen's good graces passed directly through that little girl. He directed a much warmer look at Shen Mingxia as he picked the little girl up.

"Ai, that is Shen Mingxia," said Sen.

The girl frowned a little, which made Wu Meng Yao's heart skip a beat, but it was all innocent enough.

The girl slowly sounded out the name. "Shen. Ming. Xia."

"That's right," said Sen.

Wu Meng Yao glanced over at Shen Mingxia and recognized a lost cause when she saw one. The other woman only had eyes for the little girl. She wore a huge smile on her face like she didn't even realize how close to utter destruction they had come. The little girl smiled back at Mingxia.

"I'm a beautiful orchid," the child announced.

"Oh, aren't you just," agreed Shen Mingxia with an enthusiastic nod.

That elicited an actual smile from Lu Sen, which frustrated Wu Meng Yao to no end. She'd left the sect, come all this way to make amends, and Shen Mingxia was getting smiles. That was just so *unfair*. On top of all of that, he was even better looking than the last time she'd seen him, which was a tall order. No doubt the product of all those advancements he'd seemingly crashed through over the last several years. Improvements that most cultivators had to wait an eternity to enjoy had piled up on him like gifts from the heavens. It was almost difficult to look at him and not simply gawk. With a start, she realized she was doing just that and averted her eyes before he noticed.

"Alright, everyone," said Sen. "I think it's safe to say that we aren't going to accomplish anything more today. You should head home."

The mortals all started to shuffle around and deposit spears on... Wu Meng Yao studied the wall a little more closely. It looked like hangers had simply grown out of the stone so people could place the spears there. She noticed a similar arrangement where halberds hung. Beyond that, there were hooks where people had hung up their wet coats and cloaks to dry. Cultivators talented with earth qi could do such things, but the mortals seemed to take the conveniences for granted. And why wouldn't they? It was clear that this setup had been in place for a while. What she couldn't figure out was why someone as powerful and infamous as Judgment's Gale was teaching mortals to use weapons. Maybe he'd tell her, if she could ever thaw that cold unhappiness she'd seen on his face when he first recognized her.

Turning to say something to Shen Mingxia, she discovered the woman gone. Looking around, Wu Meng Yao found the traitor fussing over the little girl, who Sen had put back down on the ground. Feeling like there was a plot against her, Wu Meng Yao watched her student win another look of quiet approval from Lu Sen. The trio were quietly joined by another little girl who was holding what looked like a ball made of shadow. *Another daughter?* The other little girl seemed hesitant, her eyes locking on Lu Sen for approval. He gently rested a hand on the girl's head and introduced her.

"This is Li Zhi," he told Shen Mingxia.

Seemingly bolstered by Sen's presence and introduction, Zhi walked over to Shen Mingxia and Ai. The little girls immediately co-opted Shen Mingxia to play some kind of game with them. *Thank the gods there are no sect elders here to witness this*, thought Wu Meng Yao. She wasn't sure that either of them would ever live the encounter down. She kept her distance while Lu Sen had a number of brief conversations with the mortals. One of the mortal women eventually went over to claim the girl, Li Zhi, who immediately ran away and hid behind Lu Sen's leg. It seemed this was some kind of ritual because the little girl started giggling as soon as Lu Sen began looking around like he was confused.

"Oh no!" he cried in the most theatrical of worried voices. "Where can Li Zhi have gone?"

The little girl giggled louder and louder as Lu Sen managed to look everywhere except at where she was standing.

"Whatever will we do if we can't find Li Zhi?" he moaned as he dropped his face into his hands.

The other little girl took up her part in the ritual.

"Shadow dog!" shouted Ai. "Shadow dog can find her!"

"You're right! Shadow dog can do it!"

Wu Meng Yao had no idea what they meant by shadow dog until she felt a surge of qi from Lu Sen, followed by what looked like a literal dog made of shadow leaping into being out of nowhere. She felt her mouth hanging open at the sight, not sure if she should be horrified at the outrageously wasteful use of qi for a child's game, or astounded at the nonchalant way that the man formed and directed the shadow construct. It bounded around the huge building like an actual dog, looking as though it was sniffing for a trail. The little girl, Li Zhi, wasn't even bothering to hide anymore. Instead, she was standing right next to Lu Sen jumping in happiness at the sight of the shadow dog. After what seemed like an unnecessarily convoluted trek through the completely open space, the shadow dog suddenly turned to where Li Zhi was standing, its void black tail started wagging back and forth, and it trotted over to her.

"Shadow dog found her!" shouted Ai.

"Yes, he did," agreed Lu Sen, as the little girls petted the construct.

With the ritual completed, the mortal woman bundled up the little girl for the cold weather. Wu Meng Yao expected Lu Sen to disperse the shadow construct, but the other little girl immediately climbed onto it. She watched in stunned silence as Ai rode the shadow construct as if it were some kind of horse. She was pulled from her thoughts by the voice of Lu Sen.

"You've advanced to core formation. Congratulations."

She turned to face him. The words had been neutral. Safe. A topic that any cultivator would respond to. She nodded.

"Thank you. Although, it seems no star burns as brightly as yours in the heavens' eyes when it comes to advancement."

She had thought it was a safe enough comment, but Lu Sen grimaced at the words.

"Perhaps," he said, apparently ready to put away even the pretext of polite conversation. "You've come a long way, Wu Meng Yao. What do you want?"

CHAPTER THIRTY

DON'T WORRY ABOUT IT

As Sen waited for an answer, he watched the woman's face. She seemed almost confused as she looked around at the building, and then over at Ai riding on the shadow dog. When she did finally look at him again, it was only for a few moments before her eyes shifted to look past him. He glanced over his shoulder to see Shen Mingxia curiously staring at the pit of shadow balls he kept there for the girls to play in. The woman looked from the pit to Ai on the shadow dog, and then back to the pit. She reached down and picked one of the balls out of the pit. Sen felt Mingxia extend her spiritual sense and her qi. A look of muted awe crossed her face and she looked toward Sen. When she saw Sen and Wu Meng Yao looking at her, she jumped, squeaked, and hastily dropped the ball back into the pit. Sen snorted. Feeling amused, he held out a hand and formed another of the shadow balls. He threw it to her.

"Study it all you like," he said. "Who knows? Maybe you'll get an insight from it."

He turned his attention back to Wu Meng Yao and found her watching him with an intense look in her eyes. *Yeah*, he thought, *that's not off-putting at all.* Sen remembered that last conversation they'd had back in Emperor's Bay with a lot more clarity than he'd like. He remembered her telling him that he frightened her. It didn't sting the way it used to, but it wasn't the kind of thing that a person just shrugs off either. When Sen found his patience starting to wear thin, it must have shown on his face because Wu Meng Yao blurted out a hasty question.

"Is she your... Is she your daughter?"

Sen had to think hard about that question. It wasn't a question about where Ai stood in his heart because that answer was locked in stone. She was his, and anyone who tried to take her from him was going to discover that he was the kind of man for whom phrases like *scorched earth* and *no survivors* were literal possibilities. No, the real question was whether he wanted any sect to possess a confirmation that he saw Ai that way. After a moment of thought, he knew with certainty that he did not to want to confirm that kind of relationship to any sect. Instead, he lied by saying something true.

"She is under my protection."

From the way Wu Meng Yao took a step back from him, she understood that questions on that topic would not increase her odds of a long, happy, healthy life. Sen thought that taking this approach was probably even better than simply saying she was his daughter. Saying Ai was under his protection meant that any action against her wouldn't mean the *possibility* of retribution but the absolute *guarantee* of it. With his reputation, that was a risk that most sects would go out of their way to avoid. Sen didn't particularly want to reinforce a reputation as a merciless, blood-soaked agent of doom. If someone threatened Ai, though, that's exactly what he'd become. However, Sen didn't have any particular grudge against Wu Meng Yao, so scaring her to death was probably out of bounds. Besides, he got the impression that she'd just asked him the first thing that sprang to mind. He did his best to tamp down the impression that he'd murder people for asking the wrong questions. He softened his tone.

"Meng Yao, you didn't come this far from your sect on a whim. Why are you here?"

Part of Sen worried that she was here on some kind of misguided mission to recruit him to the Soaring Skies Sect. Although, he had saddled Elder Deng with that list of demonic cultivators. Maybe she'd been sent with a message about that. Looking back, he felt a little bad about doing that to Elder Deng. The old man hadn't been all that friendly to Sen, but Sen also hadn't been that good for the Soaring Skies' reputation. A wandering cultivator coming in, killing their sect members, and piling them up in the street like trash. Murdering one of their elders while also exposing said elder as a demonic cultivator. He'd probably set them back a few centuries in terms of the honor and prestige of the sect. In hindsight, it was downright miraculous that he'd gotten out of that city alive. Although, Lo Meifeng had threatened to bring down the wrath of Fate's Razor on them all, so maybe it wasn't that miraculous.

"The last time we spoke—" said Wu Meng Yao before she trailed off.

"I remember," said Sen with more than a hint of dryness in his tone.

"Yeah," she answered, wincing a little. "I was unkind to you. It wasn't until after you were gone that I understood what you'd done for me."

Sen blinked at her. *I have no idea what she's talking about*, he thought. He scoured his memory and tried to think of anything he might have done *for* her. He hadn't given her anything. That was in the days before he made a habit of picking up absurdly powerful plants and reagents out in the wilds. No matter how hard he thought, he just couldn't imagine what action or event she was referring to. In the end, he did the only thing he could do. He shrugged.

"Well, things worked out fine, I guess. Don't worry about it."

Wu Meng Yao stared at him, her mouth working a little, but she seemed utterly at a loss. Shen Mingxia spoke from behind him with an amused voice.

"He doesn't remember," she said.

"What?" asked Wu Meng Yao.

"Isn't it obvious? He has no idea what he did for you. For us."

Sen looked back to see Shen Mingxia holding the shadow ball he'd given her. She was still studying it, apparently.

"You don't remember?" asked Wu Meng Yao with an incredulous expression.

Sen gave her a helpless look. "I really don't. I mean, it seems like it was important, and I'm glad it helped you, but a *lot* has happened to me since then."

Wu Meng Yao stood completely still for a few seconds before a little laugh escaped her lips. Once that laugh was out in the world, though, it was like the sect woman couldn't keep the rest of them in. She laughed until she was wiping tears away from her eyes.

"I should have known," she said.

"Known what?" asked Sen, even if he wasn't sure he actually wanted to know.

"What you did was life-changing for me," said Wu Meng Yao.

"For both of us," chimed in Shen Mingxia.

"But the life you live is so—" she started, only to pause.

"Absurd?" offered Sen.

"I was going to say extreme or maybe intense. Your life is so intense that you don't even remember doing life-altering things for people."

Sen frowned. She wasn't necessarily wrong, but he also wasn't sure that she was right about this either.

"Yeah, but did I actually *do* anything? Did I personally do anything for either of you? I mean after that business at the Silver Crane. Because I honestly can't think of a single thing."

"You told Elder Deng I could be trusted," said Wu Meng Yao.

Sen nodded at that. "Sure."

She looked at him expectantly.

"What?" asked Sen.

"You told one of the most powerful people in my sect that I could be trusted."

"I know. I told him that because it was true."

"So, you do remember," said Wu Meng Yao.

"I remember saying it," said Sen.

That was when Sen's brain finally caught up with the conversation that Wu Meng Yao had been trying to have with him. He hadn't been thinking about it in the big picture. To him, it had been an offhand statement of fact and maybe a way to help Shen Mingxia get some decent training. But, to Elder Deng, a man confronted with the fact that his sect had been infiltrated by at least one demonic cultivator, those words had probably carried a lot more weight. Coming from Sen, coming from the student of Feng Ming, those words must have sounded like a ringing endorsement. He could imagine how it came across to Deng. *Yeah, I think your sect is filled with garbage, but I found one diamond of a person that I think is trustworthy.* Sen didn't know exactly what that meant for her at the sect, but it must have been pretty good for her to go through all the trouble to find him. When he thought about that last conversation they had, he realized that she must have been harboring some deep guilt about the whole thing.

"I see," said Sen, before he decided that it didn't change anything. "Well, I'm glad that worked out for you. Don't worry about it."

The look of shock and even offense on Wu Meng Yao's face was not what Sen had expected. He'd figured he could send her back to her sect, free of guilt, and never to trouble him again.

"I spent years searching for you so I could try to make amends. And you don't care?"

That hadn't been what Sen was trying to say, but he could sort of see how it might look that way from her position. He'd just meant to give her an easy out. *Why are these things always so complicated?* The problem was that he didn't know what she did want.

"That's not it. I genuinely appreciate what you've done, and that you want to make amends. I'm just not sure what you expected me to do about it. I mean, honestly, what can I do other than tell you it's fine and send you home?"

"Well, for starters, you could—" she said before a look of uncertainty crossed her face.

Sen narrowed his eyes at her. "You thought that *I'd* have a plan for something like this, didn't you? Some task that I'd want done? Some quest you could pursue? Something that would put us back on even terms?"

"Do you?" asked Wu Meng Yao in a weak but hopeful voice.

"No. What kind of a person has a plan ready to go for this situation?" asked Sen as he pinched the bridge of his nose.

He looked over at Ai who was still cheerfully riding around on the shadow dog construct. He had it bring her over to him. She hopped down off the construct and waved at it as it dispersed. Sen wondered if she thought it was sapient. *Now, there's a question,* thought Sen. *Could I make it sapient? I wonder how I'd do that, assuming it's even possible.* He tucked that thought away for future consideration as he started making sure that Ai got her winter cloak settled around her. He very pointedly did not look at Wu Meng Yao while he did that. She had seemed both embarrassed and out of sorts, so a little time not being under direct scrutiny was probably a good thing. He finally turned his attention back to the sect cultivators.

"Do you two have rooms yet?"

"No," said Shen Mingxia.

"Follow me. There's an inn in town. They probably have some rooms open. It's not a great inn, but it's dry, warm, and the food isn't terrible. I need to get you settled, so we can go home. Are you ready to go home?" he asked Ai.

"Home!" she agreed enthusiastically.

"I don't suppose we could—" started Wu Meng Yao.

"Definitely not," said Sen, shuddering at the very thought of what Fu Ruolan might do if he brought two sect members into her domain.

CHAPTER THIRTY-ONE

QUEST-GIVING

F alling Leaf just stared at Sen with those green eyes of hers for a while, her hand gently stroking Ai's hair as the little girl slept in her lap. That sleep was peaceful, for which Sen was deeply grateful. The awful nightmares of the first couple of months had slowly faded away, largely Sen suspected, in lockstep with Ai's increasing feeling of safety and security. These days, the nightmares were the rare exception. To Sen's immense relief, those nightmares often featured threats conjured by the girl's imagination instead of the far-too-real human monsters of her past. Sen's eyes were drawn back up as Falling Leaf shook her head.

"What does the foolish human girl expect you to do? The guilt isn't yours."

That had been Sen's general feeling about Wu Meng Yao as well, but there was something comforting in having the ghost panther agree with him. He'd been wrestling with the problem of what, if anything, he should do about the sect cultivator since he left her and Shen Mingxia back at the inn. It was strange to have such different reactions to two people. Wu Meng Yao had immediately made herself into an issue, albeit a very minor one on the scale of Sen's usual problems. He'd been certain that she'd drag some huge calamity in her wake that would inevitably require him to do things he'd rather not do. The reality was much more mundane and annoying than disastrous and deadly.

He'd actually been happy to see Shen Mingxia. It was a relief to know that she had escaped the kind of unwanted attention she'd faced in the sect before. Based on her advancement, she'd been the recipient of some good training, good luck, or both in the interim. Sen could even allow himself a tiny bit of satisfaction that he'd played some small role in making *that* happen. Sen was willing to admit that the woman's reaction to Ai *might* have disposed him to like her a little more than he otherwise would have. Of course, Mingxia had been willing to simply say a heartfelt thank you and leave it at that. If she was harboring some of the same feelings as Wu Meng Yao, she did a much better job of hiding them. As for what Wu Meng Yao expected from him, that was the mystery.

"I really don't know," admitted Sen. "I can see where she's coming from, a little bit, but I don't think it's my problem to deal with. On the other hand, I don't want sect members in town all the time, bothering people, or bothering me."

"Then give her something to do. Some task that she won't like that will eventually make her leave. Or, better yet, a task that will drag her away for a long time. Send her after a difficult-to-reach treasure."

"*I* don't know where to find any treasures. Where am I supposed to send her?"

Falling Leaf sat in thoughtful silence for a while before she smiled the kind of smile that makes people shiver.

"Send her to the Mountains of Sorrow. The Caihong said that there are many caves and many treasures hidden near the peaks of those mountains."

Sen lifted an eyebrow at the ghost panther. "I'm fairly certain that Uncle Kho said that there were also all kinds of monsters crawling around near those peaks."

"What better test of her sincerity?" asked Falling Leaf.

"I'm so glad you don't get angry with me all that often," observed Sen. "Well, I suppose I have to send her after something."

"Just tell her that it's a shadow qi treasure that she'll recognize as soon as she sees it."

Sen mulled it over. "So, you figure that they'll go looking, realize how stupidly dangerous it is, or realize I sent them there just to get them out of here, and go home?"

"They will if they have any sense," said Falling Leaf.

"What if they find something?" asked Sen.

Falling Leaf rocked her head to each side a few times. "Then, I imagine that you'll get a shadow treasure with no effort."

Sen laughed gently and shook his head. His gaze shifted when Ai stirred a little.

"Do you want me to take her?" asked Sen.

The ghost panther didn't actually hiss at him, but Sen got the impression it was a close thing. Instead, Falling Leaf gave him a flat look.

"She's fine where she is."

Sen lifted his hands in a placating gesture. "I was only offering. Just trying to be helpful"

"If you wish to be helpful, fetch one of those tedious history scrolls that the Kho gave you and read it to me. Since it seems I am truly to be stuck in this form forever, I should make an effort to know some of your human history."

Sen was startled by the request but did as he was asked. Reading it out loud wasn't that much better than reading it in his head, but Falling Leaf remained attentive. She even asked questions from time to time. After they put Ai to bed, Sen brought out his writing kit.

"I thought you were done teaching me," said the ghost panther.

"Done is a strong word. You know enough to get by, but it's a skill you need to practice occasionally."

"Very well," said Falling Leaf, sitting down at the table. "What shall I write?"

"You heard a bunch of that scroll earlier. Write down some of what you remember."

That earned Sen a skeptical look, but Falling Leaf dutifully picked up the brush and began writing. At first, he just watched the characters appear on the scroll and marveled at the crisp control that went into forming them. After a little while, though, Sen really focused on what Falling Leaf was writing. Sen couldn't be sure without going and getting the scroll he'd been reading, but it appeared that Falling Leaf was writing what she'd heard nearly verbatim. Sen's memory was good. In fact, it was very, very good compared to his mortal days, but he didn't think he could have pulled off the feat he was witnessing.

"You remember all of this?" he asked.

"I was listening carefully," she said as she turned to look at him. "I always listen carefully when you speak."

Sen felt inexplicably nervous under that look and shifted in his seat. Then, Falling Leaf broke the moment when she continued.

"You should try it sometime."

"Very funny," said Sen as Falling Leaf smirked to herself.

WU MENG YAO looked a little horrified at Sen's words.

"You want me to go to the Mountains of Sorrow and retrieve a treasure from one of the peaks there?"

Sen nodded. "Yes. That's about the size of it."

The woman swallowed hard. Sen did his best not to look at Shen Mingxia because she was giving him a very skeptical look.

"Which peak?" asked Wu Meng Yao.

"I don't know exactly which peak. It's supposed to be one of the peaks near the main pass through the mountains. I mean, if I knew exactly where it was and how to get it, I'd just go myself."

"Do you have any other information?" asked the sect woman.

Sen was starting to feel bad about the whole subterfuge, but he carried on with it. "It's a potent shadow qi treasure. It's in a cave. You should expect terrible weather, powerful spirit beasts, and probably some dangerous formations and qi traps. It's perfect for a fresh core formation cultivator. I get a treasure. You're freed from your debt. Everybody wins."

Wu Meng Yao's brow furrowed. "Do we need to leave immediately?"

Sen wanted to say *yes*. Oh, he wanted to say it so very badly, but he'd seen the map. There was basically nothing between where they were and where he was sending them. No major cities. He wasn't sure there were even any towns or villages. Sen might want them gone, but he wasn't cruel enough to force them to travel in the dead of winter to places where there simply was no shelter. After all, they couldn't simply raise a galehouse and hole up for a month if they needed to. He shook his head.

"It'll hold until spring, I expect."

A tiny little part of Sen hoped that she'd decide to go back to Emperor's Bay until the weather broke, but it wasn't to be. She offered him a relieved smile.

"Well then, we'll just have to find ways to make ourselves useful around here until then."

Sen tried to smile back and almost made it. Wu Meng Yao stood.

"I'll get us something to drink," she announced.

The moment she was gone, Sen felt Shen Mingxia's eyes boring into him. He looked over at her and did his best to maintain a calm, neutral expression.

"There's no treasure, is there?" she demanded.

"Oh, there's definitely treasures up in those peaks," said Sen.

"But not the one you're talking about."

Sen said nothing.

Shen Mingxia glared at him. "Are you trying to get me and her killed?"

"What? No. *Your* job is to wait until you get to the mountains and then tell her that I'm a cruel liar who sent you after a nonexistent treasure."

Shen Mingxia opened her mouth and the only thing that came out was a baffled, "Why?"

"Because it's not my job to fix her guilt," said Sen.

Shen Mingxia frowned but eventually nodded. "Okay. I can see that. But why all of this? Why not just say that to her?"

"Do you really think that if I just say, this is not my problem, go home, she'll actually do it? Because that would make my life so much easier."

"No," admitted Shen Mingxia. "There's almost zero chance of that."

"That was what I thought. This way, I waste a bunch of her time and send her on a fool's errand. You put a stop to it before it gets really dangerous. She stops feeling guilty and just thinks that I'm an ass for doing that to her."

"You *are* an ass for doing this to her."

"As a wandering cultivator, you work with the tools you have. Besides, it's not like I have anything real for her to do. You're not dealing with a sect here. It's just me. I don't have jobs or missions or whatever you call them to hand out to people."

"Still, this was the best you could come up with?"

"Figure out something better," said Sen. "You have until spring."

CHAPTER THIRTY-TWO

FIRST TEST, PART 1

Sen had barely begun to walk away from the inn when his spiritual sense alerted him that there were spirit beasts near to the town. They were much too close to be doing anything but preparing to attack. *I guess this day was always coming*, he thought. *Now, we find out if I've been wasting my time or not.* Sen activated his qinggong technique and flashed over to where the town had set up a gong. It was usually tucked away and only brought out for festivals, but Sen had made the argument that it could serve another purpose. It could be an alert for the town that danger was at hand. Sen flipped open the box that was there to offer the mallet some basic protection from the weather, seized the mallet, and struck the gong three times. By the time the third reverberating note was washing out over the town, Sen was crashing into the practice hall and hurriedly storing weapons in a storage ring.

This was bad planning, he realized. He never went anywhere without his weapons. In fact, he kept backup weapons on him at all times. Granted, the mortals couldn't make use of storage rings, but they could keep spears close at hand. Needing to run to a building outside the city to arm themselves was a huge waste of time during which people could die. Of course, solving that problem meant getting more spears. *Well, it's not like I don't have the money*, thought Sen. *Maybe I'll call it a loan to the town, and they can pay me back a copper tael each year until the end of time.* Having grabbed all the weapons, he shot back toward the town. He only paused long enough to toss Wang Bo over his shoulder. The young man was fast on his feet and lived the closest to the practice hall, so Sen wasn't entirely surprised to find him racing for the weapons. Sen did have to suppress his laughter at the high-pitched yelp the young man made when he was seemingly seized by an all-but-invisible force and carried back to the town. Sen went over the wall and dropped down on the inside of the gate. He was gratified to see that about half of the people he'd been training were racing toward his direction. If all was going according to plan, the rest would be at the other gate. Sen put down Wang Bo, who looked a little nauseated and swayed on his feet. He turned and pointed to one of the people who was racing toward him.

"Go to the other gate. Fetch the rest. The threat is here."

More poor planning, thought Sen. *There should be a specific signal for which gate they should meet at.* The realization that people would have needed to carry spears to the far side of town just so the townspeople could arm themselves drove home just how badly he'd thought all of it through. He consoled himself a little with the knowledge that no one else had thought of these things either. Plus, it wasn't like Sen had ever gotten any practical training in defending a town or city. He wasn't a general. He was just a wandering cultivator. He summoned an armful of spears and shoved them at Wang Bo. Then, he summoned an armful for himself. They started passing the weapons out. Sen could feel the rest of the people coming from the far side of the town. He handed out a few more armloads of weapons and tasked people with arming the new arrivals.

He strode back to the gate and turned to face the townspeople. He waited and did his best to look calm and project confidence.

Once everyone was assembled and armed, he swept his gaze across the people. Some looked scared. Some looked excited. Some of the people who had fought the last spirit beasts to attack the town looked grim but determined. He saw Wu Meng Yao and Shen Mingxia drift toward the gathering. He'd have to stop them from interfering unless things went terribly, terribly wrong. Taking a deep breath, he clasped his hands behind him. *I need to give them something to focus on*, he thought.

"There are spirit beasts close to the town. They might just be passing by, but I'm not willing to sit back and simply *hope* that's what happens. These are your homes, your livelihoods," he locked eyes with Li Hua for a second, "and your families. The fight will be hard. I can't promise that none of you will be hurt. I can't promise that no one will die. But you are the line between those spirit beasts and everything and everyone you hold dear. You are their shield. You are their sword. Will you fail them?"

The townspeople stared at him as though transfixed. He waited. It was Dai Bao who broke the silence.

"No!" shouted the grizzled man.

"Is Dai Bao the only one? I ask you again. *Will you fail them*?"

That time, fifty voices shouted out at him as one. "No!"

Some of them shouted in fear. Some shouted in defiance of the threat bearing down on them. Yet, they were united. It was the most he could ask for.

"Good," said Sen, giving them all a nod. "Through the gate and into your teams."

He turned and pushed the gate open. The townspeople flooded past him, their eyes blazing with purpose. Wu Meng Yao and Shen Mingxia came up on either side of him. Shen Mingxia watched the mortals organizing themselves with a thoughtful look on her face. Sen felt Wu Meng Yao extend her spiritual sense. She gave Sen a perplexed look.

"I don't understand. You could kill those spirit beasts without even trying. Mingxia and I could do it without any help."

Sen glanced over at her. "What about next time?"

"What do you mean?"

"I mean that I'm not always here. You won't always be here. But they will," he said, gesturing at the people beyond the gate. "They'll be here every day. They'll be here the next time spirit beasts come looking for easy food or easy prey. So, I'm trying to give them the skills they need to protect themselves. This will be the first test."

"You don't want us to interfere at all?" asked Shen Mingxia.

Sen almost agreed, but the look of deep concern on the woman's face made him think better of it. He had two sect-trained cultivators just hanging around, at least one of them positively aching to be useful to him. Sen had fought with enough sect cultivators to recognize that, while he might not care for their attitudes on the whole, they were generally competent to above-average fighters. Simply telling these two to stay out of it completely was a poor use of available resources. Yes, he wanted the townspeople to get some valuable experience. Yes, he wanted them to be the ones to make the actual kills. No, he didn't want either of those things to result in preventable deaths. And with three cultivators on hand, pretty much every certain death scenario for a mortal was preventable. Sen was new to this quasi-leadership role he'd adopted, but even he could see that allowing deaths for no reason other than "teaching" would undermine the townspeople's trust in him at best, and seem like a basic betrayal of trust at worst.

"The whole point of this is to help them build up some experience and confidence, so leave the fighting and killing to them. With that said, you can intervene to save lives. Get people out of certain death. Push the beasts back to let the townspeople regroup. That kind of thing. If something too powerful shows up, I'll deal with it. Or you two can."

Shen Mingxia looked relieved, while Wu Meng Yao looked eager. *Man, I should have sent her on that stupid fake quest immediately*, thought Sen. Still, he'd be lying to himself if he didn't feel the pressure of responsibility on him reduce just a little bit. He knew that spirit beasts killed mortals all the time, the same way that cultivators killed spirit beasts and each other all the time. It was the way of the world. But he was at a remove from all of those people, cultivators, and spirit beasts. He hadn't tried to get to know the townspeople all that well, but he'd inevitably become a casual acquaintance to pretty much every student. He considered a small handful of them as actual friends. Dai Bao, Li Hua, and Li Zhi, Wang Bo and his parents, and a few others. Thankfully, only some of them were getting ready to fight, but Sen recognized that this was a test for himself as much as it was for them.

During that first fight with the spirit beasts, it had been easy to limit his intervention. He didn't really know any of them. Now, he did, and he needed to find out if he could stay his hand when things got bloody. Intervening for anything short of certain death would tell the townspeople that he didn't trust them, didn't trust what he'd taught them, which would make them doubt what he'd taught them. It was going to be hard because Wu Meng Yao was right. He could end the approaching spirit beasts by himself from the exact spot he was standing. The townspeople would never know, but he would know. He needed to be a little cruel right now so that they would learn, and so that they would be better prepared later. Sen put on a mask of cool confidence as he stepped through the gate.

He watched as Dai Bao went from group to group, offering words of encouragement and making sure everyone's weapon was in fighting condition. During the first battle, there had been so few people that Sen broke them up into three-person teams. With fifty people, that was impractical. After some discussion with Dai Bao, they'd settled on five-person teams. Three people carried spears while two wielded halberds. It was a cold calculation, but that meant that up to two people could theoretically die and leave a team still capable of fighting or, barring that, retreating with some possibility of survival. With ten teams, it also meant that they could hold some teams in reserve to rotate in if the battle raged on for more than a few minutes. Sen remembered how tired he had been during the earliest days of his training and how fatigue made him sloppy. He had quickly learned that those memories were accurate for mortals in general. Even healthy, fit adult mortals grew tired very fast compared with a formation foundation cultivator like Shen Mingxia. He expected that would prove more true in a situation like this, where the combat would be far fiercer and demanding than their most brutal practice sessions.

"They're almost here," said Wu Meng Yao.

Her comment wasn't necessary. Sen could feel them even more clearly than she could. At least the woman had lost that eager expression. It seemed the reality of the situation was finally sinking in for her. Mortals were about to fight spirit beasts. Sen caught Dai Bao's eyes and nodded.

"Here they come!" bellowed the man. "You don't let them see so much as a wisp of fear in your eyes. They don't know it, yet, but they came here to die!"

CHAPTER THIRTY-THREE
FIRST TEST, PART 2

I t was all Sen could do to keep his breathing steady. If this had been his fight, he knew he would have been calm, collected, and focused. He might have even been a little excited. But this wasn't his fight. Not really. He was mostly a spectator to the danger. His eyes traveled across the backs of the townspeople, and he couldn't help but pick out the ones he knew and liked best. He could almost see the fear rolling off the people who had never been in any kind of a real fight before. Sparring was useful, but it wasn't the same as real fighting.

Sen had learned that lesson back on the mountain when he'd made his long trek to form his killing intent. Training helped prepare you, but it couldn't ever replace the actual experience of fear trying to claw its way out of your chest, the thunderous pounding of blood in your ears like a drum that refused to be silent, or the pressing need to simply be doing something, even if doing nothing was the best choice. That was a fight he couldn't help the townspeople win. That was a fight that would happen in their own minds and hearts, and they each needed to find something inside themselves that gave them the strength they needed to overcome their fears.

When the spirit beasts finally burst out of the forest, Sen very nearly broke every promise he'd made to himself and the townspeople, all so he could go on a one-cultivator killing spree. It was a small pack of those gods damned bear-cats. He could kill them. He'd vowed to kill them. It'd be nothing, nothing at all, to cut them down like the waste of life and qi that they all were. It would be right. It would be good. It would be... Sen didn't realize he'd started to move until he felt a hand seize his arm. He stared down at that hand in blank incomprehension before his eyes followed the arm back to the confused face of Wu Meng Yao. In a blink, Sen came back to himself.

"What are you doing?" she asked. "You said not to interfere. That this was for them to learn."

Sen looked down and saw his hand wrapped around the hilt of his jian so tightly that it was amazing the weapon hadn't been damaged. He forced himself to let go of the hilt. He ordered his lungs to take in air. *She's right*, he told himself. *This isn't about you.* He took a few more steadying breaths and nodded to her. She didn't release his arm immediately.

"What was that about?" she asked.

Sen glared at the advancing bear-cats. "I hate those things."

He was gratified to see that the bear-cats didn't quite know what to make of the group of armed mortals standing between them and the town. The spirit beasts shuffled back and forth a bit before the biggest of the group hiss-snarled something in what Sen presumed was the bear-cat language. Letting go of their reluctance, they surged toward the townspeople.

"Do you think they can beat six of them?" asked Shen Mingxia, the doubt clear in her voice and on her face.

"I don't know. Neither do they," said Sen. "That's the whole point of this. Besides, even if we weren't here, they'd still have to fight them."

While Sen had harbored some dim, vain hope that that fight would be over quickly with the mortals earning a decisive victory, life was rarely so clean. Many of the townspeople were clearly unnerved by the charge of the spirit beasts, so their reactions were slow. The teams were pushed out of shape as some people acted immediately while others remained frozen, if only for a moment or two. The groups who had been in front were pushed back toward the reserve groups until a voice cut through the noise and chaos.

"Fight!" screamed Li Hua.

Her face was a mask of untempered rage, and her spear lashed out at a bear-cat to draw blood. That single word seemed to break the semi-paralysis, but the townspeople had lost whatever advantage the bear-cats' initial confusion might have bought them. It would all be uphill from here. Even that one split-second hesitation to unleash her battle cry nearly cost Li Hua her life. The bear-cat she'd wounded turned and swiped at her. It was only the descending blade of a halberd that made the spirit beast shy away. Of course, that part was according to plan. Only a very exceptional few mortals stood a real chance against any spirit beast in a one-on-one confrontation. Sen had done his best to drive that one idea into their mind.

"You will not win against spirit beasts with brute force. You must kill them by attrition. It's not the stuff of legends, but if you cut a spirit beast a thousand times, it will die. You do that by working together. Distract. Harass. Cut. Then, when it's bled so much it can't move, you cut off its head."

As he kept his eyes moving across the fight, he saw the townspeople enacting that plan, more or less. Fear had a real grip on some of the people. Some were simply more talented than others. Sen and Dai Bao had done their best to spread the talent out, but there was no way to predict who would succumb to fear. It meant that some of the fights were lopsided. The bear-cats were savage, but they weren't stupid. They could recognize where the threats were coming from and would attack the weak links. That forced the others to intervene, putting them closer to claws and teeth. On the whole, though, the strategy was working. Sen did wonder if this strategy could possibly endure the attack of a truly powerful spirit beast, but that wasn't what he'd been teaching them to fight. If something truly powerful came looking for trouble, the best they could hope for was to buy time for people to flee.

Much as he had expected, Sen could see that people were getting tired. Spear thrusts were getting sloppy. Halberd swings were coming later than they should. Then, it happened. Wang Bo stepped on something and stumbled. If he had stumbled sideways or backward, it would have been fine, but he stumbled forward. Right toward the waiting jaws of a bear-cat. Sen had restrained himself when people were taking minor injuries, but it took him less than a fraction of a second to analyze where everyone in Wang Bo's group was positioned. No one would be able to intervene in time. Sen activated his qinggong technique and gleefully put himself between the screaming Wang Bo and the bear-cat. The spirit beast seemed utterly perplexed as its jaws closed around Sen's arm and found precisely no give in that body cultivation-hardened flesh. It was everything that Sen could do not to simply kill it on the spot, but he restrained himself to simply jerking his arm and sending the beast bouncing away on the ground. He turned and looked at the stunned group. It had probably looked to them like he'd appeared from nowhere.

"Fall back," he told them. "Send a new team forward."

When Wu Meng Yao and Shen Mingxia saw what Sen had done, they followed suit. They intervened for two other groups that seemed to be the most hard-pressed by the fighting. The exhausted townspeople didn't need any convincing, simply retreating toward the wall. Three of the reserve groups came forward and none of them looked excited anymore. They'd seen what fighting spirit beasts really looked like and realized that it wasn't glorious or anything like the stories they'd heard. It was just danger and blood. The advantage was that they'd had more time to master their fear, and they were fresh. The bear-cats were all injured to one degree or another, which made them a little slower.

It wasn't a lot, but a little could mean everything in a fight. Once the new teams were situated, Sen fell back. He kept his attention and spiritual sense mostly on the battle, but there were injuries to tend and spirits to bolster. He went to each team, bandaged the more serious wounds he found, and passed out water. Before moving on to a new team, he met the eyes of every person while he made the same speech.

"You fought. You survived. The town is still safe."

That straightened backs and even triggered a few grim smiles.

"Now, rest," said Sen "You may be needed again before the end."

The fight seemed to drag on forever to Sen, although he knew that each group wasn't fighting for very long before they needed to be cycled out. What he couldn't understand was why the bear-cats didn't simply withdraw. It would have been the smart choice, at least on the surface. He knew that if they fled, he would hunt them down in the forest and slaughter them all, but he didn't think that they could know that. Instead, they stayed and fought. *Maybe, they really are just that vindictive*, thought Sen. *They'd rather stay and die with the hope of killing a few people than retreat.*

Sen saw the life of one of the bear-cats wink out in his spiritual sense just a moment before a cheer went up from the resting teams. Sen was about to order that team back, but Dai Bao beat him to it. While the townspeople were happy, Sen knew that the bear-cats would become wilder and more vicious after one of theirs fell. The only saving grace was that the spirit beasts had been thoroughly bloodied. The townspeople couldn't land many deep cuts, but, just as he'd told them, enough cuts would do the job. Sen watched on in cold approval as, one by one, the bear-cats fell. Wu Meng Yao still had to intervene one more time to save someone. Sen thought she acted a little too hastily, but he decided he'd rather that she act prematurely than not act soon enough. Shen Mingxia had appointed herself the person in charge of deciding when to have teams trade out. Again, Sen thought she was acting a little sooner than necessary, but it probably prevented some injuries. Ideally, there would have been group leaders to make calls like that, but it was just one more thing that Sen hadn't thought of. *I guess everyone is learning some things today*, he thought.

Sen was a little surprised when it was Dai Bao who struck down the last of the bear-cats. He'd handed off his spear and commandeered a halberd. The roar he let loose as he brought the blade down on the bear-cat's neck could probably have been heard clear to the far side of the town. For a long moment, there was just the sound of the man taking heaving breaths. Then, he thrust that bloody halberd toward the sky and loosed another roar, this one of victory. The rest of the battle-weary townspeople momentarily forgot their wounds and their exhaustion. They all thrust their weapons into the air and took up that triumphant cry. Sen would have been content to leave it at that, but Dai Bao turned to look at Sen. There was something searching in the man's expression that Sen didn't quite know how to interpret.

"Say something, you idiot," hissed Wu Meng Yao under her breath.

"Like what?" he muttered back, trying to not move his lips.

"They want your approval."

Oh hells, thought Sen. To buy himself a few seconds to think, he clasped his hands behind his back and walked toward Dai Bao with a stern look on his face. When he reached Dai Bao, he could see individual droplets of blood that had splattered across the man's face. Sen inclined his head to Dai Bao and then turned to look at the rest of the townspeople. *I should say something inspiring*, thought Sen. *Inspiring is good, right? What the hells do I know about inspiring people?* Realizing that the right words were not going to find him, Sen just pushed forward and hoped he didn't screw it up too badly. He infused his voice with a touch of qi so it would resonate.

"You fought bravely. You fought well. You protected each other, and you protected your home. You, farmers, shopkeepers, woodcutters, mortals, took up arms and slew spirit beasts. It's easy to fight when you have the power and strength of a cultivator. You fought with nothing but your skill, your will, and your heart. After what I saw today, I can tell you that you carry the hearts of legends inside of you. And I could not be prouder of what you achieved here today."

Oh, please let that be enough, prayed Sen.

The explosion of savage, joyous cheering that washed over him told him it was.

CHAPTER THIRTY-FOUR
HOW DID WE DO?

While Sen hadn't been able to predict exactly when another spirit beast attack would come to the town, he had known with certainty that one *would* come. With that knowledge in hand, he hadn't wasted his time. He'd made a habit of making at least some healing elixirs that mortals could use every week. With entire months behind him, he had a deep stockpile of the things just sitting around in one of his storage rings. That made it fairly easy for him to hand them out with the assistance of a few of the only lightly injured townspeople. When Sen went to hand one to Dai Bao, the man actually shuddered at the sight of it. Sen had to simultaneously suppress a laugh and a wince of sympathy. The grizzled man gritted his teeth, took the elixir, and downed it. Sen watched in mild amusement as Dai Bao squeezed his eyes shut in anticipation of a mountain of pain. A mountain of pain that did not appear. The man opened his eyes and glared at Sen.

"You could have told me this one wouldn't hurt."

"I thought it would be a nice surprise," offered Sen without a hint of contrition in his voice.

Dai Bao glared a little more before he grudgingly nodded.

"Well, that's true. To be honest, when I was taking the last few potions you gave me, I thought you were just torturing me for fun. I knew they were supposed to be healing me, but I always hurt so much it was hard tell. Today, though," he said, hefting the halberd he'd used to dispatch the last bear-cat, "I saw what it was all for."

"Worth it?" asked Sen.

The grizzled man looked torn as he considered the question. Sen didn't blame him. It had been a *lot* of pain. Dai Bao looked over the other townspeople he'd fought with, and then out to the corpses of the bear-cats.

"It was," the man finally said. "Although, I don't think I could have made myself do it if I'd known what I was in for."

"A common sentiment for so many worthwhile things, I would think," said Sen.

"That's the heavens' truth," said Dai Bao before he gave Sen a discouraged look. "I heard what you said after we finished, but how did we really do? Honestly."

Sen had expected this question. "Everyone survived. Since that's probably the most important consideration, you did well."

"But?"

"These were very weak spirit beasts. To put it in cultivator terms, they were qi-condensing spirit beasts and just barely. If any of them had advanced to the point where they could manifest qi techniques, this would have gone very differently. Those things," Sen gestured angrily at the bear-cat corpses, "are mean, and their qi techniques are nasty. The stronger ones can cut you open from a dozen feet away with a single swipe of their claws."

Dai Bao's eyes drifted over the rest of the townspeople who had fought. Sen imagined the man was picturing them with torn open stomachs or their throats ripped out by things that never got close enough to hit with a spear.

"So, this was pointless?" asked Dai Bao.

"No. It wasn't pointless. Stronger spirit beasts generally don't care about mortals who aren't easy prey. They particularly don't want to run into cultivators, who see them as a big pile of resources to collect. So, they tend to stick to the deeper wilds where even cultivators don't want to go by themselves. That isn't to say that a stronger spirit beast won't wander out of the deep wilds occasionally, but the odds are pretty low that *your* town will ever see one. I can't promise that every spirit beast you see will be as weak as these were, but many will simply leave if it's too much trouble."

"So, that's the goal? To make it too much trouble to try to get into town?"

"Essentially, yes. Ideally, you'll be able to kill them. Beast cores are good for trade. But making them leave is almost as good."

"Why didn't you explain all of this before?"

"Would it have made fighting them any easier?"

"Well, no."

"If you knew, would you have worked as hard? Would they have worked as hard?" asked Sen, nodding to the rest.

"Oh," said Dai Bao, his face scrunching with unhappiness. "Isn't that a little cold?"

"Probably. On the other hand, I'm trying to get you ready for a time when I'm not here. Would you want to depend on people who were only putting in a half-effort because they thought they only needed to scare something away instead of kill it? What if something comes that won't be scared off, like what came today?"

"I understand why you did it," grumbled Dai Bao. "Doesn't mean I have to approve."

"You can tell them if you think they should know," said Sen. "I won't try to stop you. I'll even admit it."

The grizzled man eyed Sen critically for several long seconds, and then he sighed.

"You would, wouldn't you? Knowing it would be useless or even destructive, you'd still admit it. Well, don't bother. The ones who are smart enough to figure it out will understand it. The ones who aren't smart enough to figure it out probably don't need to know."

"If you're sure," said Sen.

"Are all cultivators bastards like you?"

Sen lifted an eyebrow. "Not worried I'll strike you down?"

"You haven't killed anyone, yet. I doubt I'd be first on your list if you were going to start."

"Well, that's certainly a fact. I can't say for sure about every other cultivator, but we're all pretty cold bastards in my experience. Just goes with the territory. You have to be very selfish to challenge the heavens."

Dai Bao gave Sen a dubious glance. "If you're so selfish, why help us at all?"

"I'm sure I had some deep, obscure reason that will inevitably advance my cultivation," said Sen in a pompous voice. "Or, you know, I haven't perfected my selfishness, yet."

"Of course. I'm sure it was one of those," said the grizzled man before he frowned. "We had to fight them for a long time. I know it wasn't actually forever, but it felt that way. How long did it take?"

"A couple of hours, give or take."

"If those things were so weak, I don't know that we could have kept that up for another hour or two or five."

"It's hard to say. Experience counts in fighting. This was the first time out for most of them. I'm not saying the next time will be easier, but it does get easier the more often you do it. I also have some thoughts on speeding things up at the beginning. It'll take a bit of investment."

"We don't have much to invest."

Sen waved it off. "Let me worry about that part for now. I'm not looking to make you all penniless. There are some other things we can do that won't cost you anything but a little time and training. As for fighting longer, well, there are things you can do, but I'm not sure how practical it is. Or how willing people will be."

Dai Bao snorted. "Right now, those people would do anything you ask them to."

"What about you? Having exposed my wicked deception, where do you stand?"

"I'm not a child. Leaders keep things to themselves. Sometimes, it's for a good reason. Sometimes, it's for a bad reason or no reason at all. I can stand in front and play at being their leader, but I can't teach them what you can. As long as you keep teaching them, I'll keep standing in front."

Sen nodded. He supposed that was the best he could really hope for in the situation.

"Don't sell yourself short. They think of you as their leader more than you seem to think. Honestly, I'm surprised the town elders haven't made more trouble about it."

"What makes you think they haven't?" said Dai Bao with a partly amused, partly annoyed expression. "I'm just old enough to not care what they think, and they *can't* do anything to you. They won't dare do anything to make life harder for the people who stood out here today and fought."

"No, I don't imagine that would go very well for them," said Sen, summoning some silver tael from a storage ring. "We can worry about all of this another time. Take them to the inn and buy them food and drinks. Let them celebrate. They did earn it."

Sen held out the coins to Dai Bao who almost choked at the sight of the money. Sen supposed he might have overestimated the costs, but he'd already offered the money. It would be petty to take some of it back. The grizzled man hesitantly took the money.

"If there's any left?" asked Dai Bao.

"Think of something to buy that will benefit them all," said Sen, his mind already drifting to other matters.

He could see Wu Meng Yao hovering nearby. No doubt, she was waiting until Sen was alone so she could pounce and, well, he didn't know what. Annoy him, probably. He spoke on trivial topics with Dai Bao for a few more minutes before saying he'd come back in a few days and releasing the man to bestow well-earned rewards. As soon as the grizzled man began to walk away,

Wu Meng Yao started toward Sen. He gave her a cheerful, toothy smile, waved, and activated his qinggong technique. Sen admitted that he'd be lying to himself if he didn't find the look of startled outrage on her face hilarious in the split-second before he vanished from sight. He just didn't have the time or patience for her at that moment. Besides, it was getting late and there was a little girl who was no doubt impatient for his return. That was way more important than dealing with whatever Wu Meng Yao wanted to talk about.

CHAPTER THIRTY-FIVE
PRIME YOUR MIND

S en stared down at his own hand. He shook his head violently in the negative. *It can't be that simple*, he thought. He had to force himself to repeat the action. He waved his hand through the shadow the tree was casting. His eyes were locked on the snowy ground beneath. The sun overhead made the shadow of his hand crisp and clear as it simply disappeared into the tree's shadow, and then reappeared on the other side. *I refuse to believe that it's that stupidly simple*, he raged mentally. Yet, it was. All of the cultivation instincts he had honed over the years told him that this was the answer he'd been looking for. It *felt* right. Part of Sen wanted to go and scream at Fu Ruolan for withholding this piece of information from him. Yet, he recognized the futility of that. She had made the point to him, repeatedly, that he was approaching the transition into the nascent soul stage. That transition would require self-knowledge, as well as cultivation insight.

Sen wasn't certain how much self-knowledge he had acquired through the months of fruitless, dead-end ideas and experiments. It may have helped to reaffirm his willingness to keep pursuing something he knew was possible no matter how many setbacks he faced. He supposed it had reinforced his patience, sort of. But he hated that she hadn't simply told him. It felt like an almost vindictive act because the answer was so simple. Sen forced himself to take a couple of deep breaths.

"If it were really that simple, you wouldn't have taken this long to figure it out."

As it was, he barely felt like he could take credit for figuring out how the shadow walking technique worked, at least in theory. It had ultimately been Glimmer of Night who gave him the final inspiration. Sen had mostly just been sitting there watching the spider make the latest in a seemingly infinite number of variations on a web pattern. The spider had refused to divulge the actual patterns to Sen with some cryptic statement about Sen's current position in the web of all things. So, Sen had circled back to a question for which he'd never gotten a wholly satisfactory answer.

"Can you explain to me again how it is that the Great Matriarch's web touches all realities?" asked Sen.

Glimmer of Night had delivered what Sen had slowly come to recognize as the spider's annoyed look.

"I have tried many times and many ways," answered the spider.

"Just one more time, and I'll never ask again," pleaded Sen.

He'd never relinquished his belief that the key to understanding shadow walking was buried somewhere in that conversation if he just found the right way to approach it. Glimmer of Night fell silent for long enough that Sen thought that it was the spider's passive way of saying no. It turned out, the spider had just been deep in thought. He looked at Sen.

"Observe. Perhaps this will make clear what words have not."

The web the spider had been working on disappeared and a much simpler web appeared strung horizontally between trees. The spider pointed at it.

"Our reality."

Another web appeared almost right on top of it. "Another reality or plane or dimension. Pick the name you like best."

Another web appeared. Over the next minute, a couple of

dozen webs appeared stacked nearly on top of each other. The spider gestured at it.

"Existence in sum."

Sen frowned but nodded. He understood in general terms that the spider had made a wildly oversimplified scale model of, well, everything as construed as webs. Then, another web appeared, anchored by nothing and to nothing. It was vertical and passed through the middle of all the other webs. Sen watched in fascination as the vertical web slowly began to turn like it was affixed to an axis. It passed through the other webs without disturbing them, as though they were made of the same material, which Sen abruptly realized that they were. Of course, that web qi had no trouble passing through other web qi. The only real challenge would be making sure the qi didn't intermingle so much that it lost form.

For someone like Glimmer of Night, with his vast experience, that would pose no challenges. Sen had stared at that construct for a long time, a sick feeling growing in his stomach as he realized the truth. That was when he'd walked to the nearest tree and run his little experiment. Now, he was just trying to stay calm. He'd only figured out part of it. He had the what, but the how was something else. He supposed he even knew that, but only in the big-picture way. He had the feeling that the details were going to matter a lot with a technique like this.

"Well, you finally got there," said Fu Ruolan, unmasking her presence and stepping into view.

Sen almost made a jab about her lurking, but it would have just been unwarranted spite talking. Instead, he gave her a level look.

"How do you know I figured it out?"

"Well, if you couldn't get there after Glimmer of Night's rather interesting display, I'd have questioned your mental capacity. Also, there's just no hiding the white-hot anger you're feeling. Everyone gets that look on their face the first time they realize their teacher kept something seemingly easy and obvious back from them."

"Then, why do it?" demanded Sen.

"Because it *isn't* easy or obvious. If it were, you wouldn't have struggled for so long to put it together. How many times did you have conversations about how the Great Matriarch's web touched all reality?"

"Many," said Glimmer of Night. "Very many."

"If you were to have those conversations now, it would seem easy. Obvious. But you had to prime your mind. You had to explore the other options and reject them. You had to be ready to consider possibilities beyond your prior experience. Until you were ready to do that, nothing was going to make things clear to you. If you had quit, which most do, then it would have been evident that you were unfit for the technique and unlikely to pass into the nascent soul stage."

"What?!" exclaimed Sen.

Fu Ruolan gave him a self-satisfied smile.

"Did you think that you were the only one who could conduct tests? Granted, your tests with the mortals have been more straightforward, but they were still tests. As for my tests, why conduct only one when I could conduct two."

"And if I had failed?"

"I would have taught you other things for the next few years, sent you on your way, and likely never given you another thought. But, as I expected, you did not fail."

"So, does everyone approaching the nascent soul stage get a test like this?"

"Oh, don't be silly. Most cultivators who enter the nascent soul stage only have the vaguest idea of why they succeeded, just as most who fail are equally baffled by that failure."

"But you have a test?"

"I have a method. The test is different for everyone."

"If this method is so effective, why haven't you shared it?"

Something cold passed over Fu Ruolan's face then. It comprised old pain, bitterness, and anger. When she spoke, her voice was a metal rasp passing over stone.

"Why should I? Why should I ever help those people?"

Sen honestly didn't know who she meant by *those people*. Sects? Wandering cultivators? Humanity as a whole? She could have meant any of them or all of them. Sen also realized that he had unintentionally stepped into one of those areas of Fu Ruolan's life where he *did not want to go*. He had ultimately come to the conclusion that Fu Ruolan wasn't mad in a traditional sense, nor was she sane in a traditional sense. Some things brought out the less sane aspects of her personality, while some things encouraged her more rational side. Sen had identified certain topics that were more likely to bring out this angry, vengeful, and probably unhinged version of Fu Ruolan. He likey could have deduced that his last question would do it. He just hadn't thought it through before he threw the question out there. However, given that her killing intent was bearing down on him and he could actually feel damage accumulating inside his body, he wanted to calm her as fast as possible.

"Peace," he said. "It's your method. If you don't wish to share it, that is your decision. I should not have questioned your choice."

Fu Ruolan snarled, "It is my decision!"

Sen just waited as calmly as he could. After a few seconds, Fu Ruolan's expression became one of pain. She hunched a little as her killing intent slowly bled away. It appeared that the effort of suppressing it hurt her as much as unleashing it had hurt him. When the nascent soul cultivator had regained full control of herself, she met his eyes.

"I'm sorry," she said. "That was uncalled for."

Sen hesitated for a moment before protective ruthlessness took over. "Liu Ai is curious. She trusts you. She *will* ask you questions. What you just did to me would have killed her before she even had a chance to scream."

The look on Fu Ruolan's face was undiluted horror as those words sank home. Sen didn't relent.

"I brought that on myself. I know better than to ask a question like that. I also know how to walk it back. She won't know better. I *can't* put her at that kind of risk. So, tell me now, and tell me the truth, is this something you can keep under control?"

"Of course!" snapped the nascent soul cultivator.

"What if she asks why you don't have children? What if she asks where you come from? What if she asks why you live out here alone?"

Fu Ruolan looked like she'd just been stabbed repeatedly. She didn't say anything as Sen's gaze bore into her. Sen could see her eyes tracking back and forth like she was reading something in her mind. There was genuine pain and distress in her eyes when Fu Ruolan looked up at Sen.

"I don't know," she answered.

Sen nodded. "Thank you for being honest."

"What will you do?" asked Fu Ruolan.

"The only thing I can do. I'll take Liu Ai somewhere else. I imagine Falling Leaf will come. Glimmer of Night can make his own decision."

The spider, who had watched the entire exchange with his usual impassive gaze, shrugged. "I'll stay for now."

"What of our agreement?" asked the nascent soul cultivator.

"What about it?" asked Sen. "I'll keep my word. It'll just be a whole lot less convenient."

Sen turned to walk away when Fu Ruolan called out after him.

"When will you leave?"

He wanted to say *immediately*, but he knew that wasn't practical.

"Tomorrow. We'll go tomorrow."

CHAPTER THIRTY-SIX
MEANWHILE...

Ma Caihong had never bothered much with the little town at the bottom of the mountain. There had simply never been anything there to interest her. Plus, it was tedious to deal with mortals as a nascent soul cultivator. While she hadn't been a great beauty in her youth, she had been fair enough to turn a few heads. The miracles of cultivation refined her modestly appealing appearance over the last several thousand years. Now, like most other nascent soul cultivators, she possessed an almost unearthly beauty that had a peculiar effect on the minds of many mortals. Simply walking among them was enough to start riots in some places. The people in Orchard's Reach weren't quite that bad, but they were close. Yet, since Sen had departed, she had found herself visiting that charming little shop owned by the woman who had helped him as a child. While she'd never admit it to Jaw-Long and most certainly wouldn't admit it to Ming, she'd visited much more often than was necessary.

It was a disappointment on most visits. Sen did write, but it was sporadic. The delivery of scrolls and other missives was also notoriously unreliable, and that was taking into account the outrageous sums that she had learned Sen often paid to try to improve the odds that they arrived. At least the workers at the shop had stopped bursting into tears whenever they had to tell her that there were no parcels, letters, or scrolls for her. They seemed to have finally realized that she wasn't going to strike them dead or burn the shop to the ground if they offered her bad news. She could be as petty as any other cultivator in the right circumstances, but there was a difference between being petty and being *petty*. Those mortal workers had literally no hand in how frequently or infrequently her wayward student chose to put brush to paper. She wasn't going to punish them for something they couldn't hope to control.

Yet, every once in a while, a letter did arrive. Most of them were frustratingly short and even more frustratingly short of details. They served more to say that he was still alive than impart any news. When he did mention some new minor miracle he had worked, there was never any of the salient information about how he had accomplished such a feat. If someone else were doing it, she'd think they were intentionally trying to make her angry. Yet, it was so quintessentially Sen to simply overlook the impossible as something that was, in terms he would use, kind of hard until he figured it out. When the improbable was an everyday occurrence, and the inexplicable rained down around you like the heavens were determined to make you a figure of myth, what was one more master-stroke of cultivation insight that would make you the darling of any sect? It was nothing, which was exactly how he treated it when those things happened. So, she was left to sigh, shake her head, and try to work out on her own how he'd done something.

So infrequently it nearly qualified as a holiday, that young man would seemingly feel the pull of some kind of quasi-filial duty. He would write out long letters that provided detailed retellings of his recent, to him at any rate, adventures. It was with no small measure of excitement that she raced up the mountain with one such dispatch in hand, massive explosions of snow erupting in the wake of her footsteps. She had been greedy in her initial excitement and read through the beginning before making herself stop. Jaw-Long deserved to see it at the same time she did. She burst into the house and went directly to the library where she could sense her studious husband.

"Put that nonsense away," she ordered, as she strode into the room.

Jaw-Long gave her that indulgent, loving smile that still made her heart beat a little faster.

"And why should I do that, dear heart?"

"Because I have a letter from Sen. A real letter," she said, summoning the scroll from a storage ring.

She smirked as Jaw-Long carelessly thrust the book he'd been reading onto the nearest shelf.

"You have my complete attention."

They stood together reading the letter. Sometimes, they shook their heads and laughed at some youthful folly. Other times, they shook their heads at just how much and how fast he'd grown into a frighteningly ruthless cultivator. A few times, they had to restrain one another from immediately setting out to use a rain of lightning or rivers of poison to explain to one fool or another exactly how *not pleased* they were with the way Sen had been treated. Not that such options were off the table. Far from it. They were just temporarily set aside for future consideration. There was a letter to finish reading if nothing else.

Then, they had gotten to the very end of the letter. Sen had explained in terse terms what had happened at the mortal village. She could almost feel his lingering fury over the events and the casual mistreatment of that child wafting up off the scroll from those characters. He went on to explain that he had taken the child in and reassured Jaw-Long that he was teaching her to read and write. Mostly, though, he just talked about the girl, Liu Ai. He described the things that made her smile or laugh. The kinds of foods she liked, and the things that made her scrunch up her face.

When she saw that little girl's inexpert, painstakingly written name signed at the bottom of the letter, Caihong felt like someone had reached out and seized her heart. She turned to give her husband a firm look.

"We're going now."

The gods bless him, Jaw-Long didn't so much a miss a beat.

"I'll get our things."

THEY WERE SITTING around a table and laughing together. He knew them of old, those foxes. *Old friends*, sneered Laughing River mentally. They looked like they felt safe. Secure. Untouchable. Yet, here he was, mere feet away, and they had not recognized him. He'd left Sen behind, for now, recognizing that he had crossed some line in the cultivator's mind. It wasn't ideal, but so few things in life were. If life were ideal, his people wouldn't have suffered so much, or faced such a staggering failure of leadership. He didn't exclude himself from being painted with that particular brush of shame. You couldn't live as long as he did without carting around a mountain's worth of mistakes and regrets. He'd just like to make sure he didn't ascend before making sure that the disciple of Fate's Razor didn't follow him into ascension with a grudge in his heart. Having seen what the boy was capable of in core formation, he shuddered to imagine what kind of unstoppable monster that young man would be as a peak nascent soul cultivator. However, that was a problem for future Laughing River.

The Laughing River of right now had more immediate problems that were simply aching for solutions best delivered with tooth, claw, and blade. Any leader worth a damn knew that you couldn't suffer traitors to live. And for all that he had been an absentee leader, he was still the oldest and strongest of the nine-tail foxes. He was their leader by right. It was high time he reminded them of why it was that the name Laughing River was one to conjure fear by. Laughing River let his mind settle for a moment. He was angry about what these foxes had done, the lies they had told about him to advance themselves. He knew he couldn't let that anger rule him, though. Fuel him, certainly, but not rule. When his emotions had finally settled into a kind of dull background noise, he rose from the table he'd been sitting at. He took half a dozen calm steps, and then the sword at his hip was suddenly in his hand and passing through the neck of Summer Vale.

It had happened so fast that the other three at the table looked on in confusion until Summer Vale's head dropped away from her body. Laughing River idly noted that she had a vaguely confused look on her face. He kicked away the chair containing the now headless corpse and snagged a less bloody chair from a nearby table. He placed it with deliberate care and sat down, giving the other three foxes a big smile. The aptly named Mountain Stone looked positively livid, his face going red right down to his massive neck. He was the single biggest fox that Laughing River had ever met, and there had long been rumors of some kind of dalliance outside the fox bloodlines. Moon Behind Clouds wore a wary expression, but she usually did. The waifish woman had one hand under the table, no doubt gripping one of the many daggers she kept on her person. The final fox at the table was the calmest. Pines in Winter wore a bland, almost bored expression that suggested he'd seen worse and been just as uninterested in it.

"If you wanted to court death, fool, you should have just said so," said Mountain Stone.

"The four of you—" Laughing River shook his head like he couldn't believe he'd made such a foolish mistake. "I mean the three of you have done quite well for yourselves. Although, I suppose I made it easy by not being around to deny your lies."

"Who are you?" demanded Moon Behind Clouds.

"You don't recognize me? After all those nights we spent together?" asked Laughing River in a mock tone of sadness. "Were you just lying to me all those times you said I was a better lover than your husband? I mean, I expect everyone is a better lover than he is, but I thought I was more memorable than that. Such is the folly of ego. Although, maybe I shouldn't take it to heart. It turns out that you're an accomplished liar."

That finally drew a reaction from Pines in Winter who couldn't seem to decide if he should be angry at his wife or the stranger throwing out insults and accusations. Laughing River decided he'd played the mysterious stranger for long enough, so he continued.

"Oh, maybe it's this silly disguise I'm wearing," he said, wiping his hand across his face and dispelling the technique that was half-illusion and half-transformation.

Mountain Stone looked like he had just taken a hard shot to the groin. Moon Behind Clouds went deathly white. Pines in Winter just swallowed hard before he rallied.

"Laughing River. It's been some time. We all thought you were dead."

"Well, I'm sure you *hoped* I was dead or at least gone for good," said Laughing River in a cheerful tone before his voice lost any trace of kindness. "No. Such. Luck."

"We did what we had to do," said Moon Behind Clouds.

Laughing River gave her a look of infinite pity. "Are you under the false impression that this is a trial? Do you imagine defending yourself well enough will mean I spare you? This isn't a trial, lover. You are all guilty. This, my boon companions, my dearest, most trusted old friends, is the execution."

Mountain Stone surged to his feet. "You old fool. Do you really think you can take all three of us?"

Laughing River looked up at the towering fox and shook his head. "You always were stupid."

All it took was a momentary effort and the illusion that he had kept them all trapped in for the last two hours vanished. Where there had been the common room of an inn filled with boisterous locals and buxom girls handing out drinks and food, there were now only two dozen hooded figures, blades in hand. While most people would have considered the armed figures the greatest threat in the room, the three foxes at the table with Laughing River stared at him in terrified awe. They were all masters of illusion in their own right. They had thought themselves beyond the reach of such trickery. In one act, Laughing River had shown them how laughably inconsequential their skills were in the face of his power. He slowly stood and regarded the three of them with cold eyes.

"I just came to say goodbye. It's what you do when old friends are dying," he said, before he looked at one of the hooded figures. "Kill them."

It was a fight, but not a very long one. One of the hooded figures came over to Laughing River when the grisly work was done.

"What now?" they asked.

"We're going to the old stomping grounds of a recent acquaintance of mine. A place called Emperor's Bay. We have some extended kin there who require a bit of reeducation."

CHAPTER THIRTY-SEVEN
I AM BEGGING YOU

"She's really yours, isn't she?" asked Shen Mingxia.

Sen looked at her briefly before returning his attention to Liu Ai and Li Zhi. The girls were running around outside the galehouse he had erected adjacent to the practice hall. While he didn't think any spirit beast would be stupid enough to try to snatch one of them with him looming nearby, he wasn't about to take any chances with their lives. Not that he'd let them stay outside too long. He had the sense that the winter weather was drawing to a close, but it wasn't done with them yet. Even if he could stand outside in it without worry, he was keenly aware of how fragile those small lives were.

"What makes you ask that?"

Instead of answering, she just stood next to him and observed the girls' free-spirited play. "It's the way you watch over her. It's obvious. Even when you aren't looking at her, you always know where she is. Then, there's—"

Sen lifted an eyebrow at her. "I know why you think it. I'm curious what made you ask. Simple curiosity? Orders from Wu Meng Yao? Reconnaissance for your sect?"

Shen Mingxia's expression tightened for a moment before she

sighed. "Wu Meng Yao is, how to put it, *aware* that you prefer my company to hers. But she hasn't asked me to try to get information out of you."

"Gods, I hope she doesn't think that you'll somehow charm me into liking the Soaring Skies Sect with a nice smile."

"Nothing so pointless," said Shen Mingxia, flashing that nice smile at him. "I think she might be hoping that I'll charm you into liking *her* a little better."

"I like Wu Meng Yao just fine. I always liked her. If all she wanted was to be my friend, everything would be fine. It's her intentions I find problematic."

"You say that like her intentions are evil."

Sen laughed a little at that. "I know they aren't evil. They're just misguided."

"You know she's not a bad person. You don't need to humiliate her with this made-up mission. You could give her something real to do. Are you honestly telling me that there's nothing you can think of that she could do for you? She's not some nobody foundation formation cultivator like me. She's a core cultivator."

Sen bit back an angry reply. They'd been talking around the problem for the last month, but this was the first time either of them had directly addressed it. Plus, that word, humiliate, had given him pause. He hadn't thought about it in quite that way. Sen definitely wanted to aggravate Wu Meng Yao enough that she'd give up on her ridiculous ideas about balancing the scales between them and go home. Still, he questioned if the imaginary task he'd handed out would really end in some kind of shame. *Yeah*, he admitted to himself, *it would be humiliating*. Not scar her for life humiliation, but it would still leave a wound. He had to give Shen Mingxia some credit for standing up to him. To describe the difference in their cultivation as stark would be radically understating things. By calling him out about what he'd planned, she wasn't risking simply annoying him. She was risking death. At least, that's what she'd be doing if she was dealing with some sect core cultiva-

ERIC DONTIGNEY

tor. She probably suspected that he wouldn't do something terrible to her, but those were shaky grounds to take a risk on. Especially when you were taking a risk on someone else's behalf.

"Don't sell foundation formation short," chided Sen. "Some of the things I'm famous for happened when I was a foundation formation cultivator."

"I'm aware. I was there for one of those of things," said Shen Mingxia. "The difference is that I am not you."

"I assure you that's a blessing. And just what would you suggest I have Wu Meng Yao do? I could have her run more errands like that trip to the capital to buy weapons and deliver messages. How many more of those do you think it'd take before she felt like she'd done enough?"

Shen Mingxia grimaced. "A lot more."

"That was my thinking as well."

"Let her join your sect," said an exasperated Shen Mingxia, "for a while anyway. Say she's a visiting elder who's here to teach."

Sen felt his jaw drop as he fully turned to look at the woman. "What in the world are you talking about? I don't have a sect."

Shen Mingxia arched an eyebrow at him, turned, and gave the practice hall a long look. She faced him again.

"You will. Soon. You must know that there are already cultivators in town just trying to work up the nerve to come and ask."

"I know about the cultivators. I was thinking it was about time to encourage them to move on. They've been behaved so far, but we all know that won't last."

The expression on her face wasn't quite pity, but it was close enough to make Sen's skin crawl.

"You could chase them away, but they won't be the last. You're too famous. They'll just keep coming because who wouldn't want to be taught by the Heavens' Scouring Blade?"

"Please tell me that's something you just made up. Please, *please* tell me that no one else actually calls me that."

"Oh, they do. I know a bunch more if you want to hear them."

"I'd really rather not."

"I think my favorite may be the Hand of Chaos," said Shen Mingxia with a gleeful little grin.

"I am begging you. Please stop."

"Alright. I'll stop taunting you. The point still stands, though. This problem isn't going away unless you go back to traveling constantly."

"It's not like that's a real solution. I mean, obviously, traveling didn't do much to keep me out of trouble," complained Sen.

"There you go. May as well just start a sect," said Shen Mingxia, "and let Wu Meng Yao be useful in it."

"I don't want a sect. I hate sects."

"Yes, what a terrible life you lead. So famous and talented that people will come to you, shower you with gifts and money, and all for the chance to learn at your feet. It's a real tough road you're on there."

"Wait? What are you talking about? Gifts and money?"

Shen Mingxia gave him a look that said he was being exceptionally slow on the uptake. "Yes, of course, they brought gifts and money. How else are they supposed to convince the mighty and elusive Judgment's Gale to take them on as students? The time-honored tradition of bribery. I assume that's how most sects finance themselves when they first get started. If nothing else, it'll make it cheaper to help the mortals protect their town."

That brought Sen up short. He truly did not have any interest in teaching other cultivators anything, but the idea of using their resources to support things he did care about held a certain appeal. Of course, if he took their money, he'd be obligated to actually teach them things. It would give Wu Meng Yao something to do, though. That came with the pitfall that she'd still be around, but at least she'd be busy with something. She didn't lurk quite as much as Fu Ruolan had used to lurk, but she was pretty bad about it. He did worry about getting distracted from his initial goal of training up the local mortals, but the reality was that most of them had gone as far as they were ever going to go with the spear. It wasn't a lack of willingness. There just came a point where someone reached the limits of their native talent and physical ability. There were a few standout talents that he could take farther, but that was more on them to put in the work than it was on him to do anything.

"I don't know anything about training cultivators," said Sen, trying to deflect the conversation.

"But you had vast experience in training mortals and setting up a system for them to defend their town from spirit beasts?"

"Does it matter that I just don't want to?"

"Sure. If you don't want to, don't do it. Just understand that people are people, cultivators or not. If you say no all the time, it will discourage some, but it will make others even more determined."

"Great," muttered Sen with zero enthusiasm.

Shen Mingxia laughed. "Okay. I had my say. I won't bother you about this anymore."

"Ever?" asked Sen with a lot more enthusiasm.

She gave him another of those nice smiles and said, "Today."

Sen gave her a sour look before his head turned to the north, and he grunted to himself. Shen Mingxia gave him a questioning look. He held up a hand to keep her from asking anything immediately.

"Ai! Zhi! It's time to go inside!"

The girls gave him the pouty looks that sometimes made him relent, but Sen just waved them over. They took a little longer than was necessary, but they came over. He squatted down so he wasn't towering over them.

"Are you hungry?" he asked.

Both girls grew visibly happier at that question and nodded.

"Okay, well, you should head inside because I'm going to make us all something really delicious soon. Plus, we'll even have a special guest with us."

"Who?" asked Ai with curiosity burning in her eyes. "Is it Auntie Mingxia?"

"She's certainly welcome to join us, but that isn't who I meant. I meant her," said Sen as he pointed.

Fu Ruolan stepped out of the forest and glanced around. She gave Mingxia a cool, neutral look before she directed a bright smile at Ai.

"Auntie Ru!" squealed Ai, rushing over to tackle the nascent soul cultivator's leg in a hug.

Zhi had walked in Ai's wake but seemed more hesitant. That hesitance vanished when Fu Ruolan snuck the children some small candies that she'd gotten somewhere. Sen studiously pretended not to see it happening. Sen noticed Shen Mingxia trembling, pale-faced, and silently mouthing the words *Auntie Ru*.

"You feeling okay?" asked Sen.

"No warning that a nascent soul cultivator was about to descend on us? You really are an ass, sometimes," growled Shen Mingxia.

CHAPTER THIRTY-EIGHT
THE REALITIES OF SECT BUILDING

"She's not wrong," said Fu Ruolan.

After they had all eaten and Fu Ruolan had spent some quality time listening to Ai regale her with tales of walking through town, "training" with Dai Bao, and drawing orchids in the snow, the nascent soul cultivator had withdrawn to talk with Sen. The two had reached an odd sort of unspoken agreement after Sen had moved himself, Ai, and Falling Leaf to the new galehouse. Things had been incredibly tense that first week. Fu Ruolan had been keeping herself under such rigid control that it looked unhealthy.

It had taken a while for Sen to realize that she was trying to prove, maybe to herself, maybe to him, that she could keep herself from doing anything drastic. Sen had finally relented and brought Ai with him one day. He hadn't left the two of them alone, but Fu Ruolan had seemed to take the gesture in the right spirit. Even so, Sen had been astounded when the woman had come to them for the first time. Her visits were unpredictable, and he didn't ask about it. They made Ai happy and seemed to soothe some inner turmoil in Fu Ruolan. That struck Sen as just about the best possible outcome in the situation.

Of course, as soon as the elder cultivator withdrew from the girls, Shen Mingxia promptly became the designated doll for Ai and Zhi. They took turns putting, thankfully imaginary, flowers and ribbons in the woman's hair. If Mingxia minded, there was no sign of it on her face.

"She's not wrong about which part?" asked Sen.

"About all of the parts. If you really need some excuse to send that girl away that isn't a complete fiction, there are plenty of real treasures in places far less lethal than up on the Mountains of Sorrow."

"You know where they are?"

"When you get to be my age, you have whole lists of treasures you're going to go and get when you have the time. I bet all of your other teachers have them too. I'd even be willing to bet that we all have at least a few of the same ones on our lists."

"So, why don't you go and get them?"

"It just never quite rises to the level of a priority. Every once in a while, you find out you actually *need* some particular treasure. That's enough to get you out there and looking. Once you have it, though, you want to use it. You go home and run whatever experiment you were going to do or use it to reach that next level of advancement. By the time all of that is done, you've fallen into old routines."

Sen couldn't help but nod. He'd been running around, advancing at a breakneck pace, and rarely getting so much as a second to consolidate his gains, but that wasn't true for everyone. Uncle Kho had spent centuries up on his mountain, only leaving on the rarest of occasions according to Master Feng and Auntie Caihong. Even if he had one of those lists, his routines kept him firmly in place. Sen could even see that happening to him. *Oh, heavens, that would just be glorious*, thought Sen. *Years or decades with nothing to do but focus on refining my skills and enhancing my qi understanding? Not constantly forced into situations where I have to kill? Where do I get in line for that?* Sen was so caught up in that beautiful daydream that Fu Ruolan snapped her fingers right in front of his face to reclaim his attention.

"Where did you just go?" she asked.

"I was just imagining what it would be like to have no one bothering me for years at a time. Focusing all my energy on improving as a cultivator. It was beautiful," said Sen.

"Yeah, well, it's not as great as it looks from the outside," said Fu Ruolan, her eyes drifting over Liu Ai. "Company isn't always a bad thing."

"Speaking of company, Glimmer of Night isn't bothering you, is he? I don't expect he would, but I did bring him out there."

"The spiderkin is wholly preoccupied at the moment. I think he had some minor breakthrough in—" she hesitated. "Honestly, I'm not sure what it is that he's doing."

Sen gave the woman a startled look. "Did you ask?"

"Oh, I asked. He even explained it."

"And?"

"I said he explained it. I didn't say I understood him."

"I know that feeling," said Sen with some sympathy, all too familiar with how impenetrable the spider's explanations could get. "If he does become a problem—"

"I'd just ask him to leave. It wouldn't occur to him to be combative about it."

"That's fair. What about all of this," Sen shuddered, "sect nonsense?"

"Do you really need me to explain what was already explained to you?"

"Not exactly. I need you to explain to me what I don't know. Yes, there are some dubious advantages to loosely taking on some students, but what are the pitfalls of having a sect? Official or otherwise."

Fu Ruolan gave Sen a considering look. "I'm glad to see that your mind and paranoia haven't abandoned you entirely in our quiet little corner of the kingdom."

"I came by my paranoia honestly. I'm just trying to use it to best effect these days."

"Well, the most obvious pitfall is that other nearby sects won't like it. Most of them don't have the raw power to do anything to you, let alone make you stop, but you might draw the ire of the Vermilion Blade Sect. They could cause you some real trouble."

Sen lifted a hand, formed a vermilion blade in the air, and dispersed it. "I think I have a functional accommodation with them. It should hold for the time being."

"Now, that *is* interesting. You mentioned having a run-in with one of their members. Did you leave out a few details there?"

"I left out a lot of details there. Most of them tedious."

"Stories are like that. They get dull in the details. The bigger concern you have to worry about with the other sects is that they won't target you personally. They'll target whatever students you take on."

"What does that accomplish beyond making me angry enough to do something about it?"

"This is where never joining a sect is going to work against you. There are a lot of rules that are simply understood by sects. One of those rules is that conflicts between juniors are left at that. Let's say that girl over there," said Fu Ruolan, "gets into a fight with a foundation formation cultivator from some local sect."

"Her name is Shen Mingxia."

"Yes, I'm sure it is. So, the girl gets into a fight and gets hurt. The understanding is that you, as a vastly superior cultivator, to say nothing of being a sect patriarch, will not take it upon yourself to hunt down and kill the foundation formation cultivator who injured her."

"What could possibly motivate me to accept that stupid rule?" asked Sen.

"I think you can figure that one out on your own."

Sen did know why. He just didn't like it.

"I imagine," he said, "the desire to avoid having core formation or nascent soul cultivators battling in the streets of this little town would probably top that list."

"Exactly. Just like the elders of other sects don't want someone like you showing up to do battle in the streets of whatever towns or villages are to be found near their compounds. And there are nuances to all of these rules. Now, let's say the girl—"

"Shen Mingxia," repeated Sen.

"*The girl*," insisted Fu Ruolan. "Let's say the girl isn't injured in a fair fight with someone of her approximate cultivation level. Let's say that she's ambushed by three cultivators of a higher advancement. Things get a lot murkier in a situation like that since there was a clear intent to do permanent harm. Now, you might have grounds to go hunting those three to express your displeasure. If you do, though, the expectation is that you'll dole out a more or less equivalent amount of injury. If you kill them outright, we're back to powerful cultivators battling in the streets and killing mortals by the hundreds."

"And you're saying that there are a lot of these unwritten rules?"

"Dozens."

"I hate everything about this."

"As you should," said Fu Ruolan. "That's without even considering the problem of people showing up to challenge you for control of the sect."

"Who would want these kinds of headaches?"

"The kind of people who love power and can't be bothered with details. I will say that you have a big advantage on that front. Your reputation as someone who ruthlessly slaughtered every enemy who got in his way as he crossed the kingdom will serve as a rather potent deterrent for most. Which leaves you with the more nebulous problem of poaching."

"Poaching?" asked Sen.

"Sects tend to think of the nearby territory as theirs to recruit from. There's a reason that they keep a certain distance from each other. They won't like it if you start plucking up all the young talents."

"I'm not planning on recruiting at all. So, problem solved."

"They won't see much difference between you actively trying to get students and students ignoring them to flock to the infamous Judgment's Gale."

"There is an *enormous* difference between those two things," said Sen, already feeling the aggravation accumulating in his chest.

"Yes, and if they were using logic to understand the situation, they would acknowledge that. But they won't be using logic. They'll just see you as impinging on what is theirs."

Sen leaned his head back and thought hard for a little while. Something finally occurred to him that he thought should have been obvious.

"All the people who are coming around or will be coming around to get me to teach them or start a sect with them. I assume that at least some of them are aware of these issues, right?"

"It seems likely. The wandering cultivators may not know the nuances, but any current or former sect cultivators will certainly know," agreed Fu Ruolan.

"Then, why would any of them do it? Knowing it's likely to draw all kinds of trouble down on their heads and mine, why would they even want to start down this road?"

"Some will do it because you're a folk hero. Stories have a way of infecting people's minds. Most will do it because you're powerful, and they're desperately hoping that they'll be able to grab ahold of a piece of that same power."

"Can't you get power in any sect?"

"Can and will are, as you put it, enormously different things. Sect politics can hold a cultivator back just as effectively as it can push them forward. If people have tried the sect route and found the experience disappointing, they'll hope that things will be different with you."

"Have I mentioned how much I hate everything about this?"

"You have."

Sen grit his teeth. "It was worth saying twice. I also think that this is way more trouble than I want to deal with."

Fu Ruolan started to speak, but Sen saw her eyes go out of focus for a moment. Then, they snapped back into focus and a look of cold anger crossed her face. She stood and gestured for Sen to come with her.

"What's going on?" asked Sen as he fell into step beside her.

"I have unwanted guests. Two of them. Both nascent soul cultivators."

Sen came up short. Two nascent soul cultivators?

"Oh," said Sen feeling abruptly sheepish. "About that. I think I know who it is."

CHAPTER THIRTY-NINE

ARRIVAL AND
INTRODUCTIONS

F u Ruolan glared at Sen. "You *invited* them here?"

"No! No, no, no," said Sen. "I just sent them a letter telling them what's been happening to me in recent... Um, years. It's the first time I've been stationary for a while."

"You should have told me they were coming."

"I didn't *know* they were coming."

The awkward conversation was mercifully cut short as Ma Caihong and Kho Jaw-Long descended from the sky supported by nothing but the power of their qi. They alighted on the snowy ground outside the galehouse and looked around. Uncle Kho seemed very interested in the practice hall. Auntie Caihong smiled at Sen. Neither of them seemed terribly concerned by the thunderous look on Fu Ruolan's face, which Sen wasn't sure was altogether wise.

"Do you two make a habit of invading other people's territory?" demanded Fu Ruolan.

"Be still, Ruolan," said Auntie Caihong in an amused voice. "We aren't here about *you*. We came to see Ai."

"Be still," said Fu Ruolan in an icy tone. "How dare y—"

Her voice choked off as Uncle Kho went over and pulled the woman into a hug.

"It's good to see you again, Ru. Even if that temper of yours hasn't improved at all."

Sen stood in mute shock as Fu Ruolan's cheeks turned bright red. Then, a lot of hazy things snapped into sharp focus. The woman's constant comparisons to Auntie Caihong. The quiet resentment that Fu Ruolan seemed to hold for Ma Caihong. Sen had always just assumed it was jealousy over Auntie Caihong's talent, and that may have been a part of it. As he watched the woman slap at Uncle Kho in a way that looked more playful than serious, it became evident that wasn't all of it.

"Let me go, you lightning-wielding oaf," chided Fu Ruolan, while she didn't actually do that much to escape.

Sen traded a look with Auntie Caihong and saw the truth in her eyes. She knew, and she was wholly unperturbed by it. It was also evident that Uncle Kho *didn't* realize it. Sen wasn't sure he'd share Auntie Caihong's calm in similar circumstances, but he guessed that she must have long ago worked through any doubts she had about her marriage. Uncle Kho released Fu Ruolan from the hug and stepped back. She tried to glare at him but only managed a weak, sour expression.

"You could have at least sent word you were coming," she complained.

"To where?" asked Auntie Caihong in a slightly too-sweet voice.

The women locked gazes for a moment and universes of information passed between the two in that brief look. Sen resolved, then and there, that he would never, *ever*, for any reason, ask any of them a single question about what he had just figured out. There was the very pertinent reason that he simply didn't want to know, followed by the profoundly pressing reason that he didn't want to get involved. He'd seen what happened when Master Feng and

Auntie Caihong argued. He had zero desire to be present for a similar performance between Auntie Caihong and Fu Ruolan.

This absence of desire was fueled in no small part by the knowledge that Master Feng's self-control was substantial, while Fu Ruolan's was not. After all, Master Feng had retained his wits enough to go take out his anger and frustration on dangerous spirit beasts. Those beasts probably hadn't had it coming, but it was better than obliterating a small town. He had his doubts that Fu Ruolan would show similar restraint if pushed to her breaking point. Yet, the sometimes-unstable nascent soul cultivator surprised him with her reaction.

"You obviously knew where to come. You could have sent a message to him first," she said, pointing at Sen.

"Sen is rather famous for his wandering ways. There was no way to be certain that any message we sent here would actually reach him," murmured Uncle Kho absently, wholly oblivious to the undercurrents in the conversation as he stared at the training hall. "Sen, what is that?"

Oh, how Sen wished he shared that ignorance. However, the question gave him the golden opportunity to change the subject, and he seized it like a starving man seized food.

"That's the training hall," said Sen, and then he kept talking to prevent anyone else from saying anything. "I put it up so the mortals would have somewhere permanent to train. I went out and found some fire treasures to put in the floor to keep it warm in the winter. I thought about using a formation, but I couldn't work out how to make formations that the mortals could easily use and adjust. But you're here now, Uncle Kho, so I'll definitely want to see if you have any ideas that might work. I've been training the mortals with the spear. I imagine you'll want to take a look at what they're doing. I mean, clearly, they can't meet cultivator standards, but they all work hard, and I'd appreciate any advice you could give me. I've never really trained people before, so it's been a steep learning curve. I certainly have a new appreciation for how patient all of you have always been with me. I—"

"Sen," interrupted Auntie Caihong. "Are you feeling well? You're babbling. I don't think I've ever seen you babble before."

"Agreed," said Uncle Kho with a worried look on his face.

"Did you break him?" said Auntie Caihong as she turned to look at Fu Ruolan.

Except, Fu Ruolan was staring at Sen like she'd never seen him before. Instead of answering Auntie Caihong, Fu Ruolan spoke to him.

"Did you suffer a head injury recently that I'm not aware of? I know cultivators are resilient, but you shouldn't ignore those."

"I'm fine," said Sen.

He would much rather that they thought something might be wrong with him than continue down their previous conversational path.

"Are you sure?" asked Auntie Caihong, as her spiritual sense and qi washed over him. "Well, I don't sense any injuries."

She gave him a speculative look that let him know they would be discussing his current condition in more depth later. Sen realized that he might have glossed over a few too many details in that letter he sent.

"Well," he said, putting on a forced smile, "let's go see Ai. I'm sure she'll be excited to meet new people."

Suiting actions to words, he started walking toward the galehouse and hoping that the power of adorableness would distract everyone even more. He felt a little bad using Ai that way, but it was going to happen anyway. So, he might as well put it to productive use. As soon as the group entered the galehouse, Sen remembered that there was another guest already inside. Shen Mingxia looked like she'd just swallowed something very sharp and jagged as the presences of two more nascent soul cultivators were added to Fu Ruolan's presence. Before Sen could do or say anything, Auntie Caihong grabbed his arm.

"There are two of them?" she asked, her eyes sparkling.

Sen didn't quite know what she meant until he followed her gaze to where Ai and Li Zhi were using bits of charcoal to draw on paper that Sen had purchased. It only occurred to him now that whoever made that paper would probably be horrified to know that Sen used the ridiculously expensive product to keep small children entertained.

"Oh, no," answered Sen. "The one on the right is Ai. The one on the left is Zhi, her friend from the town."

"They are so precious," said Auntie Caihong in a hushed whisper. "Introduce me."

"Ai," called Sen. "Come here, please. I want you to meet some important people."

Ai looked up, saw the new people, and immediately jumped to her feet. She ran over to them. She started asking questions before Sen got a word in.

"Who are you?" she asked Ma Caihong. "Where are you from? Why are you so pretty?"

Sen cut in before the torrent of questions could continue.

"Ai, this is my Auntie Caihong."

"Your Auntie?" asked Ai.

"Yes," said Caihong, kneeling down. "I'm Sen's auntie, and I'm very pleased to meet you, Ai."

Caihong reached out a hand and gently touched Ai's hair.

"Oh, you have such beautiful hair."

Ai suddenly found her shyness, because she ran over to Sen and hugged his leg while smiling at Auntie Caihong. Sen reached down and ruffled her hair, which made the girl giggle.

"There's someone else I want you to meet," said Sen and pointed. "That is my Uncle Kho."

Uncle Kho beamed. "Hello, Ai. You can call me Uncle Kho too."

She gave Uncle Kho a little wave before she whispered in a

voice that everyone could hear, "Uncle Kho is tall, but not as tall as you."

The two men traded questioning glances before Sen asked, "Am I taller?"

Kho got a thoughtful little frown and shrugged like it wasn't that important.

"Probably."

Sen heard another whisper then, one he was pretty sure no one was meant to hear. But cultivator-enhanced senses being what they were, everyone heard it.

"He's going to get me killed."

Whatever color Shen Mingxia had left in her face drained away as three sets of nascent soul eyes turned to her. Then, Auntie Caihong got a vaguely predatory look that sent chills down Sen's back.

"Hello dear," said Auntie Caihong as she stood back up. "I'm Ma Caihong. And who might you be?"

The only reply she got was a tiny, little squeak.

CHAPTER FORTY

PANIC, CHAOS, QUESTIONS... AND MORE PANIC

Shen Mingxia just stared at Ma Caihong with her eyes so wide that Sen worried she might damage them. Then, the woman lurched to her feet, slammed her hands together, and bowed so low she was basically looking at the floor.

"Lady Ma Caihong, this unworthy one is Shen Mingxia. I apologize for—" Her words trailed off when it finally seemed to occur to her that she hadn't actually done anything wrong. "It is the greatest honor of my life to meet the esteemed Alchemy's Handmaiden!"

When no one said anything, Shen Mingxia lifted her head just enough that Sen could shake his head at her in disapproval. Taking pity on her, Sen walked over, grabbed her arm, and pulled her up straight. He gave Auntie Caihong a reproving look because he could see that little twinkle of amusement in her eyes.

"Auntie, this is Shen Mingxia. You'll have to forgive her. Being in a sect has clearly *damaged her mind*. Shen Mingxia, you've met my auntie. That is Kho Jaw-Long, or as I like to call him, Uncle Kho."

"Kho Jaw-Long," muttered Shen Mingxia, before her eyes threatened to do unnatural things again. "The Living Spear!"

241

If Sen hadn't kept a firm grip on her arm, she would have done another of those incredibly awkward-looking bows. Instead, she sort of flopped forward at an angle and her arm spun in Sen's hand. She lurched around and bumped into Sen's chest. She stared up at him, and he could read the near-perfect panic on her face. He just shook his head again. Sen planned to wait for her to calm down. When she just kept shaking and staring up at him like he was the only boat in a flood, he knew he'd have to act. He lifted his free hand and poked her forehead with a finger. The tap seemed to jar loose a bit of sanity, which Sen came to understand might have been even worse. She started whispering at him.

"Sen, you need to get me out of here. You need to get me out of here right now! Do you have any idea what they're going to do to someone like me?"

Ignoring her pleading, Sen spoke in a bland voice, "Uncle Kho, are you planning to kill Shen Mingxia?"

Uncle Kho, who had gone to sit on the floor next to Zhi and was exclaiming over her pictures, glanced up.

"What? Why would I do that?"

"No reason. I was just asking. Auntie Caihong, were you planning on running some terrifying experiment on her with your alchemy?"

Ma Caihong looked like she desperately wanted to say *yes*, just to see what would happen, but Sen's narrowed eyes put that idea to rest.

"Of course, I'm not going to run any experiments on her. The poor thing is a formation foundation cultivator in a sect. That seems far worse than anything *I* could do to her."

Shen Mingxia was still staring up at him, although he could feel that her heart wasn't racing quite as fast.

"They're really not going to do anything to me?" she whispered.

"One, they can hear you. Two, they're my family, and you're my guest. Three, you're Ai's friend. Of course, they aren't going to do anything to you," said Sen before he thought it through a little more. "Well, they aren't going to hurt you. I make no promises about the kinds of questions they may ask you."

Sen would never know if it was his comments, his clear lack of concern, or the reassurances from the nascent soul cultivators that let Shen Mingxia finally get a grip on her emotions. She did finally seem to realize that she'd pressed herself up against Sen like he was some of kind sheltering wall. She hurriedly stepped back and her cheeks went a little pink. Giggling, Ai came over and grabbed the woman's hand.

"Auntie Mingxia, you made funny faces."

"Yeah. I sure did," said Mingxia weakly.

The little girl pulled the reluctant formation foundation cultivator over to where Uncle Kho and Zhi were sitting. Sen walked over to Auntie Caihong.

"Be nice," he muttered.

"It was just a little fun," she said.

"Not for her."

"I suppose that's true. I'll make it up to her," said Auntie Caihong before she looked around the galehouse. "Where's Falling Leaf?"

"She said she was going exploring today. We're a bit close to the town for her liking and the forest is right there. I expect she'll be back before too long."

"Idle curiosity, why is there a sect cultivator in your home? You don't usually get along very well with them."

"She's here because...You know what? That's a really long story, and if I'm going to tell it, I should bring in that core cultivator who's lurking outside. You should feel free to have fun at that one's expense."

"Sen!" exclaimed a scandalized Shen Mingxia.

"Oh, fine. Don't terrify her. Actually, we should do that tomorrow. The girls are going to be all riled up with new faces here. No need to add to that chaos."

As if to prove his point, the girls ran over to him yelling in unison. "Shadow dog!"

"Sen, make shadow dog," pleaded Ai.

"Please, Uncle Sen," chimed in Li Zhi.

"I don't know. Have you been good girls today?" asked Sen.

The two girls stared up at him with identical expressions of pure innocence and nodded. From the look he saw on Auntie Caihong's face, he thought she wanted to just scoop them both up and keep them forever. Sen stroked his chin in thought.

"What will you give me for performing this mighty magic for you?"

"Hugs," said Ai.

"Hugs!" said Sen. "How could I possibly turn down a treasure like hugs? Very well, I will summon forth the great shadow dog."

Sen made a big show of concentrating before thrusting his hand at a corner. The form of a dog the black of deepest shadow sprang out and looked around.

"Yay!" cheered the girls.

Sen leaned down. "Where are my treasures?"

The girls both threw their arms around his neck for a moment before crashing across the room toward the dog. Fu Ruolan finally rejoined the conversation at that point.

"It looks like you've refined that one," she said.

Sen nodded. "It's getting better. I still haven't figured out how to make it sapient."

"Sapient?" asked Uncle Kho, rejoining the group. "Why would you want to make it sapient?"

"It'd make a good guard for them," said Sen.

"What use is a shadow guard?" asked Auntie Caihong. "Would it come and warn you?"

That was when the Zhi climbed up onto the shadow construct and it began a slow meander around the interior of the galehouse. Ai walked behind them with her hands wrapped around the construct's tail. Uncle Kho and Auntie Caihong look mildly stunned. Fu Ruolan looked on with an air of smug satisfaction so thick it was almost tangible.

"Sen?" asked Uncle Kho.

"Yes?"

"Is that charming little girl riding on top of a shadow dog that you made?"

"Well, it's not really a dog. It's just a construct I made to look like a dog. If I can crack that sapience thing, though, I could make them a real shadow dog."

"I think you missed the important part of my question," said Uncle Kho. "You made that shadow construct solid enough that it's safe for her to ride it?"

"Oh, yeah. That thing will stay tangible like that for five or six hours as it is. It was kind of a rush job. When I really focus on making one, it'll last for a whole day. The problem is that I have to make it move around and interact with them. If I don't, it just stands there. Not much fun for the girls when it's like that."

"How long have you been working to master this technique?" asked Auntie Caihong.

"It's not really a technique. This was just something I figured out how to do on the side while I was trying to figure something else out. I mean, it's got some uses in a fight, but it's kind of slow to make anything practical. So, I mostly just use it to make things for the girls to play with."

"Like what?" asked Uncle Kho.

"All kinds of things. Balls are pretty easy to make. I do flowers. Stuff for them to climb around on. It turns out that you can make a big, fluffy cushion out of shadow even easier than using air qi. And it makes sure they don't get hurt when they fall. I make them houses to play in sometimes."

"You make them *houses*?" demanded Auntie Caihong. "Tangible houses that they can move around in? Made from shadow?"

Sen nodded. "I do scale them down a little bit so they can reach everything. I also make sure everything stays a bit soft so there's nothing they can injure themselves on. You know, it's actually easier to do it that way than to make something that's completely rigid. Took me a while to realize that."

The longer Sen talked, the happier he saw Fu Ruolan get. He couldn't bring himself to blame her. She'd had a hand in making this all happen. He supposed she was taking a bit of pleasure out of having taught him something that Uncle Kho and Auntie Caihong found so impressive. The fact that this was just a byproduct of trying to figure out the true technique probably added a bit more enjoyment to the moment. *There's probably some ego involved with it too*, thought Sen. Fu Ruolan was a nascent soul cultivator who had, as far as he could tell, been living in the shadows of Auntie Caihong, Uncle Kho, and Master Feng for a very long time.

He wasn't sure if this felt like a balancing of some old inequity to her, but she was genuinely happy for once. Far be it from him to steal that from her. Sen did smirk to himself as he reached over and grabbed Shen Mingxia as she tried to sneak out while everyone was distracted. He pulled her over and draped an arm around her shoulder. It was everything he could do to keep the laugh inside as she stared murder at him. Ignoring her glare, he plucked the piece of paper she was trying to hide from her hand and glanced at it. His heart melted a little at what he saw.

"It's a rather good likeness. Don't you agree, Auntie Caihong?" asked Sen, handing over the picture and ignoring the elbow that Shen Mingxia rammed into his ribs.

The nascent soul cultivator took the paper and peered down at the picture of Ai that Shen Mingxia had rendered in shades of black and gray. The girl wore a happy little smile while she pondered something unseen in the distance. Auntie Caihong looked up at the struggling foundation formation cultivator that Sen still had locked into place with his arm around her.

"Come with me, dear," said Auntie Caihong. "We have something to discuss."

"What?" wheezed Shen Mingxia.

"I wish to buy this. We need to discuss a fair price."

Sen gave Shen Mingxia a big smile. "See. Nothing to worry about."

Shen Mingxia's expression told him that she was certain he had lost his damn mind.

CHAPTER FORTY-ONE
PAYMENT

It wasn't long after Auntie Caihong dragged a weakly protesting Shen Mingxia into a corner to negotiate for the picture that Falling Leaf arrived. Sen couldn't help but chuckle a little at the startled look on her face. The scene she had walked into was a little bit more exciting than what she was used to seeing. Two little girls were sitting on a shadow dog, cheering wildly as Uncle Kho made a tiny figure made of lightning dash across the wall, leap over windows like they were great chasms, and do battle with an appropriately sized shadow dragon that Sen controlled. Having fought a dragon or two in his day, Sen naturally knew that the appropriate size was enormous relative to the puny human figure that Kho had created. Sen was also using shadow construct appendages that he'd temporarily affixed to a wall to help prep some food for a meal. The sheer noise and chaos had been too much for Fu Ruolan. She had fled back to the quiet of her home. It seemed that the ghost panther was at a loss about what to address first. Finally, she turned to Sen.

"Sen, why does the Mingxia look as though she's about to start crying?"

"She's afraid of Auntie Caihong and Uncle Kho. Mostly Auntie Caihong, I think."

Falling Leaf considered that statement for a long beat before she said, "Wise."

The epic battle between lightning man and shadow dragon played out for a couple more minutes before the great beast fell. There was more elated cheering from Ai and Zhi. Uncle Kho looked over at Falling Leaf and smiled. The girls followed his look and ran over to the ghost panther, their words tumbling over each so fast that only the occasional *lightning*, *shadow*, *Uncle*, and *Auntie* were understandable. In the end, it was just a wall of noise that crashed into Sen and Falling Leaf. Sen knew he'd need to rein everyone in soon. The girls were getting overexcited, but he supposed that was part of being a child. It was also a little entertaining watching the ghost panther try to adjust to the sudden change in circumstance. She'd come a long way since the first time they'd met Ai. Then, she'd simply frozen up, uncertain what to do or say. Now, she was more accustomed to the children, but their sheer exuberance at that moment was a bit more than she knew what to do with.

"Okay, girls," said Sen. "I think it's time for quiet playing. I see some paper over that doesn't have flowers or birds or anything on it."

Seeing the obvious disappointment on their faces, Sen decided to take advantage of his guests.

"If you're good, Uncle Kho might even make something else out of lightning."

The girls immediately whirled to look at Uncle Kho, who stroked his beard thoughtfully. He dragged it out until Ai and Zhi were practically dancing on their toes.

"If you're good," he finally agreed.

Of course, it wasn't quite that easy, but Sen eventually managed to get the girls settled down with the paper and charcoal again. He was about to go back to Falling Leaf and Uncle Kho, who had settled into chairs and were chatting about something, but Auntie Caihong turned and looked at him.

"Sen, can you join us please?" she asked.

He dutifully changed course to join the alchemist and the miserable Shen Mingxia. The foundation formation cultivator alternated between giving him pleading looks and ones that promised vengeance as he approached. He supposed he'd had more than his share of fun at her expense. It was time to extract her from this situation she'd been wholly unprepared to face.

"Yes, Auntie Caihong?" he asked.

"We were discussing what would be an appropriate payment for the picture. Do you think you can make her one of your elixirs with this?"

Caihong lifted a hand and summoned a delicate flower from one of her storage treasures. Sen didn't recognize the flower, but he could feel it positively bursting with air qi. That was the kind of natural treasure that sects normally had to organize entire expeditions to retrieve from the deep wilds. It was also the kind of treasure that he thought they probably reserved for their core formation members. Knowing Auntie Caihong, though, she'd likely just picked it because she thought she might be able to do something with it someday. He briefly examined it with his senses and qi, confirming what he already knew, and then gave Shen Mingxia a questioning look.

"You're certain that an air qi focus is the way you want to go?" he asked her.

It seemed that she didn't even hear the question at first because her eyes were locked onto the flower. She looked worried that it was some kind of an illusion that would disappear if she so much as blinked.

"Mingxia," said Sen with a bit more force.

She did blink then and turned her attention to him.

"What?" she asked sounding confused.

Sen shook his head a little and repeated his question. She gave it the kind of deep consideration that all decisions affecting the rest of one's life should get by immediately nodding.

"Yes. Yes! I am very completely certain!"

Sen looked at Auntie Caihong. "Sure, I can make her something."

"Good," she said and gave him the flower before walking over to show off her newly acquired picture to Uncle Kho.

Sen swiftly stored the flower in his own storage ring to preserve its potency. The exaggerated disappointment on Shen Mingxia's face nearly drove him into a fit of laughter, but he fought it back. She didn't deserve that.

"It's best to keep plants like that stored until you're ready to use them," he explained.

"I know," said Shen Mingxia. "It's just, how often am I ever going to see something like that in person?"

"Well, I mean, I've got a storage ring full of things like that if you ever want to see some," offered Sen in a bid to be helpful.

Shen Mingxia closed her eyes and took several deep breaths before she said, "It's very hard to know you some days."

"What? Why?"

"Seriously? If I came back to the sect with something like that flower, well, I'd never be allowed to keep it. But I would also get massive rewards and all kinds of cultivation resources. And you're telling me that you've just got a pile of things like that sitting in a storage ring."

"Um, yes?" said Sen, uncertain if honesty was the best choice.

"Sitting in a storage ring," said Shen Mingxia in a clipped voice. "Sitting. Doing nothing. Just there for your convenience if you ever decide that you have some use for *inconceivably valuable* natural treasures."

"I am an alchemist. Gathering natural treasures and doing things with them is pretty much the whole job."

She pointed her finger at him, grimaced, and said, "It's really easy to forget that you're an alchemist. Still, a whole storage ring with treasures like that? Why don't you just go sell or trade some of them to the big sects in the capital? Hells, you could throw an auction all by yourself. You could finance ten new sects with the gold and resources they'd throw at you."

Sen blinked at her a few times. A look of burgeoning comprehension crossed her face. She closed her eyes again.

"It never occurred to you to do that, did it?"

"In my defense, I've had a lot of things to deal with since the last time we met."

"That's the heavens' own truth."

"Okay," said Sen after glancing around, "everyone is preoccupied. Let's get you out of here."

"Yes, please."

Shen Mingxia visibly relaxed once they were outside and away from the nascent soul cultivators. She shuddered, and Sen didn't think it had anything to do with the cold. She peered at him and seemed oddly shy.

"What will you make with the flower?" she asked hesitantly.

Sen shrugged. "I don't know yet. It depends on you and what you're looking for."

"I don't understand."

"I *can* make all kinds of things with the flower. I can think of ten or fifteen things right off the top of my head. I could make something that would enhance your air qi affinity, for example."

"Really? I mean, I heard about things like that, but it's not something I ever saw at the sect."

"That may have more to do with the alchemists at your sect than anything else. A pill or elixir like that has to be made specifically for someone. It's not like healing pills. You can make those in batches and expect them to work more or less the same way for everyone. So, it makes sense for the alchemists at your sect to focus their time and energy on making things that everyone can use. I imagine they reserve specialized pills and elixirs for the inner sect disciples, core members, and elders."

"I guess that makes sense."

"Of course, I don't care about any of that. I can make whatever I want. That doesn't make the things I'd think to make with that flower into things *you* need. It also doesn't make them things you could survive taking. We'll have to talk about it. I'll take a look at your qi, your channels, and your dantian. We'll take it from there."

"Can you make me something that will help me advance?" she asked, eager and reluctant at the same time.

"Yes. The question is whether that's a good thing or even the most advantageous thing. I could make you something that would help you advance right now. I can probably also make you something that would help you break through to core formation and form a stronger core when the time comes."

Sen held out his hands, palms up, and moved them up and down like they were balancing things on a scale. He continued.

"I get it. Everything in cultivation is focused on pushing forward. Not losing momentum. I'm just saying that rapid advancement isn't always a good thing. Advancing too quickly can have consequences."

"Easy to say when you've advanced so quickly."

Sen nodded in acknowledgment of the point. "It came at a steep price. Most of it paid in pain. Don't misunderstand. I'm not saying I won't help you advance now. I will if that's what you decide you want. I'm only suggesting that you consider the state of your cultivation. Look at all of the options. *Then,* make the best choice for you."

Shen Mingxia stood there in thoughtful silence before a little smile formed on her lips. She pressed her fists together and bowed.

"Yes, senior," she said with merriment in her voice.

"Ugh," groaned Sen.

"This humble Shen Mingxia is grateful for the patriarch's advice."

"Gods save me."

"You had that coming, and you know it. Leaving me alone with that terrifying woman."

"She's just Auntie Caihong."

"I don't even know what to say to that," muttered Shen Mingxia as she turned and walked away.

CHAPTER FORTY-TWO

TALKING

The rest of that evening passed in a glow of food, carefully curated conversations that steered away from anything too dark for the girls, and familial warmth. While Uncle Kho and Auntie Caihong were very nice to both girls, it was clear that they were more focused on Ai. Falling Leaf surprised Sen by taking up the slack and lavishing extra attention on Zhi, who eventually drifted off to sleep in the ghost panther's lap. Even after the girls were put to bed, Ai possessively hugging a shadow ball, and Zhi snuggling a stuffed doll she took everywhere with her, the conversations stayed on the light side. Everyone knew there were more serious conversations coming, but no one seemed to be in a hurry to start them. That suited Sen just fine. Eventually, he did ask a question that he didn't necessarily need an answer to, but that he knew Fu Ruolan was going to demand within two seconds the very next time he saw her.

"So, how long were you thinking about staying?" asked Sen.

"Looking to get rid of us old people already?" asked Uncle Kho as the corners of his eyes crinkled in amusement.

"Not at all," answered Sen with a smile. "But, if you're only thinking of staying for a few days, it doesn't make sense for me to make you your own galehouse."

Auntie Caihong gave him a wry smile. "That name. It's a little on the nose."

"I didn't come up with it," said Sen. "And I have to call them something."

"I suppose that's true. I was thinking that we might stay for a while. Ming is bound to show up at some point, so we need to make sure that Ai loves us best before he turns up being all gruff and grandfatherly."

"Caihong," said Uncle Kho in an amused but chiding tone.

"What? You've seen how he is with children. Honestly, it's annoying. The man's name alone is enough to send hardened sects screaming in terror, but children take one look at him and decide he's just the best thing that walks the world."

Sen looked to Uncle Kho and asked, "Is that true?"

"It's not exactly that way. She's exaggerating thi—" started Uncle Kho before getting cut off.

"Yes!" insisted Auntie Caihong. "It's *exactly* that way. It's like he's using a technique on them."

"Is he?" asked Sen.

"No," admitted Auntie Caihong. "Which may make it even more annoying."

"He makes them feel safe," said Falling Leaf, chiming into the conversation for the first time in a while.

"What do you mean?" asked Sen.

"He is a dragon in all but name. Ancient. Powerful beyond reason. A living, breathing nightmare for his enemies, but he would never see children as his enemies. It would never even occur to him that they could *be* his enemies. At worst, he might simply dismiss them. Should violence come, though, they can sense that he would shelter them beneath his wings. And what more absolute safety could there be than the Feng's protection?"

Everyone considered that in thoughtful silence for a few moments before Auntie Caihong spoke up.

"How am I supposed to go on being unreasonably annoyed with him now?" she demanded of no one in particular.

Sen and Uncle Kho both chuckled while Falling Leaf gave her a curious look. They spoke deep into the night before Sen finally excused himself to go outside and raise another galehouse, although one that strongly resembled their home on the mountain in structure. After he finished, he turned to find Auntie Caihong and Uncle Kho standing nearby simply staring at the new structure.

"If you can make something like this," asked Uncle Kho, "why don't you make one for yourself?"

Sen considered the question and asked, "What would I do with it? It's just me, Falling Leaf, and Ai. Falling Leaf doesn't want anything. I don't need anything that I can't put into a storage ring. And Ai is happy as long as it's warm, dry, and I don't forget to make her a new shadow ball every now and then. I mean, maybe I'll make something bigger when Ai is older or I find somewhere that I want to live permanently. For now, it'd just be empty rooms."

Auntie Caihong shook her head. "I knew we focused too much on your training. There is more to life than cultivation, Sen."

He offered her a helpless shrug. "Maybe there is, but I haven't had much time to think about it. If it makes you feel any better, I'm sure Jing would be just as horrified by my humble little home. He'd probably tell me it wasn't befitting someone of my power and stature."

"Jing?" asked Uncle Kho.

"He means the king, dear," said Auntie Caihong.

Uncle Kho stroked his beard. "Oh, that's right. Some kind of strategic alliance there?"

"Nah," said Sen. "He's just my friend."

Auntie Caihong giggled, and Sen gave her a questioning look. She waved a hand in the air as if to shoo some errant thought away.

"I was just imagining all of the nobles across the kingdom spitting blood if they'd heard you say that. They wouldn't be able to decide if they were horrified by your lack of ambition, envious of your position, or terrified that the king could call on your aid."

"It'd be all three," said Uncle Kho. "He wouldn't be wrong, though. About having a place befitting your power and stature. It is sort of expected that people getting as close to the nascent soul stage as you are will conduct themselves a certain way."

"Yeah, well, I get the feeling that most people at that point have had a long time to develop other interests," answered Sen.

"That's probably a fair assessment," admitted Uncle Kho.

Auntie Caihong looped her arm through Uncle Kho's and directed a smile at Sen. "We'll go get settled in. There's no need to talk about everything tonight."

"Goodnight," said Sen and watched as Auntie Caihong and Uncle Kho disappeared into the house he'd made for them.

"How long will they be here for?" demanded Fu Ruolan.

Sen almost rolled his eyes at her. She'd lasted four seconds after his arrival before she'd asked the question. Since she'd lasted nearly twice as long as he'd predicted, he felt she should get some credit for that.

"They weren't specific. They said *a while.*"

"A while? Could they have been any vaguer?"

"I guess they could have shrugged at me," offered Sen.

He reassured himself that he'd provided that answer with nothing but pure helpfulness in his heart. Not that his pristine intentions were understood by the out-of-sorts nascent soul cultivator who glowered at him.

"I don't like having them here," said Fu Ruolan.

"You'll notice that they aren't *here*," answered Sen. "They're back at the town and, as near as I can tell, completely focused on keeping a certain little girl entertained. Far be it from me to say that I understand the motives or plans of my betters because history tells me that I assuredly don't. However, I don't think they're particularly interested in bothering you. They didn't even ask me where you are. Does that sound like they're planning to make some kind of unannounced visit to your home?"

Fu Ruolan grumbled something unintelligible before she fixed Sen with a hard look.

"You just keep them in line."

Sen returned her hard look with a lifted eyebrow and said, "Sure, that sounds probable. I'll just order them around, and they'll do what I say."

"I came all the way out here so I wouldn't have to deal with people," complained Fu Ruolan.

"You also bartered that manual to make me stay. Auntie Caihong and Uncle Kho coming here was always a possibility, and you had to know that. It's also quite likely that Master Feng will come and visit at some point, which you also had to have predicted."

Fu Ruolan pursed her lips. "Perhaps. It doesn't make it any less distracting for you or annoying for me. You know full well that I have reasons to avoid others."

That was a point that Sen couldn't deny.

"I'll make sure they know that you don't want any guests to come calling."

"That will have to do."

"I will say that I specifically invited my Grandmother Lu to visit. I don't see how she could bother you, but I don't want it to come as a surprise."

"Grandmother Lu? The elderly body cultivator you told me about? The one who," she seemed to search her memory, "started some kind of business?"

"That's her."

"I'm not concerned about her. Aside from the distraction she'll provide. You have more than enough of those already. You're supposed to be learning, not adopting mortal towns and starting a sect for infatuated cultivator girls who bat their eyelashes at you."

Sen struggled to formulate an appropriate response. Part of him wanted to laugh at her description of the sect she thought he was starting. He'd more or less decided that he wasn't going to start a sect. He was going to start something else. Something less likely to draw the ire or unwanted attention of established sects. He just needed to think it through a little longer and maybe consult with Uncle Kho a bit. Another part of him wanted to deny that he'd adopted a mortal town, but there was more than a little truth in that. He didn't have anything like official control, but he'd more or less bypassed whatever served as local government and instituted a militia. A militia that was likely more loyal to him than it should be.

Those hadn't been his goals. All he'd really wanted to do was give the mortals there a fighting chance against the kind of low-level spirit beasts that were likely to assault the town. Yet, there was a stark truth that whoever controlled the loyalty of the military controlled the area. For the moment, that meant him. Not that he thought the people he was training would ever do anything to harm the town. They all lived and worked there. That didn't mean that the local elders would see it that way. They probably saw him as equal parts resource and threat. On the one hand, he was providing the locals with what could only be described as excellent training. Training he was providing free of charge, at that. On the other hand, he was an outsider and cultivator with a powerful hold over anyone who passed through the training hall. They were also far from the reach of the kingdom's centers of power. It could very well look to them like Sen meant to set himself up as some kind of local king or warlord. And that was a problem he wasn't entirely sure how to remedy.

"What are you daydreaming about?" snapped Fu Ruolan.

"I was just wondering if the local elders think that I'm getting ready to use their town as the foundation for trying to set up my own little kingdom."

"Why in the world would you be thinking about that? That's completely... It's completely—" she trailed off as she thought it over. "Actually, that's probably more plausible than it sounds on the surface."

"Any advice?" asked Sen.

"You'll need a lot more people than you have if you plan on taking over a piece of the kingdom," said Fu Ruolan in a completely serious voice. "Wars are messy business. You need a lot of bodies for them."

Sen gaped at her. "I meant any advice on how to convince the elders that's *not* what I'm doing. I'm not, by the way. Just to be clear."

"Oh. My mistake. I wouldn't care if you did. I'm not particularly attached to this kingdom. It didn't even exist when I was young," mused the woman. "Plus, it'd be very convenient if you were the local king. I could ask for favors."

"I'm not setting myself up as a warlord just so you can have me post soldiers to keep people away!"

"Calm down. It was just a thought. A really nice thought."

Sen pinched the bridge of his nose. "Any advice on accomplishing my actual goal."

"There is this one ancient stratagem you can try."

"Which is?"

"It's a mysterious, poorly understood technique called talking."

CHAPTER FORTY-THREE

ACADEMY, PART 1

" Again," said Sen.

The townspeople, under the guidance of Dai Bao, started the form over again as Sen and Uncle Kho watched. The elder cultivator had seemed both curious and dubious about Sen's project to train the mortals to defend themselves against spirit beasts. As they worked through the form again, he could see Uncle Kho's gaze turn considering as he evaluated the townspeople. He reserved judgment, though, electing to maintain his guise as a simple visitor for the moment. He'd gotten more than one curious look from the practicing mortals, but they all had enough respect for Sen not to push for more information than he was willing to share. Sen was struggling not to send everyone home just so he could sate his curiosity about Uncle Kho's thoughts, but he resisted the urge. Everyone had made time for this, despite the demands of their own jobs and lives. He could do them the basic courtesy of giving this an honest effort.

So, he slowly walked around the group and made mental notes. He saw some incremental improvement here and there, but nothing fundamental had changed. The handful of people capable of going further would need more direct instruction, while everyone else had reached their peak. Sen wondered if this was what running a sect was like for the core sect members and elders. Did they invest just enough time and effort to pick out the handful of unpolished gems, and then focus their attention on those few? He had the worrying feeling that, while things might not be *quite* that simple, the transition from outer sect disciple to inner sect disciple was probably handled in almost exactly that fashion. However, while most people's skills weren't progressing, other things that were just as important to surviving a battle with spirit beasts were improving. Things like stamina.

During the first month or two, everyone's endurance had been pitiful. It wasn't that everyone was in terrible condition. A few, the ones who spent most of their time working with their minds rather than their hands, had been almost beyond hope. Most of the townspeople worked hard at some kind of manual labor. The problem was that the labor they were doing didn't necessarily translate into strength in the right parts of the body or sustained endurance. Wang Bo had been a good example. Sen knew that the young man could go out and do the labor related to cutting down trees all day long. On top of that, he was still young even by mortal standards. He was likely at the very peak of what would be his strength and health. Yet, in the beginning, an hour of sustained practice with a spear had left him nearly beyond exhaustion. He was forced to use muscles he didn't normally use, or use them in ways he didn't normally use them. It had been like that for nearly everyone.

Now, everyone who had lasted in the training could keep it up for a couple of hours. Sen had watched as this part of the community had grown leaner and stronger. While it wasn't a substitute for body cultivation, he believed that using a rotation strategy would let them outlast most low-level beasts. Whether they believed it was another matter. They had lucked out so far that no other beasts had attacked the town, so the question hadn't been put to the test as of yet. After the group finished the form, Dai Bao had them pair off and do some light sparring with blunted spears Sen had made for the purpose. Everyone present had developed enough skill and control not to injure each other out of pure ignorance or carelessness, which meant Sen no longer felt a need to oversee every spar. Instead, he moved between the pairs, sometimes just watching and sometimes offering pieces of advice.

The small group he'd identified as having more potential, a group including Wang Bo and Li Hua, he instructed to stay when everyone else left. It took a bit for the practice hall to clear out, but eventually the only people remaining were Sen, Uncle Kho, and the people he'd told to stay. That group of five people shuffled nervously as he approached them. He hadn't told them why he wanted them to stay, so he couldn't rightly fault them for their nerves. He gave them all a gentle smile to try to alleviate their nerves. It didn't seem to help. *I guess I better just get on with it*, he thought.

"You five have the most room left for growth. So, I'm going to offer you the opportunity for some additional training," he said and held up a hand to quiet any immediate questions. "There will likely be some changes happening here soon, which means that this extra training will come with extra responsibilities. I know that all of you have responsibilities already, so don't rush to agree. If you don't have the time or the energy to take on more, I *will not* hold it against you. Give the matter some thought, and then let me know your answers."

He could see the questions burning in their eyes. They wanted to know about the training and the changes he'd been very vague about. He waited to see if they'd give in to that curiosity or if they'd do as he'd asked. It was a test of sorts to measure their self-discipline. Wang Bo's lips twitched several times as Sen looked at him with some bland amusement on his face. The young man finally wrangled his curiosity into submission and left after a hasty goodbye. The others wandered out, casting curious looks in his direction, until he was left facing just Li Hua. He lifted an eyebrow at her.

"Yes?" he asked, certain she'd ask about the changes.

"Who is that man?" she asked, nodding toward Uncle Kho.

"You know who he is. That's Uncle Kho. You've met several times now."

"I know that's how you introduced me to him. But who is he? Why is he here?"

"Oh, now those are two very different questions."

"Will you answer either of them?" she pressed.

Sen considered her for a moment before he looked over to Uncle Kho and shrugged. Those weren't Sen's secrets to tell, so he manfully made it someone else's problem. Uncle Kho smirked at Sen, clearly aware that Sen was dodging responsibility, and walked over. He politely inclined his head to Li Hua.

"It's nice to see you again, Li Hua," said Uncle Kho. "I gather you have questions."

"I, that is, yes. I do," she said, suddenly nervous as Uncle Kho gave her a very direct look.

"Go ahead," he said.

Sen kept his face perfectly neutral. Uncle Kho was having a little fun at her expense, which Sen didn't approve of but couldn't see a way to object to at the moment.

Li Hua hesitated before she blurted out, "Who are you?"

"Kho Jaw-Long," answered Uncle Kho immediately.

Li Hua blinked at him with an uncertain look on her face. It was clear the name didn't mean anything to her, but equally clear she had sensed something about the man that unsettled her. She seemed to be looking for a question that would provide some clarity and was having limited success.

"Are you a cultivator? Like him?" she ventured, even more hesitant.

"A cultivator? Yes. Like him?" asked Uncle Kho with a look toward Sen. "No. He's much more talented than I am."

When Sen rolled his eyes, Uncle Kho amended his statement.

"In some areas."

There was a long silence after that, which prompted Sen to speak. "Just ask, Hua."

Sen wasn't sure if he'd ever addressed the woman so casually before, but it seemed to hit her like a thunderbolt. She straightened and her eyes went a little wide. She hurriedly posed her other question.

"Why are you here?"

"In this town or in this building?" asked Uncle Kho, a merry sparkle in his eyes.

"Both?" she asked, her voice a little higher than usual.

"I'm in this town because Sen is here and he's adopted an adorable little girl that I wanted to meet. I'm in the building because Sen asked me to offer my opinion on this project of his and the overall aptitude of his students."

Li Hua frowned. "Why would he ask you about that?"

This time it was Uncle Kho who looked at Sen and shrugged. It was up to Sen how much he wanted to reveal about that particular relationship.

"Because Uncle Kho is the person who taught me how to use a spear."

That answer seemed to solve some mystery in the woman's head because her face cleared up.

"Oh! I see. That makes sense."

Sen frowned at Li Hua. "What did you imagine he was here for? To kick me out and take over?"

"Of course not," said Li Hua, but the pink in her cheeks exposed the small lie.

Sen shook his head. "I'm going to be here for at least a couple more years. So, no, that isn't the change that I was talking about."

She stammered a few embarrassed, half-formed sentences before Sen mercifully told her to go collect Zhi from Auntie Caihong. Li Hua all but ran out of the building.

"I'm kind of surprised you told her your name," said Sen.

"I don't need to hide. Most people know better than to bother me."

"And you do have that reputation to fall back on."

"I'm not sure you're in a position to talk about reputations."

"Don't remind me," groaned Sen.

"Not enjoying fame?" asked Uncle Kho with a bit of sympathy.

"Not at all. How did you deal with it?"

"I moved to a remote mountain and killed everyone who came there to bother me."

Sen took a moment to think before he said, "Yeah, I guess I already knew that."

Uncle Kho smiled and gestured around at the training hall. "So, what was this all about? I watched you today, and it doesn't seem like you need any feedback from me. You picked out the people with real talent just fine. You've brought the rest up to a point of basic competence. Certainly enough to delay spirit beasts if not kill them outright. Or is this about you starting a sect?"

"It's related. I want to start something that is sort of like a sect, but I'm for sure not starting an actual sect. It's a hundred headaches and responsibilities that I don't want. Especially when the benefits are so thin."

"No desire for the blind adoration and obedience of others?"

"Gods, no. Plus, there's this nascent soul cultivator who just hates them. I don't want *that guy* showing up with an ax to grind."

"Yeah, I've heard about him," said Uncle Kho with a smirk. "If you started a sect, he'd definitely show up sooner or later."

"Then, there's all the terror and screaming and foundation formation cultivators openly weeping. Who has time for that?"

"It does sound tedious. Although, there's a rumor going around that you already killed one nascent soul cultivator. What's one more?" asked Uncle Kho with laughter in his eyes.

"Oh, you know how it is. Achieve one minor miracle and

everyone expects you to do it again. People are so greedy. Besides, you have to join a sect to get any benefits from it, and mortals can't join."

"So, what it is that you do have in mind that is apparently like a sect, but not actually a sect, and that mortals can join."

"I'm thinking that I'll open an academy. A weapons academy with a focus on the spear and the jian."

"And you'll let mortals join."

"I will."

"What about cultivators?"

"That *is* the question. I don't know. If I let cultivators join, I'd have to train them myself or recruit other cultivators to serve in that capacity since I can't have them mixing with the mortals. Even if they promise to behave, I don't believe for one second that some cultivator wouldn't fall into that superior attitude almost immediately. If one of them injured one of the mortal students, I'd have to act, which could well mean a mountain of trouble I'd rather avoid. I could maybe bypass some of the problems by only accepting wandering cultivators, but that could create its own problems."

"Like sect cultivators showing up to challenge your students because they're wandering cultivators with no real backing?" asked Uncle Kho.

"Exactly, which would mean that *I'd* have to be their backing, and I don't feel like dueling all the time. The other option is that I'd accept wandering cultivators and sect members. If I do that, I can exert some control over the problem, but I don't see how to avoid making it a problem in the first place. Basically, dealing with them would be a serious drain on resources. Plus, I'd have to monitor them to make sure they don't abuse the mortals in town."

"So, why not make it a mortal-only academy?"

"I really thought about it. It's what I wanted to do originally. But it won't work," said Sen.

"No?"

"There are already cultivators in town wanting to become the students of Judgment's Gale. If I open an academy and exclude cultivators, I'd be right back to dueling all the time."

"It seems like you've at least thought about the problems. So, what do you need from me?"

"Advice. Assuming you couldn't just leverage your fearsome reputation to keep everyone in line, how would you limit the problems?"

Uncle Kho stood in quiet contemplation for several minutes, idly stroking his beard, and making noncommittal noises from time to time.

"You can't avoid the problems. Not completely. These are people we're talking about and some of them are stupid. Some will think that the rules don't apply to them because they're nobles, or cultivators, or because they come from a sect. So, one option is that you make rules that include incredibly harsh punishments, and then enforce them mercilessly. You will end up having to kill a few people and deal with the consequences of that. Most people will fall in line fast enough if you execute a few who can't follow basic rules like *do not bother the mortals*. You can also ask for oaths to the heavens, but that's a losing proposition. Even those with no ill intent will avoid taking those oaths. They'd rather miss out on an opportunity than play dice with the heavens."

"They don't want to risk the heavens interpreting their oath?"

"Would you?"

"No," admitted Sen. "I definitely would not. Any other thoughts?"

"Some logistical ones. You should charge cultivators outrageously for joining because they're going to be a hassle for you."

"I'd planned on doing that."

"You should also create a separate training space for them," added Uncle Kho.

"Right. That would let me limit their interactions with the mortal students as much as possible. I suppose I'd need to provide somewhere for students to live as well. It's not like the town has a lot of extra housing."

As they talked through the necessities, Sen became increasingly sure that this was the right choice. It should let him avoid actively antagonizing the sects in the region, train more mortals, and it would even give Wu Meng Yao something real to do. It would also give him an excuse to turn away cultivators who wanted cultivation training while also providing them with an alternative. It wasn't perfect, but very little in life was perfect. He could live with a little imperfection if it let him manage some of his problems.

CHAPTER FORTY-FOUR

ACADEMY, PART 2

Sen focused his not-inconsiderable will on suffusing his entire body with shadow qi under Fu Ruolan's watchful gaze. Her focused attention didn't bother him. In fact, he was grateful for it. When she'd first described the process for her version of shadow walking, Sen had thought it would be easy. He'd swiftly learned that there was a reason only a handful of people could perform it. It was a relentless battle against nature and his own body's desires. Sen had remolded that body again and again, infused it with everything from earth qi to heavenly qi, and the results spoke for themselves. He was the strongest and fastest he'd ever been. But it came at a cost. Every last piece of him had all of those different qi types as intrinsic components. On top of that, nature didn't want human beings, or even body cultivators, to be made up of only one kind of qi. They were born as beings touched by all forms of qi, however lightly. Trying to superimpose shadow qi on top of all of that, through all of that, was proving a challenge that Sen wasn't sure he could overcome. With an exhausted explosion of breath, Sen released the shadow qi he'd been controlling.

"I can't keep going," he said.

"That was much better. You were much closer this time," said Fu Ruolan.

He wanted to deny those words. It hadn't felt much better. He didn't have any intuitive sense that he was any closer to success. Sen still nodded in acceptance. Fu Ruolan did not give false praise. She called false praise a misguided and futile attempt to bolster the incompetent. Sen wasn't sure he agreed with that position. Having spent a lot of time with children recently, he firmly believed that praise should be lavished on them whenever they put honest effort into doing something. Of course, he was no child, nor was he a traditional student.

He was a highly experienced cultivator getting direct instruction from an even more powerful and experienced cultivator. Instruction that was pushing the very limits of his current capacities. Sen suspected that this technique wasn't even meant to be used by core formation cultivators. Either way, the expectation for someone like him *had* to be different, and he would get limited value from praise he hadn't earned. He knew it. Fu Ruolan knew it as well. So, he accepted her words as true. Even if he couldn't properly see the progress he'd made, it wasn't a sign that it didn't exist.

After he'd had the initial insight, her explanation of how the technique worked had been little more than a confirmation of his suspicions. It was simplicity itself at the conceptual level. Turn yourself into a shadow and step through to the in-between place, where you can release your shadow form and become corporeal again. Walk over to the shadow you want to come out of, become a shadow again, and step into the real world. Assume your human form once more. Easy. Sen had assumed there was more nuance involved, but he'd drastically underestimated the difficulty.

On the surface, it was a constant source of frustration. Yet, there was a part of him that found it oddly satisfying that this was something that wasn't easy for him to do. He didn't relish struggle when it seemed to be for no reason, but this kind of struggle had value. It burnished the will and his self-discipline. Improving those couldn't be anything but good for him. *Then again*, thought Sen as he tried to push through a fatigue that had settled in his bones, *there is such a thing as overtraining. Even for me.*

"You're complaining in your head again, aren't you?" asked Fu Ruolan. "You've got that look about you."

"Of course not. I never complain."

"I suppose you want to stop for the day and get back to building your sect for lovestruck cultivator girls."

"It's not a sect," said Sen for at least the thirtieth time. "It's not just for cultivators, and it's not just for women."

"You say that, but I remain unconvinced."

"I noticed," said Sen.

"Fine. I suppose you've put in an adequate effort, and you're clearly not up for another try. Be on your way."

"I was planning to visit with Glimmer of Night. Ai is with him."

"Oh, well, I haven't seen the spiderkin in the last few days. I should probably join you."

"As you say."

The pair walked over to where Glimmer of Night had constructed an incredibly complicated... Sen wasn't sure that the word *web* truly encompassed it. It crisscrossed dozens and dozens of trees and went up at least fifty feet. The spider watched on as Ai inexpertly climbed on it. Sen's heart almost stopped when she slipped and fell. Then, he saw that there was a tightly packed mesh of qi about three feet off the ground that would prevent her from coming close to an impact. After she sank into the mesh, Ai let out a wild cry of glee as the mesh snapped back into place and launched her back up into the air. The little girl cheerfully began climbing around on the web again.

"I guess she's not much of a spider," observed Sen as they approached.

"She falls on purpose," said Glimmer of Night. "She likes the bouncing."

"Of course, she does," said Sen with a shake of his head.

He didn't want Ai to be afraid of everything, but he wondered sometimes if she wasn't afraid of *enough* things. There were actual dangers in the world and, someday, he'd have to let her go and find out about them. He shoved that thought away hard. *Someday, maybe*, he admitted to himself, *but not today*. Ai eventually noticed them and "fell" again, before scrambling toward them. She flopped off the edge of the mesh and came over to Sen.

"Did you see?" she asked, eyes bright with excitement. "I bounced!"

"I did see," said Sen. "Did you thank Uncle Glimmerite for making this for you?"

"Uh-huh," she said, her little head bobbing up and down.

"That's good. I have an idea. Maybe you should show Auntie Ru how to climb on it," suggested Sen with a look of pious innocence on his face.

The nascent soul cultivator was not fooled. She directed a narrow-eyed look at him, but the enthusiastic way that Ai grabbed her hand and dragged her toward the web construct delayed any immediate vengeance. Sen snickered a little to himself.

"It seems unwise to antagonize her that way," said Glimmer of Night.

"Oh, she doesn't hate it half as much as she pretends to. Besides, it's good for her."

"I don't believe I would ever treat a matriarch that way, good for her or not."

"To be fair, neither would I," said Sen. "Those matriarchs of yours don't seem to have much of a sense of humor."

"They do not. Humor is not highly valued among my people."

"You're missing out."

The spider was quiet for several moments before shrugging. "Perhaps."

"So, I've been meaning to ask you something. You know that you're welcome to come and visit us whenever you want, right?"

"I—" the spider paused. "I did not."

"Well, that explains it. I wasn't intending to abandon you out here."

"The humans in the town do not seem to like it when I visit."

"They'll just have to get used to it. Changes are coming here, and you'll probably be one of the politest of them."

"So, you mean to open your sect for lustful, doe-eyed cultivator waifs?"

Sen turned shocked eyes on the spider who wore his usual impassive look.

"Why would you call it that?"

"That is what Fu Ruolan called it when she described it to me."

Sen was struck completely speechless for almost ten seconds before he burst into laughter.

"Of course. *Of course*, she described it that way."

"I take it she was engaging in humor?"

"No," said Sen. "I think she probably meant it, but that's not what I'm doing. I'm opening a weapons academy. Mortals and cultivators alike are welcome to join. As are you."

"I see. Then, why did she call it that?"

"She doesn't approve of the idea. So, describing it in less-than-flattering terms is an indirect way to show her disapproval."

"Why does she disapprove?"

"Mostly because she thinks it'll be nothing but lustful, doe-eyed cultivator waifs."

"Will it?" asked the spider in evident curiosity.

Sen opened his mouth, thought about it, closed his mouth, thought some more, and finally said, "I don't think it will. That's not the plan, anyway."

After that, the two fell into a comfortable silence while Ai explained to Auntie Ru how to climb on the web. Sen had to give Fu Ruolan credit that she didn't lose her patience with the explanation or even get frustrated and simply use her qi to fly nearby.

Sen didn't know if that was progress, but it was enough for the moment. Sen let the two of them play while occasionally asking Glimmer of Night questions about the spider's ongoing quest to, if Sen understood correctly, discover a new aspect of truth through a newly discovered web pattern. Glimmer of Night had not achieved his goal but seemed undaunted by the ongoing work. If nothing else, it seemed that the environment and the work had allowed the spider to evolve his spirit beast core a little. He was radiating a more condensed qi energy than before. Before it got too late, Sen finally called an end to the play and headed back to town.

CHAPTER FORTY-FIVE

ACADEMY, PART 3

S en shook his head as he silently observed Wu Meng Yao trying to observe the galehouse. He'd been standing about three feet behind her for five minutes. He'd also been *hiding*. He realized it wasn't a fair test, but she had been lurking a lot the last few days. Maybe it was because spring was just about there. He wasn't sure if she wanted to ask him about the task he'd set her or if she was just curious, but the amusement value in the whole situation had long since faded.

"That's creepy, you know," said Sen.

Wu Meng Yao jumped at least six inches off the ground and whirled to face him. Qi started to gather around her hands for some kind of technique. When the shock faded and recognition set in, she dispelled the gathering qi and directed an aggravated look at him.

"It's not funny to sneak up on people like that."

"It's not funny to spy on people's homes either," observed Sen.

"I—" she started only to falter when Sen raised an eyebrow at her. "Fine. I was spying."

"Any particular reason or just basic voyeurism?"

Wu Meng Yao turned bright red in embarrassment. "I'm not a voyeur!"

"It was a joke," said Sen in a bland voice. "Which you were obviously in no frame of mind to enjoy. Come with me."

"Where?"

"Does it matter? You're going to follow me either way."

"I guess it doesn't," said Wu Meng Yao, falling into step beside him.

"Have you been preparing for your trip?" asked Sen.

"I've prepared as much as one can for a trip like that. Which, incidentally, isn't much because *no one* does it."

"Oh, that's not true. Merchants go over those mountains all the time."

"Yes. Over. On an established trail and with guards. Guards frequently obtained from a sect. Over. Not up," said Wu Meng Yao in a voice that was almost complaining.

"A valid distinction," agreed Sen. "Idle curiosity, why have you been spying on my home?"

"You don't know?"

"I have my guesses, but they're just guesses."

"Shen Mingxia didn't tell you?" asked Wu Meng Yao, genuine bitterness in her voice.

"I didn't ask her," said Sen.

He chose not to comment on that bitterness. There were too many possible reasons for it. Plus, he had more than a sneaking suspicion that asking about it would open him up to a lot of information he didn't want. Wu Meng Yao didn't strike him as particularly volatile but emotions could run deep in anyone. Plus, if her emotions were that close to the surface at the moment, asking about them could inadvertently end with her revealing things she'd later wish she hadn't. No, it was better to just leave that alone for the moment.

"You have two legendary nascent soul cultivators who just dropped by for a visit. How could I not be curious?"

"You could have just asked to meet them," noted Sen.

"How? You've been avoiding me."

"Have I?"

"Yes! You have," she said with a fire in her eyes that abruptly went out. "I get why, though. I keep making things awkward, and it's very clear that you don't enjoy awkward."

Sen stopped walking so he could turn to look at her.

"Do you know *anyone*, anyone at all, who does enjoy awkward conversations?"

"No," she admitted with a slight wince.

"Okay. I was wondering if I missed something along the way," said Sen, resuming his walk.

There was a short silence that Wu Meng Yao apparently found intolerable because she asked a question that Sen had sort of expected.

"Why are you so much nicer to Shen Mingxia?"

"She doesn't make things awkward," answered Sen.

"That's it?"

"Isn't that enough? She treats me like a person. So, I respond in kind. What have I ever done to make you think that I care about all that hierarchy nonsense that sects impose?"

It seemed that she didn't have an answer to that question, which was for the best since they'd arrived at Sen's intended destination. They stood outside the door to the practice hall. It was almost exactly the same as it had always been, save for the addition of some characters on the wall. Sen stood there and looked at those characters until Wu Meng Yao took the hint and read them aloud.

"Deep Wilds Academy. What's this about?"

"I'm going to train people here."

"You're starting a sect?"

"Academy," corrected Sen. "A very specific kind of academy. I intend to teach the spear and jian here."

"No cultivation training?"

"I don't want to say never. If the exact right person walked through the door, I might, *might*, take on a student for cultivation training. But that's not what this place is for. This place is intended to teach the spear and jian to anyone who comes along. Mortals and cultivators alike."

Wu Meng Yao was silent for a full minute before she spoke again. "That's smart. If you're not training anyone to be cultivators, then people from any sect could come here to learn the spear or jian from the infamous Judgment's Gale. At the same time, the sects won't worry that you're trying to recruit away their best disciples. Assuming they believe it."

"Oh, I'm sure they'll send spies looking to prove that I'm really running a sect here. As long as they pay the outrageous fees I'll charge, they're free to spy all they want. There won't be anything to find."

"Have you considered the possibility of assassins? You aren't exactly everyone's favorite person."

"I can't pretend that everyone loves me. But I've survived assassination attempts before. Even one from a nascent soul cultivator."

"Wait! What? Seriously?"

"Yeah, it's been an interesting few years. It happened when I was in the capital a while back. There were a lot of people there who didn't like me. He just tried to do something about it. It didn't work out for him."

"Did you leave the city before he found you?"

"No. I killed him when he wouldn't leave the city, but I'd prefer it if you didn't spread that one around. Somehow, it's not common knowledge yet. I'd like to keep it that way."

Wu Meng Yao was staring at him with her mouth a little open. "You're serious. You killed a nascent soul cultivator, as a core formation cultivator?"

"He didn't leave me a lot of options. Well, no, that's probably not true. I expect that there were options, but I wasn't necessarily thinking all that clearly at the time. Mostly, I killed him because he deserved it, and because I wanted him dead."

"If that were common knowledge, you might not need to worry about assassins. Who would dare?"

"There's always someone who dares. I also know that I'm not invincible. Yes, it's possible someone might come here looking to kill me, but that's true literally everywhere I go. I don't think that I'm in substantially more danger here than anywhere else."

"You have things here to lose."

Sen gave her a steady look. "You mean Ai. You think someone might do something to her to get to me?"

"It's possible."

"No. Anyone capable enough to have a serious chance of killing me is going to be someone who does that kind of work professionally. That means they'll be professional enough to recognize the *ocean* of vengeance that would drown them if they did something that stupid. I would erase them and anything they ever touched. That's assuming that Auntie Caihong or Uncle Kho didn't get there first. The word *safe* would simply vanish from their world. Anyone not professional enough to recognize that is going to be dead, or desperately wishing they were dead, before they can actually do anything to her."

Wu Meng Yao swallowed hard before she said, "I'm glad to see that the last few years have toughened you up. You were so soft and forgiving before."

Sen met her eyes and then snorted. "And you missed my whole angry time. This is soft and forgiving compared to those days."

"I'm struggling to imagine that."

"You met Lo Meifeng, right? She can tell you all about how full of joy I was then. But, we're way off topic. There's a question that you need to answer."

"What's that?"

"Do you really want to go do the imaginary task I gave you, or would rather stay here and teach?"

"Imaginary task," said Wu Meng Yao a little numbly. "The treasure up near the peak? It's not real?"

"Nope. I made the whole thing up. Well, actually, I expect that there probably is some incredibly powerful shadow treasure in one of those caves, but I don't know that for sure."

"You... You made it up? You were going to let me go to those mountains and risk my life for a treasure that *doesn't even exist*!"

"Of course not. I was going to let you go most of the way to those mountains. Then, Shen Mingxia was going to tell you the truth."

"That little traitor."

"Don't be too hard on her. She's owed me since before she even met you. And she's been trying to convince me to find something else, something real, for you to do since day one. You must be doing something right there because she's loyal."

"Oh," said Wu Meng Yao, looking a little chagrined. "Still, why would you do something like that?"

"Is that a real question?" asked Sen.

"No! But I'm still angry about it. You could have just—"

"Told you it was fine and not to worry about it?"

"Yes!" she snapped before the realization hit.

"Well, before you go off and feel angry with me for, well, however long that's going to be, back to the question at hand. Imaginary task or teaching here?"

"Teaching what? To who?"

"You're competent with the jian. So, you'll teach that. As for the who, it'll be the lower-level cultivators who come here. I cannot spend all of my time teaching, and cultivators can only learn from other cultivators. So, if you feel like you've got some debt or obligation to me, you can work it off that way."

"I can't afford to stay here indefinitely."

"You'll be provided a place to stay, food, and some kind of stipend. It can be gold, some reasonable cultivation resources, or a combination."

The sect cultivator didn't say anything. She just kept staring at Sen and biting her lip.

"Do you need a day to think about it?" Sen finally asked.

"I want lessons," she blurted out. "The same lessons the other core cultivators get."

"Yeah, that's fine."

"If I'm going to be teaching, it only seems fair that I—" she trailed off. "It's fine? I don't understand."

"Well, that sounds like a personal problem that you should take up with the universe."

CHAPTER FORTY-SIX
ACADEMY, PART 4

Sen had been making excuses to avoid this task. He knew he'd been making excuses to avoid it. Of course, it helped that his excuses were, by and large, to do things like go train with Fu Ruolan, train the townspeople, evaluate Wu Meng Yao's true skill level, and shore up some of her weaknesses. Most important to his way of thinking was spending time with Ai. In other words, he wasn't inventing mindless goals or wasting time. It was just that he could have, at any point, taken a break from any of those things to go and deal with this particularly troublesome task. If only it didn't involve cultivators. *You've got to get over that,* Sen reminded himself. *If you're opening your academy to them, you're going to have to deal with them and all the things you don't like about them.* For all that, he still hoped that they would all decline when they found out the truth. Of course, that meant actually taking the step of talking with them. Sighing, Sen walked into the inn. He didn't even bother looking at them. He just pointed.

"You, you, and you. Come with me," he commanded, then turned and walked out.

They knew who he was. Half the town knew him on sight, even if they hadn't spoken directly with him. So, it was a foregone conclusion that the cultivators who had been in town for weeks and weeks had made a point to learn who he was. Oddly, none of them had gotten anywhere close to the practice hall or even, as near as he could tell, spoken with any of the mortals he was training. He didn't know if that was an overabundance of caution or just what they deemed a healthy measure of respect. He wasn't sure what, if anything, he would have done if the cultivators had approached any of his mortal students. He supposed it would have depended on how those interactions had gone. If the cultivators had been polite, he expected he would have let it go. If they had been more like the majority of cultivators Sen had encountered over the years, he probably would have turned the whole thing into a bloody, painful object lesson before *helping* that cultivator leave town. If that help resulted in them bouncing down the stone road for half a mile, that would have been very sad. For them.

His spiritual sense told him that the three had hesitated briefly, then hurried after him like ducklings chasing their mother. Now, they were walking along in his wake. Several times, he heard one or another of them take a breath like they intended to speak, only to change their minds at the last second. He led them out of town and to the practice hall. Sen had told the townspeople to take a day off, so there wouldn't be any interruptions of this meeting unless something big happened. Although, with Uncle Kho and Auntie Caihong nearby, Sen felt a certain swell of pity for any spirit beast foolish enough to come looking for trouble. Uncle Kho would likely destroy it from a distance with lightning just to make sure the spirit beast didn't disrupt whatever fun he and Auntie Caihong were having with Ai and Zhi.

Sen had initially felt like he was taking advantage of the elder cultivators since they always offered to look after the girls when he had something to do. When he'd suggested that he could take the girls for a day, he'd been met with such plaintive, hurt looks, that he'd felt compelled to explain that he didn't want them to feel like he was using them. That had immediately soothed their feelings.

Then, Auntie Caihong had metaphorically patted him on the head, told him he was a good kid, and shooed him out to go be productive. So, he had gone and fetched the cultivators who had been hanging around and acting like a mental lodestone for him. He took them inside the training hall, cycled almost unconsciously, and gestured. Three stone chairs rose from the floor. He turned to face them and sat. A fourth stone chair rose up to catch him.

"Sit," he said.

The three cultivators traded glances before taking seats. Sen looked them over. They all had the air of perpetual youth about them that made guessing their actual ages problematic. The one to the left was a young man with intelligent, dark eyes, and odd, short-cropped hair that looked more red than black. To Sen, he felt like he was somewhere in late foundation formation. Sitting next to him was a positively tiny woman. She was so small that Sen might have mistaken her for a child if he'd been distracted. The chair was big enough that her feet just sort of dangled over the floor. He frowned and concentrated for a moment. The chair slowly reduced in height until her feet could rest comfortably on the floor. She inclined her head to him in thanks. He judged that she was hovering at the cusp of qi-gathering and foundation formation.

He turned his gaze to the last person and found himself grateful that there was at least one man in the trio. The woman in that chair looked at him with defiant blue eyes. He'd heard about blue eyes, light hair, and extremely pale complexions. He knew that they were more common beyond the Mountains of Sorrow. He'd just never seen them before, let alone all on one person. It was almost jarring and might have even left him off-balance if not for seeing Falling Leaf's eyes so often over the years. She was the only core formation cultivator in the group, which suggested that she was much older than the other two and probably much older than Sen himself. He let the silence drag out for an uncomfortably long time, just to see how they'd react. The man and the tiny woman both started to fidget, but the blue-eyed woman never twitched. She just waited.

"Why are you here?" Sen asked.

The other two gave the blue-eyed woman surreptitious glances, clearly expecting her to take the lead in whatever discussion was about to happen. She didn't disappoint them.

"I am here to learn from Judgment's Gale," she announced.

"Really?" said Sen.

"Yes," she answered, confidence incarnate.

"And did he invite you?" Sen asked in a dangerous, casual voice.

She faltered at that. The man turned a shade of green, while the tiny woman seemed to be trying to make herself even smaller. Splotches of red appeared on the blue-eyed woman's cheeks. It was a bit of a relief for Sen since it suggested that there might be a human being in there somewhere if he dug deep enough. He just looked at her and waited for an answer. He wasn't about to let her off the hook.

"No," she admitted.

"Yet, here you are. Here you all are. I won't lie to you. The only reason you're sitting here right now is that you behaved politely in town. This place is, for the moment, my home. I am protective of it. I have no tolerance for cultivators who believe that being cultivators gives them a right to abuse mortals. I have exceedingly limited tolerance for cultivators who believe that being in a sect makes them special. Any attempt to abuse the mortals here or to force those of a lower cultivation to do *anything* they do not wish to do will have lethal consequences. Have I been unclear in any way?"

The core cultivator and the red-haired guy both looked a little stunned as they shook their heads. The tiny woman, on the other hand, looked ecstatic, as if she'd gotten great news that she hadn't expected. Sen continued.

"I said all of that for a reason. I'm about to tell you things you don't want to hear. So, I wanted you to understand what happens if you make a bad decision afterward. Despite what you may think, I'm not starting a sect. Nor do I expect that I will ever *want* to start one. I am also not interested in taking on disciples."

"But... But I am very skilled," objected the blue-eyed woman.

"Of course, you are," said Sen. "You're a core cultivator. You don't reach the core formation stage if you're incompetent. I'm not making a judgment on your worth as cultivators. There are a hundred sects out there that will be happy to do that. I'm informing you that no one who comes here looking for cultivation instruction will get it from me."

The red-haired man finally piped up and swept his arm around at the training hall.

"Then, what's all this?"

"This," mused Sen, "is an academy. Or the beginnings of one. It will serve to train mortals and cultivators in the fine arts of wielding spears and jian."

"Just weapons? No cultivation?" asked the tiny woman, finally deciding to join the conversation.

"Just weapons," agreed Sen. "Or, for you, I suppose just the jian. Even with cultivator strength, I don't believe a spear would serve you particularly well."

The red-haired guy snickered a little and whispered, "Spears aren't for tiny people."

The tiny woman's cheeks went bright red with either anger or embarrassment, and she stared down at her lap. That lasted until Sen let his auric imposition crash down on the man. He looked at the panicked face of the man who was struggling to draw so much as a breath beneath that crushing force.

"Her size is a fact," said Sen. "A fact over which she clearly has no control. Your rudeness is entirely a choice. One with which I am *wholly* unimpressed."

He turned his attention to the tiny woman who was staring at him like he was some kind of hero. He inclined his head to her.

"My apologies," said Sen. "While you may not get what you wanted by coming here, you most certainly didn't come to be insulted. Since it happened in my training hall, I will see to it that you receive appropriate compensation."

"Thank you," said the startled tiny woman.

Sen noticed the blue-eyed woman was watching all of this with keen interest. He finally turned his gaze back to the red-haired man, who was turning dark red. Sighing, Sen lifted the auric imposition. The barely conscious man slid out of the stone chair and lay on the floor gasping for breath. They all waited with varying degrees of interest while the red-haired man regained his breath and composure. Rising, the man cast a fearful look at Sen before turning to the tiny woman, clasping his hands before him, and bowing.

"I offer my sincerest apologies. I spoke carelessly and callously. It was unkind. I beg your forgiveness."

Sen was impressed with that apology. There was no way to know what motivated it, but it sounded sincere. The tiny woman looked a little flustered by the words, but she managed a nod.

"Of course," she murmured.

After the red-haired man sat again and refused to meet anyone's eyes, Sen continued.

"I'm still deciding on exactly how I'll decide who can and can't join the academy. For the moment, I'm allowing any mortal or cultivator to join, assuming they have the strength to actually wield the weapons. The fees for cultivators are substantial since they require training from other cultivators. Cultivators that I must recruit and pay. While I don't expect any one student to bear those costs alone, the fees will be in line with the costs. I may reduce those fees based on students providing other services."

"Such as?" asked the blue-eyed woman with a suspicious look.

"We're relatively deep in the wilds here. This town may be

more or less safe from spirit beast attacks. It doesn't mean others are. Cultivators can move fast enough to provide aid in an emergency if we can figure out a way to get messages between towns fast enough. The town can use a sturdier wall. Cultivator strength would speed up the process of building one. Things like that."

"Oh," said the woman, looking almost confused. "How practical."

"My grandmother is a strong advocate for practicality. Now, the three of you know what is and, more importantly, what is not on the table. You can make your decisions accordingly."

The red-haired guy almost ran for the door as soon as Sen finished speaking. The tiny woman went to leave, but Sen waved her over. She approached nervously like she wasn't sure what to do or say. He led her away from the blue-eyed woman who seemed intent on staying and talking more.

"There's still the matter of compensation for the insult," said Sen. "Is there anything in particular that you need? A cultivation resource for your breakthrough, perhaps?"

"I... I just... I don't know," she said, looking like she was on the verge of tears.

Sen frowned before a possibility struck him. "No master to guide you?"

"There was a woman, in my village, that taught me some things. But I'm farther along than she ever got."

Sen nodded. "I see. So, now you're in the world trying to figure out your path forward. May I examine your dantian and channels?"

The woman blushed like Sen had suggested something altogether different.

"Alright," she squeaked.

It barely took him three seconds to learn what he needed to learn. Her dantian and qi channels looked to be in good condition. Whatever the woman from her village had taught her, it had been sound. She was focused mostly on water, but he thought that she had some affinity for wood as well. He resisted the urge to give her advice and then thought better of it. He could blatantly ignore his own rules this one time because of what that fool had done. He also saw that all it would take to push her from qi-gathering to foundation formation was the tiniest nudge. He could make her something right here that would do the job. He nodded, mostly so she'd have some sign that he was done.

"You're familiar with tribulations?" he asked.

She looked very, very nervous at the word. "Yes. The heavens send lightning to test you?"

"That's more or less true," said Sen as he pulled out his pot and created a stand from stone for it to sit on. "There are some things you may not know about but should. Tribulations are most common at the transition between major stages of cultivation, like the one you're at. Tribulations *don't* happen every time someone moves between stages. I've been through several advancements where there was no tribulation. The lightning also isn't the same for everyone. The heavens adjust the tribulation to your advancement. If you're strong and your early foundations are good, which yours are, it's highly probable that you'll survive one."

As he spoke, Sen created fire beneath the pot and began summoning things from his storage ring. He realized that he hadn't been using alchemy to make anything new for a long time now. He missed it. He also saw that his words had helped to sap some of the fear in the tiny woman's expression. Sen thought that ignorance about something like the nature of tribulations was probably almost as dangerous to a cultivator as having a shoddy foundation. He chose the ingredients he used with care, striking a balance between wood and water qi-attributed plants and reagents.

"You may also be under the impression that you must choose only one qi type and focus on that," said Sen. "That's patently untrue."

He held up his left hand while using his right to continue stirring what was in the pot. Over his left hand, a ball of water appeared, followed by a sphere of fire, then shadow, and then lightning.

"That focus on only one kind of qi is traditional but not a requirement. You have a natural water affinity, but you also have a wood affinity. Don't discard that second affinity unless you have no interest in it."

The tiny woman was staring at his left hand in pure awe, and even the blue-eyed woman had moved closer at that display.

"I don't know any wood cycling techniques," said the woman.

"They're simple enough to find," said Sen, focusing on the pot for a moment to allow his intuition to guide the process more fully. "I'll find one for you. Consider it part of your compensation."

Satisfied that what he'd made would be enough to push her into foundation formation and maybe help her along a little, Sen removed the pot from over the fire that existed only because he wanted it to. He bled the heat from the elixir and filtered the final product through a cheesecloth and into a stone vial. He sealed the vial and handed it to the woman.

"That should be sufficient to move you into foundation formation," he said.

"What about the tribulation?" she asked.

"There's no predicting them, but you should take that elixir away from buildings and other people. I can't interfere with a tribulation. When you're ready to take that, though, I can go with you away from town. Make sure nothing interferes."

The woman wore such a look of profound relief that it made Sen uncomfortable.

"Thank you!" said the tiny woman.

"You're welcome," said Sen.

Seemingly at a loss, the tiny woman bowed and hurried away, cradling the vial in her hands. Sen turned to face the blue-eyed woman.

"Yes?"

"Some might say that was excessive compensation for the insult."

Sen shrugged. "I can compensate her as much as I feel is necessary."

"That was a kind thing you did for her."

"Which part?" asked Sen, reaching down to pick up his pot.

"All of it."

Sen looked up, but the blue-eyed woman was already gone.

CHAPTER FORTY-SEVEN

ACADEMY, PART 5

S oon Zi Rui's heart still thundered in his chest as he fled from the training hall. Never before in his life had he been so casually suppressed by another person. It had been an astonishing display of raw, unknowable power that would have been even more impressive if it hadn't been directed at him. He didn't even have a name for *what* Judgment's Gale had done to him, let alone an inkling of *how* the man had done it. That pressure had been all-consuming, like a mountain had taken a personal dislike to him, compressed all of its weight into one spot, and dropped it on him. It wasn't just the incredible pressure, or the fact that he couldn't breathe, but that his qi had been utterly stilled inside of him that had been so terrifying. He couldn't have fought back. Not that fighting would have proven any kind of challenge for Judgment's Gale. That much was obvious. Whatever that technique had been, it hadn't taxed the man at all. He'd simply carried on talking with the others.

However, that pure inability to put up even a token resistance had shaken Soon Zi Rui to the core. He had been completely helpless, his life hanging on the whim of a living legend who was *not* legendary for his forgiveness. He'd been surprised, not to mention thankful, when he regained himself enough to realize that the crushing, existence-ending pressure had lifted. Not that he could really remember what happened at the end. Had one of the others intervened? Convinced the blue-robed titan to stay his wrath? Or had Judgment's Gale simply lost interest? Soon Zi Rui just didn't know and didn't dare to ask. The insult had been stupid. He hadn't thought about it. He'd just said it, the way he'd said similar things a thousand times before. Except, the other thousand times, it hadn't been met with the instant arrival of death held in abeyance by only a hair's breadth. He'd offered an apology because it was deserved, and also because he had no desire whatsoever to test the patience of that man a second time. Such a mistake could only lead to certain, dishonorable death.

For all that, he hadn't been barred from entering the strange academy Judgment's Gale meant to open. Even if Soon Zi Rui couldn't receive direct instruction about cultivation, even learning about the sword or spear from the man would be valuable in ways that would last the rest of his life. It was a risk worth taking. He just needed to be mindful of his tongue. Ruthless. Implacable. Deadly. Those were the words spoken about the man, and he was exactly what Soon Zi Rui was expecting.

Mo Kai-Ming left the training hall in a daze of wonder. She stared down at the vial in her hands, almost refusing to believe it. The key to foundation formation, to a new world of possibility, a key that eluded her for years, now sat in her hands. She hadn't known exactly why she'd sought out Judgment's Gale. Mostly, it had been desperation. She'd tried a few times to join sects, but they all wanted people who could fight as well as cultivate. She'd never learned to fight and knew that it would never be one of her strengths. Physical size mattered less and less as cultivation progressed, but she was a qi-gathering cultivator. The lowest rung on a ladder that stretched to the impossibly distant heavens. They were expected to fight with swords or spears or other things she'd never so much as touched in her life.

What did a woman from a tiny village know about weapons? There had only been two bows in the entire place, both of them owned by the Ku family. Those hulking men had been the village hunters. They were stern and dutiful, but she would never have dared ask them to teach her to use the bow. She wasn't sure she could have drawn one of them even *after* becoming a cultivator. It had been something of a game at the autumn festival for people to try their hands with those bows. She had watched grown men, men made strong by the backbreaking labor of farming, fail to draw those strings back. No, she had no business even trying. Not knowing anything about true violence, she'd tarried in her village long past the time her teacher had told her she needed to venture into the world to keep growing. The world was vast and filled with dangers she did not feel equipped to face.

With each passing year, though, she'd felt something in her diminish. She didn't know what, only later learning about the idea of momentum, but she felt it leaving. It was that mysterious, diminishing commodity she couldn't name that had finally forced her to leave, to seek out sects, and be summarily dismissed by them. It had been humiliation after humiliation. Mocked by those set to test applicants. Mocked by those in towns for her size. And when it wasn't humiliation, it was attacks. She had learned about violence the hard way and learned that everyone can drown if you try hard enough. When she'd had all but decided to return to her village, she started to hear strange stories about some impossible man. A righteous man who battled evil and cured the sick, working miracles with both blade and alchemy. She'd clung to those stories, the hope they gave her, and sought him out. She'd chased those stories for years and finally, *finally*, she'd found him, only to find herself hesitating. What if he said no? What if he mocked her? She'd been trapped in indecision until he took the decision from her hands.

Then, as if she was living in one of those fantastical stories, he had worked miracles before her eyes. Judgment's Gale had come to her defense, chastised that other cultivator so severely for his mockery that she wondered if the man would ever utter another insult in his life. He had taken her aside, been so polite, and then crafted the elixir right in front of her. There was always some battered pot in the tales, although she hadn't believed that part. But the stories were true! He had used a battered old pot to make something that was absolutely bursting with qi. Such a thing could have commanded a price beyond her life, and he'd just *given* it to her. All while casually telling her things about tribulations and affinities that no sect member or other wandering cultivators would tell her. He'd even proven his words by using several types of qi in front of her. As if all that wasn't enough, he'd promised to find her a wood cycling technique and watch over her while she broke through. Kind. Generous. Honorable. Those were words used to describe him, and he was exactly what she expected.

Sua Xing Xing walked away from the training hall with only one thought circling in her mind. *What in the thousand hells did I just witness?* She had come here filled with confidence. She had heard the stories. It seemed that everyone knew someone who knew someone who had met, or been saved by, or been killed by, or been blessed by Judgment's Gale. Judgment's Gale, the eccentric cultivation genius who wandered the land doing whatever he wanted and surrounded by powerful, beautiful women. It had been so obvious, so clear to her, that she had formally withdrawn from her sect to come and find him. After all, with his reputation, why would he say no? She was powerful. She was skilled. She was beautiful, refined as she had been by cultivation. She was exactly what he looked for in companions. She had left her sect knowing that she would find him, be accepted by him, and stride in the wake of his greatness straight into the nascent soul stage. She had been so *sure*.

When she'd first arrived, Sua Xing Xing had simply assumed he would seek her out. He had to know she was there. She hadn't done anything to hide her presence. So, she had waited. As one day turned into two, and days turned into weeks, her confidence ebbed. She felt him, sometimes, coming and going. Every time, her hopes rose, only to be dashed as that presence passed her by. Again, and again, and again. She'd been contemplating whether it was time to leave when he had walked into the common area of the inn, bathed in absolute assurance. When he had pointed at her, it had felt like lightning was coursing through her body. *Finally*, she had thought. That electrifying moment had been short-lived, as he had pointed at the other two hopefuls that had been staying at the inn. She hadn't bothered to learn their names. Why would she? A qi-gathering cultivator and foundation formation cultivator? They were beneath her.

She had still been invited to join him, and any trivialities like other cultivators could be overcome easily enough. She would win him over. Except, that had failed utterly. Not only was he not impressed, *at all*, by sect cultivators, he had barely even looked at her, let alone been charmed by her beauty. If anything, he seemed annoyed by her presence. That series of revelations had made her blush in embarrassment. She had remained quiet, looking for a way to regroup, while the eccentric man described his plans to open an academy to train people with weapons. She couldn't fathom why he would want to do such a thing. Then, that fool had tossed off an insult to the little qi-gathering cultivator and everything had changed.

Up until that moment, Judgment's Gale had given off an almost feline quality of lazy indifference. The moment that insult left the foundation formation cultivator's lips, the laziness vanished, and he was focused like a raptor. She'd felt what he did then, even if she couldn't quite believe it. It was a complicated technique, the kind of thing that involved the soul, and she hadn't believed that such things were even possible before the nascent soul stage. And he'd made it look *easy*. As that technique nearly ended the life of that insulting fool, the name Judgment's Gale took on a new reality for her. She was watching as he passed judgment on someone, and it was, well, it was thrilling. It was also petrifying because it was very clear that he took all of what was happening for granted. Then, he dismissed them.

The foundation formation cultivator ran for his life, which Sua Xing Xing thought was an indication that the man might survive to see core formation. She had resolved to stay and see if she might find some other path into his good graces. Once again, he ignored her, choosing to speak with the little qi-gathering cultivator instead. Being in a room with that man was proving very hard on her self-worth. It was still a fascinating exercise, though, as he used the excuse of the insult to do exactly what he said he wouldn't do. He provided the little woman with cultivation instruction, while simultaneously performing a feat of alchemy crafting that should have been impossible given the ridiculous pot and the absurdly short amount of time he spent on it. Even so, she could feel the strength of that elixir from across the room. She didn't know how he had done it, but he had made that woman a cultivation resource that bordered on being too potent. He had been masterful, powerful, focused, and utterly uncompromising. He was not at all what she expected.

SEN TOOK a moment to store his alchemy pot and restore the training hall to its original condition. Then, he turned and looked at a particular shadow.

"What do you think?" he asked.

Falling Leaf stepped out of that concealing darkness and looked toward the door.

"About what?" she asked.

"Should I let them join?"

"The man is a fool, but most men are. If you refuse to train foolish men, you will have few students. The little one will love you forever. I don't know if that will make her a good student or a bad student, but she'll be a loyal student. The pale one—" she trailed off.

"Yeah," said Sen. "She's trouble. I'm just not sure what kind of trouble."

"She has an agenda."

"I expect that almost everyone who comes here will have an agenda."

"True," agreed the ghost panther, "but her agenda is you. She means to have you."

Sen started to say something funny, but the words died on his lips when he saw Falling Leaf's hands were balled into tight fists. They were balled so tightly that he saw blood dripping from them. She turned to look at him. There was something lethal, primal, and fundamentally inhuman in that gaze.

"She means to *keep* you."

Sen considered that look for a moment before he answered.

"I guess she'll just have to live with the disappointment of that failure."

CHAPTER FORTY-EIGHT

ACADEMY, PART 6

I *guess it's for real now*, thought Sen. All along, he'd thought of the academy as something of a safer middle ground and a half-baked idea that he could abandon at a moment's notice if it seemed like too much trouble. Once he'd decided to accept students, though, the hypothetical nature of the academy became a fixed reality. Not that everything had gone smoothly. Word had slowly spread to nearby towns and villages that there was a place to learn how to fight, which had meant a steady trickle of young men toward the academy. While Sen was aware that fighting was largely considered a man's job outside of the Jianghu, he also knew that it wasn't just men who wanted to learn *how* to fight. He'd made visits to some of those villages with Li Hua and Falling Leaf for practical demonstrations. Li Hua had been decidedly nervous, while Falling Leaf had found the entire exercise to be hilarious. After the pair of them had embarrassed the local village men to the point of coughing up blood, Sen had made the announcement that his academy was open to any man or woman who wanted to learn. It hadn't changed the numbers a lot, but some women had started to show up.

He'd also been vexed by the problem of money. Not that

money was an actual problem. He could probably run the academy out of his own funds for decades. He just didn't want to. The problem was figuring out what to charge. He was intentionally charging any cultivators who showed up what most people would consider extortionate fees. It served the dual purpose of scaring away people who weren't serious, while also letting him pay Wu Meng Yao. He still needed to find someone else to handle teaching spear forms to the lower-level cultivators, who would also need to be compensated. The problem was that he was negotiating the extortion on a person-by-person basis. Painfully expensive to someone like Mo Kai-Ming was, he knew from experience, nothing to someone like Sua Xing Xing. Just as what would be nearly unpayable by a mortal wouldn't have made Soon Zi Rui blink. Sen thought that he'd just have to settle on a number for lower-level cultivators and leave negotiating to the core formation cultivators he'd have to train personally.

On the other hand, he wasn't extorting the mortal students the way he was the cultivators. This academy had mostly been created as a way to help them defend their towns and villages. Even so, he had to charge enough to at least cover the cost of their food and hire people to prepare the food. He had considered just giving people raw ingredients a few times a week, but a few conversations with would-be students put a swift end to that plan. Auntie Caihong might have made sure that *he* knew how to cook, but it seemed that most of the young mortal men were helpless to make anything beyond tea. Plus, he had to give some consideration to the more talented townspeople he'd picked for more advanced training. They were tasked with teaching new students. The time they spent teaching was time they weren't spending on their actual professions, which meant he needed to pay them enough to make up that difference. In the end, he didn't care if the place made money, but he did want it to make enough to be self-sufficient.

At least Uncle Kho solved the heating problem, thought Sen. It had been instructional for Sen to watch as a problem that had vexed him for months took the elder cultivator less than an afternoon to solve. Sen saw it as the difference between talent and experience. He was good with formations and could intuitively improve them, which gave him a lot of advantages. But he didn't have thousands of years of experience dealing with problems ranging from the purely mundane to the mind-bendingly difficult. Not only had Uncle Kho solved it, but he'd also solved a problem that Sen hadn't been thinking about. High summer heat. While the stone he used to make buildings wouldn't absorb heat quickly, it would build up over time. So, rather than try to adjust the heat based on the weather, Uncle Kho just devised a formation intended to keep the temperature inside the buildings at a fixed point.

Of course, that simple-sounding solution had been both hideously complex in the details and a pain to implement. Sen had needed to create the actual formations inside the walls of the buildings. More specifically, he'd needed to add layers and layers of interlocking formations into the walls and then seal them up. The sheer complexity of those formations had taxed the upper limits of his understanding, as well as his abilities. He read that as just one more sign that he was nowhere even close to done learning about formations. Sen and Uncle Kho had taken a trip deeper into the wilds to acquire more fire-attributed treasures and some ice-attributed treasures. The formation could draw on those when the weather turned especially cold or hot. Then, Sen had needed to create special chambers beneath the buildings to house the treasures and contain their extreme heat and cold, which had turned into a secondary formation project all on its own. The good news was that unless something managed to damage the walls of the building, the system should function without any need for maintenance until the natural treasures ran dry. Sen estimated that would take at least a hundred years unless something drastic changed with how the weather worked.

However, the big picture details had slowly been dealt with or handed off, and training had begun. Of course, that had become a whole new pile of details to worry about. While the townspeople might only train a couple of hours a day, Sen didn't want the other mortal students left with lots of free time to wander around town and make trouble. They needed to have things to do, all day. Preferably things that would tire them out enough that only the most ambitious would inevitably get caught up in some romantic entanglements. The last thing Sen wanted was a string of angry parents showing up to scream at him because their daughters or sons had gotten a little *too* friendly with a student who was going to leave in six months or a year. So, he had them do what he had done while training. He made them run. When they weren't running, they were training. When they weren't training, they were reading. Getting enough of the same scrolls for that had taken a trip to the capital and an obscene amount of gold to hire people to rush the copying. Sen had just paid for that and considered it an investment in future sanity. The students who didn't know how to write were put in classes to learn. Then, they ran some more. The schedule was brutal enough that Sen actually worried it might prove too much for some of the older people who turned up looking to learn or to improve their skills.

Of course, he'd had to recruit more people to oversee all of those things. He'd been able to find a few in the town. There was an old man who couldn't handle physical labor anymore, was bored out of his mind, and had no sense of humor. He did, however, possess the ability to write. So, Sen hired him to teach people to write. It had gone on and on, and he'd thought it would never end. He found himself grateful that he didn't need to actually sleep every single day. Between dealing with academy problems, his own training, and being around enough that Ai didn't simply forget about him entirely, sleep was a high luxury. But, like all enormous tasks, the work did eventually come to an end. That was how he found himself standing near a building in the large complex of buildings that now comprised the academy just watching the mortal students grow increasingly winded as they ran.

"Is the grand and mighty patriarch deciding which of the children to cast out?" asked Shen Mingxia as she came over to stand next to him.

Sen rolled his eyes.

"I don't actually have anything to do at the moment," he told her.

"That sounds unlikely."

"I know. I didn't believe it myself at first but here we are."

"Don't you have a little girl to take care of?"

"Uncle Kho and Auntie Caihong are watching her. By watching, I naturally mean planning how they'll keep her."

Shen Mingxi gave him a sharp look and asked, "Really?"

"No," he laughed. "Well, probably not."

"So, instead of sleeping, or cultivating, or doing anything even remotely productive, you're watching people run?"

"They're only running because I said they had to. It only seems fair that I watch them do it from time to time to make sure I don't accidentally kill one of them."

"You're not pushing them that hard," said Shen Mingxia.

"Not if they were cultivators, but those are mortals. Things that a qi-gathering cultivator would shrug off in a few days could cripple one of them for life."

"Couldn't you just give them one of your healing elixirs?"

"Yes, but the goal is to train them. Crippling injuries run counter to that goal. Admittedly, there will be some injuries when they're learning the spear or jian. It's unavoidable. If they're collapsing from exhaustion during a run, or damaging their muscles and joints, that's not training."

Shen Mingxia frowned. "I guess I do take fast recuperation a little for granted."

"It's not just you. I expect most cultivators do that. I know I've let myself take injuries to achieve victory because I knew I'd recover."

"Wu Meng Yao did say something once about finding you battered, bleeding, and unconscious in a crater."

"I was *napping*," said Sen.

"In a crater?"

"It was a very comfortable crater."

"Was it?" asked Shen Mingxia with a skeptical expression.

"Not at all. I was in a lot of pain."

"Well, since you've got the time to chat about crater naps, don't you think it's time we talk about that flower you've been keeping in your storage ring?" .

Sen looked at her blankly for a few seconds before it came back to him. "Oh yeah! We should definitely do that."

CHAPTER FORTY-NINE
CONSULTATION

Sen led Shen Mingxia over to the building where he kept most of the people who dealt with problems he didn't want cluttering up his day. It seemed like there were more of them in there every day, some of them he had no memory of hiring, which made putting names to faces more than a challenge. As they walked through the space, Sen noticed that almost everyone was wearing a shade of blue similar to the robes he wore. It looked uncomfortably like a uniform to him. Everyone bowed and greeted him, which made him grind his teeth, but he knew that trying to put a stop to it would just create more problems. So, he endured it. Shen Mingxia looked around at the bowing people and gave him an arch look.

"Yeah, this isn't anything like a sect," she whispered.

"Thank you for that *very* helpful observation," said Sen as he led her to what had become, mostly by accident, his working space.

He summoned chairs from his storage ring for them both and sat down. Shen Mingxia looked around at the completely barren room before turning a questioning gaze on him.

He sighed. "I used this room a few times, so everyone just thought it was mine. Now, nobody comes in here except me."

"You should get a table or something. It's kind of creepy when you come in and it's just stone. Looks like a place you might take someone to make them vanish forever."

Sen looked around at the room. He supposed it did sort of give that impression.

"I'll get a table for it eventually," he said. "Now, have you decided what you want in general terms? Immediate advancement? Future improvement? Stronger affinity?"

"What would you do?" she asked.

"What would I do, or what would I recommend that you do?"

"Is there a difference?"

"There is a very big difference."

"Alright," said Shen Mingxia, her expression thoughtful. "What would you do?"

"Nothing," said Sen.

"I don't understand. You'd do nothing with the flower? Like, you'd save it for something?"

"I meant a little more generally. If I had the chance to push my cultivation forward or expand an affinity or basically any of the options you have, I'd choose none of them. And to answer your next question, it's because I don't want to advance my cultivation, and expanding one of my affinities would be more of a distraction than a benefit. If anything, I want to slow my advancement, not speed it up."

Shen Mingxia was very quiet for a time before she said, "That's a strange attitude for a cultivator."

"Probably. But that's where I'm at. So, that's what I'd do."

"That's not what you'd advise for me, though."

"No. You seem to be advancing at a perfectly sane pace. Faster than most, based on what I've heard."

"Not as fast as you or Wu Meng Yao."

"I'm a freakish anomaly who had advancement forced on me more often than I sought it out. I can't guess the details. In fact, you'd probably know better than I would, but I have to assume

Wu Meng Yao had some lucky encounters. Maybe found a few natural treasures along the way."

"She did," admitted Shen Mingxia.

"Then she's a poor example to measure yourself by. Lucky encounters and the right natural treasures have a way of unnaturally speeding advancement along."

"Natural treasures like the flower."

"Exactly like the flower."

"So, you don't think I should use it to advance?"

Sen leaned back in his chair and frowned up at the ceiling for a moment before he answered.

"There's so much a person doesn't know when they start out cultivating. So many things that are almost impossible to explain until someone is there. For example, it's hard to explain how important your own thinking, self-knowledge, and intuition are to the process. So, let me ask you this. Do you feel like you still have momentum?"

Sen watched Shen Mingxia wrestle with that question. She seemed to go back and forth with it before she finally gave a reluctant answer.

"Yes."

"You wanted to say no, didn't you? So, you'd have an excuse to push for advancement now?"

"Yeah," she admitted.

"Why didn't you?" asked Sen. "I wouldn't have known the difference."

"One, I don't believe that for a second. Two, lying to you probably wouldn't lead to good advice."

"Fair. Now, here's a harder question for you. How sure are you that you'll reach core formation?"

Shen Mingxia took much, much longer to contemplate that question. It was also clear that she didn't feel nearly as certain about her answer when she finally gave one.

"Pretty sure."

"Are you saying that because you believe it or because you were told by someone that you could?"

"Does it matter?"

Sen nodded. "A bottleneck can be mental or emotional. It's not just a question of accumulating enough qi to do it. If that's all it took, everyone would fly through these advancements. If you don't think you can or should, or if you think you don't deserve it, you'll never advance. You won't *let* yourself advance."

"Did that happen to you?"

"No," admitted Sen. "But I was trained by people who have watched hundreds if not thousands of other people fail advancements. They explained it to me. I'm willing to take it on faith that they know what they're talking about."

"I guess if anyone would know, they would."

"I have, however, been through the advancements that you're working toward. I can tell you now that you need to know, in your soul, that you're going to advance. If you have doubts, you'll hesitate at a crucial moment and the whole thing will collapse. Admittedly, a failure to advance from foundation formation to core formation isn't a complete catastrophe. At least, it's not from a pure cultivation perspective. The failed core will simply dissolve back into qi in your dantian."

Shen Mingxia gave him a hard look. "But? I assume there's a but."

"But the failure has a way of undermining people's confidence. The way I understand it, the number of people who succeed on second or third attempts at core formation is—" Sen paused. "Let's say that the number is very low and leave it at that."

Sen gave her time to think while she chewed on her bottom lip in a way that looked painful to him. It got bad enough that he worried she might draw blood. She finally looked at him again.

"So, are you going to tell me what you would recommend?"

"If you're hoping that pushing an advancement now will give you confidence later, I'd recommend that you dispel that notion.

Advancement doesn't change who you are, what you think, or how you feel. It only changes what you can do. At best, it'll give you a bit of false confidence that won't survive the first challenge."

"That isn't what I meant," complained Shen Mingxia.

"I know. Here's my recommendation. You need to *decide* if you're going to become a core formation cultivator or not. I'm talking about a true decision one way or the other. If you decide that becoming a core cultivator is something that will absolutely happen for you, then I'd recommend having me make something that will aid in that advancement. If you decide that foundation formation is as far as you're going to go, then ask me to make something that will help you make the most of what foundation formation has to offer."

Sen could see the disappointment on her face, even though she nodded.

He gave her a mildly chastising look and asked, "Were you hoping that I'd tell you to go with the elixir that would help in the advancement to core formation? Use that as a confirmation that you would make it?"

Shen Mingxia averted her eyes. "Maybe."

"Sorry. If I thought that would work, I'd have done it. Unfortunately, no one can really decide your path for you. Not in cultivation. I don't know if it matters to you, but I've seen you practicing since you've been here. Your foundations are solid. Your control is good. I think you *can* reach core formation. You have what you need on the cultivation side of things. Whether you *will* advance is in your hands."

Shen Mingxia huffed out a breath and said, "You certainly talk like a sect elder."

Sen put on a wounded expression and pressed a hand to his chest.

"There's no call to be mean."

The foundation formation cultivator snorted and looked around at the empty room again. She shook her head.

"Seriously. Get a table in here. Maybe pile up some scrolls on it. It would help a lot."

"Fine. I'll get a table," said Sen, who cycled for earth and made a stone table rise up out of the floor behind him. "Better?"

Shen Mingxia gave the table a dubious look. "Well, it's a start, I guess. Maybe you could make it look a little nicer."

"I'll make that my project when I have free time again next year. This brief window of idleness can't possibly last."

"Why is that?"

"Because the universe hates me."

"What? Do you think that a messenger is going to show up and tell you that the king wants to see you?" asked Shen Mingxia with a laugh.

Her laugh slowly dwindled at the aghast look on Sen's face.

"Why?" he asked. "Why would you ever even put that idea in the air?"

"Come on. That's not going to happen."

Sen stabbed a finger at her. "When it happens, you're coming with me. Because you have to know that the universe is going to take that last comment as a challenge, and you've now sealed it as absolute fate."

Shen Mingxia rolled her eyes. "Okay, let's say that by some cosmic twist that it does happen, why would you take me along?"

Sen gave her a wolf's smile. "So that you too can experience all of the exquisite joys of spending time in a room full of nobles and royals. Since you've opted not to join my academy, you can think of it as an alternative learning experience."

"When you describe it like that, it doesn't sound like a good thing. Thank goodness that'll never happen, right?"

Before Sen could answer, the door cracked open a little. "Patriarch?"

Sen had to resist the urge to strangle the man through the door for calling him that.

"Yes?" he called out.

"There's a messenger to see you. From the capital."

Sen glared at Shen Mingxia who was staring at the still mostly closed door with a mix of utter disbelief and pure horror writ large across her features.

"This is your fault," he hissed at her. "Pack for a trip."

CHAPTER FIFTY
SHIELD

The messenger was ushered into the room, and the immediate look of fear on the man's face told Sen that Shen Mingxia was right. The room was too stark and foreboding to be somewhere that good things happened. Those realizations simply furthered his intention to let her think that this whole thing was her fault. He knew, in his heart of hearts, that wasn't the case. In fact, he'd been expecting something like this for a while. Not that he planned to tell her any of that. Why waste a golden opportunity to mess with the woman in a way that didn't involve her fearing for her life? The look on her face had been downright hilarious. It had been so hilarious that it took a monumental effort not to laugh. Sen had risen to the occasion and kept a straight face. Laughing would have given the game away.

Still, Sen couldn't tell himself that he was surprised that someone had shown up looking for him. He'd been in and out of the capital a few times in the last year and had not stopped in to see anyone but Lo Meifeng. He hadn't even gone to pick up the formation flags he'd commissioned. Plus, by now, rumors had to have gotten back to the city about where he was in general, and that some blue-robed lunatic was starting some kind of organization out in the wilds. Maybe a sect, maybe something else, but probably something that should be paying taxes. There was going to be a *line* of people in the capital wanting to ask him questions, with the king at the very front of the line, followed closely by some sect patriarchs and at least one sect matriarch. To Sen's way of thinking, if *he* had to go deal with that nonsense, he might as well share that experience with other people, and Shen Mingxia had been in the room.

Sen and the messenger sort of looked at each other expectantly for a while before Sen realized that the other man wasn't going to break the silence first. Sen just wasn't sure what he was supposed to say. He studied the messenger, who was wearing robes of dark red and black, but Sen didn't see anything that looked like a crest or sect emblem.

"I'm Lu Sen," he finally told the messenger. "You have a message for me?"

"I do," said the man.

The messenger reached into a pouch and withdrew an extremely ornate scroll case that Sen recognized. He'd gotten one like it before from the, then, Prince Jing. *I guess that solves that mystery*, thought Sen. He took the scroll case and nodded to the messenger.

"Thank you."

The messenger got a very uncomfortable look that told Sen he'd forgotten something.

"I'm sorry," said Sen. "Am I supposed to pay you?"

"No. I am well-paid by my employer. It's just—" the man hesitated.

"It's not going to get easier to say if you wait another ten seconds," Sen told him. "Out with it."

The man winced a little and said, "I'm to wait for your response and return with it immediately."

"Of course, you are," said Sen.

Then, just to make sure she knew that he hadn't forgotten

about her supposed role in this social disaster, Sen gave Shen Mingxia a narrow-eyed look. She flushed a little and averted her eyes. Sen broke the seal on the scroll case, opened it, and removed the scroll inside. Unrolling it, he swiftly scanned the contents. It was filled with a mountain of formal language that Sen boiled down to a handful of quick sentences.

I'm having a thing for important people. Don't be an ass. Show up.

Jing

Sen considered the scroll for a while before he suppressed a groan. *No wonder he told the messenger to get an answer*, thought Sen. *He must have known that I would make a thousand excuses to not even open the scroll.* There was no getting around it. He would have to give the man an answer. As much as Sen wanted to say *no thanks*, he couldn't bring himself to do it. Jing was, at the end of the day, his friend. The man could have done a lot to make Sen's life hard. That he hadn't done any of them was something that Sen couldn't just dismiss. He looked at the messenger.

"Please inform the king that I will be in attendance. As will Honorable Shen Mingxia."

Shen Mingxia's head snapped up at that. He could see all the questions in her eyes, which he intended to ignore for the moment. Instead, he returned the ornate scroll case to the messenger, who tucked it back into the pouch.

"I will convey your message to his royal majesty," said the messenger as he offered a deep bow.

Sen nodded in acknowledgment and the man swiftly departed. Sen turned his gaze to Shen Mingxia.

"You're off the hook for the moment. We have a few weeks until we need to leave. We can push it to a month if necessary."

While that news seemed to provide a tiny bit of relief to the woman, she still looked unhappy.

"Honorable Shen Mingxia?" she asked. "What was that about?"

"People keep giving me stupid titles. I should get to do it once in a while. At least yours is accurate."

"I don't know about that," objected Shen Mingxia.

"Well, I do," said Sen, waving away her denial. "Bring your nice robes."

"How nice?" demanded Shen Mingxia with a look of panic on her face.

Sen offered her a blank look. "Very nice? Nice enough for an event at court."

Shen Mingxia pointed at the scroll that Sen still held in his hand.

"Can I see that?"

Sen handed it over. Shen Mingxia grew paler and paler the longer she looked at the scroll. Sen wasn't sure why she was so worked up about it. Compared to his last visit to the palace, this should be a bloodless affair. Apparently, that didn't matter, because she looked up from the scroll to glare at him.

"You can't take me to this," she insisted.

"Yes, I can. Besides, I already said you were coming."

"This is a *formal* event. Representatives from foreign kingdoms will be there."

Sen frowned at her for several seconds. "No, I'm still not seeing the problem."

"This is the kind of thing that, I don't know, sect patriarchs go to. Not a foundation formation cultivator from a middling sect in a middling city. I don't belong there."

That was enough to send Sen into fits of laughter.

"You don't belong there, but I somehow do?"

"You're, well, you. You're famous."

"Yeah," said Sen, "and isn't that just a gift that keeps on giving. Let me put this another way. You're talking to someone who spent his childhood eating garbage, actual garbage, from behind restaurants in a nowhere town. I trained on a mountain with people old enough to remember all the names of the kingdoms this kingdom used to be. My only real friend for that entire time was a spirit beast. Exactly how do you think that I'm better equipped for this than you are?"

"Garbage? Really?" asked Shen Mingxia.

"I'm glad to see that you're staying focused."

"I'm just trying to imagine you doing that. It's not an easy thing to picture."

"My point is that you're as competent to be there as I am. And you don't have a choice."

"What? Why?"

"You know why."

"You can't still be blaming me for this," complained Shen Mingxia. "Do you think the universe just conjured that messenger out of nowhere solely to mess with you?"

"I'd give it even odds," said Sen. "Plus, you're my shield. If someone is already coming with me, then no one will try to *arrange* for me to take them."

That drew a particularly bland look from Shen Mingxia.

"Thank you, oh mighty Judgment's Gale. Nothing adds a bit of romance like telling someone they're a utility object."

That caught Sen a little off guard. He weighed the unintentional insult he'd delivered.

"I'll buy you some nice robes to wear. Will that help to make up for my charmless comment?"

"They better be *very* nice. You know how shields are. We just don't perform as well when you don't treat us properly."

"This is going to haunt me for a while, isn't it?" asked Sen.

"That depends on how often you swing this poor foundation formation shield into the path of danger to spare yourself."

"You could have just said, yes."

Shen Mingxia giggled. "I could have, but then I wouldn't have gotten to see that look of pain on your face. Don't worry. I'm sure it won't take me more than ten or fifteen years to forgive you."

"Fifteen years!"

"It's expensive to get to core formation. I can't let a resource like you off the hook when you just give me that kind of leverage."

Sen snorted. "If I thought you meant that, I'd be checking to see if you're actually a nine-tail fox."

"You could have at least pretended to be worried. And, if I were a nine-tail fox, I'd make myself way prettier than this."

Sen caught himself before he said anything and directed an unamused look at Shen Mingxia.

"Looking to see if I'd give you more leverage?"

"You can't blame a shield for trying."

CHAPTER FIFTY-ONE

SHADOW WALKING, PART 1

S en pushed, and pushed, and pushed to suffuse his body with shadow qi. After months of effort, he finally felt like he was teetering on the very edge of success, like all he needed was one last infinitesimal iota of strength, one last smidgen of insight, and he would finally achieve victory. However, it seemed the strength was not in him. That insight was elusive. He felt suspended there as if he were a rope bridge pulled taut between opposing sides of a deep canyon. He could touch both sides but was a part of neither. As the moment stretched out, the very fibers of his being almost hummed under the strain of maintaining the effort. *I'm missing something*, thought Sen. *I know it. I can feel it.* There was too much resistance. Back on the mountain, what felt like several lifetimes ago, he would have tried more brute effort in his ignorance. Even back in the capital city when he and Lo Meifeng had been trying to escape from Tong Guanting, he had pushed his *hiding* ability beyond its limits and suffered for it. Fortunately, experience was the most fundamental of all teachers.

He knew that he might be able to dredge up a last bit of strength and force the technique to work. If his life had been on the line, he might have even done it. The costs be damned. Forcing things to work the way he wanted them to, though, was not a winning strategy. When he'd first started using his qinggong technique, it had been hard, very hard, but not because the technique was resisting him. It had been hard because the qi costs were so high. He had improved that technique with finesse, incrementally growing more efficient with it until, now, he harbored the suspicion that it would take a nascent soul cultivator to match his full speed. He needed to borrow from that experience to figure this out. Where was the resistance coming from? Where were the inefficiencies? Was the problem his entire approach?

Sen had relied on the age-old wisdom his teacher knew best until he had evidence otherwise. This was the approach that Fu Ruolan had provided. He had worked with it and worked with it, only to meet with failure. Had she, however unintentionally, led him astray? A mental head shake cut that line of thought short. *Start with the simplest explanation*, he reminded himself. The simplest answer was that he was the problem, not the approach he had been provided. He did his best to solidify his tenuous grasp on the technique and turned his attention inward. He watched the shadow qi course through his channels, dark as the void itself. He followed the qi as it bled out of those channels and entered his muscles, bones, and organs. He drifted with the qi as it spread out and approached his skin and... Understanding bloomed.

Shadow might exist under the heavens, but it carried more in common with the void, with nothingness, the very antithesis of the eternal heavens. Based on the way the divine qi in his skin was reacting, shadow qi was a barely tolerated stepchild. The shadow qi was trying, and failing, to cover over the nodes of divine qi that lived in his very skin. The divine qi was continually shredding the shadow qi to let its own light blaze, even if it wasn't visible to the eye. *No wonder I haven't run into any shadow cultivators*, thought Sen. If he had to guess, he would expect that they faced obstacles that people who cultivated other qi types simply did not. If nothing else, the heavens might simply weed them out with particularly brutal tribulations.

As much as Sen loathed his tribulation experiences, he wasn't foolish enough to think that the heavens had truly tried to kill him. It was a test. A means to discover if cultivators possessed the skill and the will to endure the demands of the next stage. The survival rate of tribulations said it all. Yes, some people died during tribulations, but they were the exceptions rather than the rule. But if the heavens *wanted* to kill people with tribulations, it wouldn't be that difficult. Send a tribulation with the strength normally used for the next stage, and the cultivator *would* die. Of course, Sen recognized that he was just speculating. It was just as possible that there were so few shadow cultivators because most people had no affinity for it. Having witnessed what was happening in his own body undermined his confidence in that possibility, but he couldn't reject the notion outright. Whatever the actual answer was, he'd have to put aside looking for it for now. It wouldn't help him solve the problem in front of him.

He needed to suppress the divine qi's natural reaction to shadow qi. Somehow. This was a demand wholly outside of Sen's experience. Cultivation was all about working with the natural tendencies of a qi type. You didn't call up wind qi and then ask it to stop moving. You didn't summon water qi and expect it to leave things dry. Complicating the problem was that he couldn't simply discard the divine qi the way he might with qi that he had cycled to produce. It had been... Sen struggled to find the right word to describe what had happened. He supposed that it had been *cooked* into his very body. It was literally part of him now. That idea brought him up short. *It is a part of me, isn't it? I can tell other parts of me what to do*, he thought. *Maybe the same is true here.* Rather than try to think of some complicated cultivation solution to the problem, he treated it more like he would if he wanted to slow down his heart. It wasn't quite an active, conscious process, but he could do it.

He bent his attention to getting the divine qi to stop interfering with what the shadow qi was doing. The divine qi threw up immediate resistance to the idea, but he kept focusing, almost yelling at the divine qi to just let it happen. Slowly, *reluctantly*, the divine qi slowed and finally stopped shredding the shadow qi that got near it. The shadow qi slid over those divine nodes and that terrible resistance he'd been struggling against simply vanished. It was so abrupt that he almost lost control of the technique. Pride and happiness swelled inside of him at succeeding where he had failed so often. That glorious moment was cut short as a sensation of falling backward was accompanied by an almost panicked shout from Fu Ruolan.

"Wait!"

Everything that Sen had been sensing in his environment with his spiritual sense disappeared in a blink. It was replaced by a world filled with things that felt insubstantial, like objects made of mist. It was a world where he feared any motion would punch straight through the membrane of reality. In short, everything felt *wrong*. His eyes shot open at the same time he lost his grip on the technique. He looked down at his own hand and watched as inky blackness receded to expose smooth, pale skin. The color in that skin jarred against the monochrome world around him where everything was a shade that sat somewhere on a spectrum between white and black. The total absence of color in anything except himself and his clothes was disorienting. That feeling was only made worse by the chaotic shapes that surrounded him that bore no resemblance to anything made by the hand of man. It made him want to squeeze his eyes shut to deny the sheer alien nature of the place any hold in his psyche. The only thing that kept him from doing exactly that was the warning that Fu Ruolan had given when she first started him down this path. He only had so much time before this place would start to kill him.

He shook off the disorientation and looked around. He was standing in a wedge of bright white that looked like, well, it didn't really look like anything. It was just a bizarre shape with hard edges. *That must be how the shadow I was in was shaped on the other side*, he thought. He was relieved that he hadn't done something stupid like start walking around. He'd do that eventually, but not when he'd come here by accident. Even his natural curiosity was hiding in a hole somewhere, not even remotely interested in exploring this unsettling place. Focus, he ordered himself. He worked backward this time and focused on suppressing the divine qi first and then suffusing his body with shadow qi. It was still hard. Every new technique was like that at first. He was sure that as he developed experience and strength, it would grow easier. Even so, it no longer felt like he was trying to lift an impossible weight over his head and keep it there. By contrast to what it had been like, this felt easy to him.

He watched with an almost detached interest as that inky blackness covered his skin again. Casting one last look around and shuddering, Sen stepped into the wedge of whiteness and stumbled back into the Fu Ruolan's home. He instantly released the technique, not wanting to chance an accidental return to that awful place. He stared around him, drinking in the familiar shapes and colors, and was overwhelmed with a sense of rightness restored. He took a few heaving breaths and then forced himself to calm down. He was back. He had made it. Everything had worked out.

"Well," said Fu Ruolan, "that was a stupid thing to do."

Sen huffed out an almost involuntary laugh. "You say that like I did it on purpose."

The nascent soul cultivator gave him a deeply suspicious look. It was clear that she didn't believe he'd accidentally moved between planes of existence. He wasn't sure that he would have believed it, either, if he was in her shoes. The first thing most cultivators did when they figured out a new technique was use it. It was the only way that Sen knew for someone to master a new technique. Of course, most techniques didn't come with the serious risk of being trapped in some awful other place where nothing made sense, everything felt wrong, and staying too long meant your likely destruction. That kind of deadly risk was usually enough to make even cultivators wary about experimenting too much, at least without experienced guidance. After studying him briefly, Fu Ruolan seemed to conclude that he wasn't outright lying to her. He had to think that his near-immediate return and manifest happiness at being back probably lent his words some credibility.

"You made it work. Congratulations," said Fu Ruolan without much enthusiasm.

"You don't sound that happy about it."

"Of course, I'm not happy about it. Do you have any idea how long it took me to do that for the first time?"

Sen could almost feel the jaws of doom closing around him at that question. He just couldn't see a way to avoid them.

"A month?" he ventured, hoping that massaging her pride might help.

"A month? A month, he says. Not all of us are cultivation geniuses kissed by the heavens like you," said Fu Ruolan, even as Sen felt those jaws locking tight. "Try *two years*."

CHAPTER FIFTY-TWO

SHADOW WALKING, PART 2

S en realized that there was absolutely nothing he could say to make things better. All he could do was make things worse. So, he said nothing. Better by far to just let her get whatever it was out of her system. Especially since he was pretty sure her instability came from not getting things out of her system a thousand years ago, or whenever the bad things happened, and keeping them locked inside her for centuries. With nothing but time to fester and a decided lack of people in her life to talk to, it was no wonder. So, rather than become another figurative or literal heart demon for her, Sen decided the smart and possibly honorable thing to do was just stand there and *take it*. None of which made it fun. Fu Ruolan stormed back and forth, gesticulating wildly when she wasn't pointing at him, and generally spewing frustrations that Sen had a feeling were only partly to do with him.

"Unbelievable. *Unbelievable*! Countless years of alchemy. Investing in the best components available. Doing everything as meticulously as possible. What does that get me? Competence. I'm competent. And then along comes Judgment's Gale, swaggering through the world, and throwing whatever comes to hand into his stupid, old, battered *pot*! And what comes out? Genius! Impossibly potent elixirs! Pills to make the heavens tremble. Not because he's earned it. Not because he's that good. No! It's just because he's lucky! Falling into the hands of not one, but three other geniuses who just poured knowledge into you like the empty vessel you are.

"As if that's not bad enough, then you show up at my door. I think that this is my chance to see what you're really made of. Is any of it you or is it all them? And you pick up shadow walking in six months. Six months! I did it in two years, and my master thought I was made of brilliance. And you do it in six months while you weren't even really trying! No, it wasn't enough to master a technique designed for nascent soul cultivators. You also found time to raise a little girl, train locals to fight, and start a damn school! It's not fair!" she almost screamed, before her voice fell into a hushed whisper. "It's not fair."

Fu Ruolan stood there, fists clenched by her side, and breathing through clenched teeth for a while before she slumped. While a lot of that had stung Sen's pride, something else was more important. At no point during that rant did she ever lose control of her killing intent. Granted, it was one time losing her temper and she might have been making a conscious effort to keep a grip on it, but Sen still took it as a good sign. When it looked like the full fury of the storm had passed, Sen finally spoke.

"Feel any better?" he asked.

Her shoulder twitched in something that might have been a shrug before she added, "Yes, actually. I do feel a little better."

"In that case, I think I'll head out for the day."

"No. Did you think I missed that look on your face when you came back? You'd do almost anything to never go back there. If I let you leave now, you never will go back. Shadow walking is too useful to let you ignore the skill out of foolish fear. No, we're going into that realm."

"That's really not necessary," said Sen, lifting a hand and taking a step back.

It wasn't that he thought she was wrong about him or his reaction. He agreed with her. He *would* do anything to avoid going back to that place and was completely fine with that outcome. That other place was simply horrible. He'd gotten along just fine without shadow walking until now. All of the other nascent soul cultivators he'd met had gotten along fine without out. His *hiding* skill was practically shadow walking already. Sen felt confident that he could live without it and never feel as though he'd missed out on anything. Why torment himself by going somewhere he didn't want to go when he could just *not*? However, he could see from the stern expression on Fu Ruolan's face that she would not be moved by such arguments. She would just say that enduring pain was part of cultivation, and she'd be right.

He couldn't even argue that it would be needless physical pain. It was just mentally taxing and emotionally jarring to be somewhere that felt so fundamentally off from all of his expectations. That didn't stop him from a mad mental scramble to try to find some kind of argument, any kind of excuse, that might convince the nascent soul cultivator that they didn't need to go there right that minute. *Or any minute, ever*, thought Sen. Try as he might, though, Sen came up empty. The real problem was that he didn't have a good reason. He just didn't want to go because the place made his skin crawl. That might be a sufficient reason for him, but it wouldn't satisfy Fu Ruolan. He did consider just fleeing. His eyes drifted to the door even though he knew that wouldn't work. Sen remembered how easily Fu Ruolan had locked him down when he'd let his killing intent get out of control. He could run, but he couldn't escape.

"Fine," he grumbled.

Fu Ruolan arched an eyebrow. "I thought you'd run for sure. You've got that look in your eye."

"We both know it wouldn't work. So, let's just get this over with."

"You think we're only going to go in the one time, don't you?"

"Yes. Why?"

"I hope you didn't have anything important planned for this afternoon."

Sen gave much more serious consideration to running, but he eventually realized that would just end with him having to enter the shadow realm tired. Sen's head dropped a little as he accepted the inevitable.

"You go first," said Fu Ruolan. "I'll follow."

Turning around and trudging back to the shadow, Sen prepared the technique. When he was ready, he stepped through. The shadow realm was just as bad the second time as it had been the first. The only real difference was that he didn't have shock to help shield his mind from the utter otherness of the place. It scraped against his psyche like claws against stone. He grit his teeth and turned to watch as Fu Ruolan entered the realm. What he could see of her skin was the same inky black color that his skin turned. In other circumstances, he'd have found watching that black bleed away a mildly nauseating experience. It seemed to sink into her like some kind of parasite. In the shadow realm, it didn't even make an impression because that looked almost normal in comparison to the mishmash of unrecognizable shapes and the absence of colors. Fu Ruolan's lack of obvious distress only made things worse. He wanted her to be as profoundly unsettled as he was. Instead, she just settled a steady gaze on him.

"What now?" he demanded.

"We just wait," she said.

"For what?"

"For you to adjust or for our time here to run out."

Sen was not at all surprised that their time ran out before he adjusted. Or Fu Ruolan's time ran out. He still felt fine but wasn't about to tell her that. He feared that she would make him stay there while she left. As much as he disliked her for making him come back to that place, he was grateful that she was there to provide at least one touchstone of a familiar reality. He was almost stepping on her heels when they left. He fervently hoped that it would be a long time before they could go back, but it turned out that the nascent soul cultivator only needed about ten minutes before she was ready to go again. And that was how he spent a very long afternoon. Moving in and out of the shadow realm, over and over again. The worst thing of all was that Fu Ruolan had been right. Sen couldn't pinpoint a moment when it happened, but there did come a time when going into the shadow realm no longer made him immediately want to rip out his own eyes. Not that the change made him hate the place any less. It just made him slightly less miserable to be there.

Fu Ruolan took the time to make tea and the pair of them sat there, drinking their tea in total silence. Sen was doing everything he could to soak up the normal that surrounded him. He'd never been so in love with colors as he was in that moment. Never before had walls, floors, and ceilings seemed to possess so much divine grace. As for tea, tea contained in the achingly familiar shape of a cup, that was a miracle to be treasured in his heart until the end of all things. He just wanted to wrap his arms around everything that was as it should be and hold it to him. Of course, that blissful moment of peace couldn't last.

"You seem to have regained your composure," announced Fu Ruolan. "So, one last minor lesson, and then I'll set you free for the day. It's time that you actually do some shadow walking."

"We haven't been doing that already?"

"Technically, I suppose we have, but going into a shadow and coming out of the same shadow ten minutes later isn't particularly useful. No, this time, we'll go in through one shadow and come out of a different one."

"Why?" asked Sen. "I mean, does it make a difference to the technique?"

"It can. The strength of the shadow on this side can affect how accessible it is on the other side. We've been going through a fairly dark shadow. You can go in through and come out of less pronounced shadows, but it's more difficult. More dangerous. Pick the wrong shadow and you can lose a piece of yourself in the transition."

"Like what?" asked Sen.

"A hand. A leg. Your head," said Fu Ruolan without much apparent concern.

With that casual pronouncement, they went back into the shadow realm. Fu Ruolan started walking away, and Sen stuck close by, worried about being left behind.

"Right now, your main concern should be finding the brightest spots on this side. Those are the darkest shadows on the other side. They're the safest ones to use. Once you're comfortable with that, we'll move on to navigating to specific shadows," she said coming to a stop and looking around. "Pick one."

Sen looked around at the various shades of black, dark gray, light gray, and nearly white. He almost pointed at one extremely bright patch, but realized it was too small. He'd never be able to squeeze his body through. He searched the area again before settling on a swath of gray that was at least lighter than most of the others, although darker than the one they had come through. Fu Ruolan watched him with a perfectly blank expression.

"That one," he said and pointed.

"You're sure?" she asked.

He hesitated, firmed his resolve, and nodded. "Yes."

Fu Ruolan shifted her gaze to the spot, considered it, and then nodded. "Very well."

The inky blackness bled out of her skin and, without another word, she stepped through. Feeling more confident that he hadn't chosen wrong, Sen reactivated the technique. Having done it dozens of times now, it came faster and easier than before, although he suspected that it would never come quite as easily for him as it would for someone without divine qi in their skin. He stepped into the gray spot and immediately felt the difference between stepping through a truly dark shadow and stepping through a less well-defined one. He had to physically push almost twice as hard and dramatically increase the amount of shadow qi he was spreading throughout his body to get back to his world. Only when he was certain that he was all the way through and not in danger of losing body parts did he release the technique. It felt like someone punched him in the base of the skull the moment the technique was gone. He dropped to a knee and had to put a hand on the ground to steady himself. He looked up to see Fu Ruolan standing there, but she looked drained.

"That's why choosing the right exit is so important," she said.

Sen did not approve of that particular teaching method, but he had to acknowledge how effective it was. He now knew exactly how bright a spot needed to be for him to safely pass through. He also knew that he would work very hard to find much brighter spots in the future. It was only after a bit of controlled breathing, cycling a bit of healing wood qi, and finally downing a healing elixir that Sen could really take in his surroundings. They were outside of Fu Ruolan's house and had come out through the relatively dim shadow of a tree. Pushing himself to his feet, Sen debated simply walking away. He wasn't going back into the shadow realm again that day. He knew it, and he figured that Fu Ruolan knew it as well.

As if reading his thoughts, she waved a hand and said, "We're done for the day."

Sen took a few steps before his conscience got the better of him. Going through that shadow might not have been as bad for her as it had been for him, but he doubted she would have picked it herself. He summoned one of his best healing elixirs, one he thought might provide benefits to nascent soul cultivators, and held it out to her. She eyed the stone vial for a moment before she accepted it. She didn't hesitate to drink it, either, telling Sen that the trip back hadn't been fun and games for her.

"Thank you," said Fu Ruolan.

After she turned and walked back toward her home, Sen turned the other way and started the much longer trip back to his. And if he glared at some of the shadows he walked past, he felt fully justified.

CHAPTER FIFTY-THREE
THUNDEROUS SKY

Sen was in the middle of jian training with Sua Xing Xing when he felt the approach of several cultivators. Cultivators that he didn't recognize by feel. Cultivators that even he might feel inclined to acknowledge if his initial impression of their strength was accurate. That was always a little dodgy at a distance. While cultivators arriving at the academy wasn't anything new, he had a premonition that this was going to be different. Different good or different bad, he wasn't sure, but since cultivators were involved, he assumed it would probably be bad. Sen had only been half paying attention to his spar with the pale woman, idly staying a step ahead of her aggressive attack pattern while he weighed what to do about the new cultivators. He made a point to meet new cultivators, if only briefly, when they first arrived at the academy.

Sen decided that it was better not to break that pattern. With the exceptions of Uncle Kho and Auntie Caihong, he was best equipped to deal with it if hostile sect members or wandering cultivators showed up. He was also less likely than they were to simply kill those cultivators out of hand if they proved annoying. He'd worked hard to not lean on their reputations as much as possible. It seemed wise to continue approaching the world that way. While Auntie Caihong might let cultivators go if they bothered her, Uncle Kho would not. If he started reducing cultivators to ash left and right, Sen would never convince anyone that this place wasn't a sect. And if the other sects believed that Uncle Kho had finally, after thousands of years, decided to start his own sect with Sen as a figurehead... Sen didn't know what the other sects would do. Nothing good. He was sure of that much. Sua Xing Xing's voice snapped him back to the present.

"You could do me the courtesy of *pretending* that this requires your full attention," she said, stepping back and checking the edge of her jian before sheathing it.

"What?" asked Sen with a blank stare.

"Exactly," muttered the woman.

"Sorry. We have new arrivals. People I should probably greet in person to avoid any unfortunate incidents."

A hint of interest sparked in Sua Xing Xing's eyes. "More cultivators?"

Sen nodded as he sheathed his own jian. He didn't bother checking the edge. The blade had been stuffed with metal qi. He would have sensed it if the weapon had taken any damage. Walking toward the door, he called back.

"This shouldn't take too long."

She was walking next to him a moment later, having used a qinggong technique to close the distance. The woman gave him a little smile.

"Why would I intentionally miss out on this?" she asked. "It should be interesting if nothing else."

Sen considered ordering her to stay in the training hall he'd designated for cultivators. While she might be playing at just wanting to see what happened, it wasn't lost on him how it would look if she arrived with him. It would imply things to the cultivators about her position here, her relationship with him, or both. Those were all implications that didn't please him because perception had a way of becoming fact, and he hadn't decided what to do about her. He didn't want people assuming that they could influence him *through* her. On the other hand, the new cultivators were making their way toward the mortal training hall. Exactly where he didn't want them to go and interfere with people.

He decided to just let it go this time, mostly because he didn't want to take the time to argue with her. Seeming to sense his resignation, her smile widened just a little into something that bordered on self-satisfied. That almost made him change his mind then and there. Of course, they were most of the way to the mortal training hall by then. *Damn cultivator speed*, he complained to himself. As they neared the door, Sen saw three people who were all very obviously from some sect. They wore matching dark gray uniforms with yellow patterns stitched into them that resembled lightning. It didn't mean anything to Sen, but it clearly did mean something to Sua Xing Xing. The woman took one look, stopped short, and took a sharp breath. He gave her a look, but her gaze was fixed on the one who looked like he was in command. The one about to shove open the door. *Can't have that*, thought Sen.

"You aren't students here," said Sen in a qi-reinforced voice loud enough to make leaves shake free from nearby trees. "That building is off-limits to any who aren't invited."

The trio by the door turned to look at him. He braced himself for the usual young master posturing. Instead, the trio ignored him almost entirely while staring at Sua Xing Xing in open-mouthed shock. The leader, a handsome man with narrow features and piercing eyes took a step forward. He couldn't seem to rip his gaze away from the woman standing next to Sen. For her part, she had drawn herself up and was leveling a cool, dispassionate gaze at all of them.

"Xing Xing," said the leader in a soft, disbelieving voice. "You came *here*?"

"That is my affair and none of yours," she said in words chipped from ice. "You don't belong here, Sheung Tian Kuo."

"I don't belong here," said Sheung Tian Kuo in a low dangerous voice. "None of my affair? We were supposed to—"

"*Were*," repeated Sua Xing Xing. "No longer."

If this were happening almost anywhere else, Sen would have simply backed off and enjoyed the show. Unfortunately, it was happening at his academy with very fragile mortals far too close for the kind of destruction that would ensue if a fight broke out. Now that they were close enough, Sen could better judge the strength of the newcomers. In terms of pure spirit cultivation, Sheung Tian Kuo was actually sitting a little higher than Sen at true peak core formation. The pair who stood a respectful step behind were closer to Sua Xing Xing's level. All of which meant a lot of potential destruction if things turned violent. Given the way Sheung Tian Kuo was glaring and even shaking a little, that felt like an almost inevitable outcome.

"If the two of you have some personal matter to settle, do it elsewhere," said Sen in a voice that was more command than suggestion.

Sheung Tian Kuo turned his attention to Sen and fought a visible battle for self-control. It was a battle that he seemingly lost because the next words out of his mouth sounded almost designed to trigger an immediate duel.

"Do not speak to your betters until spoken to, you jumped up little nothing. The Thunderous Sky Sect goes where it will, when it will."

Sen's first instinct was to simply kill the man where he stood and be done with it. There was a theoretical gap between them, but Sen had bridged much bigger gaps than that. Plus, this place was *his* in ways that the newly arrived cultivators clearly hadn't discerned yet. On the other hand, the man was distraught. Sen didn't know the details but the broad strokes were clear enough. There was some kind of romantic history between Sheung Tian

Kuo and Sua Xing Xing. A romance that she had apparently ended, and he hadn't gotten over yet. Sen generally thought that how people acted under stress was often a better indicator of their true nature than how they acted while calm. However, it left the issue of how this might have gone down if Sua Xing Xing hadn't decided to make an appearance something of an open question. The longer Sen stood there, simply staring at Sheung Tian Kuo like some kind of undesirable insect that he'd stumbled across, the less certain the other man looked. It was like Sen's mere gaze held a weight that was slowly crushing the other man's confidence. It was Sua Xing Xing who finally broke the silence.

"Elder Yu would be *ashamed* of you."

Sen watched as those words struck the three sect cultivators like a condemnation from the heavens. Sheung Tian Kuo lost every bit of color in his face. The other two looked abruptly nauseated. Sen thought that he might want to meet this Elder Yu one day. A person who could evoke those reactions in core cultivators at the mere suggestion of their disapproval, well, that was someone formidable. That the elder would feel such disapproval at what Sen had come to think of as standard sect behavior also told him that the stories he'd heard that not every sect was a collection of useless, awful people might hold some truth. Sua Xing Xing continued without a trace of mercy in her expression. Sen stared at her as she seemed to become an entirely different person. A person he might actually be able to like a little bit.

"Using the honorable name and reputation of the Thunderous Sky Sect as a club. Seeking to disrupt the education of others. Hurling insults at your host. Have you forgotten *everything* that you were taught?"

Sheung Tian Kuo flinched back from the rebuke. He held out a hand toward Sua Xing Xing as if imploring her to stop. She was not moved. Her face was stone as the next words fell from her lips like an executioner's blade falling on the neck of a disgraced foe.

"You shame us all."

As Sheun Tian Kuo's face went a little slack and sweat broke out on his forehead, it was obvious to Sen that those two had been extremely close at some point. It was the only way she could have known exactly how to break the man with a handful of cold, precise statements. It also told him some things about her. Things that he wasn't sure how to interpret. At the very least, it was a statement about how completely she had severed that relationship in her heart. What she had just done wasn't something you did to someone you still cared about. At the same time, she seemed to be deeply concerned about how the man's actions would reflect on her old sect. That was a relationship that she hadn't severed so neatly. Sen took all of that as a warning not to put too much trust in her. Divided loyalties were a dangerous thing. As for Sheung Tian Kuo, he lowered his head, stared at the ground, and quietly mumbled to himself about honor and shame.

The other two Thunderous Sky Sect cultivators looked at each other for some hint of what they should do. Sen could just barely hear them conferring in hushed, frantic tones. Finally, one of the pair stepped forward. The man gave Sua Xing Xing an uncertain look while she continued to exude imperious displeasure and towering disdain. Seeing no shelter from the storm there, the man turned his eyes to Sen.

"This one is Lim Haitao," said the man, clasping his hands and bowing.

Sen gave the man an infinitesimal nod and said, "I am Lu Sen."

Lim Haitao straightened, but he didn't get a chance to speak before Sua Xing Xing spoke.

"He is also known as Judgment's Gale, the Heavens' Scouring Blade, the Hand of Chaos, and—"

"I'm relatively confident he knows who I am," said Sen, cutting off the litany of names.

"I beg the forgiveness of Judgment's Gale. This," said Lim Haitao with a helpless little gesture around him, "was not our goal or task. I ask that we be allowed to withdraw and tend to our brother disciple."

Sen considered those words for a moment before he asked, "And just what was your task?"

When he saw the man swallow hard, Sen just knew he wasn't going to like the answer.

CHAPTER FIFTY-FOUR

THE TRUTH

L im Haitao bent every last bit of his self-control on
maintaining a calm expression, yet, the question rang in
his ears like a death knell. *And just what was your task?*
The man called Judgment's Gale had asked the question in a
neutral tone. Too neutral. It was the pause before the club of
disaster fell to crush the unworthy beneath its uncaring might.
From where he stood, Lim Haitao felt decidedly unworthy, and
Judgment's Gale felt far too much like a hammer poised in the air,
simply waiting for the signal to unleash doom. He had harbored
the desperate hope that Sister Sua might intervene on their behalf.
She had left the sect, true, but on cordial terms. She had witnessed
the entire incident as well. He hadn't issued any threats or insults,
nor tried to use the name of the Thundering Sky Sect in an inappropriate way. Nor had Shao Anhe let foolishness slip from her
lips.

However, it seemed that mere association with Sheung Tian
Kuo had painted them with the same brush of guilt in Sua Xing
Xing's eyes. When he had dared to look at her, all he saw was cold
fury burning in her eyes. That meant that their only hope of
escaping from this unmitigated catastrophe rested in the hands of

Judgment's Gale. Except, that man had just asked a question to which Lim Haitao did not want to provide an honest answer. Not that he was prone to lying. Quite the contrary. The sect frowned mightily on dishonesty in all but the direst of circumstances. No, he contemplated lying because a true answer could only bring them closer to certain death. In any other circumstance, he wouldn't have been the one trying to save their lives. He wouldn't have spoken at all, except perhaps to introduce himself if things went smoothly.

Now, three lives hung on what he did next, and he had no idea what the right thing was to do. *Curse you, Sheung Tian Kuo,* thought Lim Haitao. *You and your stupid obsession with that woman has damned us.* When a look of mild impatience passed over the face of Judgment's Gale, Lim Haitao knew he had to make a decision. He resisted the urge to look back at Shao Anhe. She was no better prepared for this than he was. In the end, a lie was too risky, too easy to expose. It only took one slip of the tongue, one moment of carelessness, and whatever tiny shred of trust or credibility he and the sect might have with Judgment's Gale would evaporate. The truth would have to do. He just wished that he hadn't heard so many stories about the man who was staring at him. Stories that never seemed to end well for those who roused his ire. Gathering his courage, Lim Haitao spoke.

"We were sent to," he swallowed again, "inspect this academy."

The look of detached annoyance that Judgment's Gale had worn disappeared as something implacable entered his eyes. The man's lips compressed into a hard line, and it felt to Lim Haitao that the very air seemed to squeeze him in sympathy with the other cultivator's anger.

"Inspect," said Judgment's Gale.

It was the same word, but it wasn't. Lim Haitao had tried to make the word sound as mundane and innocuous as possible. Nothing that important. Just a boring little procedure that no one needed to concern themselves with at all. When Judgment's Gale said it, it sounded like a filthy obscenity that had been dragged up from the depths of a cesspit. It sounded invasive. It sounded unclean. It sounded like another step on a very short road to a cliff's edge.

"You came here expecting to simply walk into my academy and *inspect* things. You expected me to allow that?"

"Yes," said Lim Haitao, his voice a rasp of fear.

Judgment's Gale walked toward him until he loomed like a tower. *The stories never said he was this tall*, thought Lim Haitao, aware that fear was making him irrational but uncertain how to stop it.

"Tell me, Lim Haitao of the Thunderous Sky Sect, what would your elders do if I came to your sect and demanded to *inspect* it? Would they throw open their doors and divulge their secrets to me? Lavish me with gifts? Would they welcome my inspection with grace and provide me with a feast afterward?"

Part of Lim Haitao wanted to flee beneath that implacable gaze and those impossible questions. If it just meant leaving Sheung Tian Kuo behind, he might have even done it. But fleeing would also mean abandoning Shao Anhe, and she had done nothing to deserve being left to the mercies of this man. The problem was that he didn't even need to consider what his sect would do. He knew. The Thundering Sky Sect would never tolerate such a thing. The insult alone would demand an immediate and deadly response. It made him wonder why they had been sent here to offer a similar insult to a man known for taking vengeance. It seemed... It seemed inconsistent with the temperance that the sect taught from the very first moment someone entered as an outer disciple.

That realization begged an uncomfortable question. *Had* the sect sent them, or had Sheung Tian Kuo decided to come here for his own, rather obvious, reasons? Had the man somehow discovered the location of Sua Xing Xing and simply invented the inspection as an excuse to come find her? If so, why drag others down into the thousand hells with him? There was no way to know and no point in asking the fool who was still muttering about shame and honor.

"Well?" demanded Judgment's Gale. "What would they do?"

"They would demand your immediate death," said Lim Haitao in a hollow voice.

He never saw the man move. He only felt the hot spray of blood on his face. His heart stopped for a moment before he realized that the blood wasn't his. Lim Haitao turned and watched as Sheung Tian Kuo's lifeless body fell into several large pieces. Judgment's Gale looked down at what was left of one of the Thunderous Sky's most promising disciples, and then he looked at Lim Haitao. The man's expression hadn't changed at all, which sent Lim Haitao's heart to pounding. *Does he mean to kill us all?* There was no fighting power like that. Even if Sheung Tian Kuo had been sensible, he doubted that the results would have been any different. Sheung Tian Kuo had been a peak core cultivator, had moved and fought like one, which had made him extraordinarily dangerous. But he would have stood no chance against that kind of speed. Lim Haitao tried to steel himself, to face death with the bravery expected from one of the Thunderous Sky Sect, but he couldn't find that courage inside himself while facing down a man who found peak core cultivators easy prey. In the end, the best he could do was stop himself from visibly quaking in terror before the gaze of Judgment's Gale.

"This academy is not open for inspection," said the towering figure, who gestured toward the road with the still bloody blade in his hand. "Now go or I might decide to hold you all accountable for this insult."

Lim Haitao had to fight the urge to kowtow in pure relief. He fell into a deep bow instead.

"This Lim Haitao thanks the honored cultivator for his forbearance."

Shao Anhe copied him a moment later. He felt it as something in the air seemed to bleed away and a sense of impending death went with it. When Judgment's Gale spoke again, he sounded weary.

"Just—" he hesitated. "Just leave."

Shao Anhe fell into step beside him, and they did their best to maintain a shred of the dignity of the Thunderous Sky Sect as they walked away. At least, they did while Judgment's Gale and Sua Xing Xing could physically see them. The moment they passed beyond direct line of sight, the pair exchanged a look and, by unspoken agreement, they activated their movement techniques and fled at speed. They didn't speak or stop running for several hours, determined to put enough distance between them and Judgment's Gale that he would decide it wasn't worth chasing them down if he changed his mind. They eventually set up camp and started a small fire. Neither of them really needed the fire for warmth, but there was a deeper kind of chill inside Lim Haitao that the fire seemed to help stave off with its cheerful light.

Shao Anhe wore a troubled expression as she asked, "What will we tell the elders?"

"The truth," he said. "We'll tell them the truth, and pray to the heavens that they don't send us back there to die."

It seemed that idea hadn't crossed her mind, because Shao Anhe sat up straight and stared at him in horror.

"They wouldn't do that, would they?"

"We insulted a very powerful cultivator. A cultivator that I imagine the elders would prefer to stay on good terms with. Arguably, we shamed the sect. Is it that hard to imagine that they might decide that the best way to deal with all of those problems is to give us to him? Let him take his vengeance on us and good relations may be restored."

"We're core cultivators," she said in shock. "We're not that... That—"

"Disposable?" asked Lim Haitao.

"Yes!" shouted Shao Anhe.

"Normally, no, but these aren't normal circumstances. We're

talking about a man who could very well send The Living Spear to instruct our sect in what he sees as appropriate behavior. That instruction is likely to leave very little standing in its wake. Compared to a threat like that, what value is there in the lives of a couple of core cultivators?"

Shao Anhe didn't say anything, but he saw her eyes drift out to the road. He sympathized with what she was thinking, having thought something very similar not that long ago.

"I won't stop you," he said. "If you want to go, I won't stop you."

Shao Anhe didn't meet his gaze when she stood.

"I'm sorry," she whispered. "I won't let myself be sacrificed to make up for a dead man's stupidity."

Lim Haitao watched her disappear into the darkness and part of him wished he had the courage to join her.

CHAPTER FIFTY-FIVE

JUST A VISITOR

Almost the second they were out of sight, Sen mentally dismissed the two cultivators he'd let go. They might become a problem down the road, but the dead thing on the ground in front of him was much more likely to become a problem. It had been a situation without a way to win. If he simply let them all go, it would signal weakness. He'd find himself hounded by entitled cultivators who would think they could come to the academy and do whatever they wanted. The other path was no more palatable, it just offered the slightly better chance of preventing people from showing up and being insufferable. Still, it had been a while since he'd last had to kill another cultivator. He hadn't missed it. He didn't move or speak until Sua Xing Xing stepped close and reached toward the body.

"What in the hells do you think you're doing?" asked Sen.

She froze, straightened, and turned a very cautious look toward him. "I was just—"

"It was rhetorical," said Sen. "Nothing on that corpse belongs to you."

She shot him an affronted look. "If not for me, do you really think you would have won that fight?"

347

"If not for you, do you think there would have been a fight? Do you think they even would have been here? I don't."

Sua Xing Xing opened her mouth but couldn't seem to find an answer.

"As for your question," he said, "yes. I most certainly would have won the fight with or without your intervention. None of which matters to this discussion. I'm the one who did the killing, so I get whatever dubious rewards there are to have."

Sua Xing Xing's eyes drifted down to the jian Sen still held. She seemed to take it for an implicit threat, and Sen supposed that it probably was one. Her eyes moved from the sword down to the body. A flash of frustration crossed her face before she smoothed it to calm acceptance. Maybe the man had something that she thought was hers, or maybe it was something that she thought would embarrass her. Then again, she might have just known about a treasure he possessed that she wanted. Sen almost asked before he decided that he didn't care what it was. She wasn't getting it. He wasn't so foolish as to lay all the blame on her for the way things had gone. He sincerely doubted that she had come along for the express purpose of alienating those cultivators. That didn't change the fact that her mere presence had immediately and irrevocably escalated the situation. She wasn't getting rewarded for that.

Sua Xing Xing bowed and said, "As you say, patriarch."

Did he detect a bitter undertone to the word *patriarch*? Sen wasn't certain, but he wouldn't have been surprised. Core cultivators usually got what they wanted when they were out in the world away from their sects. *She'll just have to treat being shut down that hard as a new and novel experience*, thought Sen. There was a calculating part of him that hoped she would use this whole matter as an excuse to leave. It was, however, a dim hope. She might have seen all of this as an unexpected opportunity, but he doubted her failure to seize the opportunity would influence her long-term agenda. He gave her a flat look.

"I'm not a patriarch," corrected Sen. "This is an academy, not a sect."

"Of course. My mistake. I apologize, founder," she offered with a sickly-sweet smile before turning and walking away.

Founder was only nominally better than patriarch, but Sen lacked the mental energy to pick that fight. It just wasn't worth the effort. If she needed to poke at him to assuage her bruised pride, then so be it. Instead, he focused on the body. An examination with his spiritual sense and qi revealed three storage treasures, as well as an amulet that did... He could tell it did something. He pocketed all of them and took the man's sword. He'd have to look in the storage rings and maybe ask Auntie Caihong about the amulet, but that would have to wait. He didn't want the townspeople walking out of the training hall to find a dismembered body. Sen cycled for earth qi to open a deep pit beneath the corpse pieces. They dropped down into the hole, where he incinerated them until nothing but ash remained. He closed the hole and used a bit of wood qi to encourage a fast bit of minor plant growth. It would be obvious to everyone that something had happened there but the details should remain obscure.

Sen looked down and was surprised to find he was still holding the jian. He used a flash of intense heat to burn away the blood that still coated it. That kind of heat would have warped a mortal-grade blade or melted it outright, but it barely warmed the enhanced metal of a blade made for those in core cultivation. With a flick of his wrist, the ashes fell away from the jian. He sheathed it, and then tried to remember what else he needed to do. The altercation had pushed all other concerns out of his mind. He looked around at the buildings in a futile search for inspiration or maybe even just someone to ask where he was supposed to be right then. He was usually supposed to be *somewhere*. There was a telltale *tink* noise of something hard bumping against glass that drew his eye to one of the windows in the mortal training hall. He saw a cluster of faces pressed to the glass. When he turned his gaze directly on them, they all disappeared with varying looks of guilt, fear, and surprise.

Sen debated just going back to the galehouse. He didn't want to talk to the townspeople, or the small band of cultivators who had joined the academy, or anyone else who saw him as a cultivator first. He just wanted to see Ai and listen as she regaled him with stories about pictures she drew, or how she'd discovered some new bug, or how Uncle Kho had taken her flying. That wish was so powerful that he'd walked nearly twenty feet before he stopped himself. As much as he loathed the thought of explaining *anything* to *anyone* at that moment, he knew he needed to do it. Otherwise, rumors would spread. There were enough fake stories about him in the world already. He didn't need to add to that pile because he didn't feel like talking. Sen allowed himself ten seconds to just tilt his head back, look at the clear sky overhead, and take calming breaths. Then, he made himself walk to the doors of the training hall and go inside to do what needed to be done.

No one was training. People were standing around in small groups and, there was no other word for it, gossiping. A silent, awkward hush fell over the space when he entered. Everyone stared at him with all of their questions barely held back behind their teeth. That silent regard was damning. The day before, they would have asked those questions in a tumultuous upswell of incomprehensible noise. The day before, they saw him as, maybe not one of them, but not an incomprehensible and dangerous outsider either. Now, he saw the fear that held their questions in check. He wasn't Sen to them anymore. Now, he was a cultivator, or the founder, or —may the heavens shield him—the patriarch in their minds. A remote, distant power that might offer some level of protection and teaching, but one that might also turn on them in a moment of capricious malice.

Maybe this had been inevitable from the moment he started to train the townspeople. That distance between him and them wasn't just in their imaginations. He had avoided it recently, but a cultivator never truly escaped the Jianghu. It was always going to come looking for him unless he followed Fu Ruolan's example and hid himself away deep in the wilds. He'd let himself overlook the truth for a time, but he did live in a different world from the mortal townspeople. He was, as he had once told Jing, just a visitor in their world. And now his world had arrived on the doorstep of these mortal bystanders. He might not owe them an explanation, but they still deserved one.

"I'm sure you're all wondering what just happened out there," he said in a voice that even he thought sounded tired. "I'll tell you what I can."

So, he gave them an unvarnished, if incomplete, version of the facts. He omitted the information he'd inferred about the relationship between Sua Xing Xing and Sheung Tian Kuo. He also withheld his suspicions that this hadn't been a sanctioned action by the Thunderous Sky Sect. That was a different kind of rumor he didn't want spread around. If it hadn't been sanctioned and he kept that information from spreading, it could give him a bit of leverage if someone else from that sect showed up in some official capacity. If it had been sanctioned, spreading falsehoods was a sure way to *guarantee* that someone would show up with retribution in mind. No, silence on that matter only benefitted him and, while they'd never know, the townspeople. No one interrupted his explanation. When he finished, everyone held their tongues, proving to him that they saw him differently. Helpless to alter that change, he did the only thing he could. He lived up to their expectations.

"Return to your training," he ordered.

CHAPTER FIFTY-SIX

STARS

"They looked at me like a stranger," said Sen, trying to keep the hurt out of his voice.

Falling Leaf turned her head to peer at him for a moment before she went back to looking at the sky. They were sitting on top of the mortal training hall, which had long since gone dark and silent for the day as everyone went home. The stone remained warm beneath them, despite the unusual chill of the night. Sen had retreated to the galehouse after telling the townspeople what had happened with the sect cultivators. Always happy to discuss what she had done during the day, Ai had proved the balm to his soul that he'd imagined she would be. Her uncomplicated joy at everything from finding a pretty rock to experiencing the phenomenal powers of Uncle Kho and Auntie Caihong was a sharp and welcome contrast to the murky complexities of so much else in his life. For her, everything was simple, because everything was a miracle.

He had taken refuge behind the light of her joy for a time, and let it blind him to all else. But that kind of refuge was, by nature and necessity, a temporary one. After he had put her to bed and entertained her with shadows dancing on the wall, everything he'd been hiding from was still waiting for him. However, that brief respite had muted the sharp stab of immediate pain and allowed him to see it a little more objectively. It still hurt because he thought he'd made at least a few friends among the townspeople. That he'd pushed past all of the accumulated garbage that came with the word *cultivator* and been seen as a person. The deathly silence that greeted him inside the very training hall he now sat on had put the lie to that fantasy. Falling Leaf kept her gaze firmly fixed on the stars when she spoke.

"Did you imagine it would end any other way?" she asked.

The words were said gently, with kindness, but also with a tone that suggested she was not surprised. Sen grimaced.

"Yes. No. I just... I guess I just wanted it to," admitted Sen. "Was it too much to ask?"

"The Caihong tells me that those are made of fire," said Falling Leaf, gesturing at the stars. "She says that they are very far away, but burn so hot and so bright that we can see them here. She also says that many of them are so large that they could consume our world without even noticing."

Sen gave her a perplexed look, wholly uncertain where she was going with this talk of stars and fire.

"She told me the same thing."

"Campfires are also made of fire, yet you would not expect a star to be a campfire. Nor would you expect a campfire to be a star. They are the same, but they are also not the same. It shouldn't be a surprise when a person fails to mistake one for the other."

Sen gave Falling Leaf a wan look. "I take it that I'm the star, expecting people to see me as a campfire?"

She nodded. "You want the mortals to treat you like a mortal. Perhaps it's because you are still so close to your mortal life. Those memories are fresh enough, close enough, that they seem right to you. But you are not like them anymore. Expecting them to see you as one of them, to treat you as one of them is unfair. It's dangerous."

"What? What do you mean?"

"While you might welcome them treating you as ordinary, what other cultivator would? Do you imagine training them to treat cultivators with such casual disregard can end well for them?"

Sen had to swallow hard when he considered it from that angle. He hadn't looked at all the possible consequences. All he'd thought about was how much he hated the way mortals reacted when they found out he was a cultivator. Even worse, this was a lesson he should have learned long ago in Inferno's Vale. Hadn't the Matriarch of the Order of the Celestial Flame explained it to him? She tolerated all of the obeisance that she clearly despised because the alternative was *worse*. Falling Leaf was right. It would be dangerous for mortals to treat other cultivators the way he wanted them to treat him. It would get them killed. There were a few exceptions. Master Feng would probably find it amusing. Uncle Kho and Auntie Caihong might tolerate it within limits. Most cultivators, though, would see it as flagrant disrespect and a grave insult. The kind of insult that would justify murdering mortals who would otherwise enjoy the safety of being beneath notice.

"When did you get so wise?" asked Sen.

"Is it wisdom to see what is obvious?"

"If you expected all of this, why didn't you say anything?"

"Some things can be learned by example or explanation. Other things are only learned through pain. I could have told you. You might have even stopped. But you wouldn't have believed. This was something that you could only learn through pain," said the ghost panther.

There was a current of empathetic understanding in her voice that snuffed the dim flame of anger that Sen wanted to feel. This wasn't a sentiment that she had heard from someone. It was a lived truth for her. He didn't know which of her many difficult experiences she was thinking of right then. After a thoughtful moment or two, he realized it didn't matter all that much how she had come to that conclusion. She believed it with deep conviction. Sen leaned back until he flopped against the roof of the training hall.

"So, I just live with it?" he asked. "I just live with the fear, and the false respect, and kowtowing?"

"The respect doesn't have to be false. You can earn that. You *have* earned that from many here. As for the fear and the kowtowing... Yes, you just live with it. You live with it because that's what's best for these people. You can live apart, but they must live in the world as they find it."

"I hate it, you know."

"I know."

Sen rubbed his face with his hands in an act of mute frustration. *All this power*, he thought, *and I'm still helpless*. He once again imagined finding some mountain of his own and building a manor in the sky like Uncle Kho's. That particular dream felt both closer and farther away in ways he couldn't articulate, even to himself. Knowing that continuing the conversation would only lead them in circles, he picked a new topic.

"I'll have to head to the capital soon," he said.

Sen could almost feel the tension in Falling Leaf's body at the mere mention of the capital. While Sen had disliked the place, she loathed it with a near-religious fervor. He didn't keep her in suspense.

"You don't need to come."

She didn't collapse in relief, but he did hear her release the breath she'd been holding. Not that she was necessarily happy about the turn of events, though.

"Who will keep watch over you in that terrible place?" she asked with a guilty edge in her voice.

"I'm not expecting this to be a violent visit. And, if it does turn into that, I can always ask Lo Meifeng for help. She's not one to shy away from bloody business."

Falling Leaf nodded. "She is capable enough in a fight."

355

"And if things turn really, really ugly, I have one or two favors I can call in."

"The sects?"

"The sects," agreed Sen.

"Can you trust them?"

"I doubt it, but the people who matter owe me, and they know it."

"You mean to take the Mingxia with you?"

Sen snickered at the very thought. "I do."

"This is an unkind thing you mean to do," chided Falling Leaf.

"Probably," said Sen. "There is value in experience, though."

"Why not take the other one?"

"Wu Meng Yao? Mostly, it's because I need her here. Teaching. Someone needs to be in charge while I'm gone."

Falling Leaf made a dissatisfied noise. "And what about the *other*, other one?"

"I have no idea what to do with or about her."

"You could take her with you. Perhaps someone will kill her," said Falling Leaf with far too much enthusiasm.

Sen didn't particularly like Sua Xing Xing, but he definitely wasn't to the point where he was hoping someone would violently help her reach her next incarnation. She was outrageously selfish, self-involved, and arrogant, but that was an accusation that could be laid at the feet of just about every cultivator alive. Himself included. Aside from overstepping with the body of Sheung Tian Kuo, the woman hadn't actually done anything wrong that Sen knew about. She hadn't hurt or even been noticeably unkind to the townspeople. She hadn't destroyed anything that didn't belong to her. She'd abided by his rule that higher-level cultivators couldn't order around those with a lesser cultivation. It was just her personality. She *bothered* people, and Sen didn't think that should be enough to warrant death. Then, a notion struck Sen that he almost dismissed before he turned a gimlet eye on Falling Leaf.

"The reason you want me to take her along is so she won't be here to aggravate you, isn't it?"

Sen sat through a pregnant pause with his gaze locked onto the ghost panther.

"No. Of course not," said Falling Leaf in the most blatant and badly delivered lie he'd ever heard.

CHAPTER FIFTY-SEVEN
YOUR WORD IS LAW

"It's a protection amulet," said Auntie Caihong, eyeing the small object critically. "It's actually quite a good one. This would probably stop an attack from someone in the early nascent soul stages. Just one attack, mind you, but that can be enough to let you escape. Where did you get it?"

"I took it off that sect idiot I killed," said Sen. "Which sort of begs the question of why it didn't stop me from killing him."

Auntie Caihong handed the amulet back to him with an amused smile.

"You have to activate it. He clearly didn't."

Sen nodded in understanding. Sheung Tian Kuo hadn't been in a right state of mind to do anything as practical as activating some kind of protection. It did lead Sen to a different question. He looked at Auntie Caihong who guessed the question before he uttered the words.

"I guess none of us got around to teaching you about these things," she said, looking a little apologetic.

"Not so much, which is unfortunate. If I had known things like this existed, I'd have gone looking for one. I could have used something like this when—" Sen hesitated as a flood of memories where he was on the cusp of death passed through his mind. "I could have used about twenty of these."

"It's one of those things that we *should* have remembered to tell you about. Sadly, it's easy to forget about them when you haven't been able to use one in a thousand years. Once you become a nascent soul cultivator, there is a depressingly small number of people who can make those kinds of tools for you. The higher you climb, the fewer people there are, and the more likely it is that you'll have offended them at some point. Although, those kinds of permanent protection tools are rare even for lower-level cultivators."

"Why is that?"

"Because they're stupidly difficult to make," said Auntie Caihong with a laugh. "This is wildly inaccurate, but think of it like trying to set up a protective formation. Then, imagine squeezing it into that tiny amulet, and providing it with enough power to stop a strike from a lesser sect patriarch."

"Oh," said Sen, looking down at the amulet with new appreciation.

He thought, given enough time, he could set up a formation that would meet those requirements, but it would be big and complicated. It would take several layers to provide enough stopping power and cover the main types of qi. Then, there were the power requirements. It could be done using beast cores if he had enough of them on hand. Otherwise, he'd need to set up an entire, probably larger, secondary formation to gather environmental qi and feed it into the defensive formation. The idea of trying to do all that in something only slightly bigger than the end of his thumb made his mind reel a bit.

"They aren't *as* difficult to make for lower-level cultivators because, if you're handing them out, it's only meant for something in the next stage," offered Auntie Caihong.

"Right. You don't need as much power when you're dealing with a foundation formation cultivator's techniques as you do for techniques from a core cultivator. Still, how do they power them? That's the part I can't quite wrap my head around."

"I honestly don't know all of the details. Some of it is finding the right materials. We're alchemists, so we go looking for the right plants and reagents. Someone who makes these trinkets would go looking for the right metals and gemstones, I expect. If you start with something that already has powerful qi, it's a big shortcut. Beyond that, though, you're getting into the land of specialized techniques, processes, and secret knowledge. That's why sects are usually the only place you get things like that. They can recruit people with the right kinds of affinities and build a tradition inside the sect. It's also why they don't hand them out to just anyone."

"You said that you can *usually* only get them from sects. Why usually?"

"Oh, people find them in old ruins sometimes or inherit them from teachers. Those aren't the kinds of things you can plan for, though."

"In other words, don't just give it away?" asked Sen.

"Definitely not. It won't be useful forever, but it's certainly a useful toy for you to have for right now. Even if it just blunts an attack from a higher-level cultivator, as sturdy as you are, that might be enough to save you."

"Fair enough. Oh, is any of this of interest to you?" asked Sen.

He summoned a small pile of pills and elixirs that he'd found inside Sheung Tian Kuo's storage rings. While a few of them were interesting to Sen because they used strange ingredients, nothing had really stood out to him. Sen waited while Auntie Caihong frowned down at the pile and examined everything with her qi and her spiritual sense. She reached out and picked up one of the small vials containing one of the pills that used strange ingredients. She frowned at it.

"Now, this is interesting," muttered Auntie Caihong.

"It's odd, but isn't it just a healing pill?" asked Sen.

"Oh, the pill itself isn't that interesting. The interesting thing is that I know who made it, and they're supposed to be dead. Remind me. What sect was this cultivator from?"

"The Thunderous Sky Sect," answered Sen automatically.

"What were they doing here? That sect isn't even in this kingdom. They're in the far south."

Recognizing a rhetorical question when he heard one, Sen didn't interrupt Auntie Caihong's thoughts. She mulled over whatever problem was plaguing her before shaking her head.

"I suppose it doesn't matter for right now," she finally said. "Nothing that won't hold for a decade or two, at any rate."

"A decade or two?" asked Sen. "Isn't that kind of a long time for a problem to hold?"

"Maybe for mortals," said Auntie Caihong before giving him a grin, "or young prodigies. I can lose a decade on an interesting experiment. Why do you think other cultivators overreact every time a nascent soul cultivator makes an appearance? It's normal for them to disappear into secluded cultivation for decades or even a century or two."

"Not in the capital," grumbled Sen.

"Those sects are so big that they need a lot of active management and control. Smaller sects in more out-of-the-way places tend to roll along without as much direction from the top. Speaking of the capital, though, are you sure this little visit you're planning is a good idea?"

Sen huffed out a breath. "A *good* idea? Probably not. But I owe Jing. I caused a lot of trouble the last time I was there."

"Has it occurred to you that he may be planning to use you for some end of his own?"

"I'm sure that's exactly what he's planning to do."

Auntie Caihong gave him a look that was both stern and concerned.

"Cultivators and mortal politics don't mix, Sen."

"It's a little late for that. I already stuck my nose in. I can't pretend now that it didn't happen."

"Actually, you can do just that."

"I don't follow," said Sen.

"This is the problem with advancing as fast as you have. You skipped over learning a lot of lessons other cultivators take for granted. You are powerful, Sen. Frighteningly powerful for your stage of cultivation. You're also primed to join the ranks of the nascent soul stage before too long barring some manner of calamity. Whether you recognize it or not, whether you want it or not, you have largely transcended the concerns and institutions of this world. Frankly, when it comes to mortals, your word is *law*. Whatever debt that king thinks you owe him means precisely nothing if you say it means nothing."

Sen stood absolutely still as those words washed over him like icy water. It wasn't even that she was saying things he didn't know. He knew that mortals often viewed cultivators as powers and laws unto themselves. He knew that even kings tread with care around certain cultivators. He'd just never quite made the connection that any of that applied to *him*. He was just a street rat who caught some very lucky breaks, not some unearthly being who decided fate for others. He was just a wandering cultivator who couldn't stay out of trouble. Sen sighed at the self-deception. That was the story he held in his head to make himself feel better. He *wanted* to just be a street rat and humble wandering cultivator because those things were simpler. Unfortunately, he hadn't been a simple anything since the day he met Master Feng. Of course, the flip side of all of that was that he could decide to be involved.

"That's probably true," admitted Sen. "I could just tell him to go away and never bother me again. All things being equal, that's probably even the smart move. Just remove myself from the situation."

Auntie Caihong rolled her eyes and said, "But?"

"He's my friend. An actual friend. He helped me when he didn't have to, so now I'm choosing to help him when I don't have to. Plus, whatever he's planning, I'm fairly confident that it isn't aimed at harming me. If I had to guess, he wants me there as a kind of implicit show of force. It might be nothing more than a reminder to the nobles, or maybe he's trying to send a message to another kingdom."

"And how far are you willing to take it? Will you just intimidate his enemies? Or will you go to war with his armies? How far does that friendship extend, and how much blood are you willing to spill to keep it?"

Those weren't questions Sen had asked himself, so he had no answers to give. He thought for a moment and then shook his head. They weren't the kinds of questions you could resolve with a few seconds of deep thinking.

"I don't know," he admitted.

"You should decide before you get to the capital. You may need to know those answers, so you can draw a line at the right place."

"I will give it some thought. Speaking of needing answers to things, is Uncle Kho around?"

"He is," said Auntie Caihong with a gleam in her eye. "Do you need him?"

"I do," said Sen suspiciously.

Smiling brightly, she said, "Oh, well, I guess I'll just have to go steal Ai from him."

"You know you can't keep her, right?" asked Sen in an exasperated voice.

"I know," said Auntie Caihong. "I'll just borrow her for a little while."

"What's a little while?"

"Not too long," said Auntie Caihong with a wave of her hand as she disappeared deeper into the galehouse replica of her home. "Just until she gets married."

"What?!"

CHAPTER FIFTY-EIGHT

SPEAR TALK

Uncle Kho wore a decidedly grumpy expression when he came out to the courtyard where Sen was waiting for him.

"Uncle Kho," said Sen cautiously, nodding at the elder cultivator.

"You interrupted storytime," complained Uncle Kho.

"Storytime?"

"Yes. Storytime! I tell her stories about the adventures I've had, complete with tiny lightning people to act it all out."

Uncle Kho held out a hand, palm up, where a tiny version of him made entirely of lightning appeared. The miniature Uncle Kho thrust a spear in Sen's general direction, and a slender forking arc of lightning leapt the distance to hit Sen in the ear.

"Ouch!" shouted Sen, rubbing his ear with a hand. "Was that necessary?"

Drawing himself up and assuming a mantle of supreme dignity, Uncle Kho said, "Yes."

"Okay. I'm sorry I interrupted storytime."

Uncle Kho's dignified visage cracked into one of amusement. "I suppose I've had my revenge. You needed something?"

"I do," said Sen before he reconsidered. "What kind of stories are you telling her? I mean, it's nothing too scary or gruesome, is it?"

"Of course, it's not. What kind of person do you take me for?"

"Well, it's just... I've heard some of your stories. There's a lot of destroying entire sects, and lightning leaving the earth a scorched ruin for miles in every direction."

Uncle Kho lifted a finger, frowned, and then nodded.

"That's fair," he said. "I just tell her about things like me fighting spirit beasts."

"Oh," said Sen with a rush of relief. "She likes stories where monsters lose."

"Yeah. I figured I'd save those other stories for when she's older."

"For the best, I expect. On the topic of when she's older, you have told Auntie Caihong that she can't just keep Ai, right?"

Uncle Kho gave him a look of such profound pity that Sen found himself shuffling his feet a little bit.

"Sen, *you* can tell her that if you want, and you're feeling especially brave. I, your much older and wiser teacher, know better than to challenge powers that far beyond me."

"You're a nascent soul cultivator. Aren't you preparing to challenge the heavens themselves to ascend?"

"Yes. I picked a battle I at least have a *chance* of winning."

"I have no answer to that," said Sen.

Uncle Kho let out a light chuckle and said, "So, what are we talking about today?"

"A couple of things actually. The less interesting question is, would you be willing to step in and do a little teaching while I'm gone?"

Uncle Kho's brow furrowed a little. "Explain how much teaching we're really talking about here."

"The townspeople are covered. The advanced students can handle running them through drills and the like. Wu Meng Yao is dealing with most of the sword instruction for the cultivators who are here. I still need to recruit someone to teach the lower-level cultivators the spear. So, that's who you'd be teaching. The cultivators. I've limited them to the first couple forms you taught me."

"That sounds simple enough," said Uncle Kho, his expression smoothing out. "So, you were serious about not providing cultivation instruction here?"

"I was. I mean, didn't you agree that a sect would be more trouble than it was worth?"

"I did. I just didn't think you'd actually take that advice."

"Why wouldn't I?"

"Youth, mostly. Young people often ignore the very good advice their teachers and elders offer them. Also, founding a sect can have an appeal that overrides good sense. There *is* a kind of prestige that goes along with it."

Sen supposed he could see it, but the appeal was lost on him. He had more than enough fame to suit him. He didn't want to add anything more to that absurd legend that was growing up around him.

"Nope," he said. "Still too much trouble for not enough benefits. So, are you in?"

"As long as it doesn't go on for too long. It's sort of a pain to hide the fact that I'm a nascent soul cultivator when I'm in the same room as other cultivators. If people figure it out, they'll become very tedious."

"I'm hoping this trip won't last very long. I expect that traveling there and back will take a lot longer than my actual stay in the capital."

"Good plan. The less time you spend in places like that the better."

"Places like that?"

"Places where mortal power and large sects converge. It's easy to get dragged into things that have nothing to do with you in places like that."

"That sounds like the voice of experience," noted Sen.

"I didn't move to that mountain just because I like the view. So, you said that teaching was the boring question. What's the interesting question?"

"What's the next spear form?"

Uncle Kho quirked an eyebrow at him. "What makes you think that there is one?"

"Intuition. I've been working with the spear a lot lately, and I can just feel that there's something more after what you taught me."

That statement brought on a protracted silence that made Sen nervous. When he did finally speak, there was a contemplative air around Uncle Kho.

"So, that's where you are. I did wonder if you'd get there. Not everyone does."

"And where is there, exactly?" asked Sen.

Instead of answering, Uncle Kho posed a question of his own.

"What do you think a form is?"

Sen squinted in confusion and said, "A series of prescribed movements designed to impart fundamentals of motion, defense, and attack."

Uncle Kho nodded. "An accurate enough answer, but you're thinking about it too individually. Most of the martial forms that cultivators practice didn't originate with cultivators. They originated with mortals. We might enhance them with cultivation, but go far enough back and you'll find mortals with sharp sticks trying to find a better way to survive. Another way to think of the forms is that they're general patterns that work for most people. After all, what good is a form to a mortal army if only one person can do it?"

"Not much good, I'd imagine," said Sen.

"Precisely. So, all of those idiosyncratic forms designed by geniuses for their own needs typically fall out of use as soon as they die."

"While the forms that work for everyone live on."

"Yes. At a certain point, though, if you go far enough with any weapon, you bump up against the limits of those general forms. You intuitively know that there's something more, or rather that there's something else that would work better for you. Something designed around your exact strengths and weaknesses."

"You're saying that I need to create my own... What did you call it? My own idiosyncratic form?"

Uncle Kho shrugged. "No. You can use what I already taught you to excellent effect, probably for the rest of your very long life. Innovation isn't inherently a good thing. It can even be a bad thing if it draws your attention away from more immediate and pressing needs. What I'm saying is that you've gone far enough now, developed sufficient insight, that you *can* develop your own form if you decide you want to."

"If I want to," murmured Sen. "This isn't quite how I thought this conversation was going to go."

"What were you expecting? That I decided to only teach you some of what I knew?"

"Well, yes, but not in a bad way. I just assumed that I needed more experience before I was ready to learn it."

"Nope. You're going to discover more and more that the things you learn will be things that you develop on your own. Teachers can only guide you so far because, at a certain point, everyone walks a path shaped by their own insights, affinities, and experiences. The longer you live, the farther you go, the more those paths diverge. And that's not a bad thing. If you had good teachers, you *should* outgrow them and chart a path for yourself."

Sen saw the wisdom, but there was something melancholy about it too.

"That sounds lonely," said Sen.

"Cultivation is lonely. For all that cultivators gather into sects or travel in groups, it is a harsh truth that, if you reach that moment of ascension, you will face the heavens alone. Just you. No one else can face that final tribulation for you. You cannot carry another person with you. But that doesn't mean you have to *be* alone on your way there."

Sen smiled as a memory surfaced.

"I seem to recall you saying the same thing to Master Feng."

"Many, many times. It's worth repeating, even if I know he never really hears the words. It seems that you, at least, heard them. It's a strange little family you've built for yourself, but a family all the same. After all, how many little girls get a mad aunt and a spider on speaking terms with the Great Matriarch for an uncle? To say nothing of a legendary father."

"Infamous, maybe. And I'm not sure I'm not more of an uncle, myself."

"You should just go ahead and bury that lie," said Uncle Kho.

"I suppose that makes you her grandfather."

"No. I'm just the much and rightly adored Uncle Kho. Or maybe Great Uncle Kho. Yes. Great Uncle Kho. I like the sound of that. Let Ming be her grandfather. He needs it," said the elder cultivator before giving Sen a sly look. "Although, I will give you five thousand gold tael if you tell Caihong she's very grand-motherly."

Sen lifted an eyebrow and said, "I'm going to tell her you said that."

"Please don't," said Uncle Kho as panic and dread went to war on his face.

CHAPTER FIFTY-NINE

PRESSURE

B ased on the look that Wu Meng Yao was giving him, she clearly felt less confident about the plan than he did. He gave her a lopsided smile.

"What? I sense doubt. Do you question the wisdom of your glorious leader?"

"Yes. I do question the wisdom of leaving *me* in charge here while you're gone for some indefinite amount of time," said Wu Meng Yao before a hint of a smile crossed her lips. "If you could arrange an introduction to this glorious leader, though, I would like to meet them."

Sen blinked in surprise and then laughed.

"Better," he said. "And it won't be as bad as you think. I've found someone to temporarily take over the spear training for the cultivators, and you've got the sword training mostly in hand."

"What about *her*?" asked Wu Meng Yao.

Sen didn't need to ask who that *her* referred to.

"Sua Xing Xing will be fine. I'll leave her with some instructions about how to train while I'm gone."

"That's not what I meant. You don't think she's going to listen to me, do you?"

"She better listen to you, or she can leave exactly two seconds after I get back. Like I said, it shouldn't be a problem. Ideally, you won't have to interact with her at all. I will, however, make it abundantly clear to her who is in charge while I'm away."

"I—" she sighed. "Alright."

"I'm going to be looking to recruit a few people to pitch in with training while I'm in the capital. Some for both the sword and the spear."

"You are?" asked Wu Meng Yao, sounding genuinely surprised.

"Yeah. What? Did you think I was just going to keep you here forever like some kind of slave?"

"I'm pretty well paid for a slave."

"True," said Sen, "but this was always a temporary arrangement for you. I don't know when you plan to leave, but I've always known you were going to. You have your own cultivation journey to attend to, which means going back to your sect. So, obviously, I need to find a replacement that I can at least nominally trust."

"Trust not to spy on you?"

"Trust not to try to kill me in my sleep. As long as they spy on me quietly, that'll be good enough."

"I wouldn't have thought you'd be so understanding about that," said Wu Meng Yao. "It seems like the kind of thing that would normally provoke a more extreme response."

"Letting people do some basic spying is to *my* advantage in the short run. The real risk is that someone is going to think I'm starting a sect. So, if I let people spy on me, they're going to discover that this place is exactly what I'm saying it is. And if the sects confirm that with their own spies—" Sen trailed off.

"They'll be more likely to believe it and leave you alone."

"Precisely."

Wu Meng Yao stared at him for a moment before she asked, "Why are you taking Shen Mingxia with you?"

"As opposed to you?" asked Sen with an amused smirk.

"As opposed to literally anyone else. Is there something happening between the two of you?"

The smirk vanished from Sen's face. "Do you think that's an appropriate question?"

"Maybe not appropriate but relevant. Necessary. I'm responsible for her while we're away from the sect."

"Including things that have nothing to do with cultivation?"

"If I think that it might end in her leaving the sect, yes," said Wu Meng Yao with cold defiance on her face.

Sen resisted the urge to pinch the bridge of his nose. It didn't actually help when he did that, except maybe psychologically. He wanted to just tell her it was none of her business or that it was a stupid question, but he held back. He didn't understand exactly what Wu Meng Yao's responsibilities were in regard to Shen Mingxia. However, he had to assume that it would go badly for her if Shen Mingxia died or had her cultivation damaged in some fundamental way. It would probably go even worse if Wu Meng Yao managed to lose the sect a promising disciple to some other sect or, worse still, a wandering cultivator like him. Well, maybe not *him*, specifically, given his history with the Soaring Skies Sect, but *a* wandering cultivator. So, while he was mildly offended on Shen Mingxia's behalf and his own, he decided that answering would solve the problem faster than raising more objections to the question.

"No," he said. "There's nothing happening between us. Believe it or not, even if I was interested, I'm not that obnoxiously irresponsible."

"I'm not sure what that means."

"You do. Or you will if you think it through for a second."

Wu Meng Yao frowned, and her forehead furrowed as she pondered the problem. Sen just waited patiently as she slowly worked it out. He saw it on her face when she put the pieces together.

"Being involved that way with you would make her a target.

And she's not powerful enough to defend herself if your enemies were looking for a way to get at you."

"She is not. Being a cultivator means that she would, inevitably, need to leave my sphere of influence. So, no, I have not been entertaining Shen Mingxia in my bedroom while you weren't looking. I'm choosing to restrict that part of my life to people who don't need my protection just to survive."

Wu Meng Yao looked like she was going to speak a couple of times before she finally muttered, "That seems like a very strange thing to thank you for."

"It would be," agreed Sen. "As for the original question, it's exactly the reasons I gave her. She's going to serve as a shield for me. Keep those nobles and sect flunkies from hounding me to go as my escort. Also, seeing how things happen in the capital will be educational for her. Who knows? She might even make a useful connection or two while she's there. Being on friendly terms with one or two people in a big sect could prove useful for her in the long run."

"Is that all?" asked Wu Meng Yao as she studied him carefully. "Just that?"

Sen rolled his eyes. "Fine. It may also be, just a tiny little bit, for my amusement."

Wu Meng Yao thrust a finger at him. "I knew it! You're going to throw her to that pack of ravening hyenas just so you can laugh at her."

"Ravening hyenas?" asked Sen.

"You know what I mean," she said with a truly magnificent glare. "And stop changing the subject."

"No, I'm not. I mean, ravening hyenas? Why not wolves?"

The intensity of the glare she was giving Sen went up about a hundredfold and threatened to set his robes on fire. Sen lifted his hands in a peaceful gesture.

"Yes, it will amuse me to see her interact with them, but," said Sen, "you know as well as I do that pressure is formative. A brief exposure to that kind of pressure now, while she's still developing her foundations and settling on her path, will pay off for her later."

"Pressure can be formative, but too much pressure breaks people."

"I, of all people, am aware of what too much pressure can do to someone. And my amusement doesn't extend to me watching her collapse beneath all of that pressure. If it looks like it's getting to be too much, I'll step in."

"I'm going to hold you to that," said Wu Meng Yao.

Sen was about to go find something else to do when a thoughtful look stole over the sect cultivator's face. *Damn*, thought Sen as Wu Meng Yao's glare returned. She stepped closer to poke him in the chest.

"Is that what you're doing to me by putting me in charge?" she demanded. "Putting me under pressure to help me develop?"

"That," said Sen, doing his utmost to project an air of sincerity, "would be far too much like providing you with cultivation instruction. Something that you know I do not provide here. Besides, that would have been particularly devious and rather clever planning. Do I seem like someone who is particularly devious and has clever plans to you?"

"You do now."

"I'm wounded. *Wounded* that you would think such things about me."

"That would be a lot more convincing if I didn't know that you spent most of your time with nine-tail foxes the last time you went on a long trip away from here. It seems like you might have learned a thing or two from them."

Sen let out a small groan.

"Oh, I learned some things from them. I don't know that I'd call any of it useful, but I definitely learned some things."

"Like being devious and making clever plans?"

"No, it was more like how to do witty banter and imbue unnecessary sexual tension into a conversation."

Wu Meng Yao gave him the flattest of flat looks and said, "Did you forget that we met before this? I can say, with absolute certainty, that the foxes didn't *teach* you either of those things."

Sen stood motionless and returned her flat stare with a blank, innocent expression before cupping a hand to his ear.

"What's that? Ai needs me?" he said to the air.

"I know you're lying. It's not even a good lie."

"Right now, you say?" Sen asked the air, before walking away and calling over his shoulder. "Sorry. I'll have to cut this short."

"You better not break my student!" she shouted at him.

"It'll be fine," shouted Sen as he disappeared through the door of the training hall.

CHAPTER SIXTY
TRAINING PLANS

The trees rushed by beneath him as Sen kept his qi platform moving at a steady pace. He didn't try to go at full speed because he was relatively certain Sua Xing Xing couldn't have kept up. Of course, based on the growing look of concern she wore the deeper Sen took them into the wilds, keeping up was not her main concern at the moment. She was watching the trees below and around them like she expected something to rise up and attack them at any moment. Sen supposed it was possible, but he didn't let that take away from the nice day.

The sun was up and shining, the sky was clear, and the morning air had a refreshing coolness to it that Sen let slip into the small area around him that he controlled. When he finally spotted what he was looking for, he took them down to a clear area that had a large vein of smooth stone covering most of it. He settled onto the rock and waited for Sua Xing Xing to join him. She landed close to him. Almost too close. Another sign that her nerves were getting the better of her. She looked at him and failed to hide those nerves.

"Is there a reason you've brought me to this," she gestured around her, "this awful place?"

Sen looked around curiously. Aside from this patch of rock, the surroundings were a rather lovely, if somewhat primordial, forest. Everything looked healthy and lush. He even spotted some flowers that broke up the green with tiny explosions of color. The burbling sounds of a stream wafted through the air to add a gentle musical quality to the area. He lifted an eyebrow at Sua Xing Xing.

"Awful place?" he asked.

"Yes. These are the deep wilds," she said in a hushed tone, as though afraid that something would take notice of her. "Cultivators only come to places like this in force or desperation. To come so far is to court death."

Sen pondered that declaration. He had gone far deeper into the wilds than this for months on end. He wondered if that experience had made him somehow less cautious than he should be about the dangers. He supposed it was possible. Short of a full beast tide, there wasn't much he'd seen in the wilds that gave him pause anymore. That probably *was* a matter of pure exposure and the repeated experience of fighting while alone or with only a few companions. Experiences he suspected that Sua Xing Xing did not share. She looked like she was keeping panic at bay only through pure effort. At the very least, she believed that this was the deep wilds and that destruction was imminent.

"That kind of fear won't serve you well," said Sen. "This may be the wilds, but it isn't the deep wilds."

"So, you say," she snapped back.

"So, I say. Go another hundred, maybe two hundred miles in that direction," said Sen, pointing, "and you'll start to find the true deep wilds."

"How can you possibly—" she stopped, realization making her eyes go wide. "You've been that deep into the wilds?"

"I have," said Sen before he wandered over to the edge of the woodlands and plucked a small flower.

Sua Xing Xing made another effort to suppress her fear by focusing on the flower in his hand.

"Is that some special ingredient you need for your alchemy? Is that why we came here?" she asked.

Sen glanced down at the flower held between his thumb and forefinger.

"No. It's just a pretty flower. It smells nice, too," he said, holding it out at about the height of her nose.

The sect cultivator took a cautious sniff. Then, slowly, almost as if it pained her to make the admission, she nodded.

"Fine. It smells nice. Did you drag me all the way out here just so you could pick flowers?"

"Not particularly," he said, planting the flower so it sat between her hair and her ear.

A flurry of emotions raced across the woman's face. Confusion. Uncertainty. Anticipation.

"Then, why?" she asked, her hand rising to the flower in a gesture that looked unconscious.

"I'll be leaving soon," said Sen. "I wanted to discuss what I'll expect of your training while I'm away."

That had apparently not been the answer she was expecting, because a flush of anger or embarrassment stole across her cheeks.

"My training," she said slowly.

"Just because I'm away, it doesn't mean that you get to skate on your training."

"Skate?" asked Sua Xing Xing, bafflement momentarily replacing annoyance.

"Damn foxes," muttered Sen. "I mean you don't get to stop training just because I'm not around to directly supervise you."

"I see," she said, before doing what Sen had expected. "Wouldn't it be easier to simply take me with you and continue my training that way?"

"I expect so. I'm still not doing it."

"I'm from a large sect. I know how to behave around nobles and royalty. I could be an asset to you in the capital."

"I'm sure that all of that is true," said Sen as he agreeably nodded along.

"And you never even considered it?"

"I did not."

"But you'll take that foundation formation girl from some backwater sect?"

"I will."

"Why?"

Sen dropped the affable mask he'd been wearing.

"It's quite simple. I trust that foundation formation girl. I trust her to follow my lead. I trust her not to run some agenda that only serves to benefit her."

"The corollary being that you don't trust me. You think that I *will* engage in some self-serving agenda that will bring you no benefits or actively harm you."

Sen considered that and said, "I don't know. Maybe. Maybe not. That's the biggest problem with you, aside from your general, well, you-ness. I don't know you. I don't know why you're really here. That makes trust a rather scarce commodity, don't you think?"

The woman was very still for a moment before she said, "My me-ness?"

Sen sighed. *Of course*, that was what she focused on.

"People don't like you," Sen explained.

Sua Xing Xing took a step back as if she were physically recoiling from the words. For just an instant, Sen saw a flash of legitimate hurt, pain, and regret. Then, it was gone. Covered over with the haughty attitude of a young mistress from a powerful sect.

"I don't require their affection," she said, lifting her chin and staring into the distance.

"No?" asked Sen.

"No," she answered.

"You know, I don't need to eat anymore. I barely need to sleep. Yet, I eat every day. I try to get a little sleep most days. Do you know why?"

She turned a wary eye toward him. "Why?"

"Because there's more to life than simply what's required to survive. That's a lesson I learned the hard way. In the end, I just enjoy food. I like cooking it. I like eating it. It's not necessary for me, but it improves the *quality* of my life. Having friends, family, people I trust and who trust me in return may not be an absolute requirement for my survival, but they also improve the quality of my life. I would be diminished by their absence," said Sen, and then he shrugged. "But that's just me. Do with it what you will."

"I don't have time for such nonsense," said Sua Xing Xing.

"Do I strike you as a man burdened by excessive free time?" asked Sen, but he kept speaking before she could answer. "Speaking of which, on to the issue of your training. In addition to practicing what I've already shown you, I expect you to work on this."

In a burst of motion and qi, Sen drew his jian and swept it up. A wafer-thin wall of stone almost fifty feet long and just as high shot up out of the ground. Sua Xing Xing just stared at it with a look of incomprehension.

"Obviously," continued Sen, "you don't use earth qi. So, I expect you to adapt this technique to work with your water qi affinity."

Sua Xing Xing turned incredulous eyes on him. "You expect me to do *that*? What happened to not teaching us about cultivation?"

"I didn't say a single word about how you should cultivate. I just showed you something I can do. If you manage to adapt the technique, it'll be because you taught *yourself* something about cultivation."

"This doesn't have anything to do with swordsmanship," she said weakly. "It's not a fair test."

Sen reached out and adjusted the flower behind Sua Xing Xing's ear, which made her breath catch a little. She stared at him like she couldn't decide if she wanted to yell at him or kiss him. Sen thought that being unsettled was probably good for her.

He offered her a bright smile. "Test is such a harsh word. You should consider this an opportunity. Yes, it's an opportunity to impress me with your work ethic."

"My work ethic?" Sua Xing Xing almost screamed.

"Your work ethic. Oh, by the way, Wu Meng Yao is in charge while I'm gone. She knows you'll be training on your own, so I don't expect you'll cross paths with each other too often."

Sua Xing Xing spluttered. "What? Her? You're leaving her in charge? But she's... I'm—"

"She is a teacher at the academy. You are a student. You *will* respect those roles," said Sen, his voice going very hard, "or you will leave."

Sen waited to see if the indignity of it all would actually kill Sua Xing Xing. Judging by how red her face got, she was ready to explode. She opened her mouth once, looking for all the world like she intended to curse him straight into the thousand hells before she closed it hard enough that he heard her teeth slam together with an audible crack. He could see the muscles along her jaw working furiously as she held back whatever enraged commentary was rushing through her mind. In the end, she offered him a very formal, very precise bow.

"It will be as you say," she said through clenched teeth.

Sen was tempted to make some glib comment but recognized that it would be counterproductive. He'd brought her out there, intentionally unbalanced her, because he wanted to make a few points. He'd made them. Anything else would just be him venting some of his own general dislike for her. She didn't deserve that treatment, no matter how satisfying it might feel. He was supposed to be her teacher, after all, and she wouldn't learn anything of value from him being unnecessarily cruel. Instead, he glanced up at the sky.

"We should head back," he announced to Sua Xing Xing's visible relief. "There's still a lot to do before I leave."

CHAPTER SIXTY-ONE

ELSEWHERE

Li Yi Nuo had always thought of her sect as being rural. That was until she'd gone off to meet Sen's nigh-mythological spear teacher. It had been a long journey. Longer than it needed to be. She found herself almost shaking with rage at the sheer number of times she'd been dragged into some problem that had absolutely nothing to do with her. It was like the cultivators in this part of the kingdom simply had no respect whatsoever for cultivators from other sects, even core cultivators. And that was to say nothing of local nobles finding out about her and insisting she attend one ridiculous function or another, only to find out that they were trying to use her to advance some equally ridiculous scheme of theirs. To make it all even worse, she couldn't go a day without hearing a story about *him*. Judgment's Gale. The great cultivator. The hero.

They had clearly never met the man. If they had, they would be a lot more afraid and a lot less worshipful. Li Yi Nuo sighed and chided herself for that unkind thought. If his experience in this part of the kingdom had been anything like her experience, it was no wonder the man was so deeply mistrustful of sects or anything that even smacked of official power. Such were her thoughts as she entered the town of Orchard's Reach. Looking around, she was struck by just how small the place was. She struggled to imagine Lu Sen ever setting foot in such a tiny, dirty, unremarkable place. How it had ever contained his personality, to say nothing of his person, was a mystery she feared would never be solved. *Although*, she thought, *I guess it didn't contain him in the end.*

Her impressions of the place did not improve much as she moved toward what could charitably be called the heart of the town. It got a little cleaner, but that was about the only positive change she noted. It was also clear that they didn't get a lot of cultivators in core formation coming and going. Men and women alike stared at her. Some puffed-up local tried to saunter over to her and was stopped cold with a single, imperious look of disdain that made him go white in the face. She almost felt bad for the man. She'd been in a sect for a long time, which meant she'd already grown accustomed to the presence of ridiculously attractive people. On top of that, she'd stood within a foot of Lu Sen. After all of that, the bar for what counted as attractive was just so damned high that almost everyone seemed ugly. With a sense of relief, she spotted the shop she was looking for and went inside.

A young woman who seemed only mildly dazed by her presence directed Li Yi Nuo to the manager, a stern woman of middle years who greeted her politely.

"And how may Grandmother Lu's Heavenly Wares serve the honored cultivator?" asked the manager.

"I am looking for a man named Kho," said Li Yi Nuo. "I was told that I should be able to connect with him here by one Lu Sen."

The manager brightened at Lu Sen's name.

"The young master directed you here," she said. "He must not have known."

Li Yi Nuo felt a pit open up inside of her. "He must not have known what?"

"I'm sorry, honored cultivator, but the one called Kho has left the area for a time."

Li Yi Nuo felt something trying to well up inside of her. *I came all this way*, she thought. *I came here, and it was for nothing*? It took her a moment to marshal her composure, but when she felt like she could speak calmly, she addressed the manager.

"Do you know where he went?" asked Li Yi Nuo.

The manager looked particularly sheepish when she answered. "I was told that he was going to go west. To see the young master."

Li Yi Nuo ground her teeth together to trap the thing that was ever more urgently trying to escape from inside of her. Kho Jaw-Long was going west. To see Sen. He was going to the place where she had traveled from. She felt like the universe was mocking her.

"Thank you," she said to the manager and left the shop.

Once outside, she activated her qinggong technique and escaped the wretched little cesspit of a town as fast as she could. When she was several miles away, she stopped in the middle of the road, threw back her head, and screamed in raw frustration.

Feng Ming lashed out with a kick that connected with the dragon's chest. Said chest imploded under the force of that blow, snuffing out the ancient creature's life in an instant. The massive corpse of the dragon rocketed away from the nascent soul cultivator and slammed into a mountain so deep in the wilds that no human name had ever graced the peak. After the dragon passed *through* the mountain and reduced it to a large pile of rubble, he realized that it wouldn't ever get that name. *I'll just call it Dragon's Folly*, thought Ming with a snort of amusement. He hovered in the air for a minute or two, waiting. When no one came out to greet him, he finally lost patience. Enhancing his voice with qi until it rang out like thunder, Ming spoke.

"You made me kill your pet. Now, why don't you come on out

like a good little spirit beast and have a chat with old Grandfather Feng?"

There was another long pause before a figure rose into the air to face him. The figure looked like a human man, with long, oddly pale hair, and dark eyes, but the man felt all wrong. He couldn't quite put a finger on why, but something told him that the figure before him had started out life as some kind of a serpent. The problem was that this was not the being Feng Ming had come looking for. The creature was strong, certainly, but not nearly strong enough. He sighed.

"Really? A lackey?" asked Ming. "Oh, I see. He sent out the dragon and left you as a backup so he'd have time to run away. That's some king you have. Afraid to come out and face a lone, old wandering cultivator."

"He's well aware of who you are. Why should he face you? That benefits only you," said the snake man.

"Well," said Ming, thoughtfully, "it seems your coward, I mean, your king, has been stirring up the spirit beasts. Making them angry enough to do stupid things like invade human towns and kill everyone. I think it's high time for that foolishness to stop. Otherwise, there's going to be a war."

"That war has always existed. Even if your kind doesn't know it."

"No. There has *not* always been a war," said Ming, his voice growing cold and angry. "If there had been a war, none of you would still be walking this world."

"Human cultivators," sneered the snake man. "Your arrogance will be your downfall. Look at you. You came all this way, just to die in a trap."

At those words, dozens, then hundreds, then thousands of spirit beasts rose into the sky to form a massive circle around him. Ming looked around curiously, then lifted an eyebrow at the sneering snake man.

"Is this all you brought?"

The snake man seemed taken aback at the question. "Your false bravado will not save you."

Ming looked at the jian in his hand for a minute, gave it a fond smile, and then sheathed it.

"The funny thing about being me is that, whenever I'm within about a thousand miles of another human being or cultivator, I have to restrain myself. But here, with all of you, so far from the rest of humanity, I don't have to worry that I'm going to accidentally scare some poor farmer to death or ignite a sect war just by acting. Here, I can actually stretch myself a little. Just a little, though."

The snake man narrowed his eyes. "What are you babbling about?"

Ming smiled and unleashed his killing intent. Spirit beasts died by the hundreds. Some of them simply fell from the sky, their lives extinguished. Others exploded under the pressure, sending a red rain down onto the forests below. The ones that didn't die immediately were rocked by the force of that intangible, terrible intent, and rendered all but insensate. Ming locked eyes with the snake man, who looked aghast at the carnage he was witnessing, and snapped his fingers. Thousands of wind blades appeared all around him. Except, these were not the wind blades of lesser cultivators. They weren't vague distortions in the air. They looked like solid sheets of crystal, their edges so fine and sharp that the very air screamed as it was torn asunder. It was a sea of solidified death.

The snake man understood what was about to happen and was rendered powerless to stop it as Ming seized him in bands of air stronger than any metal in the world. The snake man tried to scream a warning, but it meant nothing as the merciless will of Fate's Razor unleashed his anger. As those wind blades raced toward the assembled army of spirit beasts, a howl like something from the void itself rose around them. The rain of red turned into a flood that drenched the world below them. In mere moments, Ming and the snake man were the only sapient beings within miles.

Everything else with a mind to know had either died or was racing away like the jaws of death were closing around them. Ming floated over to the snake man.

"You tell your false king that the war he wants to start so badly is *over*. If he continues down this path, you will be hunted like prey. You will be killed like the base creatures of the land and sky. Your children will be caged and farmed like livestock. This is my promise to you," said Feng Ming, his face a mask of conviction. "Now, go."

With a trivial effort of will, he sent the snake man hurtling into the distance. *Well, that should buy us a little time, at any rate*, thought Ming. Looking around at what he'd been made to do, he shook his head.

"What a waste," he whispered. "What a stupid, senseless waste."

CHAPTER SIXTY-TWO

OBSERVATION

Sen stood motionless inside the shadow he'd wrapped around himself and watched as Wu Meng Yao conducted a class. Part of him hated to admit it, but he was pretty sure she was a better teacher. It wasn't a matter of knowledge. He was, by all meaningful measures, the better swordsman. He understood the weapon better. He knew more about using it. But it was becoming clear that he wasn't necessarily better at showing someone else how to use it. For direct instruction, she simply had a quality that he lacked. He viewed teaching students as largely a matter of correcting flaws in their stance and imparting additional forms. It was a decidedly one-sided relationship where he provided information, and it was on them to incorporate it.

It took him a while to figure it out because she never discussed it. He wasn't even sure if she thought about it. The primary difference between himself and Wu Meng Yao as teachers was that she *wanted* her students to improve. It was important to her. More than that, she wanted them to improve in some vague, holistic way that Sen struggled to understand. Almost as if she believed that if she believed enough in them, they would become better. It baffled him, even if he could see how it changed the way the students reacted to her. His students worked hard. They worked very hard, in no small part because he wouldn't accept anything less. Wu Meng Yao's students would work themselves to death if she asked them to. Of course, she never would, and he suspected they all knew that too.

He wasn't heartless when it came to his students. Sen didn't want them to fail, but it wasn't going to influence his self-perception much if some of them did. Not every student was destined for greatness. Some deficits could be overcome through sheer tenacity and hard work. He knew that much from personal experience. He also knew that he'd been lucky in many regards. He'd had deficits. Looking back, he could see them all too clearly, but they had been the kinds of deficits that hard work *could* overcome. If his body had been slightly different, his ability to intuit certain kinds of tactical realities a little less acute, his mind a little duller, he would have been one of those failures. At a certain point, a lack of talent, insight, and a hundred other things could and would bring someone's journey toward mastery to an irrevocable end. It was harsh, but it was also a fact.

Armed with that fact, Sen didn't tie himself emotionally to the success and failure of individual students. Particularly the cultivators he dealt with as students. He was looking to raise the overall competence of a large number of people to maximize the survival chances of the small towns and villages that didn't have the questionable good fortune to be located right outside of a sect. Much as cultivators faced the heavens alone, those towns and villages would face the spirit beasts alone. They needed help and training they simply weren't going to get anywhere else. Cultivators, even wandering cultivators, had a lot of options. If they didn't like what they got from him, well, they could seek their training elsewhere. It seemed that Wu Meng Yao did not share that view, and he couldn't say that he was surprised. She was from a sect and steeped in sect thinking. She probably saw helping all those mortals as the distant, secondary concern of this place, and helping cultivators as the real work to be done. She poured herself into the task.

A tiny little piece of Sen envied that capacity in her, but he recognized that he couldn't afford to think or act that way. It would become a distraction that took the academy off of the path he'd set for it. He had to think in terms of the big picture and broader goals so that other people could do things like worry about the progress of individual students. None of which made accepting that Wu Meng Yao was just better at this than he was more palatable. That was pride talking poison into his ear. He knew it. He just wished knowing that made it easier to ignore. He'd have to settle for not letting his pride drive his behavior. Plus, even if he couldn't act the way his ego was telling him to, he could offer some support. As the class was nearing its end, Sen stepped out of the shadow he'd been...

Was I just lurking? Damn it, thought Sen. *I was lurking*. He took solace in the fact that he'd also been *hiding*, so at least no one would know he'd been acting like Fu Ruolan. The class ground to an immediate halt when he stopped hiding. Everyone stared at him until Wu Meng Yao offered a bow. The dozen or so foundation formation cultivators in the class hastily followed her lead. Sen inclined his head to them and then waved a hand.

"Continue," he said.

Wu Meng Yao gave the class a withering look as they stood there not doing anything. She clapped her hands to draw their attention.

"You heard the man. Continue."

Sen could tell his mere presence made them all nervous, particularly as he circled around them like a great wolf picking the weakest deer in the herd. He zeroed in on the man with dark red hair he'd been forced to chastise when he'd first met Sua Xing Xing. He made sure to keep a cool, impassive expression on his face as he walked over to the man. Learning from past failures, he had at least made a point to find out the man's name. Soon Zi Rui tried and failed to maintain his composure as Sen cast a critical eye over him. Without saying a word, Sen reached out with his foot and nudged the cringing cultivator's foot into the proper position. Then, he adjusted the man's grip on his jian.

"You'll gain a fraction of a second on your strikes if you hold it this way," said Sen.

Soon Zi Rui gave a jerky nod of his head. Moving on, Sen took a moment with each student to offer some little nugget of wisdom or correction. He saved the tiny, childlike woman, Mo Kai-Ming, for last. She beamed up at him like he was her favorite brother. He offered her a gentle smile and some minor corrections.

"See me after you finish. I have something for you," he told her.

He said it casually like it was routine for him to stop by and tell one of the students to see him. He'd done it on purpose. He saw the way the other cultivators treated her, the dismissal in their eyes, and he didn't like it. He didn't like it at all. Simply by inviting her to speak with him, her position in the social order of the class had just been adjusted from the bottom to somewhere above the top. She offered him a surprised nod, and he retreated to stand behind and to the side of Wu Meng Yao. He'd violated the natural balance of things enough for one day. Wu Meng Yao closed out the class with a firm admonition to continue practicing hard before she turned and bowed to him again.

"And we should all thank the founder for taking the time to visit with us today and impart his wisdom," she said.

The class all bowed again, and Sen did what Falling Leaf had told him to do. He lived with it. He inclined his head to them again.

"I'm impressed. You should all thank your teacher for the very excellent instruction she has been providing to you."

Everyone in the class straightened at the words and bowed to Wu Meng Yao.

As one, they shouted, "Thank you, teacher!"

Wu Meng Yao actually blushed and seemed at a loss for what to say, so Sen stepped up next to her.

"You are dismissed," he announced.

Most of the cultivators left, although he could see all of them shooting curious looks at Mo Kai-Ming. He also saw a few jealous looks sent her way as well. He wondered if he hadn't done her as much of a favor as he'd thought. *Well, it's too late to take it back*, he thought. The tiny woman came over looking a little uncertain about what to expect. He smiled at her.

"May I see your blade?" he asked her.

"Of course," she said, hastily untying the weapon from her waist and handing it to him.

He took it from her and unsheathed it. It was a blade of decent quality for someone in the qi-gathering stage, but it would fall short in foundation formation. That wasn't the only problem with it. She was making do, but the weapon was simply too long for her. It had been obvious as the class worked through their forms. He sighed and shook his head.

"This won't do," he said. "It won't do at all."

He sheathed the jian and handed it to Wu Meng Yao, who was giving him the same look of mixed concern and confusion as Mo Kai-Ming. After a brief search through his storage rings, he summoned a jian he'd bought for this specific purpose and promptly forgotten about for months.

"I believe that this blade will suit you better," he said and offered her the sword. "Consider it a minor inclusion in your recompense."

Her eyes wide, Mo Kai-Ming reached out and took the sword. It was of a substantially better quality than the one she'd been using. Just as importantly, it was shorter. While that loss in length would come at a small cost in range, it would also come with a substantial improvement in control. He might find out he was wrong in the long run, but he considered an improvement in control to be far more valuable than a small gain in range. After all, cultivators could maintain range with speed and techniques. There was no substitute for control. Unsheathing the blade, the tiny woman's eyes went wide. She immediately put it back into the scabbard and tried to return it.

"This is too expensive. It's too much. I'll be fine with the sword I have."

Sen looked to Wu Meng Yao. "You're her teacher. You should explain it."

She shot him a look that was equal parts grateful and disapproving. It was as if she was happy he'd left the explanation to her, but also unhappy that he'd foisted the responsibility onto her. He gave her a knowing smile which prompted a brief scowl in his direction.

"This blade," said Wu Meng Yao, lifting the tiny woman's old sword, "will swiftly fail you in foundation formation. It simply isn't made to withstand the force and pressure of the kinds of fights that you'll likely find yourself in. That blade will serve you for some time to come."

"And," added Sen with a thoughtful look, "you would shame me by refusing to accept this attempt to compensate you."

Horror blossomed on Mo Kai-Ming's face. Her eyes darted from Sen to the sword she was still trying to shove back into his hands. She immediately yanked the sword back and hugged it to her chest.

"I will, naturally, of course, accept this fine weapon," she stammered.

"My gratitude," said Sen.

When it became obvious that the tiny woman didn't know what to do next, Wu Meng Yao gently escorted her to the door, returning the old jian. As soon as they were alone, Wu Meng Yao whirled toward Sen.

"You could have told me you were going to do that."

"I wanted to see how you handle things when you don't think you're being observed. I am leaving you in charge here, after all."

"And?" asked Wu Meng Yao, doing a good but not perfect job of hiding her nervousness.

"I don't know how much teaching they let you do back at the Soaring Skies Sect, but you're good at this," said Sen, stowing his wounded pride. "You should do more of it when you leave here if you get the chance. As for me, I'm satisfied that I'm leaving things in good hands."

"Oh," said Wu Meng Yao like she'd been preparing for a reprimand that never came. "Thank you."

CHAPTER SIXTY-THREE

OH, BY THE THOUSAND HELLS

"And then the blue bird ate the bug!" exclaimed Ai as she mimicked a beak snapping shut with her hand.

Sen smiled as he listened and made sure to gasp loudly at her pantomime.

"Oh no!" he shouted. "The poor bug!"

Ai's face scrunched up in thoughtful concentration for a moment before she shook her head.

"It was a yucky bug," she announced.

"Oh, well, if it was a yucky bug, then it's a good thing that bird ate it. We can't have yucky bugs around here. Should we give the bird a present to say thank you?"

"You're silly," giggled Ai. "Birds don't get presents."

"They don't?" asked Sen as if this were the most shocking news in the world.

"No!"

She looked like she might say more, but that was when Zhi ran up, grabbed her hand, and pulled Ai away to play some new game the other little girl had thought up. Knowing he was leaving the next day made it hard for Sen not to call Ai back over to him. He wanted to soak up every second he could with her. He held his tongue, though. There had been precious little play, or fun, or joy in his childhood. He wouldn't deprive Ai of a second of those things if he could help it. Instead, he looked around at the odd mix of people in his home. Uncle Kho and Auntie Caihong had claimed a spot by the fireplace and smiled over the proceedings like a pair of benevolent deities who were well-pleased by what they saw. Sen barely contained his snort of amusement when Zhi decided that Unca Kho and Auntie Caihai—a mispronunciation that never ceased to amuse Sen—needed to join the game. A decision she announced by running over to them, unceremoniously grabbing their hands and pulling at them. He snorted when he imagined the hordes of cultivators who would probably choke to death on all the blood they spat up if they ever saw such a display.

He noticed that Falling Leaf had cornered Shen Mingxia and seemed to be imparting *something* to the other woman. Was it advice? Orders? Whatever Falling Leaf was saying had made Shen Mingxia go a little pale. He decided to leave it alone unless the foundation formation cultivator started shooting him desperate looks. That had become Shen Mingxia's go-to move whenever she felt in over her head around the nascent soul cultivators or human form spirit beasts who just sort of wandered around his home and academy whenever they got bored. He was glad the nascent soul cultivators put in a little effort and masked their true power whenever they interacted with the students at the academy. Although, that had done very little to prevent all kinds of wild speculation about who they were. The only clarification Sen had ever offered was calling them his personal guests.

Li Hua, who actually knew who Uncle Kho was, had kept that information to herself. She was there and had seemed to form some kind of pact of mutual uncertainty with Wu Meng Yao. They both hovered near the large table where Sen had put out a truly absurd amount of food for people to eat as and when they wished. Neither seemed all that sure about who they should talk to or even *if* they should interact with anyone. He had hoped that Li

Hua might grow more comfortable with everyone over time, especially given how close Ai and Zhi were, but she adhered to a firm code of formality with pretty much everyone but him. He supposed it was probably safer for her to do that. It would help prevent misunderstandings with so many other cultivators in the area. He had been very clear about his rules regarding how the cultivators at the academy were to interact with the townspeople, but cultivators were cultivators. He worried it was only a question of when, not if, he'd be forced to kill one of them to prove that he meant the rules applied to *everyone*. Sen shook those thoughts away.

He looked over to where Glimmer of Night was... Sen frowned. *What in the world is that spider doing?* Glimmer of Night was facing a wall and gently running a finger across a particular spot on the stone. Unable to resist the minor mystery, Sen rose from his chair and walked over.

"Something about my wall troubling you?" asked Sen with an amused smirk.

Glimmer of Night looked at him and said, "Not troubling. Intriguing."

Sen lifted an eyebrow. "How so?"

"Whatever you did to make this wall, it changed the stone. There's a distinct crystalline pattern to it now that you don't normally see."

"I see," said Sen slowly.

It took another second before he realized that he didn't see at all. He had no idea what a crystalline pattern was beyond what he could infer from the name itself. He thought about asking but ultimately didn't. He was sure it would be interesting, but it would also consume his attention for the rest of the night. He didn't want to be distracted. He wanted to be here, present, and available to the people around him. The spider, wholly unaware of these thoughts, nodded eagerly.

"I suspect that I might be able to learn something useful from this pattern. Possibly even adapt it for my study of webs."

Sen considered it and said, "I hope it works out."

He turned to walk over to the table when the spider brought him up short.

"When do we leave tomorrow?" asked Glimmer of Night.

It was casual as if he was asking about the weather or what to eat. It caught Sen completely off guard. He hadn't planned on taking the spider with him. The thought had never even occurred to him. Taking Glimmer of Night into the heart of human civilization seemed like a monumentally bad idea. Sure, the people here had taken his presence mostly in stride, but the spider had enjoyed a bit of reflected goodwill from Sen. The townspeople had still been exceedingly wary, and it had taken months and months of the spider coming and going and generally not murdering everyone to wear down all but the most irrational suspicions. Glimmer of Night would enjoy none of those protections in the capital.

The mortals there would likely be terrified of him. The sects would probably want to capture and dissect him. Sen thought that he might be able to prevent that latter problem by sending some carefully worded messages to the sects about how he would not look kindly on someone killing his friend to sate their curiosity. The mortals, though? He didn't think he could do anything to prevent them from forming a mob. And there were a lot of mortals in the capital. Sen tried to think about the best way to approach the problem.

"I'm not sure it's wise for you to visit the capital," Sen finally said.

The spider stopped fixating on the wall and turned to look at Sen.

"Why?" asked the spider.

"Because I'm worried that the mortals would try to kill you. Even if they didn't, there's a good chance one of the sects would try to grab you, so they could experiment on you. Live spirit beasts are not common there. Powerful ones, even less so. You might be a prize they can't resist."

"How would they know?" asked Glimmer of Night.

Sen blinked a few times as his brain tried to sort out a polite answer. Sighing, Sen just gestured at the spider.

"You're kind of obvious. You'll draw attention."

The spider looked down at himself and then seemed to understand.

"It won't be a problem."

Sen shook his head. The spider kept saying things that didn't make much sense. It was starting to make him feel twitchy.

"How is that not a problem?" asked Sen.

Sen felt a small burst of qi that had an oddly familiar quality to it, although he couldn't quite put his finger on what seemed familiar. That curiosity was swept straight out of his mind as the spider transformed from a pitch-black creature covered in chitin to a young, *human* man. From one moment to the next, Glimmer of Night had gone from being something that would attract every eye to someone who could walk unmolested anywhere in the kingdom. Sen gaped at the transformation.

"What?" Sen demanded. "When did you learn how to do this?"

"On the way here. I watched the fox who lusted after you."

Sen felt like his eyes were going to fall out of his head.

"You knew this *entire time*? Why didn't you change before?"

Glimmer of Night held up an arm and scratched at it.

"It's itchy."

Sen wanted to yell at the spider for causing all of that worry in the town for nothing, but it seemed someone else had been listening because Auntie Caihong was suddenly standing next to them.

"What's this about a fox lusting after Sen?" she asked, eyes alight with the need to know.

Before Sen could redirect the conversation, Glimmer of Night immediately decided to be helpful.

"It was the she-fox grandchild of the elder fox. She lusts for him," said the spider with an enthusiastic nod. "She was very vexed that he did not wish to mate with her."

"Really?" asked Auntie Caihong, a wicked gleam of amusement in her eyes. "Laughing River has a granddaughter?"

"Yes," said Sen, his tone resigned.

"And she propositioned you?"

"Yes," admitted Sen.

"And you declined? More than once?"

"Yes," said Sen as just the memory of it all made him feel tired.

Auntie Caihong started laughing. He wasn't sure exactly what kind of laugh it was, just that it *wasn't* a laughing together sort of laugh. It left Sen feeling deeply unsettled. He narrowed his eyes at Auntie Caihong.

"I'm clearly missing something here," he said. "What is it?"

Instead of answering, she called Uncle Kho over. He disengaged from Zhi and Ai's game and approached them while giving Auntie Caihong a questioning glance. It seemed to take a supreme effort of will for her to get through the explanation without bursting into more laughter.

"It turns out that," she said, "that Laughing River has a granddaughter, and she took an interest in Sen."

"Well, I suppose most people spend a night with at least one nine-tail fox," said Uncle Kho, seeming to lose interest.

"No. That's the thing. *He didn't.* He turned her down. Repeatedly," she said as laughter started to sneak through.

Uncle Kho stared at Auntie Caihong in baffled shock for a second before turning that look on Sen. There was a quiet moment before Uncle Kho burst into laughter. Sen felt his frustration start to rise. He didn't enjoy being on the wrong side of a joke he didn't even understand.

"What don't I know?" he demanded.

Uncle Kho turned to see if Auntie Caihong wanted to explain, but she was doubled over with laughter. Shaking his head, Uncle Kho gave Sen a look that was part pity, part sympathy, and a lot of humor.

"Sen, nine-tail foxes grow bored pretty easily. So, if one expresses that sort of interest in you, giving in makes them lose interest and go away. They read it as a lack of willpower on your part or something along those lines. Declining once, well, that's usually read as a signal that you have a more serious interest in them and that you have the strength of will to carry through on it. Saying no repeatedly. Well, how do I put this?"

Auntie Caihong got control of herself just long enough to cut in with, "You basically proposed to her!"

It took five full seconds before Sen gathered himself and said, "Oh, by the thousand hells."

CHAPTER SIXTY-FOUR

DO IT AGAIN

For all that he had done his best to prepare her for it, and that he had made similar trips in the past, Ai seemed no more settled with the idea of him leaving than any of the other times he'd gone. She refused to let him out of her sight, or her grip, for any longer than absolutely necessary. She kept giving him sad eyes and a quivering lower lip without ever actually bursting into tears. She finally gave him a serious look.

"I want to come," she declared.

Even though Sen knew it was a truly terrible idea, just for a second or two, he thought about it. If he took her with him, then he wouldn't have to miss her. Instead, he made himself act like an adult. He reminded himself that while the capital might not be the worst possible place for him to take her, it had to be near the very top of the list. Just as importantly, even if he could protect her there, something he wasn't entirely confident about, that he might need to was enough reason not to take her along. Besides, even if she didn't know, he was pretty sure she'd hate the place almost as much as Falling Leaf. The children he had seen had mostly been working, which meant there would be painfully few children for her to befriend.

Here, she had friends, and she was under the protection of people that Sen had absolute faith in. The sky would burn and the world would drown in poison before Uncle Kho and Auntie Caihong let anything, anything at all, bad happen to Ai. That was assuming that Falling Leaf didn't find those poor, doomed, disastrously stupid souls first and turn them into tiny little pieces of unidentifiable red matter scattered through the forest. Sen also knew that trying to explain any of that to Ai would be pointless. The dangers were too abstract for her. Crouching down so they could look right at each other, he leaned into what she knew and cared about.

"I know you want to come. But if you come with me, who will play with Zhi?"

Ai's brow furrowed like she maybe thought he was trying to trick her, but she still looked pensive.

"Plus, who will take care of Falling Leaf, Uncle Kho, and Auntie Caihong if you're not here? Or show the birds which yucky bugs to eat?"

He thought he'd gotten her most of the way there with Falling Leaf, Auntie Caihong, and Uncle Kho, but it was that bit with the yucky bugs that drew a look of severe worry. Ai was very concerned with the number of those bugs, and she went out of her way to tell whatever birds were in sight that they needed to be eaten. The disconcerting part was the birds seemed to go and eat those bugs more often than pure chance would account for. Sen had added it to his long list of things to look into at some point. If she was somehow ordering birds around, that would be very odd. Not that Sen felt he had much room to talk about anyone else being odd. His own ascent through the ranks of cultivation was so improbable as to be laughable, at least for anyone who hadn't been there for every painful step of the process.

"The birds *do* need me," she said, looking torn. "They're dumb."

"They do, and they are," Sen agreed and steadfastly refused to unleash the smile that kept trying to push its way free.

Whatever had been holding her tears back gave out.

"I don't want you to go," Ai sobbed, throwing herself at him and wrapping her arms around his neck.

Sen stroked her hair and patted her back while she got it out of her system. When the tears finally seemed to run dry, he gave her a smile.

"I don't want to go, but sometimes I have to do things I don't want to do. You know what, though? I am going to miss you *so much*."

"How much?" she asked in a quavery little voice.

"This much," said Sen, spreading his arms out as far as they would go.

"Promise?"

"I promise, and I promise that I'm going to come back as soon as I can."

Ai seemed to weigh those words on some scale of sincerity that only existed inside of her head. Sen concluded that, while she might not be happy, she was at least mollified by the truthfulness of his promises.

"Okay," she said, her head hanging down.

Sen scooped her up into his arms and planted a big kiss on her cheek. That got a little laugh as she rubbed at her cheek.

"Tickles," she said.

"It does?" asked Sen, feigning ignorance, and then poking a spot on her belly. "Does that tickle?"

Soon, the sadness was, if not forgotten, then displaced by peals of laughter. Sen eventually, reluctantly, put Ai down.

"You should go say goodbye to Uncle Glimmerite and Auntie Mingxia."

"Okay, Papa," she said and dashed over to tackle hug Glimmer of Night's leg.

Not that Sen saw that, or heard anything that anyone said. His entire world had ground to a stop at the word *Papa*. He had never asked her to call him that. He'd never even used the word in her presence. She loved him. There was no room to doubt it. She said it in a thousand different ways every single day. That was enough. It was *more* than enough. He had never needed her to see him as her father. He was her family. She knew that. But that word held a kind of power that made anything a cultivator could do seem trivial.

It was a *truth*. An expression of a primal bond so powerful, so potent, that any attempt to describe it was doomed to fail. For her to choose to call him that left Sen feeling simultaneously like the most important person alive and like a horribly, irreparably inadequate imposter. Not that any of that mattered. Just as she had once called for him, now she had chosen him, and he would find a way to be what she needed him to be. Bowing his head, Sen reached up and brushed away the tears that had gathered in his eyes. With his senses finally functioning again, he heard Ai's gleeful voice.

"Do it again!"

He glanced over and saw Glimmer of Night transform from his human disguise back into his black, chitinous form. This led to Ai jumping up and down in pure excitement. Sen wasn't sure how long he'd been lost inside his own head, but the way Shen Mingxia was leaning against a tree and watching gave him the impression that this had been going on for a while now. He went to walk over and free the spider, but a new presence brought him up short. He looked toward the forest and Fu Ruolan stepped out of the trees. He was a little surprised to see her since she had declined to join them the night before. She strode over to Sen, watched Ai commanding Glimmer of Night to change, and snorted in amusement. Only then did she turn her full attention on him.

"The capital? Do you feel like you didn't give it a full opportunity to kill you the last time you went there publicly?"

"Oh no," said Sen. "I definitely gave it a full opportunity."

"Then, why go back?"

Sen tried out a couple of answers in his head before he just shrugged and said, "Because I told my friend I would."

Fu Ruolan sighed and said, "Well, don't do anything stupid while you're there. I put way too much time and effort into you for you to throw it all away when you're finally getting interesting."

Sen regarded the nascent soul cultivator for a long moment. He considered how lonely she must have been, living all the way out here, isolating herself the way she had. Even if they both understood why she'd done it, he didn't expect that had made it any less difficult. He'd probably spent more time with her than almost any other living being in centuries. He was, he realized, probably the closest thing to a friend she'd made in a very, very long time. Someone who shared some of her keenest interests. Someone who could shadow walk the way she did. And now he was going away, again. He intentionally turned his gaze away before he spoke.

"I'll miss you, too."

He heard the sharp little intake of breath, the rustle of clothes as she stiffened, and finally her annoyed huff.

"Just don't die," she said in a tone that was half order, half pleading.

Sen nodded. "I'll do my best. With any luck, this will be a quick trip. I'll go, play whatever role it is that Jing has in mind for me, and then leave."

He could feel her rolling her eyes.

"You don't really think it'll go that easy, do you?"

"No, but I can hope."

"Well, just remember that a bit of—" she hesitated. "No, not a little. Giant, heaping bucketfuls of paranoia are appropriate there. Don't let your life here trick you into thinking that everyone else has stopped being awful."

Sen let out a little chuckle.

"Your faith in humanity is truly boundless."

"I have plenty of faith in humanity," said Fu Ruolan. "I have faith that they're terrible."

"Duly noted. Is there anything you need from the capital? I mean, since I'm already going."

"Nothing I can think of," she said. "Travel safely."

"I will," he said, finally turning back to her and offering her a bow.

She rolled her eyes again but returned the bow. Shooting her a quick smile, Sen finally went over to stop Ai from demanding more transformations. They didn't seem to cost the spider much in the way of qi, but Sen had no idea how many times he'd switched already. He didn't want the poor spider to simply fall over from exhaustion a few hours down the road. Uncle Kho and Auntie Caihong came over then to say their goodbyes. Auntie Caihong also took the opportunity to pick Ai up and hold her.

"I'll keep an eye on those spear students of yours. Just don't take too long, or I might get bored and decide to actually teach them something," said Uncle Kho with an amused look.

"Well, we certainly wouldn't want that," agreed Sen.

"Be mindful, Sen," said Auntie Caihong. "I know he's your friend, but you should still be cautious. Also, don't do anything that Ming would do."

That drew laughs from Sen and Uncle Kho, a baffled look from Shen Mingxia, and Glimmer of Night was ignoring them entirely because he'd found a toad somewhere and was holding it up to his eye to study it.

Ai frowned and asked, "Who's Ming?"

Auntie Caihong looked at her and said, "Oh, he's a terrible, terrible man."

"He's not a terrible man," said Sen. "He's my teacher. He's sort of like your grandfather."

Uncle Kho nodded in approval, while Auntie Caihong gave him a look of utter betrayal.

"No more lotus cakes for you," she muttered.

"Oh, now that's just mean," said Sen.

"Well, maybe I'll have forgiven you by the time you get back," said Auntie Caihong.

"I guess that will have to do," agreed Sen, before he leaned down and kissed Ai's forehead. "You be good while I'm away."

"I will, Papa."

Sen got the momentary pleasure of seeing Auntie Caihong's eyes go wide. Then, she looked like she might cry, which made Sen feel kind of bad for his amusement at her expense. Uncle Kho just beamed at the little girl.

"Where's Falling Leaf?" asked Auntie Caihong. "I thought she'd be here."

"She's hiding in that shadow over there," said Sen and pointed.

The ghost panther emerged from the shadow and gave Sen an annoyed frown. Sen excused himself and walked over to her.

"How do you always know where I am?" she asked.

"How could I not know? You're one of the two most important people in my life."

Falling Leaf pondered those words for a moment before nodding in a way that suggested that was exactly as things should be.

"The mad one is right. Be careful in that place. You have friends there, but you have enemies too."

"I will," said Sen.

Then, much as he had with Ai, he leaned in and kissed Falling Leaf's forehead.

"Watch out for Ai," he said. "And watch out for yourself. I expect to see you both healthy and happy when I return."

"Nothing will touch her," said Falling Leaf, and there was a flicker of something dangerous in her gaze.

Knowing that Falling Leaf would never actually say goodbye, Sen simply reached out and squeezed her arm for a moment before returning to Shen Mingxia and Glimmer of Night.

"It's time to go," he said.

Suiting actions to words, Sen formed a qi platform beneath himself and Shen Mingxia. She couldn't hope to keep pace with Sen or Glimmer of Night, so he'd just resolved to carry her along. The spider looked at them hovering in the air, shrugged, and formed a qi platform of his own. Sen lifted an eyebrow. He hadn't known the spider could do that. With a final wave to everyone, the trio shot down the road. They moved in silence for a short time before Shen Mingxia looked over at him. Sen braced himself mentally when he saw the smirk on her lips.

"So, are you going to do some wedding shopping in the capital?"

THE END
Unintended Cultivator
Volume 7

Sen and company will return in Unintended Cultivator Volume 8. Get it here: https://shadowalleypress.com/ UnintendedCultivator8

BLOOPERS

"Falling Leaf, this is Laughing River and Misty Peak," said Sen, gesturing at the foxes.

Falling Leaf inclined her head to Laughing River in a gesture of muted respect. She eyed Misty Peak askance for a moment before issuing a little sigh and nodding to the other woman.

"Hello," said the ghost panther.

"Laughing River, Misty Peak, this is Falling Leaf. My friend," said Sen, before he added something he thought was necessary. "I will note that, should I discover she's been drawn into any kind of fox plot, scheme, or foolishness, I will become *profoundly unhappy*."

Laughing River and Misty Peak traded uncertain looks. Finally, Misty Peak worked up the nerve to ask.

"What would that mean? You know, what would that translate to in practical terms?"

Sen gave her a stern look. "You don't want an answer to that."

She traded another look with her grandfather. "No, I really think I do."

Sen looked at Falling Leaf. She gave him *the nod*.

"What that means in practical terms," said Sen, "is that it moves out of my hands. It becomes Larry's problem."

"Who is Larry?" asked Laughing River with pure bafflement on his face.

Falling Leaf gave the pair of foxes an icy smile and shouted, "Hey, Larry! There are some people here who want to meet you."

After a moment of silence, everything in the inn that wasn't bolted down began to tremble and then jump in place. The foxes began to look around with wide, panicky eyes. Before either of them could ask the question, one of the walls disintegrated into a shower of tiny pieces to reveal the massive, majestic form of Larry. The spirit ox gave the foxes a look that would have killed mortals on the spot. Misty Peak looked like she wanted to dive under the table, and even Laughing River had gone pale at the sight.

"I'm Larry," said the ox in a basso voice that shook the building. "And I fix problems. Are you gonna be a problem that needs fixing?"

"No," said Laughing River in a voice that was two octaves higher than usual.

The morning's activities and the food seemed to overwhelm the girl's youthful vigor because she almost fell asleep while she was eating. Sen carried her limp, yawning form to her bed. She was asleep before he even left the room. He stepped outside and took a deep breath. Keeping up with Ai wasn't physically demanding, but it did require a lot more mental engagement than Sen had expected. He'd need to figure out things that she could do that would keep her mind engaged for a while. Sen left the door to the galehouse open so that he'd hear it when Ai got up from her nap and decided to take advantage of the brief lull in his day. Drawing his jian, Sen worked his sword forms. He felt Glimmer of Night approach but didn't let it immediately interrupt his work. When he finished the form he was working through, he stopped and looked over at the spider.

"Is this what you mean to teach me?" asked the spider.

"Among other things," said Sen. "The basics, at least. I can teach you some spear basics as well. We'll cover some of both, and you can decide if you like one of them better."

"Why would I need this?" asked the spider.

"Most cultivators use a weapon of some kind. It's not impossible to fight them without a weapon of your own, but it's much harder."

"And how long did it take you to learn it?"

"Years," said Sen. "But it sounds like you'll be around for years. Might as well take advantage of that."

Glimmer of Night nodded in agreement. "Will you teach the child these things?"

Sen stared at the spider as though he had clearly suffered some manner of severe damage to his spider brain.

"You're damn skippy I'm going to teach her these things."

"Because of cultivators?" asked Glimmer of Night.

"Because of *boys*! They're evil, rotten, terrible things. Every last one of them."

The spider was silent for a long, long moment before he asked, "Aren't you a boy?"

Liu Ai spared Sen more awkward conversation by coming out from behind some folding panels. She was happily trying to adjust a robe and not doing a terribly good job of it. Sen set his cup down and went over to help her, gently tying the knots and settling the folds of blue and black fabric around her. She held out her arms to each side.

"I'm a flower," she announced.

"You certainly are," agreed Sen. "A beautiful chrysanthemum."

A look of hesitant uncertainty crossed the little girl's face. "What's a kercinnamon?"

Sen could see the seamstress shaking her head in disapproval from the corner of his eye.

"Really?" said the woman. "A hundred flowers out there with short names, so you pick the one that no child can pronounce?"

"It was the first thing I thought of," said Sen.

"What a cerkanadom?" asked Ai, looking unhappy.

The seamstress crouched down and smiled at Ai. "Don't you worry about that. He's just got duck feathers for a brain. What he meant to say was that you're a beautiful lily."

Ai gave the woman a perplexed look.

"It's a very beautiful flower," said the woman, before she shot Sen a look. "Beautiful and easy to pronounce."

"I'm a lily!"

"Yes, you are," said the seamstress.

Ai pointed at Sen. "You're a duck brain."

"Yes, he is," said the woman, smiling in approval.

"Don't be fooled. I'm entirely made up. Turn your back, and I'll vanish like smoke in a dream."

"Can you—" Li Hua hesitated. "Can you really do that?"

Sen went to deny the silly idea and then thought a little harder about it. *Could I?*

"Maybe," he said. "Probably not if anyone was paying close attention."

"So, not all-powerful?"

"Not even remotely. Any cultivator who says otherwise is lying," answered Sen. "I think it's probably time for a quiet departure. Things are calming down at the gate."

"How do you know that?"

"I can hear them," said Sen as he walked over to collect Liu Ai.

She noticed him and ran over, her eyes wide.

"Did you chase the monsters away?" she asked.

"I did, with some help," said Sen, not feeling the tiniest bit guilty about the half-lie. "But it is about time for us to head home. Otherwise, we'll never get there before dark."

The girl got a pouty look on her face. Ai wasn't generally a willful girl, but Sen had learned that she could get tired or cranky like anyone else. He wanted to cut that off before it turned into something ugly.

"Why don't you show me what you were drawing?"

Distracted by the task, she reached out, seized one of Sen's fingers in her hand, and pulled him over. She proudly pointed to a misshapen, vaguely flower-shaped creation and proclaimed it a beautiful orchid. Sen nodded gravely while the other girl awkwardly stared up at him, seemingly unsure what to do. He crouched down and spoke to Ai in a very loud whisper.

"Who is your friend?"

"Zhi," said Ai. "She drew birds."

Sen peered over at what the other little girl had been drawing. He frowned and looked a little closer. They didn't look like birds. They looked like dragons. Remarkably, impossibly realistic dragons. The dragons that had been scratched into the ground started to move. Sen's eyes shot up to the little girl, who was staring at him with eyes as old as the world itself.

"What?" asked Sen, unsure what else to say.

"You didn't really think we were just going to let you wander around without a minder, did you?" asked the little girl who was clearly not a little girl.

Sen was once more struck dumb by this turn of events. He turned to look at Ai, who was also staring at him with eyes that held the knowledge of ages.

"You didn't kill those little girls, did you?" he demanded in a low, furious voice.

The false little girls both gave him aghast looks.

"Who raised you?" demanded not-Zhi.

"Honestly," said not-Ai. "What kind of question is that? Of course, we didn't kill them. They're in daycare."

"What in the thousand hells is daycare?!"

Wang Bo was shifting back and forth on his feet, his eyes bright and hopeful. Sen knew that he was missing something here, but he just couldn't put his finger on what was escaping his notice. He felt like it must be obvious. He turned to look at Dai Bao. The gruff man had barely opened his mouth to speak when impatience won out over Wang Bo's painfully limited self-control.

"When will you start?" asked the young man.

Sen frowned at him. "Start what?"

"Training us."

"Training you to do what?" asked Sen.

"To use the spears and halberds!"

Now, Sen understood. This kid had taken that offhand statement Sen had made and exaggerated it in his mind into some kind of promise that Sen would become their teacher. He didn't have time for that nonsense. He had his own training to deal with. He had little Ai to take care of and teach how to write. This was not a problem of his making, and he refused to be bound by a promise he never made. Then, Sen felt something blossom inside of him. Something that rather reminded him of Laughing River. He directed a big, bright smile at Wang Bo.

"Right now," said Sen.

"Really?" asked Wang Bo.

"Really," answered Sen. "All you have to do is pass one little test first."

Dai Bao looked profoundly skeptical at this turn of events but elected not to say anything because, apparently, he'd been born with his good sense intact. Wang Bo plowed immediately forward.

"I'm ready for any test," declared the young man.

"Terrific!" exclaimed Sen. "Let's head outside."

The three of them exited the community building, and Sen reached down to grab a handful of snowy rocks off the ground. He gave Wang Bo an encouraging smile and pointed.

"You should go stand over there," ordered Sen.

"What test is this?"

"I like to call it the Dance Dance Revo... Insurrection. That's it. Dance Dance Insurrection. All you need to do to pass is keep up for the next four minutes."

"Keep up with what?" asked Wang Bo.

Sen drew an arm back and hurled a rock at Wang Bo's feet. The rock hit the ground right in front of the young man, sending up a spray of slush, show, and displaced dirt. Within a few seconds, the ground around where Wang Bo had been standing was filled with tiny craters, and the young man was fleeing for his life.

"How long until he figures out it wasn't a real test?" asked Dai Bao curiously.

"I give it a week," said Sen.

"I've got a silver that says he figures it out in three days."

"Done."

Discover even more from Eric Dontigney, get this FREE short story!

https://shadowalleypress.com/TwoMountainsBF

THE ADVENTURE CONTINUES...

in *Unintended Cultivator Volume 8*

BOOKS AND REVIEWS

If you loved *Unintended Cultivator Volume 7* and would like to stay in the loop about the latest book releases, deals, and giveaways, be sure to subscribe to the Shadow Alley Press Mailing List.

www.ShadowAlleyPress.com/SAPmailinglist

Sign up now and get a free copy of our bestselling anthology, *Viridian Gate Online: Side Quests*! Your email address will never be shared and you can unsubscribe at any time.

Word-of-mouth and book reviews are beyond helpful for the success of any writer, so please consider leaving a rating or a short, honest review on Amazon—just a couple of lines about your overall reading experience. Thank you in advance!

You can also connect with us on our Facebook Page where we do even more giveaways: facebook.com/shadowalleypress

BOOKS BY SHADOW ALLEY PRESS

Shadow Alley Press

ENTER THE SHADOW ALLEY LIBRARY to take a peek at all of our amazing Gamelit, Fantasy, and Science Fiction books! Viridian Gate Online, Rogue Dungeon, Snake's Life, Dungeon Heart, Path of the Thunderbird, School of Swords and Serpents, the FiveFold Universe, and so many more... Your next favorite book is waiting for you inside!

ABOUT THE AUTHOR

Raised in Western New York, Eric Dontigney has lived in New Mexico, Florida, Wisconsin, Virginia, Pennsylvania, and Tennessee. He currently resides near Dayton, OH. He is a fan of photo-realism and impressionist paintings, coffee, and well-made food.

Not wishing to tarnish the good names of writers who have come before him, he refuses to name influences. He will admit to reading Neil Gaiman, Harlan Ellison, F. Scott Fitzgerald, Ayn Rand, Stephen J. Cannell, Jim Butcher, Kate Chopin, Edgar Allen Poe, Shakespeare, Camus, James Baldwin, Tim O'Brien, Ray Bradbury, Isaac Asimov, and Stephen King.

Made in the USA
Middletown, DE
02 December 2025

22205243R00253